KISS THE GIRL

A **MEANT TO BE** NOVEL

ZORAIDA CÓRDOVA

HYPERION AVENUE

Los Angeles   New York

First Edition, August 2023
10 9 8 7 6 5 4 3 2 1
FAC-004510-23167
Printed in the United States of America

This book is set in Adobe Caslon/Monotype
Designed by Marci Senders

Library of Congress Control Number: 2023934665
Hardcover ISBN: 978-1-368-05037-1
Paperback ISBN: 978-1-368-05336-5
Reinforced binding for hardcover edition

www.HyperionAvenueBooks.com

For all the mermaids who are still finding their voice. *Sing.*

PROLOGUE

ARIEL

6.21 Arthur Ashe Stadium, New York

There, standing center stage, surrounded by twenty-three thousand people, Ariel del Mar was as close to being among a sea of stars as she would ever get.

Adoring fans waved blinking LED wands shaped like clamshells and tail fins. The stage was still pitch-black, and the sixty-second countdown between songs had started. The final number did not require another costume change, or props, or backup dancers. No, the last song of their Goodbye Goodbye tour would end the way it had all started. Just them. Just Ariel and her sisters.

The only thing louder than the rhythm of Ariel's heartbeat was the crowd. All the *I love you*s and cheering rose to the rafters, melding into a powerful storm of sound that could even be felt by those tuning in to the worldwide broadcast streaming in living rooms, in bars, in crowded subway cars, and on billboards in Times Square. Ariel imagined those fans were with her, too.

Momentarily stepping away from her six sisters, Ariel approached the lip of the stage. She never felt closer to her fans and her own music than when she was performing. After 276 shows spread out over two years, Ariel had tried to prepare herself for Siren Seven's farewell concert. She wanted to hold on to that moment. To remember that she had *been* there. To know she'd given her all. To be sure it had been worth it. Hadn't it?

She'd been famous since she was ten years old, and at twenty-five, she was ready to start over. She hadn't quite figured out what "starting over" would look like. There were sponsorships, movie roles, book deals, and matchmakers all waiting for Ariel's next move. Her father had promised them all a break from the limelight, but for the first time in her life, she didn't know what the next move was, and it was thrilling. The world could wait, as long as she could sing one more song. One last song.

When the sixty seconds were up, Ariel tipped her face up to the spotlight and tried to catch her breath. The crowd roared. Her bright scarlet hair cascaded in waves over her shoulders. Sweat pooled at the nape of her neck and seeped into her iridescent violet body suit. The high waistband of her cheeky shorts was leaving a semipermanent indent against her belly button. Cool night air kissed her scraped knee where she'd ripped her sheer tights during the last number. But Ariel only flashed her best smile and waved, turning effortlessly on emerald-green platform heels. The spotlight illuminated her path across the stage, and the youngest del Mar girl rejoined her sisters. Waiting behind a row of crystal-encrusted microphone stands, Ariel fit at the center of the lineup as if she were its apex, its heart.

"You are incredible!" Ariel's bright soprano rang through Arthur Ashe Stadium.

"Of course I am," said Thea, giving her fuchsia hair a flirty flick.

Ariel shot her sister a mock-chastising glare. She thumbed at the crowd. "I *clearly* meant them."

After the ripple of laughter, Thea winked and blew a kiss.

Stella, who was usually brought to tears by any emotion, and also cute puppies, sniffled. "I just realized I'm really going to miss this."

Alicia craned her neck down the line. "*Just?*"

"Oh, you know what I mean!" Stella squeaked in defense.

Ariel's cheeks hurt from smiling. This was the last time she'd run through their end-of-show banter. "I told myself I was going to do this without crying."

The tail of her sentence warbled with emotion she'd spent two hours trying to rein in. But how could she not be emotional at this moment? Their lives would forever be divided into two periods: Before Siren Seven and After Siren Seven. Everything they'd worked on, their television show, their albums, would be referred to as "an era," if they were lucky. Or "their heyday," if they weren't.

Even Sophia, who was the eldest and never cried, wrinkled her nose like she was trying to stave off inevitable tears. She smoothed out the black silk of her ponytail, all tough-girl bravado as she said, "Come on, get it together, girls. There's no crying in baseball."

"Then it's a good thing I never made the Little League team," Elektra snarked, and their drummer doled out a *ba-dum-tss*.

"Let's get serious for a minute," Ariel said.

She couldn't quite make out the faces of the crowd, except for some of the people in the front rows and those who were illuminated by a roving spotlight. But she took a moment to lift her gaze and look out at the very top seat in the farthest nosebleed sections of the arena. She wanted the fans back there to know that she saw them.

"So, I was supposed to write something down," she confessed guiltily. "But every time I tried, I failed. It felt like rehearsing, and boy, have we done a lot of that. I guess I realized that I wasn't ready. How do we say goodbye after fifteen years?"

Sophia squeezed Ariel's hand as their fans hollered encouraging whistles and applause.

"My sisters and I have been blessed," she continued. "We know everyone says that, but I don't know how else to describe how lucky we are to have all of you here tonight. We're just a little family from

3

Queens, New York, and this feels like a dream. We have seen the world. Played stadiums and award shows."

Marilou interjected with a wink, "Won a few, too."

"We've played backyard birthdays and dingy clubs we were definitely too young to even be allowed in. We've read your letters and seen your videos. We have a room, a whole room, with your art and gifts. My sisters—and you all—remind me every day to dream of the impossible. Dream until it becomes real. Possible. Yours."

Volleys of screams filled the stage as the intro notes to their first-ever single, "Your Once Upon a Dream Girl," rang out. Ariel couldn't have timed it better herself.

"So, I've decided we are not really going to say goodbye." She pressed a trembling hand over her heart. "We're family. You're family. And family is forever. Now, put your hands together. We need a little help with this one!"

The drums kicked in, followed by sparkling chimes, the rhythmic keyboard, and then the entire stadium belting the first verse along with Ariel. She remembered the very first time they'd packed into the tiny booths at that cramped recording studio. How her dad had made them sing and sing again until their harmonies crested and rose, the perfect melody that would launch Siren Seven as a real band. She remembered taking her favorite purple gel pen and rewriting lines, the way her father would frown at her changes, then give her that stubborn smile when the song clicked into place. She remembered how it had felt the very first time they were driving across the Queensboro Bridge and the song had come up on the radio. Ariel remembered and held on tight to her sisters until Siren Seven stopped singing and it was just the crowd, just twenty-three thousand people screaming the final verse. That part, all these years later, never got old.

When it was over, the glitter confetti cannons showered the stadium and fireworks rocketed into the New York sky. The band hammered out extended solos, stage lights pulsing and spinning, until they became one collective howl of joy.

Ariel's sisters shouted their goodbyes first.

"Thank you, everyone!"

"We love you!"

"¡Adiós, adiós!"

"Good night, New York!"

"Laters, baby cakes!"

"You are everything! Everything!"

Though her sisters rushed off the stage, Ariel lingered. How could she walk away so quickly? The fans were still chanting her name. They waved their colorful wands. They danced in the shower of confetti shaped like tiny stars. She caught a fistful.

"I love you," Ariel said, and stayed there, even as all the lights went out.

MISSED SIREN SEVEN'S FAREWELL CONCERT?
WE'VE GOT YOU COVERED.

Sister Act: Did Pop Princess
Ariel Break Up the Band?

Elektra del Mar Rumored to Star in the
New Star Wars Trilogy.

24.8K LIKES

WIG SNATCHED: SIREN SEVEN SINGS
GOODBYE . . . OR DO THEY?

You Won't Believe What
Teo del Mar
Looked Like in His Twenties!
CLICK HERE *1:32pm PT*

Battle of the Bands, featuring
Star Crossed! AURORA'S GROCERY.

Doors Open at 8 p.m.

THE TUTTLE TELLER

Episode 1365:
Siren Seven: From Humble
Beginnings to Music Royalty

CHAPTER ONE

ARIEL

6.21 Arthur Ashe Stadium, New York

Backstage was aflutter with security guards, assistants, and the event managers. Ariel was fairly certain there were heads of state with smaller protection details. If she could pinpoint something she wasn't going to miss during her yearlong sabbatical from performing, it was the post-show frenzy. That and the fluorescent-lit beige halls that made every area marked AUTHORIZED PERSONNEL ONLY something out of a horror movie.

Chrissy Mahilal, a peppy Guyanese woman who barely cleared five foot one, bodychecked her way through the baker's dozen flanking Ariel and doubled her pace to keep up. Chrissy offered her boss a recycled plastic tumbler full of pomegranate-flavored electrolyte water, from which Ariel took thirsty sips.

"Reviews from the fans are coming in," Chrissy said, an exuberant trill embellishing the personal assistant's vowels. "You're trending worldwide, and the official Siren Seven gem appliqués have just been backordered. We have an invite from the owner of Ma Chérie. He's giving Siren Seven the club's premier VIP lounge."

Ariel chuckled. "The twins will love that."

Chrissy continued, scrolling with her index finger. "Trevor Tachi is back in your DMs . . ."

Ariel glanced at Chrissy. Turquoise gems glinted at the corners of her eyes, and strands of her henna-dyed hair were coming undone from her chignon. If she smiled any harder, Ariel might be able to count all her teeth. That was a bad sign.

"You know Trevor ruined his chance with me when he lied to *Entertainment Daily!* about what happened backstage at Wonderland Fest. What aren't you saying?"

"Why do you think there's something I'm not saying?"

They came to a stop outside Sophia's dressing room, where the other assistants handled the post-show chaos.

Ariel arched a shrewd brow. "I've known you for ten years. You panic-smile and straighten up like you're back in ballerina boot camp."

Chrissy grumbled and squeezed the air. "Damn you, Mistress Doroshinskaya."

"What is it?" Ariel asked patiently, though her insides bubbled with anxiety. Last show, Thea had tripped during the chorus of "Heartbreak Island" and became a meme. Before that, Stella had been photographed kissing a Hollywood starlet at an after-party, which had drawn their father's fury because she'd broken curfew and their "no unsanctioned relationships" rule. Before *that*, seven zealous fans had made their way backstage, dressed from head to toe as the del Mar sisters, and snuck past security. They'd been waiting in the greenroom and were caught smelling the band's dirty clothes.

"I have already conjured several disaster scenarios in the last thirty seconds, Christina Mahilal. *Spill.*"

Chrissy handed her phone to Ariel. "There was a leak I think you should see."

The anxiety in her gut transformed into those ugly little Troll dolls Sophia collected. They whispered her worst fears back to her, shouting, "They hate you. You're fake. You talentless hack. Thank the music gods you're over." Ariel took a deep breath and scanned the article *Voltage*

Sound had posted while she'd still been onstage. It read: ARIEL DEL MAR: POP PRINCESS SLATED TO GO SOLO.

At first, the headline didn't seem so bad. Solo careers for each of her sisters wasn't news. There had been rumors that Ariel was going to break from the group since she was a teenager. Now that they'd made their final curtain call, her sisters had new enterprises and adventures waiting for them. Ariel had spent the entirety of the Goodbye Goodbye tour negotiating her yearlong break with the head of the record label, aka her father. After fifteen years of nonstop grinding and touring and recording, she deserved—no, *needed*—a break. She was twenty-five years old and had a long list of mundane things she'd never done. She wanted to learn a new language, take cooking classes, wander through a bookstore without her beefy, though sweet, security guards waiting around the bookshelves. She wanted to have a day without a call time, without interviews or deadlines. She wanted to figure out who the hell she was without Siren Seven.

In a way, she *was* going solo. The article could have been another rumor, one in a million presumptions from people who didn't know her. But as she scanned the text, something gave her pause.

"A source from the del Mar camp claims a huge announcement is coming this Tuesday," she read just loud enough for Chrissy to hear. Sometimes these headlines were absolute fabrications or misunderstandings, like the time she liked one of the famous Chrises' shirtless photos and the next day there were hundreds of articles documenting every interaction of the "couple." But sometimes, leaks came from inside their own house when the team wanted to control a narrative. The reported date itched at the back of her thoughts. "What's on schedule for next week?"

Chrissy had their shared calendar ready to display. She gulped. "June 25. Family time. Six thirty a.m."

"When has family time ever been that early?" Ariel's post-concert high gave way to her post-concert aches. She was starving. The cut on her knee burned and her feet felt like they'd been crushed in a vise, which they sort of had been. She wanted a scalding shower and to crawl into bed. She did not want to ask her father for an explanation.

Surely, it was a misunderstanding. Another headline that claimed to know the truth behind the perfect facade of the del Mar sisters. So she smiled and kept her head high. She couldn't afford to frown or let frustration show on her face. There were too many people around, and even more people waiting to see if Ariel or her sisters would end up just like their mother.

From the corner of her eye, she caught a janitor raising her phone. Ariel waved and smiled for the photo. As tired as she was, she did mean that smile. She never took her fans for granted. Without them, she'd have nothing.

"I'll have the cars stand by," Chrissy said, and joined the other assistants.

Ariel thanked her and let herself into Sophia's greenroom, where her sisters were in various stages of disarray. Stella unzipped her iridescent turquoise booties, her bloody bandage coming off in the process. Marilou braided her rose-pink hair into pigtails. Elektra already had on the giant electric-blue headphones that matched her hair, which meant she was listening to her fifteen-minute meditation podcast. Meanwhile, the twins, Alicia and Thea, shoveled down noodles right out of a Chinese takeout carton.

For a second, Ariel took it all in. She memorized the long vanity with glamorous exposed bulbs, bottles of champagne, and stuffed animals. A box of fan mail, which she liked to read on nights she couldn't sleep. The whale sounds Marilou always played in the background. Shimmering clothes, wigs, and so much glitter that it would take professional crime scene cleaners to get rid of every fleck. Sure, Siren Seven was contractually guaranteed individual dressing rooms, but ever since they were little girls, they piled into Sophia's space because she was the eldest and none of them liked being alone.

Sophia sat at the center of the vanity, removing her signature gold hoops and loosening her black ponytail. She met Ariel's eyes in the mirror. "Hey, baby bird. You're not going to start getting weepy on us, are you?"

"Aww," Alicia chimed in. "It's our last greenroom decompress-sesh!"

Elektra tugged off her headphones and frowned. "We said we wouldn't call it that."

"I made no such promises," Alicia mumbled through her mouthful of noodles.

"What's in your hand?" Thea asked.

"Oh, just this really hot singer," Marilou said, zooming in on a Pixagram photo. "Eric Something. His band is actually really good."

"Not *you*," Thea said, pointing at the youngest del Mar girl. "You."

Marilou flicked a pale pink braid over her shoulder to show she wasn't bothered. "Whatever, I'm still sending this song to the group chat."

Ariel looked down at her closed fist, which still held the star-shaped confetti she'd caught. It was silly, but those tiny bits of shimmering plastic felt like her lucky send-off into the next stage of her life. "Nothing. Where's Daddy?"

"I saw him with Uncle Iggy backstage," Elektra said. She scraped her long nails through her blue roots, tugging out bobby pins one by one.

"Why?" Stella asked, raising a curious brow.

Ariel texted them the article. All six of her sisters stopped what they were doing and scrolled while she slumped into the empty seat in front of the long vanity. Her dark brown roots peeked out at the edge of her scarlet wig. Though her makeup had stayed intact, the shimmering scales that decorated the apples of her cheeks were sloughing off, making her look less like a glamorous mermaid and more like a dragon shedding skin.

11

"Wait. I thought you and Dad tabled the solo thing," Stella said. One of her faux lash strips had come unglued and was resting on her cheekbone.

Ariel snorted and reached over to pluck it. She was about to tell Stella to make fifty wishes, but they were interrupted.

Teodoro del Mar himself, loving father to seven daughters, hit-maker, and CEO and cofounder of Atlantica Records, waltzed through the door tailed by his VP and brother, Ignacio Sebastián del Mar. They just called him Uncle Iggy.

Teo was tall, imposing, and still maintained the stocky build from his younger years as a wrestler. He wore one of his favorite Italian suits adorned with a golden S-shaped lapel pin. His beard had gone white over the past two years of touring, and his hair was perfectly combed into a smooth salt-and-pepper wave.

The brothers wore pleased smiles on their faces. Smiles that quickly dissolved as each of the sirens stared them down.

"Mis amores, where's the celebration?" Uncle Iggy asked. He was his brother's opposite in every way, with short black curls, light brown skin, and bold fashion tailored to his slender frame.

Ariel held up her phone, and both men peered at the screen. She watched her father's face go from caught to annoyed to exasperated to serious. She couldn't say he didn't have range.

"What is this, Daddy?" Ariel asked, her voice a husky contralto. Her normal speaking voice wasn't the girlish underwater princess the world was used to hearing.

"We were going to talk to you when we got back home," Teo said in that stern but pacifying way of his, as if she were just having a tantrum and he needed to stand his ground.

"Clearly someone on your team didn't get the memo," Marilou snipped.

Ariel felt a knot of emotion in her throat. Their father always

12

changed plans without discussing it with them. Adding a tour stop here. A surprise visit to some royal there. A sponsorship she'd never truly agreed to. Why had she thought this time would be different?

"This took planning," Ariel said.

"And we said we'd hold off any plans and announcements until *after* the tour," Sophia added, tenting her long black nails.

"Technically, it *is* after the tour." Uncle Iggy held up his hands, as if they could shield him from his nieces' words.

"Come on, Uncle Iggy," Elektra huffed. "You're just smoothing things over for him, like you always do."

"Do not take that tone of voice with us, Elektra!" Teo threatened the room with his index finger and the booming clap of his baritone.

Frustrated, Ariel snapped, "And don't *you* change the subject, Daddy."

All at once, her sisters closed ranks. Ariel always felt stronger with them by her side, even though she hated confrontation. She hated watching her father get silent and upset. She hated that she was twenty-five and somehow still wanted, *needed*, his approval. Even as her body trembled, she forced herself to meet her father's eyes, the palest green, just like Sophia's and Thea's.

Teo del Mar frowned. "So, it's a mutiny, is it?"

"Please," Ariel begged. "Can you for once include us in your decisions about *our* lives?"

After a flash of shock at her words, Teo stood taller. His jaw set with his quick temper. "What do you want me to say? Fifteen years! More, if we're counting the years it took to get your first deal. What else can I say but my daughters have worked hard *every day* of their lives, to what end? To take a break? Lose momentum to go backpacking across Europe? Spend time in a panda sanctuary?"

"Hey!" Marilou cried out. "Do not shame my panda dreams."

"I'm not—" Teo pinched the bridge of his nose as his anger lost steam. "Queridas. My darling girls. All I have ever wanted was the best for you. I've worked—"

"'Since I was sixteen years old.'" Ariel finished the speech she knew better than almost any of her lyrics.

Sophia picked up the rest. "'Since your mother and I came to this country with three hundred dollars and nothing but our dreams and a thousand doors that closed in our faces.'"

"We get it," Alicia said. "We know."

Their father looked at them like they had taken him out, Caesar-style.

"We had a deal, Daddy," Ariel reminded him. "A year of media blackout. No interviews. No exclusives. No recording. Just a break to do whatever we wanted. So I'm asking again. What is this article talking about?"

"Poe Marlowe wants to write and produce your solo album, Ariel," Teo said, raising his hands in defeat.

Marilou gasped, then whispered, "Oooh, I would have killed to work with him."

All the girls shot her a glare that said *Not now*.

"See?" Teo said, bolstered by Marilou's reaction. "But he only has time in his schedule this summer. If we can get in the studio now, we can launch your solo career by December. He only works with the best of the best, and he wants to work with *you*, Ariel."

Ariel half scoffed and half laughed. "December?"

"We never wanted it to get out this way," Uncle Iggy said. "It's only six months earlier than your planned sabbatical."

Ariel should have seen this coming. She deflated a bit. "Oh, is that all?"

"The plan was for your sisters to do featured guest spots on individual tracks," Teo explained. "To transition the band instead of making it seem like a breakup."

That was it. That was the thing that pushed the del Mar women too far. The room broke into shouting. Her sisters wanted answers. What else was he keeping secret? When in their schedules would they fit recording? Sophia had already enrolled in university. Marilou just wanted peace for pandas. Meanwhile, Uncle Iggy tried to apologize, while Teo called for whatever underling leaked the news to the press to be fired.

Ariel couldn't sit down again. If she sat, she wouldn't be able to get back up. Even though the soles of her feet felt like she was walking on broken glass, she glided across the greenroom and stood face-to-face with her father.

He cupped her cheeks with his big palms. His brow furrowed, etching deep wrinkles on his tawny brown skin. When had he gotten so old?

"Ariel, my darling girl, my life. Querida—" He said that to all of them, often. Querida—*Dearest. Loved.* "We have the chance to do something that only comes around once in a lifetime. I know, I know I should have told you from the beginning, but I also know how much you love your fans. How much you love singing. You *are* the music. You would be miserable for a whole year without it."

Ariel had to concede that what he said was true. But wasn't it her decision to make? Her album to write? And if she was miserable when the year was up, it would be because she'd chosen herself for the very first time, instead of doing exactly what was expected of her. But her father's words always managed to snake into her thoughts. Poe Marlowe was a big deal. He *had* helped break out more musicians than almost anyone in the business. Wasn't she lucky? Lucky to be her father's golden girl, one of his prized jewels. Lucky to be an extension of his dream. Lucky that she got to connect with millions of people who adored her and her sisters.

What if that all went away?

What if she walked away from an opportunity others would kill for?

15

She glanced down, iridescent confetti stars still clutched in her sweaty fist, and said, "Fine."

Teo and Ignacio clapped their palms. Her sisters muttered in confusion.

"On one condition," Ariel added.

Teo glowered, then grinned. "You are your father's daughter."

"Everyone else gets their *promised* year off. They'll only do vocals *if and when* they want."

"No!" Sophia said fiercely. "You can't."

The others echoed the sentiment, but when it came to her sisters, Ariel would do anything. She'd never won a stare-off with her dad, but this wasn't just about her anymore. "Those are my terms."

Teodoro del Mar tugged at his neat silver beard. "Your terms are reasonable. We're going to make platinum, baby girl."

Ariel let herself get pulled into a tight hug as her father and uncle rattled off all the great things they were going to do. But her sisters didn't celebrate. They shared tired smiles, and everyone resumed gathering their things, quickly making their way to the parking lot where their cars were waiting. They fixed their faces for the lingering paparazzi and fans seeing them off.

As they raced across the Queensboro Bridge to the Upper West Side of Manhattan, Ariel rolled down the window and let the late-June breeze refresh her.

So what if her plans were going to be a little different than she'd intended? She had her sisters. She had her family. She was going to work with one of the biggest names in the music industry. She stuck her arm out the window and opened her hand, letting the glittering confetti get carried off into the wind.

She was Ariel del Mar, and her whole life was waiting.

THE TUTTLE TELLER

Episode 1365:

Siren Seven: From Humble Beginnings to Music Royalty (Intro)

Transcript:

The final show from the royal family of pop has finally come, and though I am UTTERLY DEVASTATED, I can't wait to see what's next for my girls. For now, I want to hit rewind with a multipart series highlighting Siren Seven's history.

My litmus test for friends has always been which Siren Seven album was the one that turned them into one of the Lucky Sevens. For little ole me it started with *The Little Mermaids*, the television show following a school of mermaid princesses as they single-handedly saved the oceans from pollution, all while falling in love with sailors and lifeguards—let's never forget my original teen crush #PrinceNick.

Famed Daddy del Mar at the helm of the media empire made the controversial decision to go out with a bang and cancel the show at the height of its viewership, turning the seven mermaid sisters into siren songstresses of the stage.

And so, Siren Seven was born. More glitter. More makeup. Bigger platform heels. Same signature wigs. No one can deny that Teodoro del Mar is a hitmaker for a reason, and his daughters are the jewels of his kingdom—ahem—record label, Atlantica Records.

Now the reigning girl group in the world has said their goodbyes with a two-year-long world tour. Hoo! Your boy racked up *miles*, but every single moment was worth it.

Rumor has it that for some, the party won't stop. Extremely credible sources tell me that a major announcement is forthcoming on *Wake Up! New York*, and you better believe I'll have the scoop for you first.

Don't forget to subscribe, tell me your theories, and hit up my TipJar$$ @Scott.Tuttle.7 so I can keep bringing you the very best Siren Seven content.

Tuttle Out!

CHAPTER TWO

ERIC

6.24 Brooklyn Bridge, New York

On the night of his twenty-eighth birthday, Eric Reyes was sitting in standstill traffic. As far as he could gather, there was a massive accident blocking every lane of the Brooklyn Bridge, and despite the surround sound of sirens and horns, an hour and a half later, they weren't even close to moving.

Load-in had been two hours prior, and he'd put his phone on silent because their manager, Odelia, had called a dozen times to yell about how hard she'd worked to book Star Crossed to headline the Battle of the Bands. Without the traffic, Aurora's Grocery, where they were supposed to go onstage imminently, was only fifteen minutes way.

And yet, aside from the stress of the situation, Eric was still in a disgustingly good mood. New York City spread out around him in all its glory. Sure, he was on the wrong end of the bridge, and he was in a gas-chugging SUV whose air conditioner was wheezing on life support, and from the sudden smell he was pretty sure their drummer just cut one, but there was no one he'd rather be with. He rolled down the windows.

Eleanor Grimsby, who was the human equivalent of a rain cloud emoji, took that opportunity to crane her long neck out the passenger window and release a horrible banshee cry at the traffic.

"I'm pretty sure goats in Long Island can hear you," Carly grumbled from the back seat. Her corkscrew curls were piled atop her head like a pineapple, and though it was eight at night, she wore her silk eye mask. Eric and the rest of the band had learned over the years that when Carly's migraine mask was on, no one should even attempt conversation.

Grimsby slowly thumbed at their drummer. "Max is the one blasting her trash TV."

Max, whose eyes had been glued to her phone as she bit her index fingernail raw, pushed her brown shaggy bangs away from her eyes. They fell right back into place. She grumbled, "I clearly love trash since I'm still friends with all of you!"

"I'm all for guilty pleasures," Eric said, his voice low and easy. "The guiltier and shameless-er the better."

"First of all, shameless-er is not a word," Carly said, removing her eye mask and tossing it into the catchall tray that was the floor of the SUV. She turned to Max and teased, "Second of all, aren't you a little too old to still like Siren Seven?"

Max sucked her teeth and muttered a curse in Tagalog they all knew by heart. "It's a recap of their *farewell* show, so I consider it homework. Also, our generation needs nostalgia to cope with crippling anxiety, so let me live, okay?"

Carly let it drop but proceeded to bang her head on the back of Eric's headrest. "*Arghhh*, why is this happening?"

Eric leaned away, but there was nowhere he could go, unless he wanted to stand on the traffic-jammed bridge. "Are you *trying* to shatter my eardrums?"

"You won't have eardrums when Odelia's done with us," Carly muttered.

"Who cares?" Grimsby asked, resting her pale blond hair on the half-open window like she'd given up on life. "This is what I call a doomed fate. Doomed."

Carly punched the ceiling of the car, and Max began drumming on every available surface. Eric knew that his bandmates, though a tad dramatic, needed to cope with stress in their own ways. However, those ways could not involve damage to his car.

"Easy!" Eric said, smoothing his hand over the interior. "She's not much, but my baby has gotten us to a hundred and one gigs in one piece."

The SUV was ancient, and by no means anything close to the vintage cars his father collected in Colombia. But it had been the first car he'd bought when he arrived in Miami at eighteen with his life savings, a guitar, and a dream. Thousands of miles and a decade later, Eric was so close to making that dream come true. So close he could taste it, palpable as the exhaust from the surrounding cars.

Carly flipped him off and blew him an air kiss at the same time. "Fine. Only because it's your birthday."

Eric grinned. Sent another of Odelia's calls to voicemail. Rubbed at the knot on the back of his neck.

Max clapped her hands on her head. "Oh shit! We're going to miss this gig on your *birthday*. Our first big tour kicks off tomorrow morning and it's already a mess. We're not doomed. We're *cursed*."

Grimsby raised her head lethargically. "Which one of you jerks broke a mirror?"

"We're not cursed or doomed," Eric stressed. "And go easy on my baby, will you?"

"*Curséd*," Max repeated, dragging it out into two syllables, and Grimsby nodded slowly, adding, "Curséd, it's French."

"Definitely not French." Eric couldn't help but chuckle. "I can admit that things aren't off to the best start."

"Best start?" Carly asked, shoving her torso between the front seats. "Let's pull up the cursed receipts, shall we? In the past week alone, one of our opening acts got E. coli. Who gets E. coli?"

"Two hundred and sixty something *thousand* people," Grimsby said.

"Why do you know that?" Eric shook his head. "Never mind. Also, Odelia already booked a replacement band."

Grimsby lifted her head, blinking once. "Our bus driver got into a car accident."

"He's on the mend." Eric's smile became strained. "And we have a new guy. We're going to get through this. We can't let a few mishaps—"

"Aaaand, the merch guy just quit," Max announced, holding up her phone. "Odelia is putting up an ad ASAP and also says that if you ignore her call again, our big tour is going to be a wake. Your wake, specifically. "

Eric let go of an exasperated breath. Not ideal, but there was no room to worry about hiring a new merch vendor when he had bigger problems. Like traffic. He wished he could see more from their position on the bridge. Several news helicopters circled spotlights up ahead. The couple in the car to the left of them had fogged up their windows, and a couple of suits had left their taxis to shout on their phones. For the first time in so many hours, Eric let the tendrils of failure snake around his heart: What if. What if they didn't make it?

No. They had to make it. The band needed this. *He* needed this. He would make them walk to the venue with their instruments on their backs if he got desperate, and while he was calm now, he was perhaps fifteen minutes away from desperate. Though he wouldn't let it show, and he definitely wouldn't contribute to the bad mood arising among his bandmates.

"We have to prepare ourselves for the worst," Grimsby said. Her big gray eyes were glassy.

Carly scratched at her throat, the way she did when she was nervous and thought she was breaking out in hives. "If Aurora's Grocery thinks we're flakes, then so will the Hazy Underground, and then we'll never be able to play the Red Zone!"

"All right. That's it." Eric swung the driver's door open. "Everyone out. Now."

Max sat up. "What the hell are you doing?"

"You know I have a fear of getting run over on a bridge," Carly said.

"I need to stretch, actually," Grimsby added in her slow, wry tone.

Eric popped open the trunk, undoing the latches to his guitar case. His guitar was the most valuable thing he owned in the entire world. Each and every time he'd faced the worst moments of his life, this guitar had seen him through. Now was no different. He secured the strap, so the body rested on his back, then boosted himself from the fender to the hood, until his boots were firmly on the top of the SUV.

Carly leaned against the hood. "Is this what you meant by treating this piece of junk with respect?"

"This is what I call being the best hype man you could have ever asked for." Eric strummed the opening chords to the first song they'd ever written together, "Adíos to My Old Love." It was the first moment he knew they had something special. Their vocals in harmony, their instruments like extensions of themselves and one another. Something that the whole world needed to see. "Look at where we are."

"In standstill traffic?" Max grumbled.

Eric hummed the opening melody, then said, "We're suspended over the East fucking River. We're in the greatest city in the world. Carly, do you remember what you said when we wrote this song?"

Carly's arms were crossed over her chest, but her frown unfurled into a shy smile. "I said we made magic."

He strummed into the chorus and stomped once. A crowd of pedestrians on the level above had stopped to watch. He winked in their direction before turning to Grimsby. Her black eyeliner was more smudged than usual, but even his favorite sad goth girl couldn't help but grin when he got down on one knee and fingered the bass notes she usually played.

"You took a bus from North Sunshine, Montana, all the way here, to this city, for what, Grimsby?" He tilted his head toward her because he couldn't hear her over the chatter of pedestrians and blaring of horns. "I'm sorry, what?"

She shook her fists, giving in to him, and shouted, "I came here to play in a sick-ass band, okay?"

Finally, he stood, balancing on the roof, and faced Max. "And you! You didn't free a thousand guinea pigs and quit your job at a major pharmaceutical company just to think we're *cursed*, did you?"

Max drummed her palms on the side of the car. "Hell no!"

"We never thought it was going to be easy," he sang, hitting a long strum that took him into the bridge of the song. "Believe in us just for a little longer."

"Your naive optimism is giving me a toothache," Carly said, but she still belted her voice into the bridge with him. The first line they wrote together.

"Believe in us just for a little longer." They didn't care who was looking on or recording. The four of them sang at the top of their lungs, cradled by traffic and the warm summer breeze.

When it was over, a trickle of applause came from some surrounding cars and onlookers from the pedestrian walk. It was followed by aggressive honking that snapped their attention to the moving cars.

"We broke the curse!" Max shouted.

They cheered, and Eric felt their joy down to his bones. He handed Grimsby his guitar and took one final moment to look out at the bright lights of the city. A final moment that was interrupted by a passing car. A bald, mustached man leaned his head out the window and shouted, "Move it along, asshole!"

"I love New York." Eric slid down the windshield and hood, landing on his feet.

Once they were packed into the SUV, they eased along. Sure, it was five miles per hour, but getting faster by the minute. He glanced at the clock. They were really going to make it.

"Sooo," Max began, "we were going to save this until after the show. I think you deserve it now."

She presented a slightly squished giant cupcake impaled by an askew candle.

"See?" Eric grinned, giving the car some gas as the traffic cleared up. "You're all mushy romantics."

"Take that back," Grimsby warned as she lit a match. "Take that back right now."

The single sparkler candle came to life, likely a hazard in the SUV, but they sang a fast Spanglish version of the "Happy Birthday" song.

"Make a wish," Carly said.

Eric smiled. Wishing was easy, but believing was hard. He'd made a thousand, ten thousand wishes over the years. Some were superficial—a bike, a complete Lego set, a six-figure record deal. The older he got, the more complicated his wishes became. He wished for his mother's pain to ease. He wished for his student visa. He wished for his father's approval. For a chance to make something out of himself. Now, surrounded by his best friends as they hurtled over the Brooklyn Bridge, he knew they were going to make it. Which was why instead of wishing for a record deal and tons of cash, he made the simplest wish anyone could.

I wish for her, he thought.

He didn't know her yet. The girl of his dreams. The girl he'd been writing every song about since he could string together catchy melodies and lyrics. He'd always been lucky with women, but all his love affairs were fleeting. He wanted something lasting. Someone to hold on to. Something real. Perhaps because it was his birthday, or because his bandmates had surprised him, or maybe because there was something in the air, but he had a good feeling about what was waiting ahead.

And so, Eric Reyes blew out his birthday candle and took a huge bite of the caramel-filled cupcake, leaving the rest for the girls to tear apart.

"Buckle up," he said, stepping on the gas as every vehicle on the bridge honked their way to freedom. "No stop till Brooklyn."

GET THE LOOK!
Siren Seven Edition

ARIEL
Color: Ruby Red

Must have: Glitter, glitter, glitter! Face gem appliqués, platform boots . . . There's no such thing as casual-wear for this mermaid princess.

Attitude: Glam girl next door!

MARILOU
Color: Rose Gold

Must have: Panda earrings, vintage eighties tee, killer boots, rose-gold lamé pants.

Attitude: Pretty in pink, with an edge!

STELLA
Color: Sea Breeze Turquoise

Must have: Ethically sourced bohemian slip dress, recycled ocean plastic bracelets, vegan leather sandals. Don't forget the crystal in your pocket.

Attitude: Chill vibes only!

ELEKTRA
Color: Electric Blue

Must have: Electric-blue everything, fifties A-line skirt, lightning earrings.

Attitude: Life of the party!

ALICIA
Color: Dreamy Violet

Must have: Violet Butterfly clips, white puffy vest, shimmer leggings.

Attitude: You're everyone's dream girl!

THEA
Color: Feisty Fuchsia

Must have: Artfully distressed jeans, hand-stitched tube top, oversize parka. Don't forget the pop of bright pink.

Attitude: The world is your oyster!

SOPHIA
Color: Back in Black

Must have: Killer high ponytail, a set of stiletto nails, bitchin' black, like a true New Yorker.

Attitude: Be the rebel you want to see in the world!

CHAPTER THREE

ARIEL

6.24 Upper West Side, New York

A few days after the last Goodbye Goodbye concert, Ariel still couldn't get a good night's sleep. She haunted the rooms of their deluxe Upper West Side penthouse.

On tour, her body had acclimated to sleeping on luxury buses, the family jet, the occasional greenroom, and even a bathroom stall (don't ask). But with her feet firmly on solid ground, she was restless. She'd tried to sleep out in the balcony lounge chairs but had woken to a pigeon attempting to nest in her hair. She'd had even less luck in the living room with the glass pillar aquarium full of gawking fish. Inevitably, at sunrise, she'd go back to her bedroom, where only sheer exhaustion would do the trick.

The evening before Ariel's big solo announcement, Marilou barged into her room and said, "Enough moping!"

"I'm not moping. I'm doom scrolling." She'd been on her phone so long, the pad of her left thumb was numb.

"Call it whatever you want." Marilou shut the door behind her. Her hair was wrapped in a towel, and she was still in her favorite rose-pink fuzzy robe. She gently kicked one of the knickknacks littering the floor. "Have you even showered? This place is a mess."

"I am squeaky clean, and unlike you, I don't leave a hundred candy wrappers under my bed," Ariel teased defensively.

Ariel would hear zero slander about her room. It was her sanctuary. Every detail carefully selected to be part of her favorite place in the world. High ceilings dotted with gold constellations—the Pleiades, the Seven Sisters, most prominent. Wall-to-wall windows showed impossible city views. Her headboard was repurposed driftwood. Her guitar collection was affixed to one wall, and there was a lounge area dedicated to her record player and vinyl collection.

Marilou shuffled to the floor-to-ceiling wall of shelves and waved at rows of books and trinkets Ariel had collected from every single city they'd ever been to. Hand-stitched embroidery wheels, custom dolls that fans had made of her, ticket stubs, awards, vintage boxes full of handwritten letters. Her sisters called her a "hoarder," but there were some things Ariel simply couldn't part with. Sure, she didn't have any use for an orphan bedazzled sneaker, but that sneaker was a memento from *The Little Mermaids* shooting days, when her character would go undercover as a "regular tween girl" on land. Years later, Ariel learned she wasn't *actually* allowed to take things from set.

"Why do you keep this stuff? You don't even play Scrabble," Marilou scoffed, picking up a single Scrabble piece—the letter *Q*— then the sneaker.

Ariel got up and snatched the shoe, setting it back beside the framed portrait of their family, the last picture of the nine of them before their mother's accident. "I don't go into your room and complain about the fact that you've never heard of a hamper."

Marilou pursed her lips, her freckles bunched like a dusting of chocolate powder on her fair skin. "Fine, but my point stands. You're like a ghost around here." She took out a tiny notebook from her robe pocket. "Oh, *Ghost in a Penthouse* would make a great TV show."

Ariel plopped onto a beanbag chair. "I can't exactly leave the house until the interview tomorrow, so I don't spoil the reveal of my 'brand-new' look."

"Speaking of new looks . . ." Marilou pulled the towel off her head and waggled her eyebrows. "You like?"

The color was a soft brown with an ombré effect that faded to rose-pink ends. Ariel curled one of her sister's waves around her finger. "I love it."

"I wanted to go back to natural, but I've been Marilou del Mar for so long I almost felt scared to let go of the pink, you know?" She shook her head. "It's silly."

Ariel glanced at her own red wig, displayed on the highest shelf. She knew exactly how her sister felt. "Not silly at all. You deserve time to figure things out."

"So do you, Ariel." Marilou wedged herself on the beanbag beside her little sister, sighing her frustration. "We appreciate the deal you made with Dad, but you're the baby. A big, twenty-five-year-old baby. Still. *We're* the ones who should be taking care of you."

"It's not your job, either. It's Dad's." Ariel couldn't go down that road yet, so she changed the subject. "Why do I feel more tired now than when we're getting on a plane at three a.m.?"

"That's because you actually love it. More than any of us. Probably more than Dad himself. You love being a musician. You've just never gotten to do it on your own terms."

Ariel couldn't deny that. "Have you seen the mock-ups Uncle Iggy sent over?"

Marilou cringed. "Yeah, I have to say, you can't pull off blond."

"I don't *want* to pull off blond. But I've been wearing a red wig since I was ten, so Dad thinks it's the right direction."

"Then don't do it. If you're going to be Ariel del Mar 2.0, do it as yourself."

"You know how he is when he gets something into his head. I'm taking one for the team."

"Yeah, but we don't matter. Dad was always going to let us go our own way. It's you he needs for the label. You have the power here."

The way Marilou said that tore something in Ariel's heart. It was followed by anger at her dad, her uncle. Ariel had always been the center of attention. And the thing was, her sisters never got jealous. They did their duty. They stuck it out so their family stayed together. Ariel could do the same for just a little longer. Couldn't she?

"Well, if this is my last night of freedom," she said, "let's go out with a bang."

Marilou cocked her brow. "You have my attention."

"Chrissy's going to this Battle of the Bands tonight at Aurora's Grocery. That band you sent me is headlining. I've listened to their new song about a hundred times."

Marilou shook her fists in excitement. "I love rebellious Ariel. You should let her out more often."

A plan started shifting into place in her mind. "Dad and Uncle Iggy have that Save the Music fundraiser tonight, right?"

Marilou grinned knowingly, already on her way out of the room. "I'll text the girls to see if anyone wants to come."

For the first time in days, Ariel had something to look forward to, even if it was one night out. She got dressed and shuffled into her en suite bathroom to freshen up. When the cameras weren't rolling, she only used a blush pink lip gloss and tinted sunscreen that brightened the warm, peach undertones of her skin.

Marilou knocked on the open door, took one look at Ariel, and said, "You're like Latina Hipster Barbie."

Ariel wore a fitted pink T-shirt and matching shorts that hugged her hourglass curves. She'd finished the look with a vintage jean jacket, clear square frames, her lucky charm bracelet, and a gold nameplate necklace that spelled out the name she shared with her mom, her own legal first name.

"Thanks," Ariel said, then added, "I think?"

Marilou was ready to go. Her civilian disguise included a baseball cap with a peach emoji stitched at the center and a leather jacket borrowed from Ariel over a black slip dress.

They went out through the kitchen. Their sisters were still in pajamas, several bottles of wine open on the table. Feasting on a smorgasbord of delicious treats, the others had declined the offer to leave the house. Ariel swiped a couple of cookies for the road as she and Marilou sneaked out through the rear elevator.

"Turn off your location services!" was the last thing Sophia shouted as the metal doors shut.

Ariel was used to taking the dumpster alley for two reasons: The doorman was Uncle Iggy's snitch, and the front entrance was cordoned off by security because their fans liked to camp outside in hopes of catching a glimpse of them. The fans had always been a part of the neighborhood's everyday life when she was home, but it wasn't a normal thing to have people waiting at the front of your house or paparazzi hiding in the Central Park bushes across the street.

Blending in as she made her way past the crowd, Ariel followed her sister into the 81st Street station. Marilou, who was used to sneaking out more than Ariel, made quick work of getting them MetroCards.

"I just realized I've never bought a MetroCard," Ariel admitted, and accepted her pass.

"And you call yourself a New Yorker." Marilou winked and hip-checked the turnstile. It took Ariel two tries before she got it.

When the train came, Ariel let the warm breeze of the subway blow away her nerves. She was out of the del Mar penthouse. She was breaking their three-day lockdown. She was going to a concert where there would be hundreds of people and none of them would recognize her. That, and the thought of the energy of the crowd, had her bouncing on the balls of her sneakered feet as they squished into two seats in the air-conditioned train car.

They'd already missed the first hour of Battle of the Bands, but there was still a long lineup. Ariel scrolled through Aurora's Grocery's Pixagram page. She particularly wanted to see the band from Ecuador that called their sound "Andean techno." When she got to the final slide, she zoomed in on the headliners—Star Crossed. The name itself made her smile. She'd already memorized the song and now hummed the catchy chorus, delighted as the subway stops sped by.

She listened to everything around her. The rattle of the train tunneling underground, the ping of doors, the hissing when they opened and closed, the chatter of people coming and going, dozens of lives intersecting and running parallel in different directions. New York was its own song. Her mind cycled through the seeds of new lyrics, imagined details from the lives of every person. It was a game she'd played with her sisters as long as she could remember, even if the words didn't make it into all their songs.

When her attention settled on a group of girls carrying shopping bags and tall cups of bubble tea, Ariel turned to Marilou. "Do you think we'd be the same if we'd grown up as normal girls?"

"We *are* normal girls," Marilou told her. "We just happen to be millionaire pop stars who have superhero personas."

"Yeah," Ariel chuckled. "That elusive normal pop star."

An hour later, they were at Aurora's Grocery, a warehouse that had been around since the eighties. They found Chrissy on the long line snaking around the block and were subject to people grumbling when they cut in with her. One of the guys behind them was wearing a Siren Seven T-shirt with Elektra's face on it. He looked Ariel dead in the eyes and complained loudly to his friends. Ariel snorted at the irony, but felt bolstered by the fact that Cranky Fanboy hadn't recognized her.

"I bet if we tell the bouncer we're with Atlantica Records—"

"Nope." Ariel shut her sister down. "We're waiting in line. We're *normal* pop stars, remember?"

"I hate waiting," Marilou whimpered, but conceded.

While Chrissy expertly distracted Marilou by asking about her hair, Ariel's attention was drawn to the grating skid of tires. An SUV that had seen better days sped right at them. The front wheels hopped the curb, scaring the Cranky Fanboy as the van skidded to a stop.

A side door of the venue swung open, nearly clipping Ariel's nose, and separating Ariel from Marilou and Chrissy. Before she could protest, a young woman with black-and-purple hair hurried out. She blocked the path as four people leaped out of the SUV like the inside was on fire.

"Cutting it close, Reyes," the black-and-purple-haired girl said.

The guy in the foursome flashed a crooked smile as he popped open the trunk. "For once I agree with you, Vanessa."

Reyes.

Eric Reyes.

Ariel recognized him at once. Star Crossed's front man began unloading the instruments, each member of the band passing them down and into the venue. Ariel winced as she realized how late they must have been for load-in. Once, early on, before Siren Seven had become a well-oiled machine, Sophia had gone off with her assistant exploring the city and showed up minutes before they had to go onstage. Teo del Mar had fired the assistant on the spot and made Sophia sit out the set. No one was ever late after that.

Now Ariel's stomach tightened as the band hauled out the last pieces of the drum set and slammed the trunk door shut. A tall goth girl hopped into the driver's seat and adjusted the terrible parking job, moving in front of a heap of garbage bags.

Meanwhile, Eric set his guitar case down and blinked like he'd been startled. Ariel's belly fluttered as he turned her way, a feeling that was followed by twinge of disappointment when she realized he wasn't looking at *her*, but taking in the line of people waiting to go inside Aurora's Grocery. Ariel recognized the spark in his dark eyes. The understanding that all those people were there to hear him sing.

Eric combed his fingers through his thick black waves. Soft streetlight bronzed his skin, shadowed the sharp lines of his jaw, the swell of his biceps as he picked up a box of what looked like merch. He handed the box down the assembly line. Despite what seemed to be an anxiety-inducing mad dash, his smile was infectious. A tender, fuzzy sensation worked its way from her toes to the corners of her lips, which unfurled into a smile that matched his.

Her reverie was interrupted by a hard jab on her shoulder.

"Um, *hello?*" Cranky Fanboy behind her said impatiently. "Your friends are calling you."

Ariel blinked and realized the path was clear, and Marilou and Chrissy had been waving at her to hurry up and close the gap in the line.

"Sorry," she mumbled, and ran to catch up.

Though she'd see Eric inside, she couldn't stop her traitorous body from sneaking another glimpse over her shoulder. He was helping his bandmate straighten out the van, while the woman he'd called Vanessa shouted for them to hurry up.

Ariel caught another movement. A man with tufts of green hair sticking out from a hoodie stopped to light a cigarette. He glanced up and down the sidewalk, eyeing everyone on the busy street. Waiting for someone? Rubbernecking the commotion? Then he bent down as if to tie his shoe, but grabbed the guitar case instead.

For the briefest moment, Ariel wondered if he was a handler from the venue. A guitar tech getting the instrument ready. But when the man kept walking in the opposite direction, she understood what was really happening.

"Stop!" she shouted, waving her arms in the air. She pointed, but the street was too crowded, too noisy from the uproar inside the venue.

Only the guitar thief heard her. He craned his neck, looking up and down the block, assessing his best point of getaway.

Ignoring every ounce of common sense and self-preservation, Ariel was possessed. Moving. Running. Closing the width of the sidewalk, she tackled the thief as he started to sprint away. The momentum of their collision landed them on the mountain of garbage bags sitting on the curb. Adrenaline made her heart thunder in her ears as she tried to stand on trash that crunched and slipped beneath her feet.

"Get off me, you lunatic!" the thief shouted.

Honestly, the nerve. She hadn't realized she was trying to get up by using his torso for support until he managed to shove her and she fell backward, landing hard on her tailbone.

As she tried to catch her breath and pushed herself up on her elbows, Ariel was aware of someone kneeling at her side. The tumult allowed her to discern blurry fragments. White shirt. Black hair. Brown eyes, startled and focused on her. Eric Reyes.

"Are you hurt?" he asked, gently adjusting the slightly askew glasses on her nose. "How many fingers am I holding up?"

She chuckled low. "I didn't think people really asked that."

Eric smiled wide. He had the kind of smile that was both friendly and mischievous. "It's a tried-and-true method. Now come on—" He waggled his fingers, narrowing his eyes to read her necklace. "Melody."

Her belly squeezed when he called her that. It was her first name, but not even her family called her by it. She dusted bits of gravel and a smooshed cigarette butt that were stuck to her palms. Despite the sidewalk sludge blurring one lens, and a fine crack on the other, she saw him perfectly.

"Three." Ariel shook her head. "But your guitar—"

"Safe. Security's got it covered," he assured her, resting a comforting hand on her shoulder. "Holy shit. You were amazing. And incredibly reckless. But mostly amazing."

35

She removed her glasses and cleaned them with the hem of her shirt. A warm feeling bubbled in her chest. *Amazing and incredibly reckless.* She'd been told she was amazing more times than she could count. But "incredibly reckless" was new. And, yes, she should definitely not have put herself in danger that way, or exposed herself to a potential viral video so carelessly, but for the first time in so long, she hadn't thought. She just *did* what felt right.

Eric helped her stand, his grip as strong as a lifeline. "Are you sure you're okay?"

"I'm fine, I promise." She'd experienced worse during Siren Seven's brutal rehearsals. "My pride and left butt cheek are a little bruised, but I'll live."

He pressed his lips together like he was trying not to laugh.

From behind them, someone shouted, "Reyes! Let's go!"

His attention strayed to the side door, where Vanessa tapped her smart watch. They had a loud exchange of fast expletives in Spanish until she threw her hands up in frustration and trudged back inside.

"Sorry," Eric told Ariel as he released her, but he wavered between leaving her there and his very time-sensitive show. "We're—"

"Late. I know."

All at once Ariel remembered the curious crowd of concertgoers. The thrashing would-be thief who cursed at her as security dragged him away. Camera flashes blinding Ariel in the dark. If anyone recognized her . . . if her *father* found out . . . Thankfully, she was as far away from the glamorous Ariel del Mar as she could get.

Marilou and Chrissy slipped past the stern guard shooing everyone back in line, and came to her side. Both women eyed Eric with unadulterated delight.

"Maybe this is a sign that I should have stayed home," she told them.

"That is definitely not the lesson here," Marilou said, wrapping her little sister in a bone-crushing hug.

"Exactly," Eric said to Ariel. "You saved me. I've never played without that guitar. Please, let me find some way to thank you."

Ariel thought about what was waiting for her the next day. The deal she'd struck with her father. She'd come all this way, hadn't she? She couldn't turn back now. She took the hand Eric offered. His thumb smoothed across her knuckles in one slow movement she felt right down to her toes. Yeah, there was no way she was going home.

"Well," Ariel said coyly, "we *did* lose our place in line."

He winked. "Lucky for you, I know a guy."

"Uh, all of us, pretty boy," Marilou added. "We're a package deal."

Eric smiled his dizzying smile and led them backstage.

ATLANTICA RECORDS TEASES BIG REVEAL
FOR ARIEL DEL MAR, EXCLUSIVELY ON
WAKE UP! NEW YORK.

**An Ice Cream Truck Breaks Down on the
Brooklyn Bridge, Causing Five-Car Pileup.**

*TEODORO DEL MAR'S SORDID PAST.
A SIDE HIS FAMILY DOESN'T WANT YOU TO SEE.*

COMMUTERS MAKE THE BEST OF
A TWO-HOUR BRIDGE DELAY WITH A
SPONTANEOUS CONCERT.

CLICK HERE

YOUR CART CALLED:
50% OFF SIREN SEVEN LASHES
AND GEM APPLIQUÉS.

**SEVEN EXERCISES TO GET
THEA DEL MAR'S SIREN CURVES.**

CHAPTER FOUR

ERIC

6.24 DUMBO, New York

Eric's body hummed with adrenaline. He hadn't even realized he was still holding Melody's hand until they were pulled apart by the backstage fray. He led the three young women into the crowded backstage halls, up two flights of stairs, and through a side door that emptied out into the VIP mezzanine area. Melody had literally body-checked some dickbag who had tried to steal Eric's guitar, Pedro. She had no idea what that guitar meant to him. The least he could do was get them into the lounge, where they could have a private bartender and concessions.

"I've always wanted to come here." Melody smiled nervously, sitting on the arm of a worn leather chair.

He warmed at the way she took in the scuffed wood of the balcony, the ancient dartboard, the grimy paint marred by a hundred bands who'd graffitied their names on the walls, the mess of cables and stage lights strung to the rafters.

"A ton of rock legends have been discovered here," he said.

"I know!" She started counting on her fingers. "Las Rosas, The Waysiders, Saint Valentine—"

"*Ahem.*" One of Melody's friends cleared her throat. Eric and Melody startled apart, and she quickly introduced Mari, her sister with the pink hair, and their friend Chrissy.

39

Eric was usually a better host, but after the day he'd had, he was made of sugar and adrenaline. He told himself that was the reason he only had eyes for Melody.

"This is pretty sweet," Mari said, making herself at home in a lounge chair and kicking up her cowboy boots on the edge of a table.

Chrissy bobbed her head along to the current band, which was still finishing its set. "Do you play here a lot?"

Eric wanted to laugh, but he realized it was a serious question. "I *wish*. No, this is our first time onstage. But I was the in-house guitar tech for a few years, so this place was like a second home. Stay right here and I'll get you all some VIP bands."

He left them by the balcony and went in search of Aurora's manager, Willie Molina, who hugged him and cursed him out at the same time.

"Cutting it close. You want to give me a heart attack, kid?" Willie asked. His thick Nuyorican accent was more pronounced when he was stressed. Which was pretty much always.

"You have no idea," Eric said, explaining the bridge, the thief, the girl. Willie eyed him knowingly, flicking his eyes toward Melody. "It's not like that."

"Sure. It's never like that." Willie chuckled and pulled out three neon-green VIP bands. "Thinking you're slick. I was young once."

Eric raised his hands in a show of innocence. "I'm just saying thank you."

"For saving your abuelito's guitar?" Willie whistled. "Marry her."

"That's your advice for everything."

"And look at me. I'm a happy man." Willie gestured to his chest, his gold ring glinting in the lounge's pulsing lights. "All I'm saying is you write all these love songs to a dream girl and ignore the cityful of real ones."

Eric snatched the bands. "Just give me your blessing and I'll be happy, okay?"

Willie's blessing, or his bendición (as he preferred to call it), was unusual. It was a New York music scene superstition that Eric had witnessed during the years he'd worked at Aurora's. Willie cupped Eric's face with his callused palms. Then he smacked him. It was a gentle, loving, light slap. Among the musicians who graced the halls, it was a blessing—the literal hand of good luck. Those artists who had received it had gone off to six-figure record deals, viral videos, opening acts for the biggest musicians. Eric had waited for years, and now was his moment.

"Thanks, Willie. For everything."

"All right, all right," the big burly man said with tears in his eyes. "Go kill it."

Eric made his way back to Melody. *Of course* her name was Melody. His mind was already trying to arrange chord progressions and a strumming pattern, all because of the sweet contralto of her voice. He also needed to get backstage to the greenroom before his band and their manager came looking for him. And yet, he couldn't quite tear himself away. He told himself it was for no other reason than to finish paying her back for her heroics. That Melody was searching the crowd to people-watch, not because she was searching for him. But as he approached, she visibly perked up, and the way she smiled almost made him trip on his own idiot feet.

He fanned out the neon-green wristbands. Mari and Chrissy snatched them up in a second. When Melody took hers, their fingertips grazed. A wild and unknown sensation struck him again, right in the pit of his stomach. He'd felt it earlier when she sat up on the street and focused on him. Her long lashes framing wide brown eyes. Those pouty pink lips she kept worrying between her teeth, like she was nervous. Eric wasn't used to this feeling. Like he was struggling to catch his breath.

"I have about two minutes to get backstage or I'm a dead man," he said, though he remained rooted inches from her. His traitorous mouth betrayed him. "What are you doing after the show?"

Eric knew what he was supposed to do—give his best performance, have a post-concert beer, and get a full eight hours of sleep. He was leaving for tour first thing in the morning. He needed to focus on the prize—the band's success. His future.

"I have to—" Melody started to speak, but her friends interrupted in sync: "Nothing!"

"Can I buy you a drink? Or pizza. Both, even." *Both, even?* Who was he? Late. That's what he was. He glanced over his shoulder and saw Vanessa, her purple-and-black ponytail whipping around her as she searched the VIP area. He guessed he should be thankful his manager had sent her daughter and not come herself, because Odelia Garcia did not play around. When she spotted him, Vanessa waved her long, black nails like a threat. He began walking backward, arms open, waiting for Melody's response.

"A drink, or pizza, or both, even, sounds great," Melody said in a rush.

Eric smiled hard. "Meet me out front after the set."

He waved one more time, then Vanessa yanked him by his shirt collar, and they ran downstairs.

"You are *un*believable," she snapped.

"So I've been told." He chuckled, which was the wrong move.

She stopped right outside the backstage doors, pressing one of her long nails into his left pectoral. She had the same deadly stare as her mother. "Real talk. You've worked so hard to be here today. Can you get back in the game?"

"I didn't get *out* of the game, Vee."

She pursed her lips. "There's a hundred people who'd be happy to hook up with you if you're looking to blow off steam before we leave for tour. You don't keep your band waiting."

I was keeping track of the time, he wanted to say, but didn't. Vanessa didn't react to excuses. So he deflected by flirting. "Why, you offering?"

"Gross." She grimaced.

He clapped his hand over his heart, trapping her hand there. "Ouch."

"You're so pretty it makes me want to throw up. Plus, we both know you're not my type."

He knew that, of course. Years ago, when her mother had tried to set them up, it was the first thing Vanessa had told him before the appetizer course arrived. They'd been friends ever since. He couldn't even be mad at her real talk, because she was right. There were people depending and waiting on him. He'd gotten swept up in the moment.

"I'm here," he reassured her. "I'm good."

Pleased, she retracted her claws and opened the backstage doors. "We backlined the gear, and my mom is making sure the techs got the set list and light cues. Let's just get you miked up. You're on in fifteen."

Backstage, the rest of the band was jumping off the walls. They wanted to know everything about the almost-robbery. There were no secrets between them, but for some reason he couldn't yet understand, he wanted to keep the details of Melody to himself a little longer. Especially as the preshow jitters flooded his system.

Once he was miked up, Eric walked to the wings of the stage to watch the last hopeful band finish its song. He'd seen dozens of Battles of the Bands. Before he'd met his girls, he'd spectacularly bombed a few, too. He *knew* how those musicians must be feeling—like their whole world depended on the roar of the crowd.

Even with the blinding white lights in his eyes, he looked out at the VIP level, hoping to catch a glimpse of his savior girl. Melody. He'd been so busy staring up there, he missed the emcee announce the winning band. They came rushing from backstage, hugging each other. Eric cheered, but he also watched the losing band trudge offstage in full defeat. He caught the drummer by the shoulder.

Eric said, "Hey, you killed it out there. This wasn't your only shot."

The kid only gave a pained smile and kept walking.

"You're such a mush," Grimsby said at his ear.

"Beneath that goth exterior, so are you." He gave her a kiss on the cheek that made her roll her eyes.

"Wow." Max finger-combed her bangs over her eyes. "I think I might throw up."

"There is no puking in rock and roll," Carly said, cracking her knuckles.

Grimsby's eyes narrowed. "That is *not* true."

"Okay, huddle up," Eric said, linking arms with his bandmates in a tight circle as the lights dimmed. "Today was the longest week of our lives. But we made it. We're here. We're together. We know who we are. So let's show 'em."

They stacked their hands on top of his and howled a cheer, just for each other.

Eric accepted his guitar from the tech. Smoothing his palm along the curve of its body, he secured the strap around his neck. He took his place in the dark. Max tapped a quick *tss* of her cymbal. The crowd perked up and whistled. He wondered—he hoped—that one of those hollers was from Melody.

A focus light slowly illuminated him. He smiled at the crowd, anxious, excited, blessed. He leaned close to the mic and waited for a break in the applause.

"Give it up to all the bands that killed it tonight, especially the Plutos for their big win." He glanced up at the mezzanine balcony again and his chest gave a tight squeeze. "Aurora's Grocery is real special for me. When I was nineteen, broke and hungry, this place gave me my first job cleaning the bathrooms. The things I've seen . . ." He flashed a smile, because that always got a laugh. Then he stroked the opening riff.

"When I showed them what I could do," he said, "I worked my

way up. Ten years later, I'm on this stage for the first time. Funny, how life works. One minute you're refilling the toilet paper, and then bam, everything changes. Tomorrow we're kicking off our *first-ever* national tour, and we're coming full circle, right back here. So if you like what you hear, we've got more of it. Come on up! Come closer. Don't be shy, now."

He felt the crowd move and shift, get closer to the stage. He glanced up again, the roving lights clearing just enough so he could see her. Melody leaning over the balcony, smiling at him. There, then gone in the shadows.

"I'm Eric Reyes. We're Star Crossed, and we're going to play you the new single off our self-titled album. This is 'Love Like Lightning.'"

Max came in with the drums, the fast tempo matching the way Eric's heartbeat ratcheted up to his throat. Grimsby's bass hit the perfect notes, and then Carly took the spotlight with the way she owned her guitar. He shut his eyes and sang, but even then he kept seeing her—warm brown eyes and pink lips— and he knew, he knew he'd written every single word of his songs before he'd ever met her, but he sang to her now, because, impossibly, it felt right.

Star Crossed didn't stop. Kicking right into "Sunset Hearts," Eric did what he did best. He performed. When he was onstage, every discordant thing that had ever gone wrong vanished. There was only the song, his friends giving it their all, and the bodies moving to the rhythm he set. His guitar was an extension of himself, as if he'd been carved from the same wood, bits of him strung and tightened to create, to belt out his heart of hearts. Seamlessly slipping into the moody sounds of "Montana Snowfalls," he watched the crowd undulate to Grimsby's bass, to Carly's strums, to Max's steady kick drum. If there was a greater feeling than this, Eric had yet to find it.

When it was over, the crowd called for an encore. He turned to the band, and each of them nodded at him eagerly. They'd never gotten that kind of roar before.

"I guess tonight is a good night for firsts," he said into the mic. "This one's for the girl who saved my life today."

He bit his lower lip and glanced up. The lights were too bright, obscuring everything. He hoped that she was still there. That she was looking down at him and smiling right back.

They reprised their opening number, sliding right into "Love Like Lightning" one more time.

As the lights cut out, they filed backstage and into the greenroom. If their preshow energy was frantic, the post-show vibes were kinetic. Odelia, who wasn't one for public displays of emotion, hugged him before heading to collect their headlining fee. Willie and all the staff who had known him for years stopped by for a send-off. Somehow beers found their way into each of their hands.

"I think that was our best show yet," Max announced to the room. She took a sip of her drink, and Eric plucked the bottle from her hand. She was so confused, she followed the foam that dribbled out until it was out of her reach. "Exsqueeze me?"

"I need a favor," he said, twisting his face into the pleading, ridiculous look of utter adoration that had gotten him out of every speeding ticket, every scolding from his mother, every bad grade and bad date. "Please. Mi amor. Mi vida."

"Do not start with that 'puppy chulo' shit with me, Eric Reyes," Max warned.

"You know it's *papi* chulo." Eric narrowed his eyes. Though he didn't mind being reminded that he was attractive, he regretted ever trying to teach his bandmates rudimentary Spanish.

"What do you want?" Max asked impatiently.

He took a swig of his stolen beer. "I need you to drive tonight. I sort of have a meetup."

"You're really going to ditch us for a date right now?" Carly asked.

"I'm asking you to ditch me, actually," Eric clarified.

"Can't you wait to get laid on the road, Eric Reyes?" Grimsby muttered.

He raked his fingers through his hair. He needed deodorant. And gum. "It's not like that. I can't explain it. I—I swear on my baby."

Max pointed her drumstick at him. "Your baby is four wheels held together by duct tape and Latino baby Jesus's mercy."

He blew out an exasperated breath. "Then I swear on Pedro."

He picked up his guitar and held it across his palms like he was some old knight presenting his sword. They knew it was serious when he swore on his Pedro. His grandfather had crafted the guitar for him out of tropical rosewood. It was the last guitar he'd ever made, and it had been for Eric.

"Damn," Carly said, rubbing her chin in consideration.

Max groaned but thrust out her open palm for the keys. She was the only other one of them with a valid driver's license. "Fine. But only because it's your birthday."

"And," Grimsby added, "we better not be raising your secret baby in nine months."

"I swear, you all have collectively dirtier minds than my entire family, and—"

"We're Colombian," the three of them finished for him.

"I need new friends," he admitted, stripping off his shirt to swap it out for the clean, if wrinkled, white T-shirt he kept in his guitar case.

His screen lit up with a call from his estranged father. Not in the mood to ruin what was left of his birthday, Eric sent it to voicemail.

He grabbed his brown leather jacket and kissed them all goodbye. Grimsby, as always, grimaced and rubbed her cheek.

"Good luck!" they cried in singsong, suggestive ways.

He shook his head but barked a laugh. "I definitely need new friends."

As he stepped into the cool Brooklyn night, he checked for his wallet, his phone, his house key. When he checked again, Eric Reyes realized that he was nervous. When he was about to start a show, stepping onto the dark stage in a room full of strangers, he wasn't *nervous*, exactly. It was preshow jitters, that spark of excitement telling him he was about to connect with an audience. This was something else. It was like strutting off a gangplank into an unknown sea in search of a feeling he only ever experienced when he was making music.

Eric had two rules, the first being he'd get nowhere without patience. The second was that music was everything. It was his life, the reason he hadn't spoken to his father in ten years. It was in his blood, grafted deep into his bones, stitched into his sinews. It was his future.

He'd sworn off real dating and all attempts at romantic relationships in the last year so he could focus on the group's new album and first big tour. The results had produced some of the best music he'd written. Besides, Grimsby liked to tell him that reputations are earned, and over the years, he'd earned his as a flirt. Someone who let women take him home for a night, but not *bring* home. A one-night stand, not a forever one.

He didn't want that to be the case with Melody. Even if she felt the same, he couldn't start something with her and then pull a disappearing act. He was *leaving* the state in twelve hours, for David Bowie's sake.

So what was he doing?

When he saw her, waiting at the corner of the block for him, he knew. It was simple. Pure. Thrilling. It was everything. He was going to meet a girl.

THE TUTTLE TELLER

Episode 1365:
Siren Seven: From Humble Beginnings to Music Royalty (Part I)

Transcript:

Here's everything you need to know about Teodoro del Mar. Ugh, I just love saying his entire name. Teo, or "Daddy" del Mar, as the Lucky Sevens call him, is no stranger to success. Before he created Siren Seven, the music tycoon was in the limelight for his eighties glam-pop duo, Luna Lunita, with late wife Maia del Mar.

As Luna Lunita, the husband-and-wife duo were big in Latin America and Europe, but never quite crossed over to the States. I was able to dig up some used vinyl from ridiculously obscure collectors in Sweden.

While Luna Lunita was only active for two years, they snatched up two gold singles and one platinum for "Amor de Mi Vida" and "Solo Tu Amor," with "Luna Mia" their biggest hit. All three scored Teo del Mar consecutive Grammys for Best Latin Pop Recording. But once the couple got pregnant with rebel girl Sophia, Luna Lunita hung up their bedazzled leather jackets and focused on family. They got BUSY, y'all.

And OH MY SIRENS, I'm here to tell you how good Luna Lunita was. Honestly? Their first album was absolute fire. My mom caught me listening to it, and even she said she remembers the lyrics TO THIS DATE. If you're a member of my private chat, we're streaming some Luna Lunita tonight. #DJTuttle.

On to the big news. I am dying for the big reveal tomorrow. If you see me in the Times Square crowd, I'll be wearing my custom Siren Seven satin bomber jacket. Now, SimonSays69 thinks that we're getting a Siren Seven movie. I mean, I would die. Literally die. S7SuperFan3452 is hoping that the news about the breakup was a hoax. Oh, I'm sorry, honey. We all are.

Personally, I'm hoping for nothing but the best for our gorgeous, gorgeous girls.

See you at Times Square tomorrow!

Subscribe, like, follow, tell me you love me ♥

CHAPTER FIVE

ARIEL

6.24 DUMBO, New York

"I believe I promised pizza."

When Ariel del Mar recognized his voice, she turned around so quickly, she nearly crashed into him. Good thing she was quick on her feet. She'd already done enough rookie football for one night.

"And I believe it was a drink, or pizza, or both, even."

Slightly out of breath, Eric raked his dark waves back. He'd changed his shirt, and when the breeze shifted, she caught the pleasing scent of a spicy bergamot cologne and sweet sweat. She remembered the way he held his guitar. How toward the end of a booming bridge he'd swing it up and rest the base against his pelvis. She had never, in her entire life, wanted to *be* a guitar. *That* guitar, if it meant being held by him. A warm sensation spread across her torso, up her neck, and to the tops of her ears. Was that a heart attack? Was she too young for full-bodied hot flashes?

"Melody," he said, and offered his arm.

Her initial crush on Eric Reyes had quadrupled in intensity after seeing him perform, and now deepened with that small, kind gesture. As she linked their arms together, Ariel realized that she was a girl taking a stroll with a guy who was the perfect combination of hot and sweet. A normal girl getting a drink and pizza. A girl, surrounded by people, who no one paid special attention to. It was glorious.

"How'd you like the show?" Eric asked, after walking a block in silence. "Please, lie to me."

"In that case, it was awful. Really, the worst show I've ever been to."

She craned her head back to watch him smile, his eyes crinkling at the corners.

"That's the nicest thing anyone's said to me."

"I mean every word."

He clapped a hand over his heart, and she felt a slight tremble go through him like he was releasing all the pent-up nerves and stress that come with a performance. "Well, it's a compliment for someone who is allegedly doomed."

"What do you mean?"

"Oh, just my entire band believes we're doomed"—he paused to think—"or cursed. Maybe both. I'll tell you about it, but I require sustenance first."

About fifteen minutes later, they were at a crowded pizza shop, Laucella's. Her first instinct was to raise her palm to hide her face. But even though she caught heads turning toward Eric, she went completely unnoticed. Ariel didn't *feel* like a different person. Yes, her stage persona was superbly *extra*. But it was like dialing herself up to full volume, not like being someone different. At least, she used to think that. Without her signature red wig, her lashes, her layers of makeup, was she still Ariel? If no one recognized her, how could she be the person she'd always thought she was?

She decided a pizza parlor around the corner from the Brooklyn Bridge was not the place for an existential meltdown.

They slid into an empty corner booth. Eighties hair bands played from a jukebox, and a tired-looking waitress dropped off menus and tap water, promising to return to take their order.

"What's your poison?" he asked.

"Half of my sisters have been obsessed with cauliflower pizza crusts, so definitely not that. What about pineapple and ham?"

Eric grinned, but wrinkled his nose. "You're one of those."

She smirked at him. "One of what?"

"Monsters who think pineapple goes on pizza," he said playfully. Everything about him was playful—the way he rapped his knuckles on the surface of the table, the way his straight white teeth bit at his plump bottom lip, and the way he glanced up at her from behind the black fringe of his lashes. Everything.

She feigned offense and pretended to study the menu. "There are two kinds of people in this world. Those who love Hawaiian pizza, and those who are wrong."

He laughed so hard, people turned around to look at them. The sudden attention made her shrink. Scratch the side of her temple, even though it didn't itch, just to cover her face.

"I have an idea," he said. "Trust me?"

He phrased it as a question, but it could have easily been a plea. Sophia had always warned her against people who were too quick to ask for trust, especially in a romantic situation. But this was innocent enough.

She held up one finger. "No anchovies." Then another. "And no mushrooms."

"You have my word."

The waitress returned, and he rattled off a combination that seemed like the best of both worlds—a large pizza topped with rosemary sausage, pineapple, and pesto. She ordered a cider, and he said, "Make that two."

"So, Eric Reyes, tell me about this curse." Ariel leaned slightly toward him on the squeaky pleather seat.

He told her about what sounded like a nightmare day. With every word she noticed the way his hands were so animated, the way his thick black waves kept flopping over his forehead no matter how many times he finger-combed them back. She wanted to reach out and brush a thick lock but fidgeted with her necklace instead.

"Wow. On top of leaving Jersey City with an empty gas tank, a two-hour traffic jam, your crew dropping like flies, someone tries to steal your guitar. I feel like you need a salt bath. My sister—" She bit her tongue before she said Thea, which wasn't a super-common name. She couldn't be too careful. "My sister Tee would probably strip you naked and submerge you in a salt bath full of flower petals and crystals on a waning moon."

The image she conjured made her entire face feel hot. His gaze darkened for a heartbeat as it flicked toward her lips and then away.

"What are you talking about?" he asked, amused. "That's my normal Friday night."

"Well, then, you need a new lucky charm. To break the curse and all."

"Oh?"

She tugged at the charm bracelet on her wrist. A thin purple braid with a tiny golden star hanging from the center. She wiggled it off and took Eric's wrist. His skin was surprisingly soft, everywhere except the permanent calluses on the pads of his fingers. The bracelet had no stretch and barely fit around his hand, but when she adjusted the strings, it was just right.

"What's this?" he asked.

She swallowed a knot in her throat. She didn't want to lie, yet she couldn't exactly tell him the whole truth. But the truth looked different from a certain point of view. From where she was standing, she felt like she was teetering on a very foreign edge.

"My sisters and I each bought one at our first parade on Coney Island. It was one of the first times we'd been in public after our mom died, and we walked past a tiny shop and picked them out. Each one had a different charm."

"I couldn't take this from you. Are you sure?"

Guilt gnawed at her for the things she left out of the story. Yes, they'd been at the Mermaid Parade, but they'd been headlining the ball at the aquarium. Since then, the only time Ariel or her sisters took off the bracelets was when they were onstage. Maybe it was because their Siren Seven days were behind her, or because she wanted him to remember her after this night, but she nodded.

"I'm sure." She ran her finger along the purple bracelet, the tender skin of his inner wrist, feeling his quick pulse. "It's time its luck rubs off on someone else."

"Melody," he said, and the tenor of his voice nearly trembled when he said her name. She was certain, then, that Eric Reyes was going to kiss her.

Instead, their pizza arrived. The waitress set the metal tray on a rack and put down their ciders with an apologetic smile.

"That is a work of art," Eric proclaimed.

And it was—topped with fresh mozzarella, rosemary sausage, caramelized pineapple, and a spiral of pesto. Ariel realized she hadn't eaten dinner, and he was likely having the post-show hunger pangs. They were each on their second slice before either of them came up for air.

"I would let you pick my pizza toppings anytime," she said, licking marinara sauce from the corner of her mouth.

Eric grinned, brushing a crumb from his lip. "Promise?"

She held out her pinkie finger, and he hooked his with hers. They remained that way for a heartbeat, until his phone rang. The name Max popped up. Ariel almost spit out her drink as she realized the girl in the photo was wearing a Siren Seven T-shirt from a few tours back.

When he excused himself to take the call, she was almost relieved. Her past was a land mine of Siren Seven. Pretending she wasn't a world-famous singer had been exciting at the beginning of the night, but she hadn't thought about how to keep it going. She liked talking to Eric. Really liked it. The only other people she was this comfortable with were her sisters and Chrissy. She wanted to be as open with him as he was with her.

Perhaps—and she couldn't believe she was considering it—perhaps she should tell him the truth. It was presumptuous of her to even think he'd care. Then she remembered how nice it was to just have a normal night, sharing pizza with a sweet, sexy, *kind* guy. Getting to know him without wondering what tabloid rumors he believed to be true. She had to be Ariel 2.0 in the morning. She could be herself, Melody, for a few more hours.

"Sorry," Eric said. "My car requires a little TLC, and Max's MO is more bull in a china shop."

"You all seem really close," she said, accepting another round of ciders from the waitress. "How'd you meet?"

Eric's eyes brightened as he picked the pineapple off his third slice. "Oh man, you'd probably never believe me."

"Hit me with your best shot, Eric Reyes."

"Challenge accepted." He got comfortable, easing against the cushioned booth, stretching out his arm along the top like they were in his living room. If she scooted a foot to the left, she'd be nestled flush against his side. But she remained perfectly still as he raised a finger in warning. "Get ready for a ridiculously unbelievable series of events."

She cocked her brow skeptically but motioned for him to continue.

"When I first moved here from Miami, I didn't know anyone in the city. On days I wasn't working at Aurora's, I was busking in Union Square. A few weeks in, this tiny Filipina girl comes up to me and is like, 'I have to take these guinea pigs to the animal shelter, but if you're still here when I come back, I want to buy you a drink.'"

"Why did she have guinea pigs?"

"She worked for a pharmaceutical company—that's another story. I didn't think I'd see her again, but an hour later, Max took me to lunch and said we should start a band."

"She found you," Ariel said. "I love that. And the others?"

"We went to a bunch of clubs, put up a bunch of Gregslist ads and flyers, but we found Carly at one of Max's cousin's debuts. It's like a quinceañera, but when you're eighteen. Anyway, Carly was playing with *that* band, and she was just, like, shredding. So good. Too good. It made the rest of the band look like amateurs."

Ariel tried to unstick her thighs from the seat, but that just nudged her a little closer to him. She chuckled lightly and said, "It's a shame there were no guinea pigs involved in that one."

"You would think."

She narrowed her eyes skeptically. "No way."

"Someone had wrapped a hamster as a present, but it chewed through the cardboard and got loose. We caught it. Saved the day. We're basically animal vigilantes."

"And the bass player?"

"Grimsby?" Eric smirked, and she realized this must be his favorite story to tell. "I was actually buying a record in St. Mark's, and a girl dressed in all black—I mean spike collar and bracelets and all—is sampling music, and I just glance over to see what she's listening to, and it's ABBA."

"My sister says goth is an attitude," Ariel said.

"Which sister, Mari or Tee?"

"Another one." She waved her hand as a distraction. "I have a lot of sisters. Continue."

"So, I just introduced myself to Grimsby and listened to her music theories and how she dreamed of writing a song that had a perfect balance of joy and ennui."

"And has she?"

Eric leaned forward, like he was telling her a secret. "I actually still haven't looked up the definition of ennui."

Ariel's cheeks hurt from grinning. "Okay, but this one has no guinea pigs?"

He lazily picked up his cider and took a sip. She was mesmerized by the bob of his Adam's apple as he swallowed, then realized what his silence implied.

"Literally how?" she asked. "There is no way."

"You'd think. Grimsby had a guinea pig as a pet, although we didn't find out about it until she moved in with us. Guess where she adopted it from?"

"No."

"Yep."

Eric slammed his bottle down for emphasis. "The same shelter where Max dropped off those guinea pigs."

"You were fated." She reached out and flicked the star charm decorating his wrist. She liked it on him. "And this story features an improbable amount of guinea pigs."

He snapped his fingers. "Great band name."

Speaking of, there was something she'd been curious about since Marilou shared his song with her. "How'd you settle on Star Crossed?"

Eric wagged a finger in the air. "I feel like I've monopolized the conversation."

"I've told you stuff," she said, defensively, but nerves tangled in her belly.

"So far all I know is that you're incredibly brave." His lips hooked into a smile. "But a little shy. Ridiculously beautiful."

Ariel had been adored in so many ways and with so much hyperbole, but when Eric Reyes called her beautiful, she felt a little dizzy. He was smooth enough not to pause—he kept going, as if he was stating a fact instead of fishing for gratitude—and continued listing the things he knew about her.

"You have at least three sisters." He tugged on his new lucky brace-let. "Sentimental." He gently removed her glasses and pushed them up the bridge of his nose. He blinked, adjusting to her prescription. "Slightly nearsighted?"

"Go on."

"And you love music."

She shrugged one shoulder and pointed at the empty pizza tray. "You forgot my incredible taste buds."

"I appreciate the mystery. I'd ask you if we could do this again, but I'm leaving on tour in"—he checked his watch— "ten hours."

"In that case, thank you for tonight. I've never done *this* before."

"Oh god, is this your first time having pizza?" He fixed that mischievous gaze on her. "Was it good for you?"

She gave him a playful shove for teasing her, even though it made her feel like she was glowing from the inside out. "I mean this. Spontaneously stay out late. I'm twenty-five, and there's a thousand things someone my age has probably done that I haven't. It's just—our dad's really, *really*, very overprotective."

"*Two* reallys and one *very*." Something made him serious, his smile faltering for the first time since they'd sat down. "I can relate."

She wanted to know more, but the waitress sidled up to their table and set the check down. "Sorry, lovebirds. We closed about ten minutes ago."

Ariel reached for her tiny wallet, but Eric shook his head.

"This is my thank-you pizza, remember?"

She rubbed the shoulder that felt ever so tender from her fall. "Oh, that? It was nothing."

"Melody," he said, holding her stare. "It was *everything*."

They looked at each other for so long, the waitress lowered herself between them slowly. Her gray curls were coming undone from her bun. She grinned despite her annoyance, and whispered, "I expect a big tip."

Eric flashed the older woman that smile of his, impossible to look away from. "Mi vida, I wouldn't dream of anything else."

The waitress took his cash and laughed as she walked away.

"Smooth," Ariel said.

He slid out of the booth and offered his hand, which she accepted as if they'd held hands a hundred times before. "That's my middle name."

When they stepped outside the pizza parlor, the night was quiet. As quiet as nights in the city got. Restaurants up and down the street had already pulled down their grates, but stragglers lingered in conversation or flagged down green outer borough taxis. She could see the Brooklyn Bridge, the winking lights of Manhattan. Hear the constant hum of traffic.

"Where's home?" Eric asked. "I can get you a cab or take the subway with you, if you're going into the city."

"Actually, give me one second." Ariel's fingers trembled as she unlocked her phone. She had dozens of texts and even more notifications. She scrolled through them as she got out of earshot.

Chrissy:
😍 how's it going?

Marilou:
Check in, bish. Dad's home.

Chrissy:
So I'm in your room, no big deal . . .

Chrissy:
But I had to pretend to be you and got under the covers because your dad knocked on the door, so when you get in, don't freak out that I'm in your bed.

Marilou:
Make sure you take a yellow taxi!

Also, I'd like to talk about a raise ☺

Ariel hit the call button, and Marilou picked up before the first ring.

"Melody Ariel Marín Lucero," she loud-whispered. "You were *supposed* to check in."

"Wow, pulling out the government name." She smiled at Eric, who was chatting with the pizza guys in Spanish. "We just finished dinner."

Marilou gasped. "Are you going *home* with him? What's it been, like a year since Trevor?"

Ariel decided to ignore that. "I'm only checking in to tell you I'm alive before I talk myself out of it."

"Aww, you're such a good little guppy."

"You're the worst. I love you, byyeee." Ariel hung up her phone and walked back to Eric.

"Everything okay?" he asked.

"My sister. We're close. Some people find that weird."

"It's not. I haven't talked to my family in—I don't know how long."

She couldn't imagine not talking to her sisters for even a couple of hours. She knew that families were complicated, but she didn't want to think about it just then. She wanted to be in the moment, to hold on as long as she could before the sun came up.

"Do you know what else I've never done?" She took a step closer and fixed the collar of his brown leather jacket.

He gave a slight shake of his head, and under the yellow streetlight, she could see the shadows along his throat as he swallowed, his single word almost breathless. "What?"

"How about I show you?" This time, she started walking and didn't have to look up to know that he was right by her side.

CHAPTER SIX

ERIC

6.25 New York, New York

"How have you never walked across the Brooklyn Bridge?" Eric asked Melody.

She scrunched up her nose. "I've never been to the top of the Empire State Building, either. It's for tourists."

He clapped a hand over his heart. "Then I suppose I am a tourist."

"I'm kidding." She gently shoved him, but there was no force behind it. Only the feel of her palm on his shoulder, like they were testing boundaries. "There's so much of the city I haven't seen. Something always comes up. Then, *boom*, you're twenty-five and feel like a stranger in your own home. I don't even know if the bridge is safe at this time of night."

"I hope so, since you, a renowned guitar hero, are here to defend me," he teased, though there was no way in hell he'd knowingly put her in danger. "Nah, when I first moved here my mother would call me with every murder report she saw on the news. I had to explain Jersey City and Texas were nowhere near each other."

Melody laughed into the night. As they began the trek across the pedestrian walkway, they settled into a comfortable silence. Eric usually liked to talk. When he was a kid, family dinners were so tense. His father reading the paper or letting his meal get cold while he took a business call in his office. His mother suffered from anxiety, and when she was too stressed to eat, he cleaned up the kitchen and sang her favorite songs. He filled the silence because sometimes the lack of noise was louder, intolerable.

With Melody, he simply walked, and he was happy settling into her soothing calm. It was like she was appreciating every moment, no matter how small. Occasionally, the sleeves of their jackets would brush, and he didn't know if it was because she was walking toward him or he was trying to crash into her again.

"My dad is sort of like that," Melody said after a while. "Paranoid about things he can't control. Distrustful about new people. He always said we were safer together as a family, but over the years he's gotten worse."

"If your father's overprotective," Eric said, shoving his hands into his pockets, "how much should I fear for my life? I mean, whatever he's got, it would be worth it. I just want to be prepared."

"Been chased by many dads?"

Eric rubbed at the scar on his elbow that he'd gotten when he was sixteen and leaped out of his girlfriend's window after her father caught them in her room. That's not the man he was anymore, but the battle scars were a good reminder.

"You could say that," he admitted.

Melody's laugh was a bright, sweet sound, and so different from the husky contralto of her speaking voice. "I'm the one who needs to worry. I've actually never disobeyed him. My sisters, definitely. Even in the smallest of ways."

"So you're the good one?" As an only child, he couldn't relate. He had to play all the roles for his parents. The good son. The successful son. The proud son. Somehow, he'd managed to fail at all of it.

"I'm not the good one," she protested. Then she pursed her lips in a way that made Eric want to stop, pull her close. Dig his fingers into the pockets of her tiny pink shorts, feel the pressure of her curves against him. "Fine, maybe I am. It's complicated."

"I'm the mayor of complicated."

"Please," she said, all skeptical. "I'm the president of complicated."

"Okay, Madame President. Tell me."

He could feel her holding back. He'd never admit to being cocky, but he could usually get women to spill their secrets, their dreams and desires. He liked to listen to their stories. Every person he connected with made him feel woven into the greater tapestry of the world, less alone. Melody had walls around her, and he wanted nothing more than to tear them down. To see the person underneath it all, because he couldn't imagine not knowing her after tonight.

"My father really wants me to stay in the family business," she said after a thoughtful beat. "I've spent all my life doing and being everything he wanted from us. Terrible hours. Team player. And he promised that after all of that hard work, I'd get to break off on my own one day. But then he changed his mind, and he says it's for the good of the family. For me."

"And now you're questioning your entire life while in the company of an extremely handsome and talented musician." Eric was rewarded with her smile.

"Something like that."

People littered the bridge, nights ending or just beginning. Dozens of strangers crossing paths without paying one another any mind. That was the beauty, and the flaw, of New York City. You could scream your fears and hopes and dreams, and people could just pretend not to hear you. But Eric heard her.

"Let me guess," he said. "He's trying to live vicariously through you."

She frowned. "Better me than all my sisters. That way only one of us has to deal with it."

"Why does it have to be you?"

She peered up at him through her broken glasses. "Because I'm the good one, remember?"

They'd made it halfway across the bridge at an easy pace. He'd never wanted the bridge to magically extend before. He'd walk all the way to New Jersey or uptown, just so he could stretch out the short amount of time they had together.

He stopped and faced the dark water, smelled rain in the damp air. "When I left Medellín, I did it against my parents' wishes. I wanted to be a musician, and my father wanted me to be a land developer like him. Sometimes I regret leaving home. I miss my mother, but for years she wasn't allowed to talk to me or risk making my father angry. I resented that. I miss Colombia, especially in the winter. Snow is the worst."

She nudged her shoulder against his arm. "You just need a good jacket."

"Maybe. But I had to keep reminding myself of what I wanted. It's not about being good or bad. It's about making your own way."

"Believe me," she said, turning pensively toward the river. "I tried."

"What do you want, Melody?"

She glanced at him, unfurling that secretive grin. His pulse raced. He reminded himself to breathe while he waited for her response.

"Come on," he encouraged. "It's only me and the whole of New York. We don't judge."

Finally, she inhaled deeply and said, "I want to be a songwriter."

The answer piqued his interest. "For yourself, or others?"

"Others. I've never said that out loud before. Not even to my sisters."

"Sing for me?" he asked softly.

"I said write, not sing."

"I have a good ear." They stared each other down, that beautiful stubborn pout of hers winning out. "Fine. I'm a patient man."

When her phone beeped, she quickly glanced at the screen before tucking it in her jean jacket pocket. "Are you hungry? I'm hungry."

He wondered, could you hunger to be in someone's presence? In that case, he was ravenous for her. "Do you like empanadas?"

Melody made an excited little gasp he should not have enjoyed so profoundly. "Yes, please. Let's do that."

As he led the way across the rest of the bridge, he felt a few raindrops. She started telling him about her many sisters as they hopped on the train, and didn't finish until they emerged on the Lower East Side. For a moment he envied her; then he thought of Carly, Grimsby, and Max. Hell, even Vanessa. He'd moved to a new country and chosen a new family that chose him back. He *had* sisters.

By the time they got to the restaurant, it was pouring. Despite his best attempts to cover them both with his jacket, Eric and Melody were damp. Three flights up, they reached Julio's, a South American restaurant that turned into a club after the dinner service, and then a secret after-hours bar after last call. Waxy fake palms decorated every corner, and the purple and yellow neon lights cast an ambient glow. They waded through the tipsy dancing revelers, finding two seats tucked away at the corner of the bar.

She hopped onto the spinning stool. He took up the seat beside her, and it was so crowded, their knees had to interlock so they could face each other. He felt a hard tug at the pit of his stomach, touching her this way. Even through the layers of their clothes, he felt her radiate like sunshine.

"How did you find this place?" Melody asked.

"I used to spend a lot of nights out." Eric waved at the bartender. "A lot."

"Used to?"

"A few years ago, I felt like the band was in a rut, so I decided to concentrate on writing the best album I could. That meant no after-hours, no dating, only the music."

"I told you what I wanted," she said, watching him with curious eyes. "What do you want? To be a rock star?"

"That's the plan," he admitted. "We've done small, regional tours before, mostly whatever dives we could book. I can't explain it, but this one feels different."

"National tours generally are," she said. "So I've heard. I mean, I assume."

"Big tour. Big album. *Big bus.* That's going to be the real friendship trial."

"I spent most of my life on the road with my family," she said, picking at a scuff on the bar top. "We moved from place to place. I was actually homeschooled for my entire life."

"You're not in one of those cults, are you?" He laughed, though she went momentarily serious.

"It's more like a sorority," she said, with a slight wince. He wasn't sure what to make of that, but, hell, for Melody, he'd likely join a cult, secret society, whatever, and sign over all six hundred dollars in his bank account.

Someone channeling the dancing spirit of Rita Moreno bumped into him, pushing him closer to Melody. She grabbed his thigh for balance, and the pressure of her touch right there had him breathless. She had no idea what she was doing to him. How her nearness unlocked something he'd buried for months—years, perhaps.

Melody picked up one of the menus and pointed at the top option. "What is a Bartender's Judgment?"

"Oh, that's when Julio looks at you and makes you your perfect drink. He's literally a wizard."

"A brujo, actually," came a new voice. A former dancer, Julio was a slender Chilean man with black painted nails who dressed almost exclusively like the eighties had never left. He stared at Melody, then at Eric, and began tossing bottles and ice and shakers around.

She leaned into his side and whispered, "Thank you for bringing me here, Eric Reyes."

"You're welcome, Melody—Guitar Hero. Sorry. You never said your last name."

"Marín."

"Melody Marín," he said. "Who wants to be a songwriter but doesn't like to sing."

"Doesn't *want* to sing," she corrected. "At the moment."

He was suddenly, unfathomably curious to hear one of her songs. To know if he was right, if the soft, deep registers of her voice would sound just as beautiful as when she said his name.

Julio returned with their drinks. For her, a pale lavender cocktail with a tiny golden fork, a maraschino cherry skewered by its tines, and a tequila sunrise for Eric with a ridiculous pink flamingo plastic toy hanging from the rim.

She chuckled. "A fork?"

"A trident," Julio said, like it was obvious, then moved down the bar to check on more patrons.

Melody bit the cherry and pointed the tiny gold trident at him. "A trident is just a giant fork."

"Julio has a giant bag of tiny toys back there. The last time I was here I got a shark, a leprechaun, and a huge plastic eggplant I'm pretty sure was supposed to be for the bachelorette party there that night."

She flushed, raised her glass to his. "What should we toast to?"

With his knee trapped between her thighs, he could hardly think straight. "To the thief who brought us together?"

Melody scrunched her nose in distaste. "To your tour. You are already a star to me."

The words stunned him. Not only because they'd just met but because she was so earnest, so bright. Almost everyone he knew had been jaded, scratched like a record by the spindle of life. He clinked his glass against hers and drank to busy his mouth, because he desperately wanted to kiss her. Wanted to taste that brightness she radiated, feel the soft curves of her mouth, her hips. He drank a little too fast to quench a thirst like he'd never felt before.

Melody murmured in pleasure after her first sip. "Oh, that's delicious. It's like burned sugar and boozy pineapple."

"See? A brujo." Eric knew he had an early morning, and he still had to get back to Jersey. But he waved the bartender down and ordered another round, plus an assortment of empanadas, which they devoured shamelessly.

"My turn," Melody said, and handed Julio a stack of bills.

"What else do you have in that tiny purse?" he asked.

"All the essential thingamabobs." She spilled the contents on the bar top. "Let's see. Band-Aids. Lip gloss. Emergency tampon. A stick of gum. A MetroCard. And now my trusty golden fork. Your turn."

He emptied out his own pockets, where he had his New Jersey driver's license, a guitar pick, a pen from his last dentist visit, and his debit card. "I travel light."

"I can see that." Melody curiously eyed his drink, and he pushed it closer to her side. She swapped hers for his.

He picked up her glass and inhaled the scent of burned sugar, lavender, and fruit. He took a sip. The rum was blended well with pineapple. He swallowed and knew that for the entirety of his time on tour he was going to think of her every any time he caught a whiff of any of those scents.

When Melody returned his cocktail, she'd left a perfect imprint of her pink lip gloss on the rim. Almost too eagerly, Eric grabbed the glass, beads of condensation coating his fingers. He pressed his lips to the outline of her sticky gloss and drank.

The neon lights above the bar bathed her in a soft purple glow. She swayed to the rhythm of the salsa song. With every passing moment,

69

she seemed to unwind a little further, unravel from whatever cocoon protected her. She was so unexpected. How the fuck was he going to walk away from that night in one piece? Sure, they could text. But he'd been there before. Someone always got bored. Someone always moved on. Usually, it was him. And he remembered Vanessa's words from earlier. He needed to keep his head in the game, and that meant focusing on the band.

Hundreds of lyrics to describe feelings, and he couldn't verbalize what *he* felt in that moment. He could only act. And so Eric Reyes did the most reckless thing he'd ever done in his life.

"You should come," he said.

Melody cocked her head to the side. "Where?"

"On tour. On our tour. Our merch vendor quit because he got engaged. I guess his fiancée is the extremely jealous type. I'm happy for them, but I wish they'd figured it out before today."

Ariel rested her chin on her palm and shot him a sly smile. "Maybe I should. Anything can happen on a tour. So I've heard, I mean."

With the idea firmly planted in his mind, Eric pushed the subject a little more. "You'd basically sell merchandise, inventory, but you'd have time to work on your own songs. Get some freedom from your family—if you want." *You'd be with me*, he thought. *You'd get to really know me.* But he couldn't bring himself to say it. "You'd be helping us out, really. Not that you need to save me twice in one day."

She stared at him like she was honestly considering it. There was temptation there in the way she worried her bottom lip. In the way she kept a firm grip on his thigh, as if for balance. "Eric—"

He heard her rejection, and he decided to make one last plea. "You should do whatever makes you happy. I've known you for only a few hours, and even I can see that whatever your father wants you to do is not it. Sometimes, the only way to find what you really want is to leave your old world behind."

Melody shut her eyes against the pulsing neon lights. He realized she was listening to the music. An old song that reminded him of home, of humid nights, of neighborhood parties that went on until the sun came up. She smiled, then looked at him. Truly looked at him, like she could see right through him in a way even his best friends couldn't always. The fear beneath his courage, the insecurity beneath his charm. The hope that kept him strung together.

"Let's just have tonight. Please?"

Eric knew better than perhaps anyone else how hard it was to chase a dream, to leave, especially when you had a sense of duty. Melody's family seemed even more complicated than his own. All he could do was offer her a lifeline, and hope their paths would cross again.

"Of course. But first—" He went to share the job listing with her but realized his phone was dead. He grabbed a napkin covered in tiny flamingos off the table. He wrote down their address, his number, and the time they were leaving. "In case you change your mind."

"All right," she said, though it felt more like a goodbye. She folded the napkin and stuffed it into her tiny purse. Then she threaded her fingers through his. He noticed her fingers had calluses that matched the ones he had from playing guitar.

When they reached the heart of the dance floor, the song transitioned from the hard electronic beats that were better suited to Ibiza into the whistling accordion and drums of a cumbia.

She guided his hand to her waist, and he tugged her close. He leaned down to rest his forehead against hers. They danced like two people who knew each other's rhythms. When the song merged into a fast salsa, the entire room erupted with people, bumping and pushing Eric and Melody closer still. He spun her in his arms, flexing the twists and turns he'd learned on the streets of Medellín. Julio poured them another round, and Eric knew, he knew he needed to be somewhere. He needed sleep. He couldn't start the day off exhausted, but he couldn't pull himself away from this woman except when they were taking sips from their cold drinks or stripping off their jackets.

When Melody danced, she changed. Her face became radiant, her smile unbothered. She hooked her arms around his neck and let him lead, his hands secure around her waist, slowly brushing his thumbs where her hips bloomed. They held each other so tightly, he felt strung out. Delirious with wanting her.

At some point, he didn't know when, the bar cleared out. There was a girl sleeping in a hammock, a man crying along to the lyrics of the song, a bus boy sweeping plastic toys and glitter into a heap.

"I love this song," Melody whispered. "My mom loved boleros."

He brushed her hair behind her ear. The past tense when she spoke of her mother made her reference seem final. He wanted to ask her what happened. He wanted to kiss her and make it all better. But when she rested her head against his heart, he didn't want to move in case he broke the spell they were under.

As the song came to a crawl, someone opened the rooftop patio door and let in the sun.

Melody gasped. "What time is it?"

He took out his phone. Remembered it was dead. He checked his watch and felt a pang of anxiety. "Seven. Fuck, Odelia's going to kill me."

"I have to go," she cried, searching the room for her jacket. She tried her phone. Also dead.

"I can take you home," he offered.

She wasn't listening to him. She pulled on her jean jacket, spinning until she found the exit.

"Melody." He knew the night was over. He had to go, too, but it was happening so fast.

She whirled to face him, long lashes fluttering like she was waking from a dream. She brushed her fingers along his cheek, then shook

72

herself into motion. On her way out the door, she said, "I have to go. I'm sorry."

Eric turned to Julio, who was cashing out his register. The bartender glared at Eric as if his next move should be obvious. He found his jacket. Ran down the rickety stairs and into the New York dawn. The sun was out, but it was drizzling, and no matter which way he turned, Melody was gone. He remained stranded there for a long moment, committing their night to memory like a hopeless romantic, a fool in the rain.

BREAKING:
POP PRINCESS ARIEL DEL MAR GOES ROGUE.

The Daily New Yorker

After a much-anticipated announcement, only six of the del Mar sisters made an appearance at *Wake Up! New York*. While the songstress sisters unveiled fresh looks and brand-new ventures, the youngest, Ariel, was a no-show.

But where is the youngest sister? Teodoro del Mar assured audiences that everything was as it should be. Has the captain of the ship lost control of his vessel? Some sources call it a publicity stunt for a new album. Others close to the sisters speculate a secret trip to rehab. Perhaps the pressure has finally cracked the polished veneer in what would be an unexpected fall from grace.

Ariel's latest beau, Trevor Tachi, suggested on his Pixagram that Ariel is heartbroken from his betrayal and is willing to go to her side to mend their rift.

Fans who'd flocked to Times Square for the big announcement were devastated by the missed appearance, with diehards even attempting to file missing person reports at local and out-of-state precincts. Security called for backup to control the growing crowds outside the del Mars' Upper West Side building.

One thing is for sure: All eyes are on Ariel del Mar.

CHAPTER SEVEN

ARIEL

6.25 Upper West Side, Manhattan

The penthouse was empty. Ariel's heart raced. She could practically feel her pulse at the tip of her tongue as she stumbled into the open living room. The aquarium pillar pulsed a faint blue light, and she walked up to it, pressing her sweaty palm to the cool glass. Several colorful fish swam toward her.

She turned on the television and clicked on *Wake Up! New York*. A red banner running across the bottom detailed her absence. It read: POP PRINCESS CRACKS UNDER PRESSURE. She turned it back off and plugged her phone into the nearest charger in the kitchen.

What was she going to say? What was she going to do? The questions spun in her mind, but every minute stretched, and she just stood there, staring at the floor-to-ceiling glass walls. She had always thought that it was the most beautiful concept—a place at the top of the world where you could see the whole of the city. But it didn't quite feel that way anymore.

The elevator dinged.

The doors opened.

She whirled around when she heard the familiar heavy tread that always made Ariel and her sisters sit up straight.

"Daddy," Ariel started.

He held up a hand to silence her and pointed upstairs to his office.

Her sisters, Uncle Iggy, and Chrissy spilled out of the second elevator. Everyone looked at her with a mixture of sympathy and dread. Instead of delaying the inevitable, she straightened her spine and marched up to her father's office.

The room always smelled of polished mahogany, lemons, and cigars, even though her father had promised he'd quit years ago. Every inch of the walls was covered with awards, gold and platinum and diamond records, framed posters of the girls' biggest concerts and record covers. At the heart of it all was a portrait of their mother. Maia Melody Lucero Marín.

Teo del Mar sat at his desk, framed by the upper Manhattan skyline. The swivel of his chair wheezed as he faced her, pale green eyes shaded by the pronounced ridge of his forehead and bushy black brows.

"Daddy, I'm sorry." Ten seconds in and she'd already started shrinking, lowering her head like she was in the presence of a king. But wasn't he that? The ruler of his music empire.

"Sorry for what?" He tented his fingers together, cocked his head just so to the side.

She could sense she was walking into a trap, so it was best to be honest. "For missing the announcement."

"Do you have any idea what we went through to get that time slot? Do you know how humiliating it was to assure a studio of executives and managers and fans that you were *running late*? Do you know how embarrassing it was to not know where my own daughter is? Who she is with? What she is *doing*?"

Ariel swallowed hard. "I had dinner with a friend, and we went dancing. I lost track of time."

His lips flattened in displeasure. "What friend?"

Much like Siren Seven's wardrobe and itineraries, even friends and relationships were approved by him. She didn't want to say Eric's name. The time they'd spent together was between them.

"No one on your preapproved list," Ariel said, her voice biting.

She'd never spoken to her father that way. Not when she was exhausted, and he kept pushing and pushing his daughters to train and sing and dance. Not when he'd changed her lyrics to "Goodbye Goodbye" without telling her. Not when he forced her to break up with a friend because the fellow teen pop star had a "dangerous" image.

The shock on his face lasted for a too-long breath. "We had a deal, Ariel. You agreed to the solo announcement. Now I have Poe Marlowe calling, asking if he should move on."

"We had a deal *before* that, or did you already forget because it wasn't what you wanted?" Her voice cracked with emotion, fissures in glass spreading, every pent-up emotion from the past fifteen years punching its way out. But she wasn't backing down.

"You will respect me, Ariel," Teo said, his voice like gravel.

"Why? You don't respect us." She rested her fists on his desk to stop trembling. "If you did, you wouldn't be manipulating me into going solo. You would have kept your deal with every one of us. All we have ever done is be your perfect little dolls. We've done enough."

He'd recovered from the shock of her outburst, and he stood to meet her eye to eye. "And what are you going to do for your little wandering year? I'm honestly asking, because I know you haven't thought about it. You've never lived in the real world, Ariel." He scoffed. "You wouldn't survive a day without all of this. You wouldn't survive without being able to make music."

"There are other ways to make music." For a moment she closed her eyes. She was back at the Brooklyn Bridge, confessing her desire. *I want to be a songwriter.* "And all of this, everything you have, is because of us. You couldn't make it on your own, so you had to push your daughters to be stars when *you* couldn't be one yourself."

Ariel clapped her hands over her mouth. She'd gone too far. She wanted to take it back, but knew it was too late.

Teo tapped his gold family ring on the table and nodded. His silent, stony anger felt a million times worse than when he shouted. "If you won't talk to me as your father, then perhaps you will as your boss. You have a contract with Atlantica Records."

Ariel's lips quivered. Something irreparable was breaking, and she couldn't stop it. Couldn't go back. "Which ended with the farewell tour. Or do you think we don't read our contracts? We're just your obedient soldiers, right? Well, I won't sign anything new."

"As long as you live under my roof, you're to follow *my* rules."

"Then maybe I won't live under your roof."

Teo del Mar sat back down. He waved his hand as if to dismiss her. "With what money?"

Everything Ariel and her sisters had earned was under their family account—and, of course, under his name. When she'd been ten, it had made sense. But now? Ariel wanted to laugh, to scream. Money. Fame. What was it worth when she felt like all her power to use it was taken away?

"I'll—"

"How will you live without someone doing everything for you? You've never been on your own. You want to be a *normal* girl so badly, but you're spoiled. You've never had to struggle. You've never counted the pennies in your pocket to make sure you could afford something to eat. You wouldn't survive a day without every luxury at the tips of your fingers."

Ariel swallowed her anger. He always deflected that way. She glanced at the portrait of her mother. She felt ashamed of yelling in her presence. Felt more ashamed of her father.

"I'll figure it out," she said with false bravado.

"Then go! Get out!" He shouted it again in Spanish as Ariel fled and ran down the stairs. The sound of things breaking echoed behind her, along with his last warning: "You'll be back here before you know it."

Her father had always been stern, but never violent. He and Ariel pushed each other as far as they could go, but before, she had always folded under the pressure. Ariel marched into her room. Her heart was in her throat as she opened her closet and found her one duffel bag that didn't have the group's logo splattered all over it.

She pulled T-shirts, jeans, underwear, shoes, not caring if anything matched or was in pairs. After years on tour, packing was like muscle memory, and even though her mind was numb, her hands knew the basic things she'd need. She found a new pair of glasses, the duplicate of the ones she'd broken. She was already wearing her necklace. For a moment, she startled when she grabbed her naked wrist. Remembered Eric had her bracelet.

When she couldn't find her passport, she reached for her phone so she could text Chrissy. All she could hear in her mind was, *You wouldn't survive a day without every luxury at the tips of your fingers.*

It hadn't been ten minutes, and she was already asking for help.

No, she wouldn't let him get into her head, the way he had a million times before. There was nothing wrong with asking for help. But the more she looked around her room, the more trapped she felt, despite the glass wall. She reached for her favorite book, and instead knocked over an entire shelf of her trinkets and things.

Ariel sank down and picked up the glass menagerie she'd collected over the years. The little seahorse had broken.

"Ariel?" came a small voice. Marilou.

One by one, her sisters and Chrissy poured into the room, then closed the door behind them.

"How much did you hear?" she asked.

"Everything?" Chrissy said.

"Bajillion-dollar penthouse—" Thea said.

"Paper-thin walls," Alicia added, finishing her twin's sentence.

Sophia squeezed Ariel's shoulder. "That was freaking amazing. Legendary."

"Yeah, we had no idea that was in there," Elektra added.

"It's everything we've wanted to say, only you were like, you can't tell me what to *do* anymore, *Dad*," Stella said, getting too into the role.

They all stared, and Stella chuckled. "Sorry. Too soon."

"Are you really leaving?" Marilou asked.

"I have to." Ariel shook her head.

There was a collective sigh.

"I thought so," Sophia said. "You're both so stubborn."

"Hey," Ariel said indignantly. She fished out the napkin on which Eric had scribbled all the information she needed. "I have a job offer."

She explained about Eric and the tour. If she left soon, she'd catch up to them before they took off. "I know what you're going to say."

"All this for a *guy*?" Elektra said, rolling her eyes.

"No," she said firmly. "It's not. All of this is for me. I mean, I've never met anyone like Eric, but it's more like he left a door open, and I want to see what's on the other side."

Marilou tucked a strand of Ariel's hair back. "Are you sure? Being on tour with someone you're into makes things complicated."

Alicia tossed a pillow at her pink-haired sister. "Just because Dad fired the assistant choreographer you got caught making out with doesn't mean Ariel will make the same mistakes."

Ariel let go of a tired laugh. "How can I be the next version of myself when I don't know who I am without you all? Without Siren Seven?" She gathered strength from the pride in her sisters' eyes, took a deep breath. "When I got in that taxi this morning, I made it to Times Square with minutes to spare."

Her sisters balked and blinked at her confession.

"I could have gotten out," Ariel said. "I would have been late, and without the 'new look' Dad wanted. I could have waltzed onto that stage. But I had this moment where I thought—I have one chance to stop being Ariel del Mar and figure out what I want."

"Are you sure about this?" Marilou asked. "You don't even know this guy. What if the band bus already left?"

"Then I will figure it out." Ariel smiled for the first time since she left Eric at the bar. She wouldn't be able to explain it to her sisters. All she needed was for them to trust her. "I'll have my phone. I'll stay in our chat."

"Not with that phone, you're not." Sophia handed her a leather envelope. Inside were stacks of twenties and a new smartphone that was several models older than her current version. "I've had a runaway duffel since Mom died. I just wasn't as brave as you."

The realization that Sophia had made it so close to leaving hit Ariel like a sledgehammer. How many of them had thought of leaving but ended up staying? One day they would all have to talk about it, but for now, she had to go her own way.

"I can't take this," Ariel said, pushing the envelope back to her eldest sister.

Sophia waved a sharp black nail. "Don't do that. It's *our* money. Plus, you'll need cash so Uncle Iggy and Dad can't track your cards. Don't worry, I'm working on a way to separate our accounts from Dad's."

"Here." Stella offered up the lucky amethyst crystal she always kept in her bra. "To protect you from bad vibes."

Ariel wrinkled her nose. "Thanks. I think?"

Alicia made her take a dress she'd designed for her recent fashion line with Thea, even though Ariel insisted she didn't need fancy clothes on an indie rock tour. Marilou placed her favorite baseball cap on Ariel's head. It was pale pink and had a tiny red crab emoji on it. Thea offered up her stress plushie, which was a foot-long stuffed shark, and

Elektra gifted her a new notebook—from her collection of 101 empty notebooks. Each gift was worth everything, and a send-off she hadn't been prepared for. She'd thought they'd stop her, but no one understood her better than her sisters.

"I feel like I'm going on a quest," Ariel said, and her voice wavered with emotion.

"Wait!" Chrissy said. She crossed the room, opened a safe, and pulled out a plastic folder. "Here's all your documents."

She pulled Chrissy into a hug. "Thank you. I'll make sure—"

"Oh, I know. Raise, baby."

One by one, Ariel hugged them goodbye. She shouldered her bag. She had a million and one memories in her bedroom. Half a lifetime of things she'd collected. But for the very first time, she was going to leave it all behind. She'd prove her father wrong. His way wasn't the only way. She had to believe she could make her path. And there was one person who could help her. If he was willing to wait.

"What about the crowds outside?" Marilou asked. "They've got the building surrounded."

Thea, who was the closest to Ariel in build and height, picked up Ariel's ruby-red wig from the vanity stand and looked at herself in the mirror. Her lips quickly took the shape of a mischievous smile. "I've got an idea."

Ariel del Mar Steps Out After Announcement Fail! Where Is Ariel Going?

Pop Princess Was Seen Leaving Her Apartment Building with a Suitcase and Getting into a Limo Headed for MacArthur Airport.

BAD BLOOD BETWEEN DADDY DEL MAR AND ARIEL. WE'VE GOT THE TEA.

 Del Mar Sisters Sleep in Glass Coffins. Footage from a Source in the Building.

CHAPTER EIGHT

ARIEL

6.25 Jersey City, New Jersey

Ariel emerged from the train station in Jersey City with five minutes to reach Star Crossed's meeting point. She'd tried to text the phone number Eric had scribbled on the napkin, but had received no response. The only legible part of the scrawl was the address, so she must have deciphered the numbers incorrectly.

She'd gone too far to not take the chance. Years of life on the road had conditioned her to dial up her energy on just a handful of hours asleep. Orienting herself by the map, she ran down the busy street, her duffel bouncing against her hip, as fast as her feet could carry her.

When she rounded the corner, she passed the red gate of a fire station, a row of renovated town houses, and there it was, parked in front of a small blue house that looked homey but out of place on the changing street: a giant green tour bus.

She recognized two members of Star Crossed from the concert, but after hearing Eric's stories, she felt like she already knew them. There was Max, with her shaggy bangs obscuring her eyes as she carried two giant suitcases into the belly of the bus. The tall goth, Grimsby, was loading her bass into the storage trailer hitched to the back of the bus.

As Ariel got closer, Carly stepped out of the blue house. Her black curls were tied back in a silk headscarf, and she was still wearing fuzzy slippers as she dragged a giant suitcase down the steps. When she noticed Ariel across the street, she froze.

"Eric!" Carly shouted, flashing Ariel a confused smile. "Get your ass over here. *Now*."

Ariel's stomach plummeted as she thought of the worst-case scenarios. He hadn't told his bandmates that he'd offered her the job. She'd have to go home with her tail tucked between her legs. She'd have to tell her father that he'd been right. That she was naive and foolish for taking the word of a guy she'd *just* met. For taking a chance on herself.

A half-dressed Eric Reyes stumbled out of the house, and her already frantic pulse spiked. His bronze skin was smooth and taut over lean muscles. She'd traced her fingers over the hard planes of his forearms, the swell of his biceps where tattooed flowers bloomed. A trail of dark hair made an arrow from his belly button to the white elastic of his boxers, peeking out above his jeans. She felt a visceral groan start at the back of her throat and turned it into a throat-clearing cough.

That's when he saw her. All at once, he tugged on the plain white T-shirt bunched in his hands and hurried down the porch steps. She delighted in the way his eyes went wide with surprise. How he halted impatiently at the burst of traffic that seemed to decide suddenly to speed down Mercer.

"You came," he said.

As the final car went by, they stepped into the middle of the street.

"I texted, but your drunk handwriting is pretty terrible," she said, ready to plead her case. "I just had a massive fight with my father and said a lot of stuff I can't take back, and . . . well. I'm your merch girl, if the job's still available."

Eric looked equally parts stunned and relieved. He reached down and took her duffel from her. "Welcome aboard, Melody Marín."

She wanted to launch herself at him, to wrap her arms around his neck like she'd done when they'd danced. But she remembered what her sisters had said. Whatever crush she had on Eric Reyes would have to wait. Even if her legs felt wobbly when he looked at her that way, like she was his birthday surprise.

"Odelia is going to love you." While his bandmates stared, Eric nodded in the direction of the open tour bus. "She's in the Beast."

Ariel chuckled. "The Beast?"

"Yeah. Big, green, loud. It's the first thing Grimsby called it when the driver pulled up this morning." He waved her aboard.

Ariel climbed up the steps, ready to meet the manager Eric had talked so much about. She'd been on her share of tour buses over the years, before exclusively using the Atlantica Records jet. Eric's bus was an older model. The panels were glossy plastic made to look like wood, with a worn leather bench and curtains that had likely been orange in the seventies but had been sun-bleached to a rusty yellow. It had the basics, which Eric pointed out. She had to remind herself that the Melody he knew had never been on a tour bus before.

"This is the front lounge," Eric said, tapping his finger on the small TV panel on the wall behind the driver's seat. "We don't get cable, but Grimsby is bringing her favorite DVDs. I hope you like horror."

She laughed. "I'm actually a wimp when it comes to horror."

"Finally, someone to sway the movie vote with me." He winked at her, then walked ahead two paces to the kitchen. "Fridge, microwave. Do not touch Max's caramel pudding cups unless you want to lose a finger." He pressed a button and a door slid open to reveal the sleeping quarters, twelve bunk beds split between the two sides. "If you don't see a sticky note by a bunk, then you're good to claim it."

When Siren Seven had struck it big, her sisters had shared a deluxe tour bus with bunk beds on two levels and a party lounge, which was where Elektra liked to practice her deejaying skills. They'd had mini fridges full of more snacks than they could eat and a full-size flat-screen TV that the twins always hogged for Star Wars marathons.

And yet there was something about the Beast that welcomed her. The Polaroids the band had already used to decorate the wall space between the bunks. The string of purple lights and velvet pillows in the back lounge. Eric entered first, and an imposing woman looked up at him from a table of paperwork.

"This is Odelia Garcia, our manager and a goddess among men," Eric said, very obviously buttering the woman up.

Odelia had short black hair styled in an elegant pixie cut, killer arched eyebrows, and scarlet lipstick that contrasted brightly with her satin brown skin. Pinup girl glam and somehow effortless, her silk cheetah-print blouse hugged buxom curves and tapered in at her waist, where it tucked into black silk cigarette pants. Long red coffin-shape nails clicked on the surface of the table as she sized Ariel up, and she did not look impressed. There was something slightly annoyed about the flare of her nostrils and the strained smile she shot Eric.

"What stray have you brought me today?" Odelia asked, her voice like crushed velvet.

"Meet Melody Marín. The one I told you about."

Ariel wondered what exactly he'd said, but focused on Odelia so she wouldn't blush. Any more than she already had, that is.

"Right," Odelia said with wary recognition. "Sit."

Eric squeezed her shoulder confidently. "I have to finish loading up, but you're in good hands."

Ariel's stomach tightened with nerves as Eric left her alone with Odelia. She realized this was real. This was happening. For the first time in her life, her father had no control of her. No idea where she was. She relaxed into the seat across from the tour manager and took off her cap. She unzipped her backpack and retrieved the leather envelope that held her cash and documents. She had never applied for a job and was unsure of what to do. Did she hand over her passport? Her Social Security card?

"No," Odelia said.

Ariel froze. "You don't need my ID?"

"N. O." Odelia leaned forward, tenting her nails. Up close, Ariel noticed the Marilyn Monroe beauty mark tattooed just below her high cheekbone. "I don't know what kind of game you're playing—"

"I'm not playing a game."

"What's your name?" Odelia asked.

Ariel couldn't help it. She looked down at her lap and said, "Melody Marín."

That was the truth. Del Mar had always been a variation of Marín, which her father had adapted for the stage even before he'd left Ecuador. Even Uncle Iggy had adopted it.

The older woman narrowed her eyes, like she could disintegrate Ariel with that stare. "You look just like her. Like both of them, really."

Her heart lurched with anxiety. "Like who?"

Odelia stilled, as if surprised she'd said that out loud. "Like your parents. Don't *lie* to me, Ariel del Mar. I know exactly who you are."

Ariel del Mar.

How could this woman, whom she'd never met in her life, know who Ariel was when no one else had looked at her twice? Then again, she was so tired she could barely remember the chaos of the past week, let alone every single past encounter. Still, her parents had their own moment in the spotlight once upon a time, even if it was nearly forty years before.

"Who are you? How did you know my parents?"

At that, Odelia glanced away. Past the tinted windows, the band was still carrying boxes from the house to the bus. "It doesn't matter. What matters is that you've found your way here on my tour bus. I don't want anything to do with your family. *Especially* not your father."

Ariel shook her head. It felt like tiny bombs going off around her. Had this woman really known her parents? Teodoro del Mar had pissed a lot of people off in his day. He had a knight-in-shining-armor complex, fighting against network executives and their old record label, until he became the man on top. The king of his own palace. Even if that palace had been built by Ariel and her sisters.

"I don't want anything to do with my father, either," Ariel said, making no move to go. "That's why I'm here. That's why I have to do this."

"Why?" The no-nonsense set of Odelia's full lips made Ariel understand why Eric admired his manager so much. It was like she could see through bullshit and lies. "Eric seems to think you're an aspiring songwriter running from a bad situation when the truth is you can have anything and anyone you could possibly want. So why would a spoiled little princess need to slum on a tour bus after jet-setting through the world in a sixty-million-dollar private plane?"

Ariel flinched. Every word from Odelia dripped with anger and resentment. What had Ariel's family done to her? And why had Ariel never heard of her?

"Harsh," Ariel said, frustrated and confused. Well, she had wanted people to treat her like a normal girl, and Odelia definitely did not treat her better because she was a del Mar. "But you're right. I could jump on some other pop star's tour. Except, outside of my sisters, I don't have any friends. I could pull strings and write a song for any label I wanted just to piss my father off, but that song would get butchered by six producers and executives by the time it's done."

Odelia shook her head, clearly displeased with that answer. "Do you expect me to feel sorry for you? You're an adult. Fight with your family on your own time, but leave me—leave *Eric* out of it."

Eric. Eric, with his dreamer heart and charming smile. She would never hurt him.

"If you really know my father," Ariel said, "you know what he's like. He's planned out my entire life. The *Little Mermaids* show. Siren Seven. I've been wearing a disguise since I was ten years old. And now he wants me to swap one disguise for another. I just couldn't do it. Not again. Over the last few days I've realized I don't know who I am when I'm not onstage or with my family. The only thing I do know is that I love music. I can give up every material thing about my world, but not that."

Odelia's anger deflated as she rested one nail on her chin. "If you want to unplug and soul search, why don't you 'Yeet, Pray, Love' yourself to Europe. Don't use that boy to fix whatever is broken."

"I'm *not* using him," Ariel assured her. Wasn't she? Even if it wasn't malicious, she was using Eric's offer of a lifeline.

"Oh no? So what will you do if I ask you to leave?"

Ariel had to prepare for the possibility. "I still won't go home. I'll figure it out."

"Boy, would I pay money to see that." Odelia chuckled, then pointed a finger at Ariel's heart. "I know what your family does. You ruin lives. That boy has been through hell and back to fight for his career. He can be vain, naive, with his heart on his sleeve. But there's a good man beneath all that leave-in conditioner. He's loyal, and he works hard. I will not let you ruin this chance for him. For any of my kids."

Ariel smiled sadly. "You really care about them."

"Do you know what the surname Garcia means?" Without waiting for an answer, Odelia rolled up the wrists of her shirt to reveal twin tattoo sleeves of Sailor Jerry–style eels. Around them were bright stars—a constellation. "It means 'the bear.' Like Ursa Major. So yes, I'm the mother bear here, and these are my cubs."

Teodoro del Mar had the same kind of ferocity. The same protective instinct. But his love was suffocating, demanding, and rigid. Ariel swallowed the foreign emotions welling up in her throat. "I promise. I won't do anything to hurt him. We're friends."

Odelia glanced away. "I've seen what the del Mars do to friends."

"I don't know what happened between you and my parents," Ariel said, "but I'm not my father. Please. I'm good with numbers. My tutors used to say that if my music career didn't work out, I could fall back on being an accountant."

"In my experience, when people are paid well, they'll give you all kinds of compliments." Odelia heaved a deep sigh. She held her index and middle fingers like there was the ghost of a cigarette there. Ariel could see she was thawing, just a little. "Have you ever had a job?"

"I'm a certified lifeguard?" She chanced a smile Odelia did not return.

"As if I'd trust you to save me in a kiddie pool. So basically, your experience is *nothing* with an internship in *nada*?"

Ariel knew this woman was making the interview difficult on purpose. But she hadn't left home because it would be easy. She'd simply have to prove that she was nothing like her father and then figure out exactly what her parents had done to cause such a visceral reaction.

"That's not true." Ariel hadn't worked a traditional job, but the results of having a "Dadager" meant she was bursting with experience. "This is a music tour. I have fifteen years of experience. I know tour schedules inside and out. And before you point it out, I know my experience is different from other people's. But life on the road is grueling. Miserable, sometimes. This is the band's first national tour? I will make it my goal to make sure things run smoothly. And from what Eric told me, you've had a lot of bad luck. If and *when* something goes wrong, I won't be another person freaking out, because I've been through it all." She sat back and forced herself not to look away from Odelia's shark gaze. "Plus, I know you leave, like, five minutes ago, and your time is better spent haranguing stage managers, not selling merch, so I'm all you've got."

They didn't move. It felt like the most important staring contest of Ariel's life.

"Seizing on a desperate moment," Odelia said, impressed. "You're more like your parents than you know."

It wasn't a compliment, and it only piqued Ariel's curiosity. Who *was* this woman?

Odelia flipped through a stack of folders. "We run for thirty-one shows, ending back at Aurora's Grocery at the end of July. Pay is seven hundred per week, plus a fifty-dollar per diem on show days."

Ariel had never had to worry about money before and was embarrassed to realize she had no concept of whether this salary was good or bad. Even before she and her sisters stepped into the limelight, when they lived in their small, crowded house in Forest Hills, Queens, she'd never felt like she had lacked material things. This was only temporary, until Sophia had their accounts separated from her father, and she would finally break free.

"Is there a problem?" Odelia asked.

"I saw on the Gregslist ad that there was a last-minute signing bonus." Once again, Ariel stood her ground.

Odelia grinned. "That there is."

"Then I accept." Ariel quelled the impulse to throw a fist into the air. Some victories were best celebrated in private.

"Welcome to the tour," Odelia said, and drew out the papers Ariel would need to fill out. "Here's the crew's contract, and a direct deposit slip. I'm sure you're familiar with NDAs. I need your ID."

"Wait," Ariel said, heart hammering. "I have two conditions."

"Oh, you do?"

"I need to be paid in cash. All of our accounts are under my father's name." Ariel couldn't meet Odelia's scrutiny as she admitted that.

The tour manager licked her canine. She looked like she wanted to say something, but only shook her head and moved on. "And you don't want him to find you. Do I want to hear this second condition?"

"You can't tell anyone my real name."

"I tell my daughter everything," Odelia said. When Ariel frowned, she added, "Vanessa G. She's my assistant, but she's replacing one of the opening acts that had to drop out. But that's not what bothers you, is it? You don't want Eric to know."

"I'll tell him," Ariel said. "But I want to figure some things out first."

"In that case I have two conditions of my own. If I even catch a whiff of you hurting this band or tour, and I mean even the slightest thing that jeopardizes us, I will leave you on the side of the road and not look back. Do we understand each other, *Melody*?"

Ariel nodded. At the very least, they had an understanding. Echoing Odelia's previous tone, she asked, "Do *I* want to hear this second condition?"

"Eric is off-limits." Odelia extended her hand, black ink peeking out at her hazelnut-brown wrists. "He's the real deal. This tour might be small potatoes to you, but for him, for the rest of them, this is their big break. I can feel it. No matter what he tells himself, Eric has a weakness for a pretty face, and I'm not going to let a passing crush and your soul-searching ruin things for him. Do we understand each other?"

This was a different kind of contract. One that didn't require ink on paper. It required her word. What was she if she could not keep her word? She remembered the way Eric had held her while they danced a few hours ago. She could still feel the brush of his fingertips at her waist, her cheekbones. It was only a *crush*. Wasn't it? She'd had a hundred crushes. She'd get over it. Even Eric had admitted that he didn't date because music was the most important thing in his life, and Ariel wasn't in a place where she could fully open up to him without revealing all of herself. This tour, this opportunity, was a delicate tightrope, and she needed to stay sharp to make it across.

This was her great escape from her old world, her chance to experience new things on her own. This was her moment, and she was going to seize it.

Ariel gripped Odelia Garcia's hand with all the confidence she could muster. "You've got yourself a deal."

@TheRealArielDelMar

Four million likes | 92,468 comments

My Lucky Sevens. I have a lot of explaining to do, but first, I owe you an apology. I know a lot of you were excited to see me on Wake Up! New York and were expecting a big announcement. The truth is, I'm not ready. I'm not ready to share the next stage of my life. Maybe I'll never be, but for the first time, I'm taking a step back to figure some things out. This isn't goodbye. I'll be seeing you. But you won't be seeing me.

Love,

Ariel ♡

CHAPTER NINE

ERIC

6.25 Philadelphia, Pennsylvania

E ric stowed his suitcase in the belly of the Beast. Odelia had gotten a deal on the massive lime-green-and-orange tour bus rental since it hadn't been repainted after a seventies rock tribute band had sold it in the spring.

What was taking so long with Melody's paperwork? They'd been in there for what felt like hours. At least Odelia was thorough, which was why she was the best at her job.

Eric closed the storage door and dusted his palms. Next came securing the instruments in the trailer. He snapped his guitar case into the guitar rack.

"Grim! Do you really need to bring your mandolin?"

When he looked up, he jumped. Carly, Vanessa, Max, and Grimsby had surrounded him like hungry lionesses.

"What do you think you're doing?" Max demanded.

"Putting my things away?"

"You hired the concert girl?" Grimsby asked, mussing up her choppy platinum hair like she did when she was worried. "Also, you packed seventeen bottles of pomade, I can bring my mandolin."

Eric let it drop. He was exhausted and excited. Two feelings that did not go well together. He'd spent the brief hours when he should have been sleeping playing and replaying his moments with Melody. He had no doubt the band would love her. How could they not? Sure, he hadn't expected her to show. But with her there—he couldn't explain it—the tour felt complete.

"I know what you're all thinking."

Carly narrowed her eyes. "Do you, though?"

Eric glanced at the front of the Beast, where the bus driver was doing what he'd called "road yoga." Whatever that was. He faced his best friends—and biggest critics.

"We were in the lurch, and I solved a problem. Isn't it better having someone we know instead of a rando from Gregslist?"

Vanessa pointed at the bus. "She *is* a rando!"

"What do you know about her?" Max asked.

"I know she's one of us. She told her overprotective old man to shove it, and she needs this gig. And—" Eric stopped himself from saying *she's the most beautiful woman I've ever met.* "And she wants to be a songwriter. Can you all just trust me? I have a good feeling about people. I found all of us, didn't I?"

Vanessa, on the other hand, didn't look so convinced. "Yeah, but you haven't wanted to bone any of us."

"You sure about that?" He hadn't, and they knew it. But he hated when she was right.

Grimsby pointed at the bus. "Odelia's the better judge of character, so if she says yes, we know we're good to go."

"Or we're desperate," Max added bleakly. Her brown eyes, barely visible through her curtain of bangs, slid in his direction. She whispered, "Doomed."

"Curséd," Grimsby added.

"I'm sure she's great," Carly said. "But we're about to be on the road for thirty-three shows over five weeks. If you Eric Reyes the situation, it's going to throw things off."

Eric held up a finger. "I'm sorry, English is my second language, but did you just use my name as a verb?"

Grimsby chomped at her index fingernail, widening her gray eyes with accusation. "You Eric Reyesed my hamster sitter."

"And our favorite bartender," Carly added. "Now we can't go back to Clayton's Saloon."

Max waved at someone behind him and said, "The widow Lopez next door."

Eric couldn't believe this. He turned and waved at one of his former paramours, who was grabbing the newspaper from her lawn in nothing but a silk robe. Having his past thrown back in his face like that didn't exactly feel great. He needed his best friends in the world, his family, to believe in him. Otherwise, who would?

"That was all from over a year ago."

"Face it, bro," Max said. "You're a rake. A scoundrel. A player who crushes, quite a lot."

"You're just murdering those lyrics," Eric muttered, rubbing his face with his palms. "We live in very close quarters and have paper-thin walls, so you know I put that behind me. There's nothing more import-ant to me than our music."

"Says you," Vanessa scoffed. "You're a sappy romantic. You literally fall in love with love. You expect us to believe you can keep things pla-tonic with your hipster pixie dream girl over there?"

"I am too hungover for this." Eric realized he'd put on his shirt inside out. He tugged it off and corrected the situation. "Okay. Let's do this in terms you all understand."

Carly perked up. "A bet?"

"I am fully capable of keeping a handle on a simple crush. An inno-cent crush." Even as he said it, he knew there was nothing innocent about the way he'd held her at the club. "And if I can't—if I slip and fuck things up during the tour"—he brushed his unruly waves back—"I will let you hold me down and shave my head."

The four of them blinked. Each of their smiles was comically devilish. Carly grimaced. "You must be into some freaky shit."

"Hair grows back," Vanessa pointed out.

"I know," Max said, snapping her fingers as an idea widened her eyes. "If you *Eric Reyes* the merch girl, then you have to agree to cover a Siren Seven song at the final show."

The others seemed thrilled at the idea. It's not that he hated one of the biggest pop sensations in the world, it's that he simply didn't understand the appeal. Sure, as a kid, he'd had crushes on them. He'd snuck into a football stadium with his friends to drink in the parking lot when they did their South American tour. But that didn't mean he liked to listen to the over-synthesized, overly saturated, glittery nightmare. He had standards. He wasn't going to sully his guitar with one of those songs.

"Deal," he said. "But if I win—and I will, because I have self-control—then I get to pick our band tattoo."

Over the years, they'd made a pact that *when* one of their songs hit the charts and they got a splashy record deal, they would all get matching band tattoos. The art was highly under contention, so if he had this power, the ability to choose, he could especially avoid Grimsby's idea, which would likely involve a guinea pig.

They all seemed to deliberate. Eric grinned. "Come on. If you're so sure you'll win, then you have nothing to worry about, right? I'm the one who should really be worried."

The bus doors swung open, and Melody descended with Odelia right behind her. Their tour manager's face looked pleased, bemused, even. The last time he'd seen her that way was when she'd destroyed them on poker night.

Then he focused on Melody. She pushed her new glasses up the bridge of her nose, and he felt his heart stutter.

Dammit.

He had to be strong. He had to be better. It was five weeks on the road. He could have a platonic friendship with Melody and get over his crush in that amount of time. His bandmates often told him that they'd all gotten over his looks after a week of living with him, which he was starting to realize was more insult than reassurance of the strength of their bond.

Eric flashed a smile at the ridiculous, gorgeous, and infuriating women in his life, and said through gritted teeth, "Well?"

Each one whispered, "Deal," just as Melody and Odelia reached them.

"Hi, everyone," Melody said, reaching out to shake their hands. "I'm Ahh—Melody."

"Ahh Melody?" Vanessa repeated, and Carly snorted.

Eric felt the protective need to defend his girl. The *Merch Girl*. But she was a crew member. She'd have to find her own footing with everyone on board. Besides, she seemed to let the snark roll off her shoulders.

"Sorry, I haven't slept since Eric kept me up all night." Melody seemed to understand what she'd implied when everyone snickered, and her cheeks flushed as red as Odelia's lipstick. Even Eric was flustered, heat pooling in his chest as he imagined it. "I mean, stayed up dancing, and there were some toys. In the drinks! I'll shut up now."

"Anyway. We're behind schedule," Odelia said, tapping her jeweled pen on her clipboard. "But it's a short ride to Philly, and these night owls can power nap. Can't have my lead singer look like he just returned from a bender in Vegas, can I?"

She grabbed Eric by his chin and gave him an affectionate tap on the cheek. Was he tired, or did the tap feel more like a light slap?

"Don't worry about me. I'll get my beauty sleep."

Max snorted. "Yeah, we know you're tired when you don't post your morning selfie."

"Hola, darlings, woke up like this," Carly and Vanessa said, deepening their voices to mimic him.

He didn't sound like that, but he was man enough to handle their teasing. What he couldn't handle was the way Melody bit down on her lower lip to stop from making fun of him. He'd almost kissed that lower lip. Hours ago, he'd been physically unable to tear himself from her after she crashed into his life. He'd thought of her on the way back home and first thing when he woke up, ready for that night to have been just one of those New York nights where everything is perfect and anything is possible until the sun came up. Now she was here. And he couldn't Eric Reyes up their dynamic. He was a professional. They could be friends, couldn't they?

"Let's introduce everyone," Eric said a little too loudly, waving over the driver.

The guy jogged over. He had a round face, short curly hair, and medium-brown skin. A wallet chain with a tiny furry creature dangled from his pocket, which he had said was his lucky Sasquatch. He'd already spilled coffee on his pale blue polo.

"Introductions," Odelia said. "Everyone, this is Osvaldo Florian, our tour bus driver."

"You can call me Oz," he said. Odelia was about to continue, but Oz actually interrupted her and kept speaking. "And we prefer entertainer coach operators now instead of bus drivers. Let's see, I'm twenty-six. This is my first tour. Just passed all my permits last week." He crossed his fingers for good luck.

Carly craned her neck toward Eric and mouthed *cursed* at him. He averted his gaze to keep from laughing.

Odelia nodded appeasingly and opened her mouth to continue. Her eyes nearly bulged out of her head when Oz very innocently kept talking while stretching his hamstrings.

"My favorite cryptids are the Sasquatch and the Loch Ness Monster. I really loved your album, so that's a plus. And I'm allergic to strawberries, most domesticated animals, pineapple, and dust."

"Thank you, Oz," Odelia said, louder than usual while trying to rein in her irritation. "Moving on—"

"Oh, and I'm a Leo."

Odelia waved her clipboard and smiled like she was one interruption from exploding. "*Happy* to have you. I'm afraid that's all the time we have. You'll get to know Melody later. Rules of the bus! Number one. No food in the bunks. We don't want any infestations. Number two. The restroom is not for use. If you need to go, tell Oz so we can pull into the nearest gas station or rest stop."

"Why did you look at me when you said that?" Max muttered indignantly.

Odelia dismissed the question with a dramatic wave of her hand. "Number three. Cleanliness. No one here is your maid picking up after you. You will keep the bus and yourself clean, or you're walking to the next tour stop."

"Why did you look at *me* when you said that?" Eric asked, then winked at Melody. Her smile was worth Odelia's exasperated sigh.

"Four. We don't have load-in crew, so it's all hands on deck." Odelia checked the thin gold watch on her wrist. "Five. While you're all adults and can do whatever you want, I need exactly seven hours of sleep or I'll be your worst nightmare, so please keep the cabin doors shut when you're in the front lounge. Last, not a rule, but a—*suggestion*. No fraternizing on the bus."

Again, she looked at Eric, then her sly gaze flitted to Melody. He was very proud of himself for not rising to the bait.

"Other than that"—Odelia's bored facade broke for one of her rare genuine smiles—"I'm very proud of you all. No matter what the world throws at you, you get back up. That's what makes you different. Let's make this a tour we'll never forget."

With that, Eric gave their quaint blue house one final look, then climbed into the Beast.

As the bus wheezed out of New Jersey, Odelia sashayed her way to the rear lounge, which she'd claimed as her office. Grimsby disappeared into her bunk, since she preferred to sleep during the day like the vampire she was. Eric should have joined Carly, Max, and Vanessa in the front lounge, but he wanted to make sure Melody settled in all right. He told himself he would have done that for anyone who had just joined their motley crew.

"Let me help you with that," he said, and she smiled as he shouldered the duffel. "I'm impressed you packed so light."

"I sort of grabbed whatever would fit. I guess if I forgot it, I really don't need it with me."

She slipped into the tight corridor of the sleeping quarters and hung her jean jacket in the narrow closet hatch.

"Wow. You already know your way around." It had taken him several tries to figure out the latches when he'd first climbed aboard.

Did he imagine the panic in her sleepy eyes? "It's intuitive."

When he adjusted her duffel, he noticed a fluffy face peeking out of the open zipper. The small stuffed shark was already half out, so he helped it the rest of the way.

"That's my sister's," she rushed to explain, taking the plushie and cradling it against her chest. "She thought I could use her stress shark."

"I think we all could," he said. "It's good that your sisters are supportive, even if . . ."

He let the rest hang between them. He knew better than most what it felt like to have a father who didn't believe in his child. Maybe that was the reason he felt so protective of Melody. Because he wanted to spare her what he'd gone through.

"Thank you." Melody squeezed his forearm once, then selected her bunk.

Twelve bunks, and the woman he was trying not to have a crush on just so happened to choose the bottom bunk right across from his. She couldn't have known, since the sticky note with his name on it had slipped off and was now stuck to his shoe.

"We're neighbors," he said, lifting his foot and unsticking the paper square with his chicken scratch across it.

Melody tucked her hair behind her ear. "Thank you for this. Really. You have no idea how much I need it."

A feeling clamped around his heart at the softness in her words. He wanted to offer her comfort. Leaving was scary, even if their situations were different. But he couldn't do that because he knew holding her again wasn't the smart thing to do. Not that he'd ever *truly* done the smart thing when it came to his ridiculous, traitorous heart.

He wanted to say something that matched the sentiment she'd shared, but nothing felt adequate. *We should be thanking you* felt patronizing. *You're welcome* didn't feel like enough. *Are you still thinking about that song that we danced to?* was way too much.

He, Eric Reyes, a man who had once convinced a Miss Universe winner to go home with him after he'd crashed an industry party, had utterly lost his chill.

"I'll let you get some rest." He was more animated than he normally was when he was so hungover, but he stuffed her duffel into the small compartment by her bunk and backed out of the corridor.

With the cabin door closed, Eric leaned against the plastic wood panel, rubbing at the tight sensation across his chest. A smile tugged at his lips, but then he realized that his entire band and Vanessa were watching him with shit-eating grins.

Eric instantly straightened, like he'd been caught doing something wrong, and forced his face into a disinterested frown. He picked up his laptop. This was what he needed to be doing. Focusing. There were a thousand things to be done. Automatic light cues to tweak. A website to update. Like Odelia said, it was all hands on deck. This tour was a make-or-break moment for them, and he had to stay in the game.

When his phone dinged a dozen times consecutively, he looked up at Max. "What are you texting me?"

"Oh, just sending you my favorite Siren Seven songs."

Carly and Vanessa snickered, while Oz turned up the volume on some podcast about alien sightings.

It was going to be a very long two hours to Philadelphia, so he put his head down and got to it. He'd done more on less sleep, and he powered through now, not stopping until Oz's shaky parking job made him look up.

That heady excitement he felt before a show overtook him. This was what Eric Reyes had been born to do. He rallied his band and crew, and they filed out of the bus and onto the venue's staff lot.

The Adam's Grove Music Hall was a converted warehouse in the crook of the Chinatown and Old City sections of Philadelphia. While Odelia checked in with the front of house staff, he and the band unloaded the gear and helped Melody with the boxes of merch. Eric introduced himself to the back of the house crew. Triple-checked their light cues, tuned his guitar, conferred with the stage manager on set changes.

Everything was perfect. He absently tugged at the charm bracelet he hadn't taken off since Melody placed it there. When she popped into his mind, he wandered from the stage, across the empty pit, and into the lobby to make sure she was settled. A friendly check-in. For friends.

The merchandise table was tucked away beside the glossy concession stands. Melody fiddled with a box cutter, turning it this way and that. Again, he had the urge to help her, his entire body alarmed at the thought that she would slice her hands open, but then she figured it out. When she noticed him and smiled, her entire face brightened. Only for a moment, then she busied herself arranging the plastic containers of branded enamel pins and stickers.

"Can you believe the bands that have played here?" Eric asked, craning his head back to get a better look at the cavernous lobby. Posters of some of the biggest names in the business were framed and bolted along the walls.

"It's incredible," she said. "Great acoustics. I mean, probably, from the size of it."

Across the hall, Max was taking a picture with the poster of Siren Seven, then trudging off backstage. Staff members were cleaning, setting up cashiers. Every bit of it was a song, a symphony of the mundane. The crackle of walkie-talkies from security guards, sharp laughter from bathroom attendants, and bartenders clocking in. He loved it.

"I've got everything covered," she assured him, pressing random buttons on the point-of-sale tablet, like she was avoiding looking directly into his eyes. Hurrying him along.

He didn't have much time to worry, as Vanessa ran up to him, the purple tips of her jet-black ponytail swishing to keep up. There was something stiff about her, an unusual tightness across her lips and brows. "Direct support isn't here yet."

He knew their second opening act was late.

"Louie from Le Poisson Bleu posted on their Pixagram that they're stuck in traffic but nearby," he reassured her. "You want to run through sound check first?"

Vanessa made a whimpering sound and nodded. Was she *nervous*? True, it was her first time performing for a real audience, but he had never seen her act this way before. Vanessa was made of steel, like her mom. "Well, your laptop keeps freezing, even though it was working fine two seconds ago."

Eric nodded slowly, assessing the situation. Not ideal, but nothing to freak out over. "It's fine, I checked the backup. You okay?"

"What makes you think I'm not?" she snapped.

Eric knew better than to answer that.

"Whatever, I need to rehearse." She spun on her black, pointy heel and marched away.

He turned to Melody, who made quick work of arranging T-shirts on the wire racks. "You want to watch Vee rehearse? She's—"

"She's coming back." Melody pointed at Vanessa.

"I can't do this," his opening act announced, barreling past him and through a set of double doors.

It took Eric a beat to understand what was happening. He glanced around for Odelia, but she wasn't in the lobby. Had he managed to lose both of his opening acts in less than forty-eight hours?

Cursèd—the word came, unwelcome.

No. He would not give any credence to a silly superstition.

"Eric." Melody said his name like she'd been repeating herself. "We have to go get her."

Together, they went through the double doors and down a long hallway that split into two directions.

Melody motioned to the right. "This way."

He was too worried about Vanessa to wonder how she could possibly know that. But she'd been right. Pacing in front of a freight elevator, Vanessa glanced back in the direction of the squeak of Melody's sneakers against the linoleum.

"Vee, let's talk about this," Eric said.

"Nope. Just tell my mom I can't." She pushed open the metal gate and stepped into the elevator. The iron hinges groaned.

"It's nerves," he pleaded. "We all get nerves."

"I need some air." She shook her head and punched the panel buttons. The whole thing tried to rattle closed, and he pressed his body against the closing door.

"There's air outside," Melody suggested. Vanessa didn't respond.

Eric cursed. He had to follow. He shoved his way inside. Melody slipped in behind him as metal slammed against metal. It was then that Eric noticed the sign stuck between the sliding gates as the elevator ascended, shuddered, and finally came to a grinding stop.

OUT OF SERVICE.

For immediate release: Star Crossed kicks off their first national tour on June 25. Combining classic rock, pop punk, and a nod to the lead singer's Latin pop origins, Star Crossed defies genre. The self-titled record follows the indie sleeper hit "Love Me Again" and "Gray Skies over Montana." French band Le Poisson Bleu is set to open, along with newcomer on the scene, Vanessa G.

On their Pixagram, lead singer Eric Reyes wrote, "I can't believe this is happening. From Colombia to the world, baby! See you on the road."

The ragtag crew was assembled in New York City. Manager Odelia Garcia says, "Musicians have to show you what they're made of. So come and get it. You won't be disappointed."

Tickets are on sale now.

6.25 • Philadelphia, PA • Adam's Grove Music Hall

6.26 • Baltimore, MD • The Intrepid Live

6.27 • Asheville, NC • River Valley Club

6.28 • Nashville, TN • The Nashville Bowl

6.29 • Atlanta, GA • Revel Nightclub

6.30 • Savannah, GA • Gator Music & Grill

7.1 • Jacksonville, FL • The Fountain Club

7.2 • Orlando, FL • House of Blues

7.4 • Miami, FL • Jesse's Live

7.5 • New Orleans, LA • The Road House

7.6 • Dallas, TX • Linda Belle Blues

7.7 • Austin, TX • Vanguard Hall

7.9 • Albuquerque, NM • First Contact Live

7.10 • Tucson, AZ • The Return of Saturn

7.11 • San Diego, CA • Rodgers Theater

7.12 • Los Angeles, CA • The Walter Estate Theater

7.15 • Las Vegas, NV • Vegas Bowl

7.16 • Portland, OR • Howling Rock

7.17 • Seattle, WA • Seattle Rock Live

7.18 • Missoula, MT • The Norma

7.19 • Salt Lake City, UT • The Canyon

7.20 • Denver, CO • Alpine Cavern

7.21 • Tulsa, OK • River Styx Crossing

7.23 • Manhattan, KS • The Little Apple Music Hall

7.24 • St. Cloud, MN • Cloud Nine

7.25 • Chicago, IL • House of Blues

7.26 • Cleveland, OH • Tenderloin Tavern

7.27 • Rochester, NY • River Run Works

7.28 • Burlington, VT • The Barn

7.30 • Boston, MA • Hunter's

7.31 • New York City, NY • Aurora's Grocery

CHAPTER TEN

ARIEL

6.25 Philadelphia, Pennsylvania

Ariel wasn't scared of much. Sure, she watched horror movies from between the slits of her fingers, and feared falling through a sidewalk grate back home, but losing any more of her family was the only thing that truly terrified her.

Until today, when getting stuck in an out-of-service freight elevator that likely hadn't been inspected since the warehouse was constructed skyrocketed to the top of the list.

While Vanessa grabbed hold of the iron gate and rattled it, Ariel picked up the ancient red emergency phone above the buttons panel. She cradled it against her chest. "No dial tone."

Eric pressed the alarm, but if it was connected to anything, it didn't ring. The lone bulb in the ceiling was blown out. He inhaled a deep breath, slid his phone out of his back pocket, and exhaled a curse. "Please, *please* tell me one of you has service."

"My phone is at the booth," Ariel said.

Vanessa held up her illuminated screen. No bars.

For a moment, they stared at each other. They hadn't told anyone where they had gone off to and were tucked away in an old part of the building. No one needed to mention that the show was set to start soon.

Vanessa loosed a string of curses that should have been audible from outer space, then slid to the floor, sitting on her heels. "Someone will come find us."

Eric pinched the bridge of his nose. "No one saw us leave."

It was then that Ariel realized she'd balled her hands into fists, waiting for him to yell and get upset. She hadn't seen him upset, she realized, but then again, they'd only known each other for a day. Why had she expected him to bash through something, or worse—blame their situation on Vanessa or her? Images of her father flashed before her eyes. His mood swings that felt like different stages of a hurricane—the raging gale, the stillness of the eye, the turbulent seas.

Instead, Eric clapped his palms together, and a new look of determination filled his eyes. "Okay. We'll get out of here. Not to worry. I'll go through the latch in the ceiling and climb to the next floor to get some help."

Ariel did not think things were going to work out the way Eric was imagining, but he was so confident and trying so hard to remain calm for them, she didn't want to dash his hopes.

He held out his hands, reaching toward the wall. "Vanessa, give me a boost."

"Don't let this go to your head, but you are two hundred pounds of solid muscle," Vanessa said, pushing herself back to her feet. "Spare me your chivalry bullshit and boost *me*."

Eric pointed at the ceiling. "If you think I'm not letting you get up there because of chivalry, you sorely underestimate how much I fear your mother."

While they were arguing, Ariel grabbed hold of the metal grate. The elevator was like one giant metal cage. She was thankful for the years of weight training and yoga that had made her strong enough to dance for three hours straight in platform boots without getting winded. She hadn't quite imagined the training would come in handy to cling to the sides of a freight elevator, but small blessings.

Eric and Vanessa finally noticed her and shouted at her to get down.

"I got it," she assured them, climbing to the bars on the ceiling and hooking the tip of her sneaker in a gap to secure her footing. Rust shavings dusted off when she gripped the handle marking the ceiling latch. She gave it a shake, but it was stuck.

"Now, *that's* impressive," Vanessa muttered.

When the elevator gave one good groan, Eric hummed nervously. "It's rusted shut. Melody, get down from there."

"Just a little farther." She needed to change her grip, but in the next attempt something sharp stabbed right at the center of her palm. The pain lanced through her, and she instinctively let go.

Ariel knew how to lean into a fall onstage and on video shoots, but those were different. She'd been prepared. She was not, however, prepared for what to do when Eric caught her.

He released a breathless *oof* as his arms tightened around her hips, right under the swell of her backside. Their position left little room for what her father called "el espirito santo." She felt his nose on her belly button, caught up in the hem of her shirt. She and Eric teetered as he kept them upright, and she clung to his shoulders for balance. Easing her down, he held his palm firm on her lower back, every inch of her body brushing against his until her feet were firmly planted on the corrugated metal floor.

"Are you okay?" he asked, immediately taking her palm to examine the injury.

For the stretch of those ten seconds, she'd forgotten about the pain. Blood pooled from a tiny cut. She righted her shirt and tried not to pant. Even in the dim light, was she imagining the flush on his face?

"This is nothing." She closed her fist tight. "I got a spiral fracture when I was fifteen."

"Yeah, well, you don't need a tetanus shot for a spiral fracture. You need a bandage." Eric dug into his pocket for a bandage but came up empty, as did Vanessa.

Ariel was just wishing she had her tiny purse when Eric tore the seams on the hem of his T-shirt and ripped a long strip that exposed his happy trail. How could someone look ridiculous and extremely sexy all at once? She decided to stare at his face instead of his exposed abdomen and focus on the concentrated furrow between his brows, on the thick fringe of his lashes, which blinked as he gently dressed her wound.

"There," he pronounced proudly.

Blood was already seeping through the makeshift bandage, but the pressure dulled the sting. "I owe you a new shirt."

"Maybe I'll start a trend." He chuckled, still cradling her injured hand in his palm. And for a heartbeat, Ariel had that feeling again. It had happened when they were in the pizza parlor, on the bridge, dancing. Like they were the only two people in the room. In the whole world.

Of course, they weren't. Vanessa made an audible gagging sound.

"Oh god." She gripped the door gate and shook hard, screaming for help. "Get me out of here before these two start—"

"*Vanessa,*" Eric warned.

Ariel felt a pang of anxiety, remembering her deal with Odelia. *Eric is off-limits.* The tour had barely started, and she'd already abandoned her post and was stuck in an elevator with two of the stars. Even if it wasn't her fault, she was guilty by association. She put an arm's length between herself and Eric, which made her back up against one of the four elevator walls. "Maybe if we all scream, we'll be loud enough for someone to hear?"

They were out of options. They screamed and screamed until their voices cracked. Until the elevator groaned precariously and they slid into three human puddles against the metal walls. They decided to take turns using the flashlight setting on their phones so that their batteries wouldn't all drain at the same time.

Ariel stopped looking at her watch after the first twenty minutes. Then Eric's low laugh rumbled through the dark.

"What's so funny?" Vanessa asked.

"At least that fish band finally showed."

The soft echoes of Le Poisson Bleu running through their sound check filtered through the warehouse to their jammed elevator. Eric hit the back of his head against the wall and shut his eyes. None of them had to say it—doors would open soon, and they were utterly screwed.

Ariel knew quite well how quickly things could go wrong on a tour. She'd lived through the gamut—backup dancers with broken legs, a stomach virus sweeping through the crew, fire alarms mid-song, that one time she got laryngitis. Getting trapped in an elevator was new, and she hated not being able to do anything but sit and wait.

"I can't believe this is happening." Vanessa sighed from her corner. "Day one. Cursed."

Eric sat forward. "You couldn't have gotten some air outside on the ground floor?"

"No one *asked* you to follow me."

"If you didn't want anyone to follow you, you wouldn't have *announced* your freak-out."

"I didn't freak out!"

"Then what is this?" Eric asked, his voice stern but understanding. "Seriously, Vee. What's going on?"

Ariel watched as the confident Vanessa retreated into herself. She'd been ready. She'd taken the time to get ready early. Black leggings dotted with hundreds of shiny crystals. Matching tank top showing off just enough cleavage. Eyes sharp with inky liner and dusted with shimmering purple.

In that moment, Vanessa reminded her so much of Sophia that it made something in Ariel's heart hurt with missing her sister. For years, Sophia had panic attacks before performing, almost without exception. Sometimes, nothing Ariel or her sisters did would help. Then Teo del Mar would waltz in and sternly remind her what was at stake, how she was a role model to her younger sisters, how they were all counting on her. Inevitably, Sophia would get back onstage.

"My sister," Ariel said softly. "She used to have these panic attacks before—going in public—and when I was little, I thought that she would get through it because she wanted to be brave for us. But now, the more I think about it, the more I wonder if she did it because she didn't want to let down our father. Like it didn't have to do with us. It had to do with the pressure he put on us."

"My mother isn't like that," Vanessa said, in a quick defense of Odelia Garcia. "I don't expect *you* to understand."

"Whoa, Vee," Eric cautioned. "That's not fair."

From the look Vanessa gave her, Ariel could tell she knew exactly who Ariel was. Of course, she hadn't expected Odelia to keep it a secret from her own daughter for long. Perhaps that would make getting through to the other singer easier.

"No, she's right." Ariel puffed a self-deprecating laugh. "I don't understand. But I know what it's like to feel like you're one step away from letting everyone down. One step from ruining *everything* your parent worked so hard for. My sisters and I felt that every day. We just got good at shoving it away. Until I cracked."

Even in the shadows, Ariel could *feel* Eric's gaze on her. She was grateful she could only see his faint outline, because the sympathy in his eyes would have been too much.

"My mom's been through so much," Vanessa said. "She worked so many jobs to make sure I had everything I wanted. Even when I was a little jerk. Even when she was tired, she'd come home, and help me sing. When we sang, when we wrote music together, it was like breathing. Then I got up there tonight. I opened my mouth, and I sounded all wrong. I cracked on my first note."

"Did you warm up?" Ariel asked softly.

Vanessa frowned, shook her head. "I'm not used to it. I was too busy thinking I was going to puke. God, I'm messing everything up."

Eric held out his hand. Vanessa looked at it stubbornly, then she took it. "You haven't messed anything up. I thought Max would get cold feet before you did."

Vanessa snorted. "Imma tell her you said that."

"Fine, then I hope they never find us," Eric said stubbornly.

Vanessa rested her forehead on her propped-up knees. "I'm so sorry, Eric."

He waved her concern off. "Your mom will figure something out. She'll probably give Poisson a longer set. Or maybe Oz will even open the crowd with a cryptid slideshow and a good backing track."

Vanessa cackled, but Ariel asked, "How do you do that?"

"Do what?" he asked, leaning forward so his unruly waves got in his eyes.

Ariel gestured at their situation. "Stay so calm."

"Oh, I'm freaking out," Eric admitted. "I think people freak out in different ways. For instance, my father slammed doors and insulted everyone in the house. My mom freaked out by not speaking, not even when she should have."

"Don't be fooled," Vanessa said. "Señor Sunshine has a dark brooding side he saves for his emo lyrics."

"I love your emo lyrics," Ariel blurted out.

Eric smiled at her. The expression on his face brought her back to the wee hours of the morning. The song, the neon lights, his lips so close to hers. How different would their night have gone if they had kissed? It was a dangerous path to go down. She needed to change the subject so he would stop staring at her like she was a star to wish upon.

"I think," Ariel began, "that since Vanessa shared something scary, we should, too."

Eric didn't hesitate. "Odelia before she's had her pan caliente and cafecito?"

"Imma tell Mom, too."

Ariel flicked the rose tattoos on his bicep with her fingernails. "You know what I mean."

Eric rubbed the place where she'd touched him. She could feel him radiating warmth. Even after load-in, he still smelled like sunscreen and citrus. She fought the urge to grab him by the shirt and quite literally *sniff* him. Instead, she pressed the center of her palm. The bright pain of the wound reminded her that she needed to keep her libido in check.

"Well, in that case." Eric raked his fingers through his dark waves. "Do you know what *I* thought when I stood on that stage for our first run-through?"

Ariel and Vanessa shook their heads.

He sighed, like the admission cost him everything, and said, "It's not like you're going to sell out stadiums."

"What?" Ariel asked after a stretch of silence.

"Those were the words my father said to me the day I left Medellín for Miami. For the last ten years I've heard those words every day. And when I look in the mirror, because my father was a lot of things, but I do get my devastatingly handsome looks from him."

Ariel's throat tightened with all the things she wanted to say to comfort him. She, a girl who actually *had* sold out stadiums and concert halls. What could she say to him that wouldn't sound patronizing, even if he didn't know the truth? She placed her hand on his, brushing her thumb across the smooth skin there. She told herself she was just soothing a friend. She repeated the thought when he turned his palm so their fingers could intertwine and she found comfort in the pressure of his touch.

"But then," he said, not letting her go, "I do it anyway. I go onstage. I remember that even if my own flesh and blood doesn't believe in me, I have a family of wonderful weirdos who do. I'm a simple man. That's all I need. Well, and a few adoring fans."

Ariel smiled hard at that.

"And you?" Vanessa asked, a slight challenge in her voice.

"I guess horror movies is out of the question." Ariel worried her bottom lip. "I mean, I've been sheltered from the world my whole life. In some ways, my father protected me from the worst of things." She was afraid that people would judge her. That her father was right, and she wouldn't be able to survive in the real world. That she was a silly, spoiled nobody. "I'm afraid—"

The elevator rattled, and for the longest second of Ariel's life, they dropped. As they jerked to a stop, Eric grabbed her arm to keep her from tipping sideways.

"We're moving!" Vanessa cried as they inched back to the ground floor. Light filled the cracks in the metal gate as a crowbar wedged through. Several sets of gloved hands pried the door open with the terrible sound of warping metal.

A cluster of firefighters waited on the other side. Behind them was the extremely unhappy venue manager and a somber Odelia.

Ariel untangled herself from Eric and took the hand one of the firemen offered. After profusely thanking their rescue team, she turned to Odelia. "I am *so* sorry."

The tour manager puffed up her chest. Ariel braced herself to get fired. To get sent back to New York before her first shift even started. But it never came. Odelia held out her arms. There was a split second where she thought they were going to hug it out. Then Ariel realized the open arms were for her daughter. Involuntary embarrassment passed through her.

"It's my fault," Vanessa said, looking at Ariel over her mother's shoulder as she gave her an abridged version of how they'd ended up in that elevator. "If they hadn't followed . . ."

"Let's not worry about that now," Odelia said, smoothing Vanessa's baby hairs from her face.

"I'm sorry," Vanessa whispered.

As an EMT cleaned and dressed her cut, Ariel observed Odelia's reaction. She'd expected the manager to flip out that there were ten minutes before Vanessa had to be onstage, but she only seemed focused on making sure her daughter was safe. Ariel tamped down the uneasiness she was feeling. She couldn't help but imagine how her father would have reacted. Teodoro del Mar would have had the venue condemned, then given Ariel a stern reprimand about responsibility, then reminded her that there were hundreds of people working, people who depended on her.

"I heard everything." Odelia glanced at Ariel and Eric and chuckled darkly. "The acoustics in here really are great."

Vanessa shook her head. "I know what you're going to say, and I want to do this. I'm ready."

"Don't do it for me, baby girl. I never want you to feel like you *owe* me anything. Ever. Even if your dreams and goals change, I will change with you. Do you understand?"

Vanessa nodded and hugged her mother tightly. "I know. And I'm sure."

Ariel glanced away from the display of affection. She squeezed her necklace and pictured her mom while the EMT attending to her finished and packed up.

"I hate to break up such a beautiful moment," the venue manager said, a vein pulsing at the center of his forehead, "but I need *someone* to get on that stage in the next three minutes."

Ariel and the others raced back the way they came. Eric shot her an apologetic smile before hurrying backstage to get miked up and change his shirt. Ariel watched the back of his glorious hair disappear. She had to remember what he'd said in their elevator-of-doom confessions. His dreams were so pure, and he was so talented. She'd had every intention of keeping her bargain with Odelia, but until that moment, the consequences for him hadn't felt real. Dreams were fragile things. Perhaps more than love and hope and happiness. She had to keep Eric at a distance. No more cute glances and hands touching if she could avoid it. Even if it hurt at first.

When she turned around, she found Oz with the merch, hiding behind the table while a long line of eager fangirls bounced impatiently. He might as well be holding a white flag.

"Oh good," he said, a slight relieved hitch in his breath. "I couldn't figure out the thing and Odelia told me to stay until they found you and this is not in my pay grade."

Ariel laughed, and it felt good to release all that pent-up emotion. She handed him a twenty-dollar bill and said, "I've got it from here. Why don't you get us some snacks and drinks."

A different kind of adrenaline fueled her as she opened up the merch table and began taking orders. There was a bright kind of energy that music fans emanated, and she loved it. The way they bunched up their hands into little fists and overflowed with happiness at being close to their favorite singers. She pulled down T-shirts. Ran out of enamel pins in the first half hour. Asked Oz to open another box of baseball caps.

When the line cleared, Ariel realized how quickly the time had passed. Vanessa's set was almost over. She'd been watching the footage on a flat screen behind the nearby bar. Purple front lighting washed the stage, where Vanessa G sat on a wooden stool with nothing but her black acoustic guitar and microphone. Her soft soprano filled every corner of the venue.

"Do you have anything from this singer?" the last customer in line, a pretty girl with a halo of red curls, asked.

"Not yet." Ariel smiled and bagged the fan's T-shirt and holographic stickers. "Follow her on Pixagram for updates, though!"

Odelia came around the booth, her sharp eyebrows nearly touching her hairline. She gave a husky chuckle. Was she actually *impressed*?

"How does it feel being on the other side?"

"Weird," Ariel answered honestly, sensing Odelia would sniff out anything but the truth. "And good. It's like I'm invisible."

"Is that what you want? To be invisible?"

She thought about that for a moment. "Not exactly. But considering I've never even been able to take a walk in the park without paps and strangers following me, it's a reprieve."

"Hmm." Odelia shifted uncomfortably. "Melody, I wanted to thank you. For what you said to Vanessa."

Ariel's smile was sad. "When you told Vanessa she didn't have to go onstage. Did you mean it?"

"I don't say things I don't mean."

Ariel didn't know whether to cry or laugh or both. "My dad would have never. I understand how you feel about him. I don't have many adults for comparison."

Odelia's sharpness softened. "Well, we're different people."

"Are you going to tell me what happened between you and my parents?" Ariel asked.

"Some things are better left in the past." Odelia pointed a long red nail at the cashier station. "Don't forget to put those receipts in the bag. And maybe wear one of the shirts, so other girls can see how it looks on you. Here, eat. You missed lunch, and popcorn isn't a meal."

Odelia left a protein bar on the table and swished away to talk to the venue manager without another word.

After the show, after the bands signed autographs and took photos with fans, after they loaded the bus and showered at the venue, Ariel filed back into the bus in her pajamas for the short ride to Baltimore.

Eric disappeared into the back lounge to talk to Odelia. The others were still wired from the show and blasted music as they spread out on the couches. Ariel pushed aside the curtain to her bunk and started to climb in so she could write in her notebook and call it a night.

"It's early, Melody," Vanessa called out. "Come hang out."

"Really?" She didn't mean to sound so eager.

"Yes, *really*." Vanessa rolled her eyes and pointed at the empty couch across from her and Carly. How did she manage to sound annoyed even when she was being friendly?

Max had her drumsticks out, tapping the ledge of the table like she was still onstage. Carly slathered lavender-scented lotion on her smooth brown skin. Grimsby was brushing her teeth with the bathroom door open, and Oz got the bus in gear.

Ariel sat, resting her notebook on her lap.

"What have you got there?" Max asked, pointing a drumstick at her.

"Oh." Ariel gathered her hair into a loose, messy bun. "You know. Dear diary, I got stuck in an elevator today and had to text my eldest sister to see if my tetanus shot was up to date."

They all laughed, and Vanessa said, "I'm *sorry*," once again.

"A parting gift before I left." Ariel smoothed her palm across the simple black notebook.

"Eric said you want to be a songwriter," Grimsby mumbled through a mouthful of toothpaste, stepping out of the narrow bathroom stall. The quarters were cramped, but dealing with limited space was familiar to Ariel, like being in Sophia's dressing room after a show.

"Right now it's just a laundry list of things I want to do while I'm on the road," Ariel said.

Carly tossed her lotion to Vanessa, who took off her many silver rings and handed them to the band's lead guitarist for safekeeping. Maybe they thought no one was looking, but Ariel caught a moment when the two women locked eyes and shared a private smile.

Carly noticed Ariel watching and deflected. "Eric also said you were in a cult, and you ran away."

As if he'd been summoned, the cabin door slid open, and Eric Reyes stepped into the front lounge.

"I did *not* say that," Eric said defensively.

Ariel didn't care. She was too busy staring at him. She blinked rapidly and tried to get her body to stop reacting so much every time he stepped into a room, because even when he looked ridiculous, he looked perfect.

Eric was dressed in nothing but a red cheetah-print silk robe. The hem barely reached the middle of his muscular thighs. Dark hair dusted his long, powerful legs. His hair was still slightly damp. He turned in a slow circle so they could take in every angle of him. The sweep of his tight derrière, his soccer-player calves, the V of his chest exposed by the thin silk.

Max whistled, and he waved his hands, inviting their teasing.

"What in the Eighties Hair Metal are you wearing?" Carly barely managed to ask, as she was laughing so hard that Vanessa had to hold her to keep her from falling off the love seat.

Vanessa broke down, too, and they both fell over, cackling. "Is that my mom's robe?"

"Okay, I might have forgotten my pajamas at home, and Odelia said she didn't want to see me half naked first thing in the morning."

Grimsby, teeth freshly brushed, joined Max at the table. "It's not like we haven't seen you run around the house buck—"

"*Also,*" Eric said pointedly to Ariel, "I did not say a cult. I said *like* a cult."

"It's fine, I swear," Ariel said to the room. Several would-be journalists had referred to her fandom and family as such. She might as well lean into that part of the truth. "Cultish."

"Like what?" Max asked, riveted. "Are we talking virgin cult? Oh! Doomsday cult? No, wait, extraterrestrials."

From the driver's seat, Oz shouted, "I was in a summer camp cult that worshipped bees once."

Grimsby nodded in that slow, slothlike way of hers. "I would really thrive in a vampire cult."

"None of the above," Ariel said, delighted in their amusement and warmth. "It was more like my dad wrote the overprotective parent playbook. "We were very sheltered. There are some things I didn't even do until I was, well, now old."

"So what's on your list?" Vanessa asked, then started laughing again. "I'm sorry, it's just—oh, my god, Eric, sit down, I cannot look at you in my mother's robe."

The only empty seat on the bus was beside Ariel. Eric looked from the spot, then to her. She inched to her corner to make room for him. Just when she'd gone an entire minute without looking at him, he was all in her space. The heat he radiated was flush against her. The bright scent of eucalyptus and soap filled her senses. He grabbed a pillow and placed it right over his lap where the red silk rode up. She felt the urge to lean into his side, the crook between his shoulder and neck where she'd sighed her troubles away when they'd danced.

"Sorry, Melody," Vanessa said, dabbing tears of laughter from the corners of her eyes. "What is on this list?"

"Because there's no limit to sex stuff," Carly added.

"Not sex stuff," Ariel said pointedly. Why did people always go there? "I'm sheltered, not innocent."

She felt Eric tense beside her, and it took every ounce of her self-control to not look up. Thankfully, the delighted round of hoots and whistles from the girls was a good distraction.

"Then what?" Carly asked, genuinely curious.

"Just small things. Normal things you can't do with a strict dad who never lets you leave the house."

Or with a thousand people camped outside of her trailers or airports. She'd done a hospital visit once, and a few paparazzi had given themselves minor injuries so they could sit in the ER. The only safe place was in the penthouse, the studio. Every event and outing was chaperoned with security. Every spontaneous moment had to be stolen. And that's what she was doing. Stealing her life back in a million moments. It was hard to explain to most people, sometimes even some of her sisters, the things she'd never experienced outside of television shows and movies. They had all been older when the del Mars became famous. With her new friends listening, she finally had the opportunity.

"I've never ridden the train to the last stop," Ariel said. "Got lost in the city. Walked across the Brooklyn Bridge with a stranger," she said, twirling her pen with her index and middle fingers. At that, she looked at Eric and found he was already staring at her. Sweet brown eyes—so *that's* what people meant when they said eyes sparkled. She'd sung songs about it but had never seen it in the boys she'd been set up with. That's because Eric Reyes wasn't one of those boys. He was a man, and he was everything she'd never imagined she could want.

"At least you can cross that last one off your list," he whispered to her.

And she did. She flipped open the first couple of pages to her growing list. She jotted it down, then crossed it off.

"Oh, so you want to do things that make you wind up in the opening credits of *Law & Order*," Max teased, brushing her bangs back with the tip of her drumstick.

Ariel snorted, then blushed. "I have others. Go on a road trip. Sit at a coffee shop. Browse a secondhand bookstore. Ride a bike, drive—"

"You've never ridden a bike?"

Ariel crinkled her nose at the memory. When Siren Seven shot the video for "Our Perfect Summer," all her sisters had to ride bikes at the beach, but only the oldest three had ever learned how. Her father had the whole set changed to a soundstage and made production mount stationary bikes in front of the green screen.

"Not exactly," she admitted, warmed by their encouraging interest. "Anyway, it's boring, ordinary stuff."

"It's not boring," Eric said, his voice low and adorably sleepy.

"Well, don't worry," Carly said, tenting her fingers. "*We* are going to teach you how to live."

BALTIMORE MUSE
How I Became a Star Crossed Lover
by Gabi Morataya

Two stops into their tour, the hot new band on the scene—Star Crossed—is *everything* I didn't know I needed from music. Don't be fooled by Eric Reyes's handsome face. The front man can *sing*. Hailing from Medellín, Colombia, Reyes has dreamy vocals reminiscent of Latin Pop stars who came before him. Their sound will make every millennial nostalgic enough to put on stretchy black plastic chokers.

The first single of their self-titled full-length album will turn any skeptic into a die-hard fangirl. While most of their set is bright, dreamy indie rock, they slow things down with the occasional heart-melting acoustic ballad. Montana-made Eleanor Grimsby delivers deep hooks with her plucky bass. Lead guitarist from Queens, New York, Carly Toles rivals Reyes with her stage presence, and Max Chin never lets the beat drop on the drums.

I'm hooked, and half tempted to follow them on the rest of their tour. I am now a self-proclaimed Star Crossed Lover!

CHAPTER ELEVEN

ERIC

6.27 Asheville, North Carolina

"**H**is 'dreamy vocals' are 'reminiscent of Latin Pop stars who came before him,'" Carly read from the review in the music section of *Baltimore Muse* magazine.

Grimsby grinned sleepily. "It's our best review."

"It's our *first* review," Carly added.

"First of many!" Max bounced off the walls, drumming her fists on every possible surface of the front lounge, but came to a stop when the next available surface was Odelia herself.

Pride swelled in Eric. Their blood, sweat, and tears were starting to pay off. Everything he'd lost and sacrificed had to mean *something*. He shut his eyes for a second and gave a silent thanks to his grandfather. Eric had to admit, when Odelia had said a reporter was coming to review their set, he'd tried to keep himself together for the sake of the others, but he'd been a nervous wreck. Now he could breathe and enjoy their free hours in Asheville, North Carolina.

"Can you repeat the part where she says I'm extremely handsome?" Eric asked.

He could practically feel every set of eyes roll. Vanessa proposed they chuck him out on the passing highway. Yet Melody. Melody offered him a smile that told him he was ridiculous, *but* she enjoyed it. At least, he hoped she enjoyed it.

The drive to Asheville on their third day of tour had been their longest—ten hours, thanks to traffic. He still couldn't quite sleep through the night. Every creak of the bus, honk on the highway, Max and Odelia's snoring concerto, and that tiny *screeching* sound from the wheels kept him up. That, and every part of his body was aware that Melody was an arm's length away, with only two acid-green privacy curtains separating them. Though she had been the first one to wake up and put on coffee to percolate the past two mornings, her bunk light had been on long into the wee hours of the night. He wondered if she was writing. If she was listening to music. If she was missing home. He wondered too much and slept too little. That's why he didn't feel all that guilty that he'd soon have a room to himself.

Perhaps then he'd be able to stop thinking of her. Of the way she'd held his hand in that elevator. The way his face had been buried in the perfect warmth of her body when he'd caught her. The alarm that had shot through him when she'd been hurt, as if *his* hand had been skewered by rusty metal. Eric Reyes had had hundreds, thousands of crushes. Why was this one so hard to shake?

"Land, ho!" Oz announced through the radio speakers.

They pulled into the parking lot of the Hotel Château de Chillon and waited for Odelia in the lobby while she got them sorted out. Melody leaned over Oz's shoulder, sliding through his pictures from his Sasquatch-search camping trip the previous summer. She seemed genuinely enthused, giggling in that way of hers, like everything was new and exciting, even when it was just a bubble gum machine at a rest stop.

Eric felt a strange pressure in his chest. Was that *jealousy*? Or was his breakfast burrito not sitting right? He rubbed his gold pendant of Saint Anthony, a gift from his mother so he'd be protected on his travels away from home, but he wasn't certain there was a saint who covered heartburn.

"All right, huddle up," Odelia ordered.

"Why do you have on your bad news face?" Carly asked.

Odelia's perfectly cat-eyed gaze slid to their lead guitarist. "I have a bad news face?"

Carly stared at her feet and took a step back. Vanessa patted her friend's shoulder, and they all stifled a laugh as their all-around manager continued.

"It slipped my mind that Robbie was supposed to room with Eric." Odelia's eyes peered into the deepest recesses of Eric's mind. "So we need to adjust our sleeping arrangements."

A thread of panic pierced right through him, but he forced his face to remain neutral.

"Who's Robbie?" Melody asked, pulling down her pink baseball cap with the bright red crab at its center.

"The merch guy who quit," Grimsby said.

The tops of Melody's cheeks flushed pink. "Oh . . ."

"A convention's happening this week, and the hotel ran out of cots," Odelia explained, turning that admonishing stare to their merch vendor. Did he imagine the warning there, too? "And my room only has one bed. Otherwise, I'd suggest you stay with me. Unless someone wants to swap."

His traitorous friends tapped the fronts of their noses, grinning like they could taste their win. Oz caught on and did the same, even though as the bus driver he was contractually guaranteed his own room and he had no clue about the bet. They truly thought so little of Eric. Well, he would prove them all wrong. He'd keep all his perfect hair. He'd keep his dignity when they lost, and he was spared from learning a Siren Seven song. He'd pick out *their* damn band tattoo—something none of them would be able to show their mothers.

Melody's pink lips curled into a shy smile. "I'm a night owl, but I'll make sure you get your beauty sleep."

Eric's tongue suddenly felt too big for his mouth. Thankfully, their manager kept giving instructions.

"That's that," Odelia murmured dryly. "Check-in isn't for another three hours. You'll have to change at the venue, and I'll have all your key cards ready to go. The hotel did give us free tickets to the convention for our inconvenience."

"What kind of convention?" Melody asked.

"Taxidermy something? I don't know, Melody, do I look like I go to conventions?"

But Oz was breathless with excitement. Odelia handed the passes to their bus driver, who looked like he'd been gifted a million dollars and a baby Sasquatch.

With that, they were dismissed and free to run around Asheville. Everyone seemed to pair up. Carly and Vanessa ran off, and Grimsby and Odelia stayed behind to work on the music video concept. Max and Oz eagerly headed to the taxidermy convention.

That left Eric with Melody. Her long mahogany waves tumbled over her shoulders. He realized he was counting the beauty marks—one under her eye, one on her chin. He mentally cursed at himself and thumbed in a direction, any direction.

"I should—" Go. He should go. But then he remembered that Melody hadn't been many places alone. She'd said it herself. She was always with her family or locked in her house like a fairy-tale princess. He'd be an absolute jerk if he left. He noticed her clutching her black notebook. Two stickers had been added—a tiny crab from Maryland and one from their opening band, Le Poisson Bleu.

Eric silenced the rational part of his brain that told him to put distance between him and Melody. "What's on your list today?"

In Baltimore, she'd gone on a food tour with Oz while the band had load-in. Not that he was keeping tabs on her. She'd just brought them back leftovers, which they'd devoured after practicing through lunch.

"Thrift store and pinball museum," she said with such delight he would have thought it sarcastic if anyone else had said it. She started toward Main Street, and he fell in step beside her. "I have been to thrift stores, but I didn't pack a jacket and Grimsby said I'd need one when we got to Montana, even in July."

"I'll join you," he said. "I need a new lucky shirt."

That, and he needed something to sleep in that didn't belong to a glamorous fifty-five-year-old Venezuelan woman. They strolled through downtown, surrounded by the hazy Blue Ridge Mountains, and found a kitschy thrift store next to a coffee shop.

The doorbell tinkled as they let themselves in. Melody's eyes lit up as she took in rows of cowboy boots, purses representing every decade hanging from the ceiling, and mannequins dressed in sequin blouses with giant shoulder pads.

A tiny old woman—Ruby, her name tag read—came around to help them and guided Melody to the jackets. "I've got just the thing for you. Your manfriend can look around."

Eric and Melody's eyes met, and she snorted. He'd never been called someone's *manfriend* before. Boyfriend, lover, one-night stand, and— the one and only time he worked as a bartender—a South Beach cougar had called him her "boy toy." The thing was, neither of them moved to correct the shop owner. Ruby hadn't meant anything by it, and it was a harmless afternoon out. He was certain that was the reason.

He browsed through old band tees, found a vintage Selena y Los Dinos shirt in his size. He had the urge to show Melody and waded through the sage-scented store to look for her in the fitting room area.

When she saw him, her eyes sparkled with mischief. "I found you the perfect pajamas."

Eric wasn't so sure if he wanted to try on secondhand long johns, but he would indulge her. "Let's see these perfect pajamas."

Melody pointed to the dressing room. Was picking out sleep

clothes something friends did? He *had* bought Max Siren Seven house slippers one Christmas, but that was a gag gift. His own curiosity had him stepping into the narrow stall. He closed the curtain and stared at an adult flannel onesie in red and green plaid so bright, his eyes began to hurt. He was positive he'd only ever seen something like this in cartoons. And yet, he shoved himself into the outfit, listening to Melody laugh from the other side of the curtain.

He stepped out onto the ancient carpet of the store and walked in a circle. Right across the butt-flap panel were the words NAUGHTY ELF. "Well?"

Melody's nose crinkled, and she gave him a thumbs-down. Ruby, on the other hand, gave him a thumbs-up. Both did nothing to hide their delight. He would drink Melody's laugh if he could. He'd only ever felt this way, as if he wanted to submerge himself into a sea of sound, about specific songs. That's how powerful and perfect her voice was to him.

"I have other options," Ruby said.

Eric shook his head with good humor. "I think I'm good."

After changing back, he did find a pair of flannel pants with the original tag still on and a new pack of white T-shirts. Melody had tried on every jacket in the store, but settled on a sunflower-yellow bomber with jackpot cherries stitched everywhere. It was hideous. And yet he'd never seen anyone more beautiful.

When she went to pay, he noticed her fumbling with a wad of cash from a leather folio. She gathered her change and smiled at Ruby as she put on her new vintage jacket.

"Did you rob a bank?" he teased, holding the jingling door open.

Melody looked alarmed at first. "Soph—um, my sister. I don't—"

"You don't have to explain."

"No, I want to try," she said. "Everything I've ever worked for is tied up in accounts my father set up for us. When we were little, he said it was the way to make sure our money was safe."

"My father did that to me," Eric said.

"Really?"

He hated thinking about it, but felt like she'd opened up, so he would, too. "My dad was a land developer. He built his own firm from nothing, and for decades he was one of the richest men in my city. I had everything. Boarding school in Switzerland, a car for when I came home for the holidays, my own horse."

"You did not have a horse."

"I did, too, have a horse. His name was Achilles." Eric remembered the privileged life he'd had once. "Then everything went away. He made one bad investment after another. We moved into a smaller home. I finished school in Medellín. That's when my grandfather moved in with us, and we spent every day—I mean *every day*—playing guitar and singing."

"And then you came here," she said.

He nodded slowly. "When I left, my dad cut me off. I wish I'd realized sooner that it was his way to control me. To mold me into what he wanted me to be."

Melody was pensive for so long, he wanted to wrap his arm around her. To let her know she wasn't alone. That perhaps he knew exactly how she felt. "Did it get easier? Being away from your family?"

"I am with my family," he said, without hesitation.

She seemed to mull that over as they reached the pinball museum. He opened the door, and she smiled. "You don't have to stay if this isn't your scene, I swear."

"Are you kidding?" As if he could tear himself from her side when she peered up at him with those bright, brown eyes. "I feel like someone needs to document this era in your life."

The museum itself took about ten minutes to run through, but the arcade section made him feel like a little kid. Dozens of machines whirred and pinged with lights and music. Clusters of kids ran around the orange carpet, hopping from game to game. Most of the adults were parents milling near the checkout counter, but there was a lone grizzled biker playing the Ms. Pac-Man game.

"It's like a casino and a circus had a baby," Melody marveled.

She gasped and ran past him to a stall called Seahorse Madness. It was one of those racing games powered by water guns. She disappeared for a second, then returned with a bag of colorful tokens and fed a few into the machine.

He followed her lead and selected one of the neon plastic water guns. His blue. Hers purple. "Ready?"

"If you let me win," she warned, "I will change my alarm to the most obnoxious sound in the world."

"Fine," he said, taking aim. "But I'll have you know I spent summers on my grandfather's farm being woken up by deranged horny roosters, so I can sleep through anything."

She hit the start button, and they were off. Tinny calypso music played, and bursts of bubbles fluttered from some automatic machine. He hadn't flicked his trigger finger that fast in—well, a while. He glanced over to Melody, her face twisted in such cute concentration, he was honestly tempted to let her win right then and there. But they were neck and neck, and he needed to prove to himself that he could treat her like a friend. He never let Max win at chugging contests or Carly win at drunken arm wrestling. Why did the idea of Melody's disappointment, just the *thought* that she'd feel let down even for a second, gnaw at him?

He knew why but couldn't allow himself to admit it. Not there, not yet.

When they were almost at the end, his green seahorse coming up by a hair, he just couldn't help it. He couldn't. He missed a click, and it was worth it for the happy little shimmy she made.

"Nerd," he muttered playfully.

"Wait." She turned her water gun on him. Her eyebrows rose in suspicion. "*Eric.*"

He held up his palms. "My finger cramped. Do you know how catastrophic it would be if I got carpal tunnel because we played Seahorse Madness?"

She rolled her eyes and got him right in the chest with a squirt of lukewarm water. That couldn't have been sanitary.

After that, he didn't let her win. Really. He bested her at foosball, at table hockey, and at virtual dirt bike racing. The arcade also boasted the rarest Star Wars pinball machine in the country, with only six ever made.

Melody saddled up and tried to get the metal ball through clusters of TIE fighters. She got increasingly frustrated when she couldn't reach a high score.

"Would it be letting you win if I showed you a trick?" he asked.

Melody stepped aside and surrendered the machine. He plinked a couple of tokens in and palmed the buttons with the mound of his hand. She studied his fingers and the way the pinball machine lit up, whirring with all the sound effects from the movies.

"I did that! Wait, show me again."

He took a step back, inviting her into the space between himself and the pinball machine. When he inhaled the rose scent of her shampoo, he ground his teeth together and put another step between them. "Here."

She rested her fingers on either side panel. He molded his hands around hers, which required him to adjust his stance for her height. He shut his eyes and thought of the least romantic things possible—that onesie he tried on, Max snoring on the bus, himself snoring on the bus. The bus. Melody on the bus. Melody.

Well, that wasn't working.

"Do it two times fast, one hard, four even faster," he said, tapping on her fingers to show her where to press down. "Then like this with your palm. But very fast. Faster."

"Two. One. Four. Got it." He felt her chest expand. Her *hum* of acknowledgment. She pushed up her bright yellow sleeves. With her bandaged hand, she only used her fingers. With the good palm, she did exactly as he'd instructed.

Eric pushed the start button for her, and she was off. Two. One. Four. Two. One. Four. Two. One. Four. The machine whirred and blared with alarms, the *pew pew* and crackling hum of space swords, until she did it.

Melody turned around and leaped into his arms. He was startled by the momentum, and to stop them from falling, he picked her up by her waist. She kicked the air for a second, before he put her back down.

"I'll share my prize with you," she said, walking down the aisles for another game.

When they turned a corner, they froze. There was a girl around six years old sitting on the floor. She had two curly puffs of hair tied with pink bows, and fat tears ran down her face.

"Do you need help?" Eric asked. He had no idea what to do around children, let alone weeping children. Frantically, he looked around for an adult, then realized he *was* the adult.

"No one wants to dance with me," the little girl said in her high-pitched voice.

Melody looked at the game with slight horror. It was a Siren Seven–themed monstrosity, all shimmery blues. Seven cartoon versions of the singers danced on a screen, and sea creatures jumped from the water, encouraging unsuspecting victims to step up to the plate and show off their moves. Two sets of shoe prints pulsed in time with the chirpy song.

"Too bad Max isn't here," he said.

Melody offered the kid her hand. "I'll dance with you."

The girl instantly cheered up, and she and Melody jumped up onto the light-up pad, arranging their feet in place. They counted down and followed the video routine on the pixelated screen. Bonus points and tiny fish burst into a rainbow of colors with every correct step. The music, though saccharine, even made his head bop along. Well, he *had* wanted the least romantic thing possible, and he'd gotten it.

And yet, watching how patient she'd been with the crying child when all he'd tried to do was find someone else to pass along the tantrum to, how kind she was to share a moment of her time and make sure the little girl didn't feel alone . . . He'd thought she was beautiful from the moment he set eyes on her. He'd thought she was brave, funny, cute, shy. Patience was different. It was something that had rarely been given to him—not by his parents or teachers. Only his grandfather and Odelia had shown him patience.

He rubbed his gold pendant and smiled as the game powered down. The kid's teen sister came searching for her, and Melody returned to him. He clapped, and she dipped into a playful curtsy.

"I'm starving," she announced.

"Good. I'm sure you're tired of losing to me."

She balked, but counted her strips of red carnival tickets. "Get on that platform. That sounds like a challenge."

"You could not pay me to dance to that crap," he said.

Melody sucked in a little gasp. Was she hurt? Was she faking?

"Don't tell me you listen to Siren Seven." He pressed his hands into prayer hands. "You, who like real music?"

"See, *I* don't judge people's music tastes." Melody shook off his reaction and shrugged one shoulder. Her cheeks blushed pink, and she wouldn't even meet his eyes as she grabbed his arm and led him to the checkout counter.

"I'm not judging."

She squinted at him. "You are."

"Fine, I am. Maybe a little." He stepped around the displays of stuffed animals, erasers, Slinkys, and all kinds of cheap, colorful prizes. "It's never been my thing. Max gives me so much shit about it."

Melody bit the inner corner of her mouth, studying him with those impossibly brown eyes. "Maybe you need to really listen."

"Maybe," he said, leaning across a rack of stuffed teddy bears. "Maybe you should make me a playlist. You know, so I can *really* listen."

"Do you want to make a playlist with me?" she asked coyly.

Eric swallowed a growl that started to form at the back of his throat. Her voice. Did she have any idea what she did to him?

Thankfully, a nearby pimple-faced teenage employee made a gagging sound. "Are you two going to check out or make out?"

Melody snorted but gathered her prize tickets from her pockets. "Check out."

"Wait," Eric said. "What's next on the list?"

"*You* have practice," she retorted. "I'm getting lunch."

As if summoned, Odelia sent a text asking where he was. Melody's phone rang at the same time, and he saw her reject her call, but not before he saw the caller ID read UNKNOWN.

Eric wavered. For the first time in years, he considered blowing off practice for just another hour with Melody. That thought alone was enough to snap him into reality. He had practice. He had a show.

He gave her all his tickets and grinned. "No erasers."

"No promises." She grinned back.

Then he left the arcade, and it took all his willpower not to look back.

That night, they packed the River Valley Club. The stage was so low, the crowd was almost close enough to touch. They danced and sang and hollered, and every ounce of energy they received, they gave right back. When he sang "Love Like Lightning," he felt every vibration of the dancing crowd, the frantic beat of his heart syncing up to the rhythm like he was singing it for the very first time.

The roar of the audience was everything he'd wanted, and he felt compelled to say "Gracias, Pedro" when the lights went out.

After the show they had a long dinner at the Japanese smokehouse next door to the venue. Locals who'd been to the concert came up, and the band geeked out when they were asked to sign napkins and take selfies.

By the time they got back to the hotel, Eric had almost forgotten that he was sharing a room with Melody.

Almost.

They grabbed their overnight bags from the belly of the Beast and took their key cards from Odelia. Because of the convention, they were not all on the same floor. Squeezing into the elevator, they all went up. Melody and Eric got out first. Carly and Vanessa whistled as the doors closed, and he said good night with a rude gesture of his hand before keying them inside.

"I call first shower," Melody announced, and dropped her bag at the entrance. She kicked off her shoes and opened the bathroom door extremely carefully.

He undid the laces of his boots and suppressed a chuckle. "Are you expecting a gremlin to jump out or—?"

"Oh," Melody said, blushing in embarrassment. "Oh, I read there are bears around here."

"I'm not a wildlife expert, but I think we're safe. Bears only stay at five-star hotels." He spread his arms to take in the room. The eighties wallpaper. The hideous curtains that matched the dizzying carpet. The single queen bed he would convince himself had fresh sheets. "Two stars."

Wait.

They both turned to the single queen bed at the same time, then to each other.

"I can fix this," he said.

With his heart thundering, he called the front desk. It took about two seconds for the woman on the other line to tell him it was the last room available, and there was nothing she could do to accommodate.

He slowly set the receiver back in place. "Apparently, the Asheville Taxidermy Convention is a really big draw."

Melody absently tapped her fingers on the wall behind her. "Is this weird?"

"It doesn't have to be," he said. "I want to make sure you're comfortable. I will go sleep in the bus."

"If I didn't feel comfortable with you," Melody said, "I would be sleeping on Odelia's floor right now. And I wouldn't have joined your seven-week tour. We're friends, right?"

He nodded, throat dry. "Right."

"I have to warn you, I've been told I hog the covers." She laughed and disappeared into the bathroom.

Eric's first thought was *Who? Who told you that?* followed by a spike of jealousy. He was not a jealous man. He'd never had reason to be. But there he was, not thinking with his upstairs brain, and getting caught up in thoughts that made him want to be careless. His second thought was of his band. He had work to do.

As he waited for her to be done in the shower, he went over the set list, forwarded interview requests to Odelia, ignored raunchy texts from his friends, and put on the evening news. Surely there was some gruesome murder somewhere that would get his mind off Melody, who was taking a shower ten paces from where he sat on an ugly once-white chair. Something to stop the vise latched around his heart when she stepped out of the bathroom and into the tiny room, steam billowing at her feet. Dressed in a baggy I HEART NARWHALS T-shirt and tiny shorts.

"Your turn."

Eric leaped into the shower and lathered up under scalding-hot water. He did his best songwriting in the shower, which his bandmates and roommates often complained about when the water bill came around. Now, as he washed the concert off his skin, he found there were no lyrics. There was just a carousel of emotions he'd never felt so intensely before, spinning and spinning until he released himself from his own denial.

As he toweled off and used the hair dryer bolted into the wall to dry his hair, he had a realization. He didn't have a fleeting crush on Melody. He full-on liked her. And he had to stop. Yes, there was the bet, and the band, and his future. But more than that, he hadn't seriously had to put his heart on the line in so long, he didn't know where to start.

Unable to sleep in the bathroom (though he would have considered it if there had been an actual tub), he pulled on his thrift store pajamas and went to bed.

Melody had taken a corner of the mattress, closer to the door. Her notebook was open on her lap. He grinned when he noticed that she was using the tiny golden fork from Julio's bar to brush out a tangle from the ends of a lock of hair.

"So, feel free to not answer this," Eric said, walking around the bed and sitting on his side. "But your father was so strict he wouldn't let you go to the arcade?"

Melody closed her notebook, wedging the fork in the center to save her place, and set it on the nightstand. She turned to face him, toes tucked under the covers. "We weren't allowed to play with other kids. At least my sisters and I had each other."

"So you've never had friends outside of your family?" Eric asked, getting under the comforter.

"A few," she said. "Friends. Boyfriends. But my father had to approve them, and he could, and did, easily change his mind."

Would your father approve of me? he wondered.

A voice that sounded like his own father answered: *No.*

Eric frowned, trying to imagine how someone more controlling than his own father could even exist. "That's terrible."

"My dad had his reasons." She reached into the covers and pulled out that tiny stuffed shark. He remembered her saying one of her sisters had given it to her.

"What possible reasons could they be?"

"My mom died when I was little," she explained, and he felt like a complete ass. "Car accident. It was a long time ago, but sometimes it feels like it was yesterday. After that, he was so careful. Like if he kept an eye on us, kept us tucked away, away from others, then we'd be safe. I always defended him. I don't know when it happened, but I got to a point where I saw that there was a whole world outside of ours, and we were parallel to it but not *in* it. You know?"

He wanted to smack himself. "Fuck, Melody, I'm sorry. I keep making these cult jokes, and I didn't know."

She reached out and placed the stuffed shark on his chest. "Here, my sister hugs Tibby when she feels stressed or emotionally compromised. She acts pretty tough, but she's a marshmallow."

"Emotionally compromised," he mused. He could relate. "Tibby? Short for Tibothée?"

Melody laughed, then clapped her hand over her mouth when she remembered it was past midnight and the walls were super thin.

"Tiburón," she said, then twisted her hands into a clawed interpretation of a shark mandible. "This thing is almost as old as me."

"Will he also protect us from the alleged bears who come to stay at two-star hotels?"

She hid under one of the pillows. "Oh, come on."

He turned on his side and rested the shark between them. "Speaking of emotional-support stuffed animals, what prizes did you get with all those tickets I won?"

Melody kicked out of the covers, her strong, sun-kissed legs something out of his wildest fantasies. She rummaged through her duffel and tossed him a squeaky plastic bathtub toy. He caught it midair. A unicorn cat. He squeezed it and regretted the terrible honking sound.

"I guess we have a tour mascot." He placed it on the nightstand and rolled onto his back. The adrenaline from the day was washing away as he settled into bed. As Melody did the same, he allowed himself one glance. Just one, to make sure she was okay. Comfortable and safe sharing the small space with him.

Her long dark hair spilled over the pillow. She folded her hands over her stomach and sighed, before turning off the light.

For a while, he could hear the buzzing of the silence, as if the space in between things—the walls, the bed, the slab of plywood they called a desk, their menagerie of toy animals—had sound.

"You know what's weird?" she whispered.

He turned to the sound of her voice, his eyes adjusting to the dark. The red light from the alarm clock at her side cast an eerie glow. A wave of anxiety washed over him. "What's weird?"

Eric could hear her move against the pillow, facing him. Saw the outline of her shadowed face when she said, "This doesn't feel weird."

Desire simmered low in his belly. For the honesty, the trust in her voice. For her.

"I know," he whispered back.

And then, it happened. A slow thud against their wall, like something slamming and pushing and banging against a headboard. Oh no. *Oh god.* Which is precisely what he heard their neighbors cry out through the walls.

"Now *that's* weird," Melody whispered.

He squeezed the unicorn cat, which squeaked loudly. "This, this is exactly what they sound like."

Melody burrowed her face into her pillow to muffle her laugher. "This is going on the list."

"Listening to two people make donkey sounds during sex is *not* ordinary. I'm just saying."

"Maybe there is a donkey, we don't know."

"You're right, we don't know. There *was* a taxidermy convention here."

"Too far."

But she laughed with him, and he laughed until his abdomen hurt, until the tension loosened from his shoulders, his whole being, and he sank into the first deep sleep he'd had since he'd left home.

SevenAteNine Group Chat

Marilou:
🙄 How's Lover Boy?

> **Ariel:**
> It's not like that.

> **Ariel:**
> And things are good. He's asleep.

Sophia:
I can't believe you're back in a
TOUR BUS.

> **Ariel:**
> We're in a hotel tonight.

Thea:
Wait, how do you know he's asleep?
YOU'RE SHARING A ROOM?!

> **Ariel:**
> He was supposed to room with the
> merch guy. He also hogs the covers.

Stella:
EXQUEEZE ME?

Alicia:
One bed?!

> **Ariel:**
> He's asleep, I told you. I'm writing.

Sophia:
Are you being careful?

> **Ariel:**
> You guys are the worst. We're friends. Period.

> **Ariel:**
> He's not what I thought. Sweet.
> Kind. He really wants this.

Elektra:
Too bad you can't mentor him.

Marilou:
OR she can. Just stealth.

Marilou:
Stealth mentoring!

Thea:
I think she should kiss him and get it over with.

Sophia:
No, Ariel should not kiss him and get it over with. Kissing him will only make it worse and complicated.

Stella:
Have you seen his Pixagram tho? YUM.

Ariel:
Why do I tell you guys anything?

Alicia:
Because we're the best and you miss ussssssss.

Marilou:
Do you know what you're going to do when you come home?

Sophia:
Still at it with the lawyers, FYI.

Ariel:
Thanks, Detective Sophia. Did you dig up anything on Odelia Garcia?

Stella:
Nope.

Sophia:
I searched through all the company records.

Marilou:
I think I can hack Dad's computer?

Thea:
Please, that thing is practically handcuffed to him.

Alicia:
Do you think she was telling the truth about knowing Mom and Dad?

Ariel:
That's what I want to find out.

CHAPTER TWELVE

ARIEL

6.28 Nashville, Tennessee

Ariel del Mar woke with a song in her head, and a man underneath her. Only one was cause for concern.

Her head rested on Eric's chest, rising and falling with his steady breathing. She could hear his strong heartbeat, and for a moment, she wanted to stay there. His arm draped around her, palm resting firmly on the swell of her hip. Her leg sprawled across his lower body. Her hand resting over his pectoral.

She tried to remember the night before. He'd fallen asleep to the honking sounds next door, then she'd texted with her sisters until she couldn't keep her eyes open. At some point, they must have rolled into each other. The room *had* been cold, she told herself. Though her heart gave a hard pang of longing, she needed to untangle herself from the rock-hard music god in her arms.

When she gently moved her hand, Eric shifted. His long lashes fluttered, as if he were dreaming. He smoothed his palm up and down her forearm, and she couldn't tear her eyes from him. No one had ever held her this way. Hard and soft at the same time, like she was something to cherish and never let go of.

Then came a pounding at the door. His eyes snapped awake, and their gazes met. She saw the panic there as he took in their intertwined limbs. They leaped apart. She threw herself a little too hard and bounced off the bed.

"Coming!" she called.

"No, wait, *wait*," Eric hissed, gathering the covers around him.

Her face burned, but she had no choice but to open the door. Oz stood there, wearing a brown bucket hat with the convention logo. His keys hung from a lanyard, and he sipped from a giant iced coffee. His brown eyes went from her to where Eric was looking like he'd lost a fight with the bedsheets.

Oz smiled knowingly, then made a zipper motion across his lips before saying, "I'm taking to-go breakfast orders, and you weren't answering your phone."

"Two seconds!" she yelped, then shut the door.

On the road by dawn, almost everyone went back to sleep in their bunks. Ariel buzzed with caffeine, so she made herself comfortable at the front lounge table. She sipped her black coffee from an I HEART CONEY ISLAND mug and watched the landscape go by as she jotted down phrases and thoughts that had the potential to be lyrics. She'd written so many songs this way, during the in-between hours of morning and night.

It was strange how the worries she'd had on a Siren Seven tour were the same ones she had as the merch vendor for Star Crossed. Was her father on an angry rampage? Were her sisters happy and well? Did her fans have enough of her? Was the music blogger who hated Siren Seven hate-listening and reviewing their last concert? The only difference was that she no longer had control over the outcomes. Her father would always find something that didn't meet his standards. Her sisters were ready to live their own lives yet still connected to her, no matter what. Her fans and haters would always want more. Perhaps the reason she still had the same worries was because she never had control over the outcomes in the first place.

There, aboard the Beast, as daybreak illuminated her inky scrawls, she took a deep breath and let those worries go. She knew they'd return, but until then, she wanted to feel present.

Grimsby joined her, refilling both of their mugs. "I didn't peg you for a black coffee girl."

Ariel raised her brow. She was used to that comment and was surprised to hear it even when she wasn't wearing a face full of makeup and a red wig. "What did you peg me for?"

"I don't know." Grimsby plopped into her seat across the table. "Sugar-free vanilla latte, cinnamon, oat-milk something?"

"Wow," Ariel said, almost snorting the bitter sludge in her mug. "I don't know if I should feel offended or not."

"Oh, I don't mean anything by it." Grimsby's big gray eyes were so expressive. They reminded Ariel of a snowy owl, blinking with surprise. "Sorry, I can be a little judgmental."

"Let's do first impressions," Ariel said, flashing the goth girl a disarming smile.

"You go first."

"I thought, intimidating and serious."

Grimsby gave her a lazy smile. "And now?"

"Thoughtful. You always give Carly your extra pillow on long drives, and refill everyone's coffee without asking."

"Fair and correct. Now you." Grimsby tapped her long finger on her pointed chin.

"Be gentle."

Grimsby grinned sheepishly. "Well, keep in mind my perception is skewed because Eric came home after a night with you acting goofy as fuck."

Ariel's cheeks warmed. "Go on."

"I thought you were unfairly pretty and unhinged."

This time, she did slightly choke on her coffee. "Unhinged?"

"I don't know!" Grimsby shrugged innocently. "I mean, *something* had to shake you loose to take a seven-week road trip with strangers. It's like people who take jobs on ocean cruises. You just pack up and vanish, you know?"

"Isn't that what you did?" Ariel leaned in, amazed to hear the bass player speak so much in one go.

"Yeah. Except when I ran away, I had nowhere to go. I was seventeen and hated my stepmom. I stole my stepbrother's car, drove it to Seattle. Left it double-parked so someone would find it, then got a job as a dog walker. So, yeah. Unhinged."

Ariel tried to imagine this goth girl walking a dozen fluffy dogs. It fit. "I don't think that's unhinged. I think it's brave."

"Maybe a little of both," Grimsby said. "To be honest, I was a little afraid that you were going to hurt Eric. He's a big softie who's been hurt before, so we worry for his big, dumb heart. He's, like, in love with love."

Hurt how? Hurt when? The questions bubbled in her throat, but she felt like she needed to ask him directly.

She drew tiny stars on her notebook to keep her fingers busy. "And now? What's your second impression?"

"Well, that same night, I thought, she's really fucking cool and brave. A little insecure. You always look at yourself in the mirror and seem surprised. Like you're seeing yourself for the first time."

Ariel set her pen down. She didn't think anyone would notice. "I guess I'm still getting used to this version of myself. Like, am I the same person if I leave behind the things that made me *me*?"

"I think I'm going to need more coffee before we try to answer that." Ariel shared Grimsby's low laugh. "Have you ever gone back?"

Grimsby frowned at her coffee. "Our show in Missoula will be the first time in eight years. Kind of freaking out. I'm still trying to decide if I should invite my family. I suppose we all have something to prove with this tour."

Ariel got up to make more coffee. Grimsby didn't know just how right she was.

The Nashville Bowl was part bowling alley and part music venue. It also had a booth for merch that looked like a carnival box. It was the biggest venue of their stops, and Ariel could feel the band's nerves as they worried about packing the venue.

Ariel took a picture of her setup and uploaded it to her new private Pixagram account. It was jarring going from a hundred million followers to only the five people on the tour bus, but it was also freeing being anonymous. She gave her sisters explicit instructions not to follow her, or the band, in case someone would notice. Besides, Ariel's new feed was full of completely uncurated images of her notebook, coffee sludge, state highway "Welcome" signs, and the unicorn cat bath toy. She also posted pictures of the band and followed the new #StarCrossedLovers fan hashtag.

With every show, the band's profile grew by a couple hundred followers. The more she got to know them, the prouder she was. They were building something, slow but steady. For her, success had felt instant. People in her face, fans wanting pieces of her. She had missed personal interactions, like in Asheville when she danced the Siren Seven arcade game with that little girl. Then she reminded herself that her father would never have allowed something that spontaneous to happen, not without a dozen photographers around, plus the family to sign a legal waiver.

When Ariel noticed Eric walking toward her booth, she focused her nervous energy on tweaking the already-perfect display on her table. They hadn't spoken about that morning, or even acknowledged that they'd slept in each other's arms. She did consider that it might mean more to her, someone with a growing list of firsts, than to a guy who was in "love with love," as Grimsby put it.

Eric knocked on the side of the booth. His easy smile made her heart stutter. "Bowling. Is it on the list?"

It was. Siren Seven had filmed a video at a bowling alley for the "Strike to the Heart" music video, but the director yelled "Cut!" just after she got in position to actually bowl, and Ariel and her sisters were shuffled off to another set.

She nodded and took the hand he offered to join the others on the second floor. Le Poisson Bleu joined, too. Louie, the French lead singer, seemed so bewildered at the game, and at Eric's impressions of *The Big Lebowski*, that he eventually gave up and announced he was going for a smoke outside.

"Would you like to join me?" he asked, offering Ariel his hand. He had slender, piano-playing fingers, which she'd seen glide up and down his electric keyboard.

"I don't smoke," she said, wrinkling her nose at the memory of the first and last time she and Marilou had tried it.

Louie winked at her, then sauntered away.

Max and Carly made a suggestive whistle, but she ignored them, as it was her turn. She waggled her fingers over the vent before hefting her shimmering purple bowling ball from the rack.

She glanced over her shoulder, where her friends were cheering her on. Eric clapped like he was watching a soccer match. Nerves bunched in her stomach, but she used that energy to focus. To aim. To feel the weight of the ball, and then let go.

Strike!

Ariel raised her fists in the air, and Carly shouted, "Beginner's luck! Switch to my team."

The rest of the hour was full of gutter balls, and the final score put her second to last ahead of Oz, but she texted a cheesing selfie to her sisters.

Sophia:
I don't remember the last time I saw
you smile so hard, my little guppy.

Marilou:
Jealous!

Stella:
Boooo, take me, please.

Ariel returned her shoes, blinking away the emotion that came with missing her sisters.

Later, at lunch, they scarfed down sticky, delicious barbecue. The last time she'd been in Nashville to perform at the The Golden Grand, Elektra and Sophia had been the ones to sneak out for live music, disguised in neon wigs and bachelorette sashes. Ariel had been too young, too scared of getting caught.

"Is anyone up for a record store?" Ariel asked as they stepped out of the Nashville Bowl.

Every one of them, except Oz and Eric, declined on account of their food comas. Ariel hailed a rideshare to PhonoGold on Nolensville

Road, Oz squished between her and Eric like a human teddy bear that kept sneezing. Good. With Oz's company it would feel like a group activity instead of a date. Then again, all her dates had been publicity stunts, even the year she spent thinking she was in love with Trevor Tachi. So what the hell could she know about the real deal?

She quickly scribbled down *Go on a real date* on her list so she wouldn't forget, then shut the notebook before either Eric or Oz could see it.

Too late. Oz, with a curious gaze, asked, "You've never been on a real date?"

"Not exactly." Heat crept up her face when Eric leaned forward, interest piqued.

Even the rideshare driver turned around to give her a once-over. "Don't worry, hon. I was a late bloomer, too. With that pretty face, you'll have 'em lined up."

"I have many follow-up questions," Eric whispered.

Ariel looked out the window and put on her best press conference voice. "I will not be taking any questions at this time."

He chuckled as the rideshare dropped them off on the curb. They escaped the warm Tennessee heat and entered PhonoGold, which claimed to house ten miles of records. The redbrick building had been built in the fifties, and smelled like old paper and incense. A couple of patrons flipped through rows and rows of crates marked with hand-drawn labels and colorful arrows.

"This place is a maze," Eric said, his rich brown eyes roaming the huge space before settling on her. "Are you looking for something specific?"

Ariel was drawn to a small display of rare fairy-tale soundtracks. "I'll know when I see it. I've only ever bought vinyl online or stolen things from my dad's collection."

"When I first moved to New York, I would spend hours looking for secondhand records." He stood beside her, using his index and middle fingers to comb through the classic-rock section. She rubbed her forearms where those fingers had caressed her that same morning. "I found a copy of *Ziggy Stardust* that was pristine."

"What about you, Oz?" Ariel asked, a little too loudly.

"Oh, I have a list," their young bus driver replied, making a beeline for the beefy man behind the counter. Oz pulled out his phone and scrolled through his notes app. "Hi, hello. Do you have anything in the vein of nature electronica?"

Eric looked amused. "What's nature electronica?"

The clerk perked up. His thick curls and big glasses gave him the look of a Samoan "Weird Al" Yankovic. His name tag read JUNE.

"Oh man. It's the best. It's like if you gave Mother Nature a computer. My faves are Zanzi, Lolatech, Pyrodyte." June and Oz faced each other and shouted, "Malichor!"

Ariel chuckled. She *loved* when people connected through music this way. "Are those bands or *Sailor Moon* characters?"

"Right? You get it," June said, setting his headphones aside.

Ariel was not sure she "got it," but she already loved him and the record store. June walked his fingers between records he kept behind the register. Ariel had no idea how he could find anything. It was like looking for a needle in a stack of slightly different-colored needles.

June's round face split into a pleased smile when he found what he was looking for. He flipped the vinyl between his palms, ever so gently laying it flat and positioning the needle on the first track. "Check it. Zanzi."

An EDM track with heavy bass played. Slow, like the notes were stretching after a long sleep. Then came the unmistakable sound of whale songs.

Eric moved slowly between the rows of vinyl. "I kind of like it."

"A lot of the artists are DJs who find these nature documentarians and experiment with the perfect tracks," Oz explained. He moved his arms to the hypnotic music, totally, unabashedly in his element. "This is what it would sound like if whales lived in outer space."

"*Yes*," June said, and reached out his fist to Oz, who met it without missing a beat.

Ariel, on the other hand, found herself moving through the aisles. When was the last time she'd listened to a song that had made her feel that same sense of reverie? As long as she could remember, she could hear melodies in her head. Her parents had always encouraged her, and she'd wanted nothing more than to see their pride when she sang her childish, made-up rhymes at the dinner table. With Siren Seven she'd expressed herself, but it was through a filter. A persona. One that came with expectations and little room to stretch and grow. It wasn't like that for everyone, but Teodoro del Mar didn't believe in messing with perfection.

Walking through the labyrinthine record store, she was uncertain about so many things—what happened after the tour, what her relationship with her father would be like when she returned home, whether she would ever have a career again. Her love of music, though—that was a certainty. But what did this version of Ariel del Mar sound like? She didn't know why, but she had a good feeling she'd get there.

Ariel's fingers itched to explore. To find a new sound, even if she didn't like it. PhonoGold had a listening wall, and she sampled the newest records, bopping along from pop to R&B to country to Celtic rock. She found a small stack of old Latin music records—Willie Colón, Oscar D'León, Celia Cruz, Maná, Carlos Vives—each one evoking memories of her mother singing in the kitchen, in the car, in the shower.

She plunged deeper into the record store, intrigued by the shimmering curtain that said RARE and underneath that: SALE SALE SALE.

The tiny room had likely once been a storage closet. She picked up a random record from the nearest milk crate. The cover depicted a woman in a taffeta dress holding a sphynx cat and read MILANDRA'S SYMPHONY. Ariel laughed, then turned around. She had the vivid urge to show the strange find to Eric.

And as if she had called him with her thoughts, he stepped through the curtain. She could *feel* her heart leap at the sight of Eric. Eric Reyes, with his smirking mouth and dreamy brown eyes. That flutter of his black lashes when he cast his eyes down before looking at her again. With him in the tiny "sale sale sale" room, everything felt a little more cramped, and warmer than it had been seconds before.

She cleared her throat and handed over the record. "Look at what I found."

"See, no one just holds wrinkled naked cats in quince dresses anymore," he said, a faux lament. "Maybe I should bring it back for the 'Love Like Lightning' music video."

"The eighties *are* back."

"I thought the nineties were back." He reached for the tiny star dangling from her black velvet choker.

"Nuh-uh. This is early aughts. Vintage. I stole it from my eldest sister." She turned and took three whole steps away to put space between them. Though his presence was calm, she felt like a live wire with him so close.

"Are we ever going to meet more of these mysterious sisters?" Eric pulled records at random. "They should come to the New York show."

"Maybe." Ariel busied herself flicking through stack after stack just so she wouldn't have to give him a real answer. *Of course* she wanted her sisters to see Star Crossed play. She was used to sharing everything with them. But this was different. This part of her life was hers, and hers alone. For a moment she considered telling Eric everything.

By the way, no big deal, my full name is Melody Ariel Marín Lucero. That cult you assumed I was part of is actually my pop group, Siren Seven, which you hate, apparently.

Would he roll with it? Would he throw her off the tour? What if his reaction fell down the middle? She knew this wasn't really about him not liking Siren Seven. It was about the things she let him assume. The pockets of truth that left room for lies. And yet, this was the most she had felt like herself since she left New York. She turned around to tell him something, anything, but realized he'd been calling her name.

"Melody?"

"Sorry. I'm in my own head."

He glanced back at the shimmering curtain, then at her. There was indecision in his dark eyes. Yes, he should leave. Yes, she should leave. No, they should not be left alone together for too long. Whatever he was wrestling with, he stayed. He took a single step toward her, within reach.

"Where do you go?" he asked softly. "When you're in your own head?"

She sighed, her hands still combing through records. "Just thinking about the choices I've made and what I'm going to do with the rest of my life. No big deal."

"Yeah, no pressure." He exhaled a laugh. "See, when I'm in my head I'm imagining my speech at the Grammys. Or the Oscars."

"The Oscars," she repeated playfully. And yet, she had no doubt he could do it. "I think you should go for the EGOT."

"Dream big, right?"

Eric's face was so open with emotion, so sincere. It was easy to meet him and assume that he was just another bro dreaming of becoming a rock star. She'd met quite a few. But Eric was so earnest, she wanted to believe with him.

The next record she pulled at random was an ABBA LP, the colors slightly distorted. She gasped, and he came up beside her to peer over her shoulder. "A misprint!"

"That is an excellent find," he said.

If she tilted her face to the side, she would be centimeters from his jawline. Why were jawlines hot? He had a day's worth of stubble, which he usually shaved a few hours before a show. She let herself imagine it for a moment, kissing him there. Pushing herself up on her toes to find his lips, the soft give of them, like biting into ripe fruit. His breathy sigh, so similar to the crescendo of his songs. Only they'd be for her and her alone.

Then she remembered her bargain with Odelia. The manager's sharp eyebrows and sharper stare replaced Ariel's kissing daydream. *Eric is off-limits*, the voice echoed.

Ariel stepped back and found herself against the wall. Every single part of her tightened at the way his eyes traced her mouth, her throat, the place where her necklace rested above her clavicles. He looked away, and she could swear he whispered a curse.

"Melody . . ."

"I'm going to get this for Grimsby," Ariel said, hugging the record against her chest like a shield against her own raging want.

Eric pinched the bridge of his nose, wincing like he couldn't believe what he was about to say, but he only spoke her name. "Melody."

"We don't have to talk about this morning," she told him. "Nothing happened."

He nodded slowly. "Right. No, yeah. I know. It was nothing. We were tired. But that's not what I wanted to bring up."

"Oh." She waited for him to continue.

"Speaking of Grimsby," he said, "I heard you two this morning on the bus."

Her cheeks burned slightly. "I should remember there's no privacy with eight people on a tour bus."

"I hope she didn't scare you with all that talk about me being a— you know . . ."

"Hopeless romantic who wears his heart on his sleeve?" she offered. Then, softer, "She said you've been hurt before."

He sighed his frustration, running anxious fingers through his hair. "It's not—it's a long story."

And they didn't have time. They should be leaving to finish back-lining the stage, and she had a job to do. But Odelia couldn't fault her for this. For listening to Eric as a friend.

"You can tell me." She touched his forearm, where rolling waves of a tempestuous sea were inked across his skin. "We're friends."

Eric touched his golden pendant thoughtfully. There was a moment when Ariel thought he might not answer. Then he held her stare, and explained, "I met someone when I arrived in Miami. It didn't work. But it doesn't go the way you think."

She chuckled. "I've never been on a real date or had a real boyfriend, so I don't have much reference."

"Wait, *real* boyfriend?" He cocked a single brow in disbelief.

"We're not on me now, we're talking about your heartbreak."

"My heartbreak can wait," he said, then paused. "That's a good line for a song. But I just need to clarify something."

She tilted her head up. "Fine."

"Did you have one of those made-up Canada ones? Why did every woman I know once have a fake Canadian boyfriend when Colombia is right there?"

At that she laughed, pressing her palm on his chest and giving him a playful shove. Coming from a big family, she missed little touches like that. Warm and loving. A reminder that someone cared, and loved you.

But when she didn't let go, when he placed his hand on top of hers so she could feel the hard pounding of his heartbeat, she knew it was more than that. She saw the moment Eric warred with himself, then closed the distance between them. His eyes locked with hers, he whispered, "It wasn't nothing, Melody. This morning. It wasn't nothing."

She grabbed the front of his shirt in her fist, tugging him to her. The heat of the room was palpable, radiating from him like an aura. She inhaled the sweet salt from his skin, the mint of his exhale, as he tilted her chin up with his rough, calloused fingers.

"Helloooooo!" Oz's singsong voice called from the other side of the curtain.

Eric quickly glanced over his shoulder, then back at her like he was contemplating whether they had any time to kiss before their friend walked in.

"I can't," Ariel said, her voice husky with want. She pulled her hand from his.

Eric put space between them and defused the tension with one of his heartbreaking smiles. "Come on, before Oz decides to buy everything in this room, too."

Ariel followed, smoothing down her T-shirt, her hair. She was almost through the curtains when she realized she had forgotten the ABBA record. She hurried back in, and that's when Ariel saw them.

Her parents.

In the last crate Eric had flipped through was an LP of her mom and dad's band, Luna Lunita, right there. She blinked the blurriness and disbelief from her eyes. It was really them. Dressed in full eighties regalia of shimmering clothes and shoulder pads, they looked incredible. She'd never seen that record before, though, which was strange, because her father had every single piece of memorabilia from his early days framed throughout the penthouse.

She picked up a couple of random sale albums to cover her parents' LP and hurried after her friends.

That night after the show, back in the bus and racing down the highway toward Atlanta, Georgia, Ariel lay in her bed but didn't sleep. She turned on the reading lamp at the corner of her bunk and carefully pulled the vinyl from out of the brown paper bag. She'd been anxious all night, wanting to be alone to better inspect her parents' album. In the dark, she took a picture and sent it to her sisters.

Seconds later, Marilou, who was always up, responded first.

Marilou:
Have a Merry Celtic Christmas? Is that ironic?

Ariel stifled a snort and took a picture of the correct record.

Ariel:
Am I losing it? I've never seen this Luna
Lunita album before in Dad's shrine.

Elektra:
Maybe it's a misprint? Those songs are on
their debut album with a different cover.

Marilou:
Also, no luck on getting on his computer, either.

Thea:
Mom looks so beautiful. I see
pieces of her in all of us.

Alicia:

Mail it! Better yet, come home! I feel like
soul-searching takes less time in movies.

Sophia:

That's because they get montages, butthead.

Ariel turned off her phone as their #SevenAteNine sister chat descended into name-calling. In some ways, ways that she'd never truly stopped to think about, they were ordinary sisters. They fought and borrowed each other's clothes and loved each other.

She had the overpowering urge to listen to her mother's voice. She pulled up a playlist of old Luna Lunita songs and adjusted her wireless earbuds.

Her mother, Maia del Mar, had had the most beautiful voice. Years later, Ariel still had the memory of being in their old house in Forest Hills, Queens. Her mom would sit on the big couch, Ariel on her lap. Sophia, still learning to play the guitar, strumming with unpracticed fingers. The twins drawing mermaids with glitter gel pens. Elektra and Thea fighting over some toy. Marilou wearing as much of Mom's costume jewelry as would fit around her slender throat and wrists. Where was her father? In his office. With Uncle Iggy, meeting with some investor, some producer, someone who would take a chance on a family with a big dream?

A dream that had never been hers, not in the way her father imagined it.

A dream that *was* Eric's.

She'd never thought that he reminded her of Teo del Mar before that moment. The thought, while deeply unsettling, passed quickly. Eric was nothing like her father. *Nothing.*

She started the track "Luna Mia" over again. It was the song that won her dad his first Grammy and opened the door for the musical kingdom he would later build with his daughters. *Through* his daughters. Weeks ago, she would not have made that distinction, she realized.

Ariel heard a scratch. She took out her earbud and reset the connection, but that scratchy little noise wasn't coming from the music. It had been there on her first night, but she had chalked it up to mysterious bus sounds. Ariel sat up, too fast, and bumped her head on the ceiling. She loosed a loud curse.

"Mel?"

Mel. One syllable from Eric, in the deliciously husky voice he got when he first woke up. She heard the rustle of his privacy curtain drawing back and quickly shoved her record back into the brown paper bag, tucking it down at her feet.

"Melody?"

Eric's concerned voice was the last thing she heard before she felt something *move.* Between her covers. Brushing against her toes. Tiny *claws* scrambling across her calves. She couldn't help it. She sucked in a breath and screamed. She must have scared Oz because the bus wavered unsteadily from side to side. One by one, the others started getting up, questioning what was happening.

Ariel tried to climb out of the bed, but her legs got tangled in the sheets and she rolled off her mattress, hitting the floor with a breathless *"oof!"*

"What's going on back there?" Oz shouted through the radio.

"Rat!" Ariel managed. "There's a rat in my bunk!"

She kicked her covers, and Eric teetered for balance, trying to help her. Groggy, cranky, sleepy noises added to the chaos as the bus shuddered and jerked hard to the left. Cars on the late-night road honked *hard*, and they zigzagged as the bus tried to right itself.

"Did we hit something?" Eric shouted. "Oz!"

Grimsby, whose bunk was above hers, said, "Oh *no*," right before everything—including Grimsby's mattress, and the girl atop it—tipped sideways.

Ariel threw up her forearms to protect her face, and Eric flung his body on top of hers. Propped up on his forearms, he formed a protective cage as Grimsby fell on them, followed by scattered items that thudded around the cabin.

Odelia was up now, shouting for Oz to get things under control. But Ariel felt the weight of another person falling on them. Eric strained to keep her from getting squished like roadkill, and if her heart wasn't plummeting right through her out of fear that they were about to crash, she'd kiss his face off. Damn any bargain. Damn everything.

But then the Beast lurched forward before coming to an abrupt stop. Slowly, everyone got up from the human trifle they'd made on the floor. Oz punched open the cabin door, wringing his bucket hat nervously.

"Yeah, so," he said. "We have a problem."

"There's a rat on the bus!" Ariel climbed back to her feet. The corridor wasn't wide enough for all of them.

"She's not a rat," Grimsby said indignantly, and frantically searched Ariel's bunk until she found the source of the commotion. In her hands was a brown-and-white guinea pig.

Oz sneezed and narrowed his eyes at the little critter. "Actually, I was going to say I hit a signpost back there. Front light is busted."

"What are you saying?" Odelia asked, and Ariel could practically see the steam emitting from her ears.

"In this dark, we're not going anywhere."

MusicMan929's Music Musings

Subscribers: 21
Archived January 4, 1998

I'm going to prove why Teodoro del Mar is a Fraud with a capital F. I worked with Luna Lunita for two years. Working with a pioneer in Latin Pop in the United States was my dream. But the more I got to know Teo, the more I realized the man has no idea what he's doing. He hasn't had a hit single since "Luna Mia." And there's a good reason!

Maia del Mar is the heart behind the whole operation, but she's taken a back seat in the business. The woman is a goddess.

I don't know what it is yet, but I am going to discover that Teo has a skeleton in his closet. One that I will expose for the world to see. He might have fired me for merely disagreeing with him, but I will have the last laugh.

CHAPTER THIRTEEN

ERIC

6.29 The Middle of Nowhere

Eric Reyes had seen his manager fluctuate between pleased and displeased, but he'd never seen what she called her "nightmare phase." Her black hair was in big rollers, tied back with a silk scarf. A couple had come undone during the crash and curled like octopus tentacles (not that he'd choose to tell her that). Without her signature eyebrows filled in or her impeccable red lipstick, Odelia looked almost vulnerable. Almost. Still dressed in her robe and furry bedroom slippers, she shouted into her phone as she paced along the side of the road.

That same road leading to Atlanta was pitch-black and empty, and the eight of them huddled in front of the bus, like it was safer to remain bunched up in the small radius of the single headlight beam.

Carly wore her sleep eye mask on her forehead. The cartoon lashes glowed in the dark. She shook her head and grimaced. "Nope. I have nightmares that start like this."

"In *Halloween Horrors Seventeen*," Max said, "the killer hijacks the family's RV and pops out from the undercarriage, and BLAM! No survivors."

"I do *not* like this," Oz whispered, hiding behind Melody, who was half his size.

Melody suppressed a laugh, but assured him, "Everything will be all right."

"That's easy for you to say." Carly crossed her arms over her chest. "All your caterwauling is the reason he almost ran us off the road and hit a freaking signpost."

"Caterwauling?" Vanessa asked, rubbing their friend's back. "Really, dude?"

Protectiveness rose to Eric's chest, and he couldn't help it. He couldn't bear the guilt on her face. "Melody didn't do anything wrong. There's no sense in blaming anyone. Monty shouldn't have been on the bus in the first place."

They all turned to Grimsby, who stood a few paces away, cradling her geriatric guinea pig like a newborn. "I'm sorry! I just couldn't leave her. What if something happened?"

Max threw up her hands. "Something almost did happen! To *us*. Plus, Oz is allergic."

"Oz is allergic to everything," Grimsby said.

"That is true." The bus driver nodded, and he had somehow become the only calm one among them. That was usually Eric's job.

He took a deep breath and regained his control. Everyone was anxious and scared. They were in the middle of nowhere, at three in the morning, with a busted headlight.

"Look, here comes Odelia," he said. "Everything *will* be fine."

But their fearless manager gave a stubborn shake of her head. Another one of her rollers fell off, and she pursed her lips with displeasure. "Every time I get connected to someone long enough to ask for help, the call drops."

"There's a gas station a few miles back," Oz said, hugging himself. "I'm sure they sell replacement bulbs?"

"Can't we make it to Atlanta without one?" Max asked between bites of her cuticles.

Oz pointed at the empty road. "Do *you* want to drive down that with only one working headlight?"

They all quietly and dejectedly stared in that direction. If it was just Eric, he'd take the chance. But with his crew?

"No," Eric said finally.

"What if we drive real slow?" Vanessa asked. "We already lost time getting turned around on the interstate."

Odelia raised prayer hands to the night sky. "¡Paciencia, Odelia, *paciencia!*"

Whenever his manager asked the heavens for patience, he knew she'd had it. Eric had to fix this. It was his band, his family.

"I'll go," Eric said. "We have an industrial flashlight in the bus. It won't take me long."

"Bro, we cannot split up!" Carly shouted.

"Yeah," Max said, backing her up. "That's how the killer will get us."

"I do not like this," Oz repeated, *"at all."*

"Curséd," Grimsby muttered, feeding Monty a grape.

"You know sugar makes her hyper," Eric said.

"It's all natural!" Grimsby shot back.

"Everyone calm the fuck *down*," Vanessa stressed, then muttered, "Sorry, Ma."

"We aren't splitting up," Carly said. "Let's *all* walk to the gas station."

Oz slowly raised his hand. "I, yet again, would not like that."

"Let's just wait on the bus until sunrise," Max offered, shrinking behind Carly as something rustled in the bushes.

"I'll go with you," Melody said. In the time they'd all been arguing, she'd retrieved her sneakers and found the emergency flashlight. "I feel partially responsible, and if we wait for daybreak, we'll fall behind schedule."

Melody didn't seem the least bit worried as she stepped out of the radius of the single headlight and started walking. It was settled.

He grinned, then realized she was leaving him behind and jogged to catch up.

"Turn your phone to the walkie setting!" Oz shouted.

Max called out, "Don't get swamp murdered!" Her voice grew more distant with every step.

Melody snorted. "I don't think we're even near a swamp."

"You know, I think that's the first time they've ever unanimously agreed with anyone."

"I mean, who wants to walk two miles there and back at three in the morning on a road in the middle of nowhere—in their pajamas, no less?"

"Us, obviously." Eric returned Melody's playful smile with a shake of his head. "I'm not going to say that Max is correct, but I can understand where she's coming from thinking we're cursed. I mean, let's go over the things that have gone wrong—"

He started counting with his thumb. "Our opening act got sick. Our merch guy bailed, we started the tour with a massive car pileup."

She flashed a coy smile. "Don't forget someone tried to steal your guitar."

"How could I forget?" He kept counting. "We got stuck in an elevator. Now this."

"Maybe you upset some cosmic forces," Melody offered. A weak, humid breeze blew her hair around her shoulders. He cracked his knuckles to busy his hands.

"Then there's the good stuff."

She swiveled the flashlight in his direction. "Good stuff?"

"If that ice cream truck hadn't broken down, I wouldn't have been there on the sidewalk, and I wouldn't have had a very reckless and brave woman bodycheck a thief, and I wouldn't have spent the most incredible night of my life—well, you know the rest."

He tried his best to stare at the stark road ahead, but he could feel her gaze on him.

"And this?" she asked. "What is the cosmic balance in this?"

"Ah. I can skip my morning workout."

Melody laughed, truly laughed, until she peeked at the shrinking view of the Beast. He couldn't figure out the flash of uncertainty in her eyes. Was she literally or figuratively looking over her shoulder? Sometimes he felt like she was holding back, scared, just a little. The more she shared about her sisters, her dreams, her father, the more abstract things became.

She stuck her arms out and let the sticky breeze envelop her. He imagined gliding behind her. Holding her as tightly as he had at the hotel in the middle of the night. He remembered those events a little differently than perhaps she did, and definitely differently than what Oz might have thought he walked in on. He'd woken in the middle of the night to find her muttering restlessly. He took a sip of water and wondered if he should wake her. Then he recalled what she'd said about that stuffed stress shark, so he gently propped it beside her pillow. She tossed it off the bed, rolling over into his side. He'd remained so still. So very agonizingly still as she wrapped her limbs around him. He was sure he'd seen a nature documentary with sugar gliders and koalas clinging to trees the same way Melody had been clinging to him. After a few moments, sleep had pulled him under, and he'd slept deeply knowing she felt safe with him.

Then he'd woken again, and his first thought had been, *This is right. This is so incredibly right.* Perhaps it was because he'd been alone for the first few months after he'd finally left home, but he had this primal need to make sure she was safe. When the bus had nearly gone off the road, his only thought had been to shield her with his own body. Even when Grimsby had fallen on his head.

Now Eric concentrated on the crunch of his sneakers against the gravel strewn across the asphalt, the frenzy of night critters serenading their walk. *Crunch. Chirp. Howl.*

"How do you do that?" she asked. "How do you stop yourself from thinking it's the end of the world?"

"*Hm.* I guess the only other option is to let things fall apart. I can't afford to do that. I mean, I'm not wildly optimistic. But I know that if I freak out, Max freaks out even more, and Carly is stubborn, but she bruises easily, and Grimsby is secretly a vampire, but a very anxious vampire."

"They depend on you." She placed one foot in front of the other, balancing on the white lane line as if it were a tightrope. Her strong legs were elegant, like a dancer's. "But who do you have to depend on?"

"I just scream when no one is looking."

She narrowed her eyes. "You live in a house with three other people. Can't they hear you?"

"I take hikes. I mean, I could probably do it in the subway and no one would look twice, but it's liberating. Like a catharsis. Try it."

"Just scream?"

He stopped beside her to give her space. "Yeah, who's going to hear us?"

She squared her shoulders and spun in place. Came up on her toes like a ballerina. (He made a note to ask if she ever *had* been a dancer.) She sucked in a deep breath, tilted her head to the night sky. A million and one stars, witness to the moment when she let go.

But she didn't do it. She wagged her finger at him, like she knew he was up to something, and kept walking.

"I think you're just avoiding my original question," she said.

"When we're rich and famous, I'll just have a huge therapy bill."

"Eric."

"I like it when you say my name like that," he confessed, his voice rough with emotion. He knew, *he knew* he wouldn't have said it if they hadn't been alone in the dark.

172

She slowed her pace, their arms brushing as they walked side by side. She toyed with her necklace. He knew she did that when she was thinking deeply, careful of what she wanted to say or ask.

"You didn't buy anything at the record store," she said.

He could take the hint. Hadn't she already whispered "I can't" just before they kissed? He shouldn't even be contemplating it. Vanessa had been right from day one, because when it came to Melody, his head was not in the game, and he couldn't have a repeat of last time.

"I have a huge collection at home," he said. "In Colombia. I left it behind."

"You haven't gone back?"

He shook his head, the ache from an old memory trying to resurface. Before it could, he changed the subject. "Don't think you're off the hook."

Melody tapped her chest. "What did I do?"

"I am"— he searched for the right word, but settled on—"curious to know how you've never been on a real date or had a real boyfriend."

Instead of *curious*, he wanted to say *desperate*. But diction was everything.

She laughed, that invisible wall going up around her. Holding back. "It's really not that exciting."

"You said, and I quote, 'I'm sheltered, not innocent.'"

She shone the light away from them, as if he couldn't practically feel the blush on her face. Yes, he remembered. He remembered every interaction they'd had over the past week.

"Tell me," he said, echoing words she'd used to beseech him at the record store in Asheville.

"Fine." She turned the light ahead, but it was so dark, so moonless, even the light from the high-powered torch was swallowed up past a couple of feet. "I've only ever dated guys my father approved of. And I say *date* in the loosest of terms. When I was fifteen, I liked a boy, and we went to a party together. Of course, my sisters were sent with me. All of them."

"I feel like there's a show about this," he teased.

She gave him a playful shove and kept going. "Even for something like a walk in Central Park, my father's assistant or my *uncle* would be nearby. When I dated this other guy—let's call him Bob."

"Blob?" He knew he was regressing into the basest thirteen-year-old version of himself, and he didn't care.

She snorted. "Yes. Bob Blobfish."

"Nice."

"I was with Bob for about a year. I was so into him. My sisters were sick of me. And I thought, wow, even my father approves. This might be it. This might be the one."

Eric felt irrational jealousy, but wanted to hear the rest. "And then?"

"Then I found out he was using me," she said. "To get to my dad. To work *for* my dad, I should say. And I just felt so foolish. Like I trusted too soon. Fell too soon. I never want to feel that way again."

Eric was not a violent person, but he felt the sudden urge to plunge the man who hurt her into the bottom of the sea. Then he wondered if that was the reason for her wall.

"Do you still have feelings for him?"

"God, no," she said, without hesitation. "It was like something cleared. Whatever lovey-dovey haze I was under was gone. I'm not an expert, but real love doesn't go away that easily. At least, that's what I want to think. What do I know?"

"You know only what you know, and learn the rest along the way."

"Who told you that that?"

"I don't know. A coffee shop inspirational poster." He smirked because her response was to playfully shove him again, though there wasn't much strength behind the push. He just wanted to feel her touch again. "I'm kidding. Odelia told me that."

"She does have good instincts."

"To be fair, 'Melody Blobfish' does not have a good ring to it. "

"I got some good songs out of it, not that those have seen the light of day," she confessed. "Hence the items on my list."

From somewhere in the distance, he heard the roll of thunder. He checked his watch and knew they needed to hurry, though the less sensible part of him wanted the road to stretch infinitely, wanted to watch the sun come up like it did the first night they spent together.

"I suppose we're both romantic songwriter types just making our way through the universe," he said. "Even if you still haven't played me anything you've written."

"I don't have a guitar," she said, though even she knew it was a weak excuse.

"Borrow mine." He turned about-face and walked backward so he could better watch her reaction. The way her lips curled with smiles that felt solely for him. "We have an embarrassment of guitars."

"I will, if you tell me one thing."

"Anything."

"Are all the songs you've written about the person who broke your heart?"

That was a complicated question. He slowed to a stop. They stood face-to-face, the flashlight illuminating their feet.

"Yes and no." He couldn't find the words.

"Tell me," she whispered, touching him on his forearm, where his tattoo of waves crested. The brush of her thumb made him shiver in the southern heat.

"Yes, because I did go through heartbreak, just not the type everyone thinks matters most. There was someone when I first moved here, but it didn't end well." He turned his hand, and her touch followed, their fingers intertwined. He wanted to tell her all of it, how much of a fool he'd been, but he also wanted to stay this way—Eric and Melody and the night. "No, because every song I've ever written hasn't been about her or anyone else. My songs are about a feeling. This gut feeling I've had my entire life, like I've been searching and searching, and I haven't found her. But I've been writing toward her."

She closed her eyes for a moment, like someone praying, wishing. When she looked at him again, he was listening to the song of the night around them—that roll of thunder again, closer. The all-consuming buzz of creatures in the surrounding grass, the frantic beat of his heart.

"I hope you find her," Melody said, smiling as a bolt of lightning cracked what seemed like mere feet away from them on the open field.

Thankfully, or regrettably, he couldn't decide which, the sky broke open. Warm rain kissed their skin. She gasped in delight, and he took in the moment. Damp earth and sweet grass. Her bright smile, her utter joy. He wanted to remember it forever.

They ran until they reached the gas station. Dripping wet, he scoured the shelves until he found a single bulb matching the one they needed. Melody grabbed an armful of snacks, remembering Oz's allergies and Carly's favorite chocolate bars. He loved that she thought about their road family.

On the way back, they hitched a ride from an older couple who'd been making an all-day trip to their granddaughter's birthday party. In the five-minute ride, Melody asked about their entire lives, and they wrote down the name of his band. His friends liked to tease him that *he* was the one in the group who could make friends with any stranger sitting next to him. Watching Melody, the way she listened with that well of patience and sincerity . . . it was different from him. Eric loved receiving attention. Melody liked to give it.

When they got dropped off at their bus, soaked but triumphant, he stared at her, smiling.

"What?" she asked, touching her face as if something was on it, as if that could be the only reason he would look at her.

And what could he say? For the first time in his life, there were no words. There was that feeling. The scent of petrichor. The strike of lightning. There was Melody.

"Oh, just," he said, "I call dibs on those double-stuffed Oreos."

"Absolutely *not*."

The doors hissed open, and they climbed aboard. Everyone packed the front lounge. Grimsby sat at the table, cradling Monty's small plastic cage protectively. The others were silent, like an intervention. He'd been on the receiving end of those once. Or twice.

"What's going on?" Eric asked.

"We can't have an animal in the bus," Odelia said, which kicked off Grimsby hugging the cage, and Carly shouting about how they'd agreed Monty would stay with the neighbor, and Vanessa pointing at the source of a very familiar squeaking sound.

"Look, it's going to town on that bath toy!"

Melody made a tiny gasp when she realized that Monty, the guinea pig, was humping their unicorn cat from the arcade. Eric tried not to laugh, but quickly descended into the chaos with everyone else.

"Do not slut-shame her!" Grimsby turned to Melody. "I'll replace it."

Melody sighed. He had the urge to brush her hair back and kiss her temple. Promise to win her another toy, to win her everything. The impulse came and went, because while everyone was laughing at Grimsby's pet, Odelia was watching him carefully. It was uncanny how much his manager could decipher with a single look.

"It's late," he said, deepening the bass in his voice. "Let's not make any life-changing decisions tonight. Let's just get to Atlanta and figure out what to do then."

Finally, they agreed.

After helping Oz change the bulb, they were off. The Star Crossed tour had to go on, guinea pig and all.

ARIEL'S PHONE LOG

Missed Call from Uncle Iggy

Missed Call from Uncle Iggy

Missed Call from Uncle Iggy

Missed Call from Uncle Iggy

Missed Call from Uncle Iggy

Missed Call from Uncle Iggy

Missed Call from Uncle Iggy

Text from Uncle Iggy:
My little darling, mi chiquitita, please come home.
Let's talk.
(Read: 1:43 P.M.)

Text from Uncle Iggy:
You've had your fun. You've made your point.
(Read: 4:04 A.M)

Text from Uncle Iggy:
Your father is sorry.
(Read: 6:21 P.M.)

Text from Uncle Iggy:
He's beside himself. I don't think I can stop him from
what he's going to do next.
(Read: 12:13 P.M)

Text from Uncle Iggy:
Please.
(Read: 8:07 A.M)

Text from Uncle Iggy:
Think of what disappearing like this will do for your
reputation.
(Read: 2:14 A.M.)

CHAPTER FOURTEEN

ARIEL

Atlanta ➤ Savannah ➤ Jacksonville ➤ Orlando

7.3 Miami, Florida

Ariel del Mar knew how easily days blurred together on the road. The Beast swept through Georgia. By then, she'd needed to buy a second duffel to make room for the gems she found at thrift stores and the gifts she was collecting for her sisters. A multicolored crystal for Thea. A vintage nineties pink telephone for Alicia. Silver earrings shaped like swords for Sophia that she found at a witchy little shop in Savannah.

She'd almost bought herself a beautiful acoustic guitar at a music shop, but she couldn't bring herself to do it. Not until Sophia sent word that their accounts were free. She had to settle for borrowing Vanessa's in between sets. The sleek black Les Paul played like a dream, and on a long stretch to Jacksonville, she'd surprised everyone on the bus by playing an instrumental of one of Vee's songs.

Eric had looked at her the same way he had that night on the pitch-black road, just before lightning struck. She'd done everything to avoid him since. Thankfully, their schedules were so packed she had a good excuse, and spent most of her downtime exploring weird city histories with the delightful, eccentric Oz. Their only interaction was the shared playlist they added songs to all throughout the day.

It was like a silent agreement, and she always, always fell asleep to it at night.

With every tour stop, more and more articles and reviews popped up about Star Crossed. More and more articles popped up about her, too. Ariel del Mar, the pop siren gone rogue. By the time they reached Florida, she had to turn off her phone because of the calls and texts from her uncle. She didn't know *how* he'd gotten her number. She was certain none of her sisters would have given it to him, but Uncle Iggy had his ways. He'd been there for every rebellion from any one of Ariel's sisters. He'd cleaned up the aftermath when Elektra got caught sneaking out of a Reykjavík hotel with her secret girlfriend. He'd somehow scrubbed a paparazzi photo taken by *drone* of a rare Nochebuena dinner at the penthouse. Ariel had often wondered if her father, the CEO, the kingmaker of Atlantica Records, would even know how to survive without his brother.

That was the thing about needing people. Sometimes, it was hard to stop. Late during the bus rides, crossing state lines, Ariel wondered if she'd gone from needing one family to needing the other. She dispelled the thought as easily as she conjured it, though, because even if she was getting close with the crew, *they* were a family. She was still a wild card Eric had drawn. More like a floating island off the coast of their continent.

By the time they were on the road to Miami, Florida, where they'd spend the first full day off at Odelia's family house, Ariel couldn't take any more of Uncle Iggy's calls and texts. The last ones read: *I don't think I can stop him from what he's going to do next. Think of what disappearing like this will do to your reputation.*

Was that all she was to them? A name to uphold. A good daughter. A good sister. The "glam girl next door."

Teo del Mar would not threaten her.

Though her fingers trembled, she typed out a message to her sisters.

Ariel:

If Daddy's so worried about my reputation, so be it.

Ariel:

Ruin it.

Ariel stared at the gray dots appearing and disappearing until someone replied.

Sophia:

Done.

🐚

The Beast pulled up at Odelia's home at sunrise. The single-floor house had a big yard and a Spanish-style tiled roof. Inside, Antonio, Odelia's seventy-year-old uncle, greeted them with a breakfast spread—fried eggs, refried beans, bacon, Venezuelan arepas stuffed with cheese, maracuyá juice, and toast.

They gathered around the table and dug in, while Ariel admired every detail of the house. The colors were so vibrant. Sunrise oranges and Caribbean blues. Painted wooden birds were strung from the ceiling in the snug dining room. Lush potted plants hung from open windows, and green vines spilled from the garden. An oscillating fan in the corner blew in the fragrance of flowers. There were whole walls of photographs—some black-and-white, and others with faded colors. It felt like an altar to their past.

"I love your house," Ariel said, helping herself to another slice of bacon. "It's incredible."

Mr. Antonio smiled, deepening the wrinkles of his brown skin. "Thank you, Maia."

Ariel froze, the wind knocked from her lungs. Maia was her mother's name. Did he think she was her mother? Her heart in her throat, she turned to Odelia, who blinked through the name slip.

No one else at the table seemed to notice.

"This is Melody, Tío," Odelia said, running soothing hands across his shoulders.

He blinked hard, one of his eyes milk gray with cataracts. He chuckled, his wrinkled hand tapping the silver curls at his temple. "Don't listen to me. I forget my own name sometimes. Enjoy your life now, because when you're my age, memories just—*zip. Flit.* Gone."

Ariel chuckled nervously and chugged her tart juice.

"Okay," Odelia said, flipping through her trusty clipboard even though she'd barely touched her breakfast. "We have the radio interview after breakfast. There are two showers, so take turns, and be quick." She glared at Eric, who grinned on a mouthful of avocado and eggs. "After that, Oz and Melody will meet us at the venue. I have a reporter from *Miami Sound* magazine coming to do an interview. We'll stay here tonight." Odelia took a breath, as if for patience. "Yes, Oz?"

"Is there room for me here?" he asked. "I know I have the hotel, but I don't want to be alone or miss the inevitable chaos from the group. I'm literally living for it."

Max reached out and patted his shoulder. "Sure thing, buddy."

Odelia visibly suppressed a smile. "You'll have to take the living room with Eric and Melody, but that shouldn't be a problem."

Despite her best efforts, Ariel glanced at Eric. Good. They hadn't been alone in days, and she'd worried about that night. But when he winked at her, she was back in the middle of that road, at the record shop, in the hotel room—

"Melody?" Odelia said impatiently.

"Huh?"

"I asked if you were okay with that."

Ariel didn't want to seem like she hadn't been listening, so she said, "Yes. Of course. Whatever you need."

"Great, you'll stay here and help with laundry and watch over Monty."

It was, perhaps, not the best time to mention that laundry was among the things Ariel del Mar had never done.

In the open laundry room, Ariel and Oz sat atop the washing machine and dryer respectively, waiting for the cycles to be done. She'd felt utterly ridiculous texting Sophia, *Hey, how do you wash clothes? Never mind there's a manual online. Oh wait, it's in German. Never mind I found a video.*

It didn't help that the machine, while new, had a million symbols that were not intuitive. She ignored the string of laughing emojis her eldest sister sent her, and felt embarrassed at her own privilege. Her father's words, *you wouldn't survive*, echoed in her ears.

"So, what's your deal?" Oz asked her, sipping the ice-cold lemonade Mr. Antonio had made.

"What deal?" she asked.

"I mean, you've told me all about the whole not-a-cult-but-sort-of upbringing, but I feel like there's more to your story. I am very good at reading energies."

Ariel wanted so badly to confide in Oz. But he and Max were the only ones on the bus who listened to Siren Seven. What if he reacted the same way he did when he mistakenly thought a tiny alligator in Jacksonville was a cryptid? Besides, she couldn't tell anyone before she told Eric.

"Why don't you read my energy and tell me?" she challenged.

He turned on the dryer and closed his eyes for a second. Then he waved his hand in the air and said, "I'm getting runaway princess. I'm getting wandering soul. I'm getting totally lusting after one lead singer."

Ariel was not amused. "You're messing with me."

"It's a very long tour, and I need a way to pass the time. Plus, I know what I saw." His eyebrows waggled suggestively.

She felt a spike of heat and pressed her cool palms on her cheeks. "Nothing happened at the hotel."

"Not the hotel, honey bunny," he said, then lowered his voice to a whisper. "The record store. Don't worry, I won't tell."

Ariel wanted to deny it. But Oz believed in aliens and monsters hiding in national parks. Anyone with that much of an open mind was easy to talk to. "Nothing happened there, either. It's for the best, honestly. He has this whole future planned out, and if something were to go wrong between us . . ." She shook her head. She would sound more serious if she wasn't practically vibrating on the washing machine surface. "I *can't* be the thing to get in the way."

"What if something goes right?"

Ariel looked at her lap and pulled on a thread of her jean shorts. What if something goes right? For someone who'd been an eternal optimist her whole life, this was the first time she could only think of the negative. Because she wasn't being completely honest. Because she was holding back a huge part of her life. Because she'd dug around her truth so deeply, the foundation was uneven. It was easier to brace for the worst.

"I mean, lover boy isn't exactly pulling back, and he'd have to shave his head if he screwed things up with you."

She nearly snorted her lemonade. "Excuse me?"

Oz made a *yikes* grimace. "Oh, you didn't know that? I guess people don't really think I'm listening when they're talking. I just have that vibe, you know?"

"Wait, go back."

Oz glanced around. Across the patio Mr. Antonio was sleeping on a rocking chair in front of the TV, and everyone else was out for their radio interviews. Still, he lowered his voice conspiratorially and said, "So *apparently*, the girls made a bet with Eric that if he screwed things up with you and blew up the tour for everyone, they would be allowed to shave his head and pick out a Siren Seven song for him to perform. He hates their music."

Ariel winced. "So I've heard."

"Whatever, I have taste," Oz said, chewing on his straw. "I'll share my ultimate Siren Seven playlist."

Sure, it hurt that Eric thought so little of her songs. Why was it that she had millions of people celebrating the music she'd made with her sisters, but this bothered her? Because it was Eric. Because she respected him as a creator. Because her stupid heart hadn't stopped racing every time she caught him looking at her.

"And if he doesn't blow up the tour?"

"Then he gets to choose their band tattoo. Location *and* design." Oz's eyes brightened with delight. "I wouldn't put it past him to choose a cartoon version of his face on their butts. Maybe a little groin action."

Ariel almost snorted her drink. "That's commitment."

"But wait," he added with a flourish. "There's more. Eric doesn't know that the band and Vanessa made a bet with *each other* about when, more or less, you would get together."

Ariel balked at that. "I don't know whether I should be insulted or not."

"Depends," Oz said.

"On what?"

"On you, obviously. That boy is in love. I told you. The vibes. They and I are one." Oz slurped the dregs of his drink and rattled the ice in his cup. "See, that's your Eric smile."

"It is not." But it was. Ariel sipped on her lemonade, sweet and tart

185

and delicious on the warm day. "I can't believe they're betting on us."

"I will say, my uncle is also an entertainment coach operator, and he used to tell me these horrible stories about bands he drove. Things would get ug-ly." Oz gave her a meaningful look. "We're only a week in. Protect your tender heart."

Ariel thought back to every almost-kiss. Was Eric being careless because of her? Was he falling in love with love? It wasn't her heart she was worried about. She knew things had to end. She was almost bracing for the impact. Ariel had also given her word to Odelia. The more she got to know the band manager, the more certain she was that Odelia Garcia was a woman of her word. She couldn't go home until she was ready. But the thing was, how would she know when she'd be ready?

She didn't want to talk about bargains and bets anymore. The only person she was betting on was herself, and she would get herself through the tour.

"Is that how you got this job?" she asked Oz. "Through your uncle?"

Oz looked at his short black nails. "Yeah. I went to school for graphic design. I want to be an artist, and thought this would be a great way to travel and make money in the meantime. The signing bonus was worth it on its own."

"Can I see some of your work?"

Those seemed to be the magic words, because Oz pulled up his portfolio on his phone. He was good. Really good. Almost everything was fantasy related, from images of dragons to reinterpretations of famous paintings like *The Scream*, only with La Llorona, the legend that had terrorized Ariel as a little girl, instead of the figure Munch had painted. Then there was a logo for the band done in a saturated prism of stars and moons.

"This is freaking awesome. You should pitch it to Odelia."

Oz shook his head shyly. "Maybe. Do you think she'd like it?"

"The worst she could say is no."

Oz sighed. "People say that but forget a no still sucks."

"Sure, but isn't the possibility of a yes worth it?" She nudged him with her toe, and he nudged her back. "Think about it."

Just then, the machines stopped. She hopped off and opened the lid. She wasn't sure what she was looking at. Everything was a rinsed wet gray blob. "Something's wrong."

Oz gritted his teeth and smiled, which gave him the appearance of a stressed-out bear. He peered in the machine and removed a black shirt she recognized as her own. "Oh honey, baby, sweetie."

"What do I do?" She didn't recognize her own shrill voice.

A soft chuckle came from behind them. Mr. Antonio was there, a grin deepening the winkles of his face. He picked up the bottle of bleach. "Sometimes the solution is making the same mistake twice."

While the clothes sat in a water-and-bleach solution and Oz changed the linens in the bus, she walked around the garden with Odelia's uncle. Even though he was at home, he wore a short-sleeve guayabera shirt and ironed slacks. There were pictures of him on the wall as a young man, sharply dressed, with a beautiful woman on his arm. Now he picked at dead weeds and plucked twigs out of hibiscus bushes, his skin weathered by the sun and time. He'd clearly been around Odelia all her life. Perhaps he could answer the questions his niece wouldn't.

"You called me Maia," Ariel said softly, then hesitated. What if he told her something she didn't want to hear? "Did you know her? My mother?"

He smiled sadly. "You look so much like your parents. I'm old, but I'm not senile yet."

"Odelia said things should be left in the past. But that's like telling someone not to do something. You just want to do it more."

Eric's face came to mind as soon as she finished those words.

187

"Then I won't tell you." Mr. Antonio reached for a pair of garden shears, cut a beautiful red hibiscus flower, and tucked it behind her ear. "I'll show you."

He followed the uneven brick path hammered into the soft earth to a dilapidated shed. Inside were boxes saggy with damp, and wooden crates of bloated old books, some labeled DONATIONS. One box was completely covered in dust. He ran his palm across the surface. Inside were shiny lamé and taffeta dresses, beaded wigs, and eighties regalia that ought to have been in a museum. Then he handed her a record. An exact copy of the one she'd bought at PhonoGold in Nashville. Her mom and dad's band.

"This is Luna Lunita." She flipped it back and forth, confused.

As promised, he said nothing. He tugged the sleeve that encased the record, still new and untouched decades after being printed. While the cover showed her parents, the perfect "it" couple, once upon a time, the image on the sleeve painted a different picture.

Three people posed for the camera: Teo and Maia del Mar, and Odelia Garcia.

It took Ariel a moment to recognize the woman she knew as a tour manager, a mother, a woman with sharp edges. On the record sleeve, her unblemished skin had a hazy quality, but her signature red lipstick hadn't changed and neither had her red nails, though they were longer now, as if she'd had to grow claws to use against the world. Eighties Odelia wore a gold blazer over one shoulder and leaned on Ariel's mother, while Teodoro del Mar looked handsome and assertive.

"Odelia was part of Luna Lunita?" Ariel asked it as a question, but here was real proof. Solid proof. She repeated it, a statement. "Odelia was part of Luna Lunita."

"Was," Mr. Antonio said in his raspy voice. "*Was* being the word. Now that you've seen for yourself, I can say I didn't tell you. I'm sure you are familiar with half-truths. Aren't you, *Ariel*?"

Ariel blinked tears from her eyes. "I don't understand."

I know what your family does. You ruin lives. Those were some of the first words Odelia had said to her. That's why she'd hesitated to bring her on tour. That's why she wanted to keep Ariel from Eric.

"I don't understand."

The old man gripped her shoulder with sympathy. Or perhaps pity. "All I know is they left for New York thick as thieves. Then Odelia returned to my doorstep with nothing but this trunk full of clothes and recalled records. She never spoke of what happened, and I knew better than to dig. Perhaps it is something you should talk to your father about, or Odelia might tell you the rest. I certainly never thought she'd let another del Mar near her, but here you are."

Ariel's throat felt tight with a repressed cry. "Did you know my mother?"

Mr. Antonio nodded once and brushed a tear from her cheek before it fell. "I met her once. Maia came to speak to my girl. To Odelia. But some hurts won't heal, and she left without seeing her again."

Ariel had a million more questions, but somewhere out front a car honked, announcing the band's return. Mr. Antonio gently pried the record from her hands. Recalled records. That's why she'd never seen them. Had Odelia taken the boxes herself? Had she quit? Worse, had her father fired her? If she confronted him, would he even tell her the truth?

She had such a clear picture of who her parents had been, and this story, this record, was a piece that didn't fit. Not without breaking the image of them first. And if she did that, she knew there would be no fixing it.

Radio Z106.3 FM

Transcript:

Alexis Dee: We are live from downtown Miami bringing you the very best rock and roll, from throwbacks to the next big thing. Today we have Star Crossed *in* the studio. You can't see them, but they are freaking adorable. Eric Reyes, Carly Toles, Eleanor Grimsby, Max Chin! Welcome. You all look absolutely petrified. I promise, I don't bite.

Carly: *We* might.

[laughing track]

Alexis: Atta girl, Carly. Tell us. First time on the road promoting your self-titled album. How are you feeling? Eric?

Eric: Overwhelmed, but in a good way.

Grimsby: We've had our share of catastrophes.

Max: But every night we get on that stage and kill it. I mean absolutely *shred.*

Alexis: I love that for you, and us. Now, your single is "Love Like Lightning," and I have to say it's dreamy AF. Eric, who was the lucky one? Or should I say lucky ones?

Eric: [laughs] Thank you, Alexis. I used to think I was writing toward this feeling I couldn't explain. This person I hadn't met but knew was out there. That one day I would meet her, and that would be it.

Alexis: Oh boy, from the look your bandmates are exchanging, I'm sensing you've already met her.

Eric: [chuckles nervously] Time will tell.

Alexis: Sooo does that mean there's a chance for the rest of us?

Carly: I think you all should come to Jesse's Live tomorrow and find out.

Alexis: I'll be there. Trust me, friends. You don't want to miss the show tomorrow night! Doors open at seven p.m. This is Star Crossed with their latest single, "Love Like Lightning." I've got a very good feeling about this one.

CHAPTER FIFTEEN

ERIC

7.3 Miami, Florida

That night, Tío Antonio cooked up a feast. Roasted chickens, plantains, heaps of avocado sprinkled with sea salt and lime. Yellow rice and fat red beans. Everyone had pitched in. Eric got to show off his killer knife skills, and Odelia made her dangerous Dark and Stormy cocktails. His best memories of his parents, when they had been happy, were all in the kitchen. Sometimes, like now, he missed them. His mother most of all. But they'd made their choices, and so had he.

The people who loved him had stuck around, and they were around the same table with him now. It felt like such a small blessing. He promised himself that whatever changed and whatever success the band reached, this would never change.

Still, he couldn't shake the feeling that Melody was upset. She smiled when Carly detailed their morning interviews, in which every single reporter and radio jockey had hit on him and shoved their calling cards into his pockets. And she laughed with everyone when Tío Antonio detailed her laundry mishap. What else had happened while he'd left her side?

"I'm curious," Oz began, setting down his Dark and Stormy with three extra limes. "How did you all know you wanted to be musicians? Like, you're all a bunch of runaways and chaos kittens, but you chose this. How did you know?"

191

Tío Antonio chuckled and pointed his fork at Odelia. "She came out of the womb singing. All the doctors said she serenaded the other babies in the nursery."

Odelia was fanning herself, but Eric could see it was all bravado in a flash when her smile fell. She glanced at Melody, and he couldn't quite tell what was going on there. Maybe *he* was the one who was off. "I used to think it was the only thing I'd ever want. But that was a lifetime ago. Then this one came along, and I had a new big love in my life."

"Mom." Vanessa playfully rolled her eyes, then thought about the question. "I knew the first time I performed at my middle school talent show. I sang Selena's 'No Me Queda Más,' and that was it."

Grimsby, who didn't think they saw her pocketing pieces of food to later feed Monty, said, "Easy. Stole my brother's copy of A Perfect Circle's *Mer de Noms*. Lady bass player, Paz Lenchantin. Never looked back."

Eric smiled, and he could practically hear the album still playing on a loop through their house.

Max drummed her fingers on the edge of the table. "Not going to lie. It was when my cousin hired a Hanson cover band for her birthday."

"No earworms," Carly said, breaking off a piece of a plantain and throwing it at Max, who leaned back on the legs of her chair and caught it in her mouth. They all had to cheer at that. Carly shimmied her shoulders. "Me? Since my old man bought me my first guitar. He was into all the old heads. Hendrix. Davis. Sister Rosetta Tharpe. Prince. It's hard to answer. But also, when I met you all."

Eric tipped his glass toward his lead guitarist. "And you tell me *I'm* the romantic in the group."

"Your turn, loser," Carly said, grinning.

"For me it was clear I wanted to be a musician when my grandfather started giving me music lessons. It was all he wanted, and it never happened for him, and I thought, I'm going to do it. For him. For me. And now for us."

Eric nudged Melody with his elbow. "Come on. We've heard you play. When did you know?"

Melody took a deep breath, pressing down on her necklace. She smiled, like she was only starting to realize her own answer. "I think—I think I never wanted to be a musician. Not at first. I mean, not in the limelight, I guess. I'm not saying this right."

"There's no right or wrong here," Odelia told her.

"Yeah, no judgment," Eric said.

Melody rubbed her temples. "I can't believe I just said that. It was never my dream to be a musician. But I always, always wanted to write songs. Music is part of me. It's stitched into everything I am. I know the power of a song, how the right one can jog your memory. How even when the world hates a song, there's always one person who will hear it and love it because they heard it at the right time, and it was everything they needed in that moment. The right song can amp you up, mellow you out. Music is literally everything. I guess I didn't choose it. Music chose me."

Eric realized he was tapping his fingers on the table as she spoke, softly, trying to remember where he learned that rhythm. *Two, one, four.* Wondering how every word matched his own feelings. The others nodded, grinning.

"I guess you're in the right place," Odelia said. "Which reminds me."

Eric's manager got up and vanished into the kitchen. She returned with a tray of cupcakes, a single sparkler candle illuminating the one at the center. Eric looked around the room but couldn't think of whose birthday it was. Then Odelia set the tray down in front of Melody, who tried to hide her embarrassed smile behind her hands.

"You shouldn't have," she said.

"Well, I did. And it's not until tomorrow, so let's get a head start," Odelia said, which was her way of saying *you're welcome.*

They broke into a tipsy, messy, Spanglish version of the "Happy Birthday" song, and Melody took a huge bite of cupcake, then tapped a bit of frosting on the tip of Eric's nose before licking her own finger clean.

"If you all get whipped cream everywhere . . ." Odelia warned.

Later that night, after everyone was showered, Eric stretched out on one of the two couches and let Melody take the air mattress. The room was lightly spinning, and he thought about what the radio jockey had asked. Who was "Love Like Lightning" about? "I'm sensing you've already met her," she'd said.

He'd said, "Time will tell."

Maybe. Maybe that time was sooner than he'd ever imagined.

The following night, before the show, Eric had a surprise for Melody. He found her in the greenroom, trying out some chords on Vanessa's guitar. When she saw him, she raised her brows. He was behind schedule, but he'd decided that was simply part of his process.

"Shouldn't you be getting dressed?" she asked, taking in his plain white tee, one from the multipack he'd bought at that first thrift store.

"Well, all my lucky shirts keep getting slashed or dyed."

She buried her face in her hands. "I'm *sorry.* I'll replace everything. I promise."

"I'm kidding. You can barely tell." He could definitely tell.

She set the guitar on the couch. "Carly thinks otherwise."

"Forget all that. I want to show you my favorite thing." And then, because he realized that his words could be interpreted in many ways, he elaborated. "I mean, the reason this venue is important to me."

Melody worried that perfect bottom lip. "As long as you promise it's not birthday related."

"I can promise it's not *your* birthday related. Just . . ." He motioned toward the door. "Please?"

She gave in and took the hand he offered.

He opened a STAFF ONLY door and led her up the steps. "Do you know I haven't taken an elevator at a venue since Philly?"

"I thought it was just me! The trauma."

Thankfully, the rooftop access was only three flights up. Someone had already propped the door open, and he made sure the heavy cinder block was in place. The last thing he needed was to get locked out before the show.

From the roof of Jesse's Live, they had a perfect view of the lazy Miami sunset. The strip of beach, the tops of palm trees, a starburst of colors he could never quite capture in a picture, no matter how many times he tried.

"I know Florida gets a bad rap," she said, "but so far it's been pretty great."

The salty evening breeze wrapped around them. From the ledge, they could see the line of people filing into the building down below. Something tightened in the pit of his stomach. They hadn't had a sold-out show yet, but perhaps this was their night. He was optimistic.

Eric checked his watch, then pointed at the beach. He watched as Melody's eyes traced the first round of fireworks in the sky. Roman candles were mirrored in the dark pools of her eyes, and she gasped as every wave of explosions grew bigger and bigger.

"I figured you've seen July Fourth fireworks," he said, hoping he wasn't coming off like a complete fool. "But you've never seen them from this rooftop." Or with me.

"This is perfect, Eric," she whispered. Then her gaze turned sly. She hopped up on the ledge to face him, sitting with her knees framing him on either side. "So, Oz mentioned a *bet* of some sort?"

It was not the thing he'd expected her to say. He exhaled a laugh. "Please don't be mad. This has nothing to do with you, but with me and my reputation."

She seemed to tense at the word, then watched the fireworks for a beat. "Tell me."

Two words. *Tell me.* It felt like a shorthand version of *trust me. Tell me, I won't judge you. Tell me, it's okay.* At least, he hoped that was the case.

"Fair. You told me your dating history, now it's my turn." Eric pressed his palms on the concrete ledge on either side of her because he couldn't stop wanting to hold her again. He took a deep breath and tried to find the words.

"My friends are right to worry that I might screw things up. I have before. Epically. I put myself out there. I got hurt. I hurt others."

"Scoundrel," Melody teased.

"Reformed scoundrel." He met her unwavering stare. He needed her to see that he meant every word he said. "I've had girlfriends since I was in grade school. Cutesy stuff, flowers from the neighbor's garden, walking with her to school. I never stopped chasing this feeling that I made up in my head. I blame my grandfather Pedro and his perfect fucking love story, but that's for a different night."

"And this night?"

"I guess this is where it happened," he said, nodding to the beach below. "I was new to Miami, taking any job I could get. I met someone after I played one of those open mic nights. She believed in me. Came to every single gig, even in the most rancid, grossest dive bar. Even busking on the street for tourists, and I thought, *that's love.*"

"Was it?" she asked softly, curiously.

"I mean you said it yourself. If it was the real thing, it wouldn't have gone away so quickly. But it did. I think the glamour started to fade. I got fewer gigs to make time for us. And the success that I kept talking about wasn't coming. She ended it, and yeah, I was a wreck, but for another reason."

She tilted her head to the side, waited patiently for him to continue.

"The night she ended things, I got a call from my mother. She never called me. Never. My father didn't allow it. I was working my bar shift, so I let the call go to voicemail."

He swallowed. He'd told the story once to his band, and not since. The guilt that came with it was always fresh when he thought about it.

"She'd been calling to say that my grandfather had passed in his sleep." He ran his hands through his hair. "I listened to it a hundred times, and it didn't feel real. I couldn't go home because of the terms of my visa, and I couldn't afford the flight, anyway. I couldn't even be there. He never got to hear me perform or see that I was trying, and that I went to New York and found my people."

Her smile was so sad, he wanted to banish it. Then he knew she understood. "I am very familiar with that kind of heartbreak."

Eric felt her knuckle gently brush his cheek. There and gone. He continued, "I was a wreck. I thought if I'd tried harder, if I'd just focused harder on the music, it would have happened sooner and my grandfather would have been able to see it."

"Eric," she said, her voice a whisper as the fireworks boomed.

He shut his eyes. She had no idea what it did to him when she whispered his name like that. He swallowed the desire in his throat and put on a good face. Though, to be fair, his was always a good face.

"That's why you thank him before every show," Melody said, brushing the windswept waves out of his eyes. "And named your guitar after him. That doesn't feel like you earned this reputation."

"Well," he said, letting the surrounding fireworks fill the silence.

"Then I went up to New York, met the band. I knew I didn't want anything serious again, and I made that clear to every woman I met. I never wanted to hurt anyone on purpose. But things had a spectacular way of blowing up in my face. Missed shows. Slashed tires. Unwanted house guests. The band got sick of it."

"See? Scoundrel."

"Reformed," he corrected. "A while ago, I told myself *no relationships*. Not even dates. Not until we hit it big."

"I think you're doing great."

"Not great enough."

Melody cast her gaze away. That invisible wall cobbling itself around her. "When will it be enough?"

Before he could answer, they whirled at the sound of the door hitting the cinder block. She hopped down from the ledge, and he behind the column that blocked them from view. Even if he was performing that night, they technically weren't supposed to be up there.

Eric had every intention of explaining how they'd just wanted to see the fireworks, but the sight waiting for them around the corner stunned him into utter silence.

It was Carly and Vanessa.

Carly and Vanessa kissing.

Carly and Vanessa kissing as a new blast of fireworks shot up, closer to their location than any of the others. It felt extremely wrong to watch, so he whirled around and collided into Melody. Which got their attention.

"What the hell are you doing?" Vanessa shouted.

"Me?" He swung back around to face them. Carly was wiping Vanessa's lipstick from her face. "What the hell are *you* doing?"

Vanessa wagged her finger like a threat. But she barely made it a few feet before she tripped over something in the dark. The cinder block. Carly and Eric reached for her at the same time, but they missed her by a hair, and she face-planted hard.

"Oh my god," Carly panted. "Are you okay?"

Vanessa cried out, holding her arm to her chest and letting out a string of curses that would have made sailors blush.

"I'll get help!" Melody was already halfway through the door when Vanessa called her back.

"No! I'm fine."

Eric scooped her up in his arms. "No, you're not."

Carly guided Vanessa's gaze toward hers. "Let me see."

Vanessa, as tough as she was, squeezed her eyes shut and kept her hand cradled to her chest. "No, no, it hurts."

"I'm getting help, end of story," Melody said again, and this time no one questioned her.

"I can walk, I promise." Vanessa kicked off her heels, and the four of them spilled out of the roof access and down the three flights of stairs.

In the greenroom, pandemonium descended. The venue manager sent someone to get ice. Melody assured them that an ambulance was on the way, Vanessa insisted she was fine, Max and Grimsby fussed over their friends.

"Will someone tell me what happened?" Odelia thundered.

For the first time since their arrival, since the history of Star Crossed, there was silence in the greenroom.

"We were watching the fireworks," Eric said.

"Without us?" Max asked, gesturing with her drumsticks in hand.

Grimsby shook her head. "Not cool, bros."

"I tripped on one of those giant bricks," Vanessa explained.

Odelia rubbed her temples and muttered, "Paciencia, Odelia, paciencia."

"Y'all are really not allowed up there," said the Jesse's Live manager. His orange tan made his teeth look practically neon white.

No one spoke again until the EMTs arrived and tended to Vanessa. They wrapped her wrist, but she'd need X-rays to determine the extent of the damage.

"Can I do it after the show?" Vanessa asked. "It's only an hour."

"I mean, technically," one of the two bored EMTs said.

"Absolutely not," Odelia said. "You can't even play."

Vanessa and Eric turned to Melody at the same time. "But *she* can."

THE TUTTLE TELLER

Episode 1371:
Breaking News

Transcript:

All right, everyone. I wasn't going to do this, but we have to talk. If you've been following what's been going on with our girl Ariel del Mar, then you know some *ish* has been happening. First, Ariel missed her appearance on *Wake Up! New York*, then she posts her cryptic message saying she needs space and is going off social media. NOW this video has surfaced of her at a Paris nightclub acting so unlike herself. There have been many copycats over the years putting on her wig and trying to pass as the superstar.

But sources from the nightclub say she was with some of her sisters, so it's really her. Ariel, partying in public? Ariel staying out at a club till six a.m.? This isn't the princess we know. I know she's come under fire and a lot of you are upset. However, I'm here to tell you she's still OUR GIRL. She's the same person who paid for the hospital bills of people affected by the Oregon wildfires. Who built a hospital in honor of her mother in the city of her birth. Who gave millions in scholarships for aspiring musicians.

We shouldn't be quick to jump without knowing what's really going on. I'll be hosting an open chat where we can discuss.

Is our girl crying out for help?

CHAPTER SIXTEEN

ARIEL

7.4 Miami, Florida

"**N**o," Ariel said. "I can't."

"I know you know my songs," Vanessa pleaded, grabbing Ariel's hand with her uninjured one. "I'm not asking you to sing. *Please.*"

Ariel turned from Odelia to Vanessa to Eric. Eric, who had opened up to her moments before. She didn't have time to process everything he'd told her *plus* this. Ariel did know Vanessa's songs. She'd been learning them on the road, but she couldn't go up onstage now. What if someone recognized her?

Then again, hadn't she told Odelia that she'd be an asset on the tour? Here she was at the center of another disruption, and she had the opportunity to save the day. No one even knew Ariel del Mar could play. Once, she'd had an electric guitar as a prop during an award show performance and had been made fun of online because it hadn't been plugged in. Her father thought giving them instruments took away from their pop star image and made them too "folk." And yes, she'd confessed the night before that becoming a musician hadn't been her dream, but music *had* chosen her. Just not in the way her father had imagined.

Ariel hadn't been onstage in almost two weeks. She didn't miss the circus or the paparazzi. The invasive and patronizing interviews.

But she did miss the energy of the crowd. She missed writing songs on her guitar in between tour stops, in the penthouse. She missed people shouting her lyrics as if they had been tailor-made for their emotions.

It was clear that she hadn't wanted a break from music. If she had, she wouldn't have gone on a music tour. She'd wanted a break from being Ariel del Mar, and being her father's perfect daughter. She had that opportunity to be a hired guitar in the background. The idea started becoming more appealing with every second, and her fingers itched for the guitar.

"I don't have anything to wear," Ariel told Vanessa.

"I have a backup black dress. It might be a little big on top, but we can cinch it," Vanessa said, turning to her mom for support.

"You don't have to do this," Odelia said, and Ariel couldn't tell who was more surprised—her daughter or Ariel.

"Mom—"

"Everyone out!" Odelia ordered. One by one, Eric, the band, the frazzled venue staff, and the EMTs (who made Odelia sign a release form before they left) emptied out of the room until just Odelia, Vanessa, and Ariel remained.

"Ariel," Odelia began, and Ariel straightened at the sound of her name. "You left because you didn't want to perform. I'm not going to ask you to do that again."

She'd watched the patience with which Odelia had spoken to Vanessa after the elevator incident, and yet being on the receiving end was different. In her mind she could hear her own father's agitation when any of her sisters was sick or exhausted or quit the band. Because they had all quit once, except for her. And then, with a few words, Teo del Mar always turned it around. Always fixed it. Always reminded them what was at stake. The first and only time Ariel had quit was the day she left on Eric's tour.

"I'll do it," she said. "I can do it. I'm sure."

Odelia smiled softly, and Vanessa squeezed her hand.

"I have some conditions," Ariel said. She was mad at her father, but she was still his daughter. The Garcia women waited and listened. "I can't sing in public."

Vanessa nodded. "The songs don't have backup vocals."

"It needed to be said," Ariel noted. "I don't want to be tagged on anything."

"We can't seem like we're not crediting our musicians. It's not a good look for us," Odelia said. "What about 'Mel'?"

"Or 'M'?" Vanessa suggested excitedly. "Or a symbol!"

"M is fine. Last thing." She leveled her gaze on Odelia and asked, "I want to know what happened between you and my parents. I know you were part of Luna Lunita."

The manager's sharp gaze darkened with anger at first, then softened when she looked at her daughter. "Not tonight. In my own time."

"But before the tour ends," Ariel added hesitantly, like she was treading on glass.

Odelia offered her hand. She was the kind of woman whose word meant everything, and so Ariel accepted it. "You've got a deal, little mermaid."

Ariel had done entire costume changes in less than thirty seconds, so getting dressed was the easiest part of the night. As Vanessa had so tactfully pointed out, Ariel's fit hourglass figure didn't fill out the top of the black silk slip dress. With a few of Odelia's pins, which drew blood as they hurried to get her dressed, they tapered the bust and used a black ribbon to cinch her at the waist.

Ariel turned, watching herself in the mirror. She'd worn one-piece body suits and booty shorts for years, but those made her feel young.

An adult-size girl-child covered in sequins and so much glitter she was sure she'd find bits of it when she was old and gray. But this dress felt intimate, an inch away from lingerie, sexy in a way that was never supposed to be part of her "brand." The twins would say that all clothes were costumes, in the end. That was the point of fashion—to show who you were. Like music, it was expression. She'd been buying secondhand things for weeks, and every time it felt like trying on someone new. This, however, was miles away from the "glam girl next door" the magazines had dubbed her.

"Hot," Vanessa said. "But don't flash anyone when you sit. They're fans, not your gynecologist."

"Vanessa!" Odelia reprimanded but snorted behind her clipboard. Ariel wasn't sure she'd truly seen the older woman laugh that way.

"No makeup," Ariel said when Vanessa launched a one-handed attack with an eyeshadow brush.

"Ay, Melody," Vanessa protested, dabbing shimmery lip gloss instead. "You still look nothing like your full-on mermaid clown show."

"Hey!"

Vanessa set her lips like she wasn't going to take her words back. Ariel was sure in that moment Vanessa would definitely get along with her sister Sophia.

Odelia returned holding a wide-brimmed fedora with a turquoise buckle. She plopped it on Ariel's head.

"Where'd you get that?" Vanessa asked.

"Bought it off some hipster in the lobby," Odelia said. "It's coming out of your pay."

"Thank you." Ariel was touched that Odelia had thought to find one more piece for her outfit to make her feel comfortable.

She remembered what Grimsby had said. How she looked in the mirror and always seemed surprised. It *was* surprising, how she was herself but not herself. Herself, but someone new. Perhaps she preferred being Melody Marín to the girl she'd been. The one who couldn't stand up for herself to her father and was practically chaperoned in her sleep and couldn't even burp without her father telling her that it was bad for her image. Melody Marín danced with a beautiful man until dawn and sat at cafés and wrote whatever songs she pleased.

Melody Marín was excited about going onstage.

Before Odelia opened the door, she darted a red nail between the girls. "Last thing. I know the four of you didn't go up to the roof to look at fireworks. You don't have to give me the details, I don't want to know. But do not lie to me again. Understood?"

There was that withering look that had petrified Ariel the day she and Odelia met. Chastened, they nodded, and hurried backstage.

The lights dimmed, and the entire venue came to life. It was like old times, and yet entirely different. There were fewer people than she was used to performing for, but even fifty excited people could feel like hundreds. She didn't have the impending feeling that she had to please *everyone*, because now she was in the background. She could simply play. Adrenaline coursed through her, making her limbs jittery.

"You okay?" Vanessa asked.

"Like riding a bike."

"I thought you didn't know how to ride a bike."

Ariel laughed. "You know it's a metaphor."

Vanessa stopped just outside the threshold. They could hear the chatter of the pit ahead. The crackle of walkies and heavy boots behind them. She smiled shyly at Ariel and said, "Thank you. Really."

"Thank me *after*."

Vanessa went onstage first, the crowd shifting their attention to her. She got up on her black stool and adjusted her mic. There was a slight murmur at the sight of her arm.

"So I sprained my wrist today," Vanessa told the crowd, her breath echoing with a touch of reverb. She really transformed onstage, a little edge, a lot of charisma. "But you know what they say. The show must fucking go on!" The crowd roared in approval. "With a little help from a friend, of course. Give it up for my girl, M."

Before Melody stepped forward, she saw him across the stage in the wings. Eric. His dark eyes raking over her, from her borrowed black boots to the hem of the dress that kissed the very tops of her thighs. Even in the shadows, his gaze seared her skin. She liked it. She *loved* it.

She strode confidently into the soft purple front light and took the seat beside Vanessa. If anyone had told Ariel that she'd be sitting there, playing backing guitar for Vanessa Garcia, she wouldn't have believed it. But she was beginning to understand that perhaps she was finding more than herself. She was finding her first real friendships. She'd have to think more on how to make those friendships last later.

In the meantime, they made music.

It was like riding a bike, and then it wasn't. Ariel strummed the upbeat intro to Vanessa's song "Storms and Silence." The vibrations of the chord reverberated down through her bones. She kept her head tilted down, watching her own fingers move and shift across the fretboard. She barely recognized her own hands, and the sensation of *rightness* was overwhelming. If her father were in the audience, would he recognize her? Would her sisters?

Every now and then, Vanessa would turn to her and flash an encouraging smile. Once, between songs, Ariel searched for Eric and found him still standing exactly where he'd been at the top of the set. She wished she could have him look at her that way always.

With each note, each song, the whistles and howls from the audience, she got back something she'd been missing since the final Goodbye Goodbye concert—the connection. Lifelines that unspooled between her and the audience. That was the power of music.

When the set was over, she handed off the guitar to a stagehand and went in search of him. She had to see him. She knew it was complicated, that they'd each made promises that felt more and more fragile when they got too close, but right now, it didn't matter.

"That was incredible!" Eric pulled her into a hug, lifting Ariel and spinning her in place.

"You sound surprised," she said, and though he set her down, she was still floating.

Stagehands cleared the equipment and made way for Le Poisson Bleu to take the limelight. In the greenroom, there was energy and chaos. Odelia hurried her daughter out of the venue to get her X-rays. Carly slugged Ariel on the shoulder and said, "What other talents are you holding out on?"

Ariel had scores of awards and die-hard fans. She couldn't leave an event or interview without someone proclaiming their undying love for her and her sisters. She'd cherished those moments and didn't want to take them for granted, but this—a forty-five-minute set on a dark stage where no one knew her beyond an elusive initial—gave her the sense that she'd earned it on her own.

She carried that feeling back to the merch booth and got to work. The venue was packed with tipsy, laughing, glittering concertgoers. She thought nothing could bring down her mood, until she checked her phone. She had dozens of messages from her sisters and Chrissy. A hot flash of anxiety burned through her as she saw the headlines and clicked through the images. They'd done as Ariel had asked. So be it.

Ariel del Mar was in the news.

Pop Princess Has a Mental Breakdown in Paris. Racks Up Thousands in Hotel Damages.

ARIEL DEL MAR CAN'T HANDLE LIFE POST SIREN SEVEN.

The Good Mothers of Texas Pen an Open Letter to Ariel del Mar: "Shame On You!"

Atlantica Records Issues No Comment Regarding Ariel's Wild Night on the Streets of Paris.

EVERYTHING YOU NEED TO KNOW ABOUT STAR CROSSED FRONT MAN ERIC REYES.

Trevor Tachi Spotted at Charles de Gaulle. Is the Couple Taking Things to the Next Level? Or Is It Over for Good?

 Fans Defend Ariel's Actions in Tribute Video.

Star Crossed Live at The Road House—7.5 New Orleans Sold Out!

CHAPTER SEVENTEEN

ERIC

7.5 New Orleans, Louisiana

They'd left Miami right after the show with a fridgeful of Tío Antonio's leftovers and news that a looped video of one of the band's performances had gone viral. In the video, Eric had flipped his head back and bitten his lip in the middle of the bridge. The video had slowed him down, frame by frame, and though he knew he looked good, everyone on the bus, except Odelia and Melody, was messing with him and doing live reenactments.

He took it in stride, scrolling through the comments. Yeah, yeah, everyone said not to read them. But he'd never been the subject of public conversation. Between the "he sucks" and "prom0te on #zaddyMuSiC" spam comments, there were those who had nothing but love. Love for Grimsby's bass and Max's tricks between sets and Carly's epic guitar solos.

Halfway through their twelve-hour drive, they parked at a rest stop; only Oz and the band got out for breakfast while Melody slept.

Eric grabbed a bacon, egg, and cheese sandwich for himself, two coffees (one sweet, one bitter), and a croissant with butter and jam, which was what Melody usually got at rest stops. Running on three hours of sleep, he stretched under the twilight sky and pounded his first coffee before joining his friends at one of the picnic tables out front.

"I think we're going to get good news today," Eric announced.

Max popped a Tater Tot into her mouth. "Here we go."

Eric grinned. "I'm serious. I had a dream about Pedro. Every time I dream about my grandfather, I get good news."

Oz nodded along like he couldn't imagine how anyone could doubt Eric. "There's definitely something to that. My grandmother moved in with us from Guatemala when I was ten, and she used to say that our loved ones speak to us in dreams. The day after my cat died, she appeared to me."

Grimsby's gray eyes went wide, and she whispered, "Ghost cat."

Eric patted Oz on his back. "I love that for you, buddy."

"Or, maybe," Carly said, "Miami is a sore spot for you and it stirred up some memories, so you dreamed of the only person who unquestioningly supported you during that period of your life."

"So young," Eric said wistfully. "So jaded."

Max drummed a beat on the table, then quieted down when the nearby truck driver shot them a cranky *it's too early for this* glare. "I believe you, Eric. Especially if it means that the label is going to give us some *cheddah cheese* for the music video. I love your concept, Grimsby, but right now it's a little out of budget."

"I have a vision, and I refuse to compromise," their goth bass player muttered.

Eric knew Max was right. "Yeah, well, right now it's pretty much found footage and us walking around the California desert."

"I might be able to help," Oz said. "I'm pretty good at graphics and minored in film."

The young driver handed his phone over, then visibly retreated into his hoodie. It was surprising that the man could talk for hours on the evolutionary theories of centaurs, but when it came to talking about himself, he was shy.

"Melody can play guitar, Oz is a freaking artist," Carly said, flipping through Oz's portfolio. She clapped—*punched*—Eric on the back. "Damn, maybe your woo-woo hunches are right."

"I didn't need a Heimlich this early in the morning." Eric coughed.

"And love how Carly forgets the phase where she consulted her tarot cards on what to make for dinner. But I agree. We have an embarrassment of riches on this tour."

Max, Grimsby, and Carly all exchanged glances. Eric knew that look. It was their intervention look. The first month they'd lived together and they hated his cologne. The date who'd shown up one day and refused to leave, claiming squatter's rights. The time he grew a caveman beard.

"What?"

"Well," Grimsby began. "Um, Max?"

Max dusted Tater Tot crumbs from the corners of her mouth. "We would like to give you the option to back out of our bet."

Eric lifted his finger from his coffee and pointed from bandmate to bandmate. "What are you up to?"

"Nothing," they said, voices syrupy and sweet.

"Did you guys get swapped out by aliens when I wasn't looking?"

"That *does* happen around these parts," Oz said uncannily, draining the rest of his sugary iced coffee concoction.

Carly crossed her arms over her chest, that stubborn gleam in her eyes. "Look, I'm usually the last person to admit I'm wrong, but I was wrong."

"Wrong about what?" he asked, though his insides churned anxiously. "Use your words. I speak three, four languages, I can understand."

"Ugh," Grimsby said. "Maybe we should let him suffer."

"We don't think you'll mess things up with Melody," Carly admitted. "We don't want you to."

"We want you to marry her!" Max added, clapping her palms.

Coffee went down Eric's windpipe, and he choked on the sip of his second coffee—this one milky and sweet. Fists pounded his back at the same time. Carly even told him to raise his arms in the air, the way they did to babies when they choked. He swatted them all away.

Eric looked at Oz, who mouthed, *"Aliens."*

"You're messing with me." He decidedly ignored the part where they mentioned marriage. "What day is it today?"

"Friday," Oz supplied.

"A *week* and a day ago, you were convinced I'd screw it up. You gave me all this shit for helping out a friend, for helping the *tour*."

"Calm down, Don Juan," Carly said. "Don't start retconning the situation. Those things were added bonuses. You invited Melody on this tour because you had a crush. We were just keeping you in line."

"We've seen the error of our ways," Grimsby said.

Eric chuckled. "Oh, I see what's really happening. You want to call this off because you see I'm going to win and you're worried you aren't going to like the tattoo I picked out for us."

Oz clapped chaotically. "Let's see it."

Eric had not, in fact, picked out their tattoo, but thankfully Oz and his portfolio were right there. He asked their driver for his phone and swiped through the pictures until he settled on one. "I'm thinking this punk-rock chupacabra might be just the thing."

"That's one of my favorites," Oz said.

Carly smirked, the way she did when Max wiped Eric's music playlists clean and replaced them with Siren Seven remixes, all because he'd had a midnight craving and eaten her last slice of cheesecake. "Oh, no no no. *I* see what's really happening."

"What?" he challenged.

Carly turned to the others, purposely talking about him as if he weren't there because she knew it drove him up a wall. "He's chicken."

"Ohhh," Max and Grimsby singsonged, and Oz came in last.

"I hate when you do that." Eric cleared his throat, still burning from the abrasion of almost inhaling his cafecito.

"This isn't about us, Señor Sunshine," Carly said. "You're scared *you're* going to fuck it up now that you don't have the bet as an excuse."

"False," he said, then said it again in Spanish, then again in Portuguese and French. He stood up. "You all don't want to admit I was right all along."

"Hold up," Oz said. "So you all agree that Melody is awesome, and Eric should go for it. What's the big deal?"

"The big deal is he's scared. What happened to Captain Optimism?" The more Carly said it, the more he knew she was right.

Their innocent, silly bet was like a fence. A short, flimsy picket fence that a good breeze could blow over, but it was still a perimeter. He was already at risk of crossing the line. The thing stopping him was Melody: *I can't.* She'd said it, and he'd backed off. Even when she looked at him that way, when she found excuses to touch him, when they were truly alone, she always pulled away first.

"I'm not scared," Eric said, seriously enough that his friends stopped teasing him. For the moment. "She's holding back. And I'm not going to push her."

"You've got it bad," Max said. "Can't blame you. She's hot, she loves music, and she's *nice.* If you don't lock it down, Carly might steal another one from you."

Carly gasped and smacked her palms on the table, her eyes wide with incredulity. "You *told* them?"

"I didn't!" Eric defended himself. "I swear."

"He didn't have to," Grimsby said.

"Yeah, we were really supposed to believe Vanessa 'tripped' while watching fireworks? No." Max put on her sunglasses like she was in the opening credits of her favorite murder procedural. "Nothing fazes Vanessa. She must have been startled or scared. And what is scarier than sneaking up to the roof and being caught in the act!" She cracked her knuckles. "I'm messing with you, Carly. I caught you and Vee holding hands during dinner."

"Well, Detective Chin," Eric said. "Melody and I *were* watching the fireworks." And spilling his guts out in a way he'd never done in his life before. No big deal.

"Because you *lurv* her." Max shaped her hands into a single heart.

"Whatever, we're on me now," Carly said.

Oz snorted. "So, wait, how come there's no warning about you and Vanessa?"

"Because." Carly shrugged. "We've been dating for two months."

"What?" they all shouted in unison.

"Look, Vanessa and I are more—pragmatic, let's say—than hopelessly romantic. We've never let relationships get in the way of the band or her music. Plus, sneaking around was kind of hot, I'm not going to lie."

"I hate all of you. Bet is still on," Eric said, stomping a few paces to take his trash out. "Let's go. Back on the road."

"Don't worry, big guy," Oz said. "I believe in you."

"Really?"

Oz nodded emphatically. "Romantic heroes are the greatest cryptids of all."

Eric laughed and tried to take that as a compliment. "I'm serious about the design stuff. I'll talk to Odelia when she gets up, but I want to buy that logo and put it on some merch."

As they piled on the bus, Melody was walking out of the bathroom with her toothbrush in hand.

"Morning." She smiled at him. That was it. Just a smile, sleepy and sweet. And it was all it took for him to feel like he'd been sucker punched with emotion.

Why hadn't he wanted to be let off the hook? He'd been so sure. So *sure* that he wasn't going to do anything to "Eric Reyes" a relationship with Melody. He knew his friends loved him, even if they'd take any chance they got to poke fun at his vanity. They were encouraging him to pursue the very thing he'd wanted. *Was* he scared? If everything went right, and he still messed it up, then it would be his fault alone. The disappointment wouldn't be solely his, but all of theirs.

No. Eric Reyes was many things, but he was not a pessimist. When he sat down at the table across from Melody, her cheeks flushed, eyes bright, he knew it couldn't be about him and what he wanted. She was on this tour to get away from a bad situation. She was guarded, protective of her past. She'd already said it: *I can't.* How selfish would he be to dive right into pursuing something with her if she wasn't ready?

And he could wait. Would wait. As long as it took. He would wait until she was ready to really let him in. Melody was worth all the time in the world.

"Max got you breakfast," he said, shoving the croissant at her without his usual finesse.

"No, I didn't," Max muttered under her breath.

Melody thanked him with a knowing smile and tapped the Plexiglas of Monty's cage. She'd been the deciding vote in whether or not to keep the horny little guinea pig instead of leaving it with Tío Antonio.

Too wired to sleep, everyone sprawled around the front lounge. Melody ripped pieces from her croissant. She had a flake on her lower lip. Eric's fingers itched to brush it away. But he could feel the smug smirks from his friends, and she got to it first.

"I've been thinking," she said, opening up her notebook. The pages had been filled with her slanted, curly script and tiny doodles. "I mean, feel free to one hundred percent say no." Her cheeks flushed rose as she shook her head. "Never mind."

"What?" He sat back, tapping the sides of his coffee cup. *Two, one, four.* "Tell me."

"I've never done it with someone else before."

He swallowed hard and sat very still, which was difficult when the bus seemed to hit a pothole. "Okay."

"And I was thinking that maybe you could help."

"Me?"

"I mean, I know you're good at it. I like what I've seen so far."

"Well . . ." Wait. What was she talking about, exactly?

"I know the tour is stacked, but I found a park near the venue."

Max chortled, and the others joined her. "You want to have sex in the park?"

"What? No!" Melody buried her face in her palms. "I was talking about writing a song."

"Yeah, *Max*," Eric said, clearing his throat. "Get your mind out of the swamp."

But his entire body still radiated heat. He needed to plunge himself into a tub of ice. And then one look at Melody made him remember what she had been asking him. He'd written most of his songs on his own, but when he hooked up with Star Crossed, it was always a collaborative process. It was his favorite thing next to performing and, well, that other kind of "songwriting."

For him, making music with someone was personal. The fact that Melody wanted to work with him brought that tight sensation to his chest again.

"I would love that," he said. "We have a couple of hours to kill after load-in."

"Great."

"Good."

He thought she might get up and go back to bed. They had another six hours on the road. Instead, she fished out the book Grimsby had just finished reading. He imagined sitting this way with her on lazy mornings. Another bus. An apartment. A house. It didn't matter where, but it would be full of books and instruments and coffee.

He caught Max glaring at him. She didn't have to say it. Perhaps he'd known it all along. The very minute she'd collided into his life like an interference from the stars themselves. Cursed not to fail, but to face the inevitable. Because that's what Melody was. That's what falling for her was—inevitable.

SevenAteNine Group Chat

Ariel:
We made the news! Paris looked
fun @Thea. Thank you.

Thea:
It's almost liberating dressing up as
you. All this uproar because I was
just dancing to one of our songs on
a table!

Elektra:
That and, you know, you went aggro
on that hotel room.

Thea:
It was cathartic. I did write them a
check, though.

Ariel:
How's Daddy?

Sophia:
Pissed

Stella:
Kind of a wreck

Marilou:
Remember that one year we didn't
get nominated for Video of the
Year even though we had the most-
streamed video of the year?

Ariel:
That bad, huh?

Sophia:
Don't worry. We've got it covered.

Alicia:
Yeah, it's my turn to play dress-up
and be the red-wig herring.

Ariel:
I owe you all big-time. Though it's shitty
to see how easy it's been to ruin me.

Ariel:
Like everyone was just waiting to hate me.

Marilou:
Fame is fickle, darling. Might as well
have fun with the papz.

Sophia:
You ready to come home?

Ariel:
No

Ariel:
But

Ariel:
Something else is happening.

Marilou:
OOOOOOH BABY. I've been
WAITING

Ariel:
😑

Alicia:
BTW, we all saw the clip of Eric
Reyes doing the lip thing. Hot.

Elektra:
Even I had to agree and I don't even
like 🌶

Sophia:
Look, you've scared Ariel back into
her little shell.

Ariel:
🖕

Marilou:
Wooooooooow.

Stella:
Maybe we should all go on tour with
a sexy stranger.

Sophia:
Are you being careful?

Thea:
I think we all still have nightmares
of your condom cucumber lessons,
Sophia, thanks.

Ariel:
It's not like that!!! Though I'm pretty sure
he thought I propositioned him just now.

Marilou:
The wrong sister went on this tour
with the music sex god ISTG

Stella:
Big Papi Chulo Energy

Ariel:
He's not like that.

Elektra:
Big show little overture?

Ariel:
Huh?

Thea:
LMAO

Alicia:
I'm going to pee on myself.

Marilou:
Our little angel

Ariel:
We're just writing a song together!!!

Elektra:
Only the most romantic thing two
songwriters can do. Riiiiiight. What
are you waiting for?

Ariel:
He hates Siren Seven. What if
he hates the real me?

Sophia:
All of you is the real you

Thea:
You're supposed to be having fun.
Not having a quarter life crisis.
Though with climate change the way
it is, it may be midlife right now.

Marilou:
You're killing my buzz, T.

Stella:
All we're saying is he's hot. He's up and coming, so he's not a dick like Trevor. Eric's interviews make him seem like a Greek statue but with a personality. But maybe he wants the things you want to leave behind.

Ariel:
You're keeping tabs on us?

Sophia:
ARIEL YOU ARE ACROSS THE COUNTRY WITH STRANGERS OBVIOUSLY

Marilou:
Yeah, you can rebel against Dad all you want, but we're still a unit.

Ariel:
I know.

Ariel:
I love you.

Sophia:
Seriously though 🌶

CHAPTER EIGHTEEN

ARIEL

7.5 New Orleans, Louisiana

N ew Orleans was sticky. Ariel hadn't sweated that much since the summer her father made them do a "dancing boot camp." Sophia had joked that it was his way of not being able to handle that their bodies were changing.

Still, sitting under a gnarly tree in Audubon Park with Eric, she didn't care how hot it was. She basked in the Louisiana sun, and was thankful for every gust of breeze, and the giant iced coffee wedged between her knees.

"Okay, listen to this," Eric said.

He finger-picked the intro she'd shown him. He hummed the rhythm of the words, trying to find his way through their cadence and melody. He changed up the tempo, and she studied his strum pattern. *Two, one, four. Two, one, four.*

"Let me try." She eagerly traded his guitar for her coffee.

She *missed* her guitars. Each one she owned back home had been a gift—from her parents, sisters, Uncle Iggy, even Ibanez themselves, after she'd mentioned in an interview how beautiful she found their instruments.

Earlier, they'd passed by a music shop in the French Quarter and she'd fallen in love with the most beautiful acoustic guitar. She'd told herself she would come back and buy it.

Eric offered up his pick, and Ariel plucked it from his fingers. She went through the intro, lending her soft contralto to the treble of his voice. They were only vocalizing around the shapes of words, but her own voice felt unfamiliar. She'd been stuck singing soprano since she was ten, something the label (her father) thought would help maintain her youthfulness despite having gone through puberty. Keep her innocent. Keep her a child.

"Sing it," Eric said. "This is a judgment-free zone."

But she couldn't sing solo. Even if he didn't recognize her after a shift in octaves, it was still too big a risk. Wouldn't it be? *Voltage Sound* magazine had called her "the voice of her generation," a sound that only comes a few times in a century. That wasn't her voice anymore.

"I'll leave the singing to you."

"Oh, come on," he insisted. "I can hear how good you'd sound."

"I'm not saying I can't sing. I don't want to. I want to write songs for other people." She plucked the E string a few times, letting the heavy warble extend, then peter out. "I said that to my dad once."

Eric leaned his body across the blanket. He plucked the same string. "He didn't approve?"

Ariel shook her head, guilt digging holes around her truth once again. "I said it at a dinner once, and he listed ten consecutive reasons why it was a waste of my time."

"I feel like our fathers would get along." He seemed to ponder that. "Or destroy each other."

She chuckled, thumbed the next string. "It was a year or so after Mom died, and he was still having these moods. Like he was the only one who lost her. Like he was the only one who expected her to walk through that door any day. I think for a long time we let things slide because of that."

"You shouldn't have had to. You were the kids."

Hearing it from Eric was different than whispering to herself, not just a seed of doubt that had felt wrong, like betraying her family.

"Speaking of disappointed fathers." Eric's phone lit up. EL JERK, read the caller ID. He pressed the red button to send it to voicemail and lay back, fingers drumming against his chest.

She set the guitar in its case and closed her notebook. It felt like the most natural thing in the world to lie beside him, propped up on her elbow.

"I guess we both have daddy issues," he said.

She wrinkled her nose. Sophia had always said she'd never date another musician because they'd remind her of their dad. Ariel had agreed. Trevor Tachi, her only tragic point of reference, had been a child actor who wanted to become a singer, and she'd told herself *never again*. But then here she was, inches away from Eric Reyes. They had both sweated through their shirts. His thin gray cotton rode up when he slung his arms behind his head, the damp material clinging to the hard planes of his muscles, and once again she was fascinated by the trail of hair disappearing into his jeans.

"My eyes are up here," he said through a low, husky laugh.

Ariel was staring. She'd been *caught* staring. She covered her face with her hand, but when she peeked through the spread of her fingers, she saw he was blushing just as much as she was.

To spare her more embarrassment, he asked, "When did you learn to play?"

Ariel took a sip of her iced coffee, which was mostly melted by then. "Mmm. I think I was seven? Most of my sisters played something. Sophia the violin. Stella and Ali the piano. Mari didn't so much play the drums, but she did like to bang on every available surface until my dad caved and bought her a drum kit."

"Did she learn?"

"No." She laughed. "It wasn't the same when she got the real thing. But I loved all of it. Guitar. My mom started to teach me, and after she died I begged for lessons, but I discovered I could just listen to a song and then play it."

"My grandfather would have told you it was your gift."

"That's what my mom said, too. She played the cuatro."

"So does Odelia, did you know that?" Eric asked, smiling at the lazy hot breeze blowing through the trees. "Random."

The reminder of her mother's connection to Odelia gave her pause. She was keeping so many secrets, and it was exhausting. Maybe that's why she named her sisters, even though he probably wouldn't be able to pick the seven of them out of a lineup unless they were all dressed up. Maybe she wanted Eric to guess. To unravel her half-truths the way being with him unraveled her heart.

"I have six sisters," Ariel confessed as she watched him watch her. He was so beautiful, she found it hard to look at him for long. Her restless fingers picked the pills from the ancient blanket they'd dug out of the bus.

"So not enough for a soccer team, but maybe enough for a band."

Her pulse thrummed at her throat. Her ears.

Just tell him, she thought. *Get it over with.*

"Any brass?" he asked. "My grandfather loved those big salsa orchestras with six trumpets and a line of conga drums."

She laughed, pitchy and nervous. She decided that she wasn't brave enough. She wasn't ready to risk losing being close to him when she went to sleep or woke up. Listening to his voice while she tended the merchandise table every night. Walking into a room and knowing he was there by the thud of his boots, the joy in his laughter. The way he took pictures with every fan who asked. He was only starting a life she was trying to say goodbye to. She had to remind herself of that every time she softened when he thought of her and brought her breakfast.

"What about you?" she asked. "Are you an only child?"

"Surprisingly, yes," he said. "I have more cousins than I've ever met. My parents had a hard time conceiving. My mom called me her miracle baby. Sometimes I wish I'd had a sibling. Then maybe I'd just be the musician brother instead of the disappointment."

"For what it's worth," she said, "I'm not disappointed."

"I should hope not. Like I said"—Eric grinned at her—"I'm a miracle, baby."

"Wow." She reached for the stubborn lock of his hair and put it back in place. His hand caught hers softly, ran the smooth calluses of his fingertips down her forearm.

"I really want to kiss you, Melody," he said, slow like honey.

Kissing Eric Reyes felt like a certainty. It wasn't about *if* but *when*. Every time, though, she remembered why she shouldn't. They said they'd be friends. Odelia warned her not to get involved with him or she'd send her back to her father. He didn't know the truth. But he wanted to kiss her—Melody her. Sophia told her that she *was* being herself, and she could convince herself that the only thing about her that had changed was her bank account and her phone number. And yet, what about when those things returned?

The buzzing thoughts in her mind faded as she let herself get pulled into him. She flattened her palm on his chest, felt the frenzied rhythm of his heartbeat. Felt the shallow intake of his breath, then the sigh of relief as she rested there on his shoulder. She could do this—be close to him. Feel the strength of him beneath her. The way he kissed the top of her head and inhaled her scent. She could stay there for hours, tracing a circle around his heart with the tip of her finger. Watch the rise and fall of his chest and, when she lifted her head, the way he licked his bottom lip, then bit down softly, as if he was trying to stop himself from saying something to break the moment.

The ominous ringtone that began to blare broke it for them.

"Sorry, that's Odelia," he said, fumbling for the phone.

She found it wedged between the pages of her notebook. The suspenseful opening notes to Beethoven repeated on a loop. She chuckled. "Symphony Number Five?"

"Also the Victory Symphony." He winked, then answered, turning slightly away from her. "¿Halo?"

They didn't need to get back for a few hours, but Ariel packed away their things. That's when she saw him, sitting on a park bench. Someone who shouldn't be there, *couldn't* be there. He couldn't.

Hoping he somehow hadn't seen her, Ariel turned around. Shoved her notebook in her backpack. Neatly tucked away Eric's guitar.

"Are you fucking serious?" Eric shouted.

She whirled at the stress in his voice. But instead of finding him angry, she saw his face split into the most radiant smile. He gave Ariel a thumbs-up, then told Odelia he'd be right over.

"What happened?"

"We sold out," he said, arms extended for her.

She stepped into his hold and hugged him. Pride overwhelmed her in a way she hadn't felt for so long. They had earned this. They deserved this. "That's incredible."

"She wants us to record some videos for social. I actually blacked out for a second. I should get back." He pressed a kiss to her temple, like he didn't think twice about that kind of affection.

"Go." She gave him a tiny push in the right direction. "I still need to buy an outfit for Vanessa's set."

He hesitated, but she hurried him off. She watched him run off through a paved road winding under ancient trees. When he was out of sight, Ariel turned around to face the man waiting for her on a park bench. She took a seat beside him. His golden-brown skin glistened in the humidity.

"Hey, kiddo," Uncle Iggy said, looking like he was in a spy thriller, ready to hand her illicit documents. He took off his sunglasses and tucked them into the pocket of his crisp white button-down.

Ariel should have been angry. How had he found her? How did he know? She should have been furious. She'd *left*. She'd made her choice.

And yet, he was the same Uncle Iggy who stayed with her all night when she had her appendix removed and her dad was across the world on a business trip. He was the one who taught her all the old boleros and pasillos her mother once loved to listen to. Her father didn't want them played in the house because it hurt him to hear them. Uncle Iggy was her confidant when her father was angry. And even if he was her only uncle, he was still her favorite uncle. So, instead of screaming, she hugged him.

She hadn't realized she missed him until she felt him tremble with relief.

"I'm sorry." Why was she apologizing?

He kissed her forehead and took a good look at her. "I don't think I've ever gone this long without seeing you."

"You shouldn't be here." She gave a rough swipe to her burning eyes.

"*You* shouldn't be here." Uncle Iggy looked in the direction Eric had left. "Especially not with him."

"Why? Because he's not on Daddy's preapproved gold-digger list?"

Uncle Iggy pinched the bridge of his brow. His light brown skin shone like it was freshly exfoliated. His dark hair was dyed black, unlike her dad, who let himself go salt-and-pepper.

"Because you're lying to him," Uncle Iggy said.

Ariel looked down at her lap. "How did you find me?"

"I saw a viral video." His voice was tight. "Who do you think scouts talent for Atlantica Records?"

"I wasn't in his video," she said.

"No, but you are in Vanessa Garcia's."

She met his eyes. Only instead of the intense, feline stare of Teodoro del Mar, Ignacio's eyes were a softer, kinder brown. "So when you say I shouldn't be here with *him*, you mean it's because his manager is Odelia Garcia, who was once part of Luna Lunita."

Despite the very tasteful Botox, his brow flickered with emotion. "You know."

Ariel scoffed. "What happened between them?"

"There are some things that are not for you to know, Ariel."

"That's your answer? I bought the recalled album. He didn't get rid of all of them."

"Is that what she told you?" he asked.

"No one's told me anything. I only want the truth."

"The truth?" Uncle Iggy deflated with a sigh. "What do you think your truth will do to that boy? Do you think he wants to know the truth of who you are?"

"It's not the same."

"Maybe. Maybe all secrets are made to hurt. Maybe you've had your fun, and it's time to come home." Uncle Iggy rubbed the back of his neck, frustrated. "I'm not saying you have to move back to the penthouse. I'll find you a new place. There's a great listing on the East Side. We could put a whole Central Park between you and Teo. We'll even push the album back."

"There is no album!" she shouted. She never shouted. People glanced at her, and she took a deep, steadying breath.

"You have a contract." His voice never wavered. He was the calm to his brother's storm. That's why they functioned so well together.

"I don't. I never signed a new one. And if he wants to sue me, fine. He's the one with the access to my money. Tell him to pay himself."

"Ariel." Hearing her name on his lips was a fresh reminder of who she had been. Who she still was. Her father's perfect doll, singing and acting and dancing for the world.

"It was never my dream," she said finally. She'd said it in Miami the night before her birthday. Her first without her sisters. But she'd never said it out loud before then, hadn't even let herself admit it. "It was never my dream."

"It's not about dreams. It's business."

"I thought it was family," she scoffed. "You can't choose one or the other when it's convenient."

"This isn't going to end the way you think it will," he said. "Have you even thought that far ahead? I'm not asking to upset you. I really want you to think about it. What about when Eric wants to meet your family? What about when your father lashes out?"

Ariel took a deep breath. "Did you tell him where I am?"

Uncle Iggy shook his head. "Officially, I'm talent-scouting in Miami. Shit, I'm surprised Odelia hasn't already told him."

"Maybe you don't know her as well as you thought."

"Neither do you." Something in the way he said that made her rein back her anger.

"You going to snitch?" Ariel asked.

"Easy. I'm still your uncle." He sighed, frustrated. "I hate this, Ariel. Tell me, what will it take to stop all of this?"

"What are you worried about? My image?" She looked around the park. No one more than glanced their way. "I was never going to be that bleached Barbie he came up with for a solo act. It's not me. I already told him what I wanted, but it's too late. Now I'm going to do it on my own terms."

He pressed his lips together, like he'd understood he wasn't going to get anywhere. "Be careful, Ariel. Your father thinks he's doing what's best, too, and look at where he is now."

"I'm not like him," she said.

Uncle Iggy gave her a kiss on the forehead, brushing away an errant tear as he looked at her with all the pride and love a father should. "Maybe. But from where I'm standing, you're turning in one costume for another."

"I have to go," she said. "You should, too. I'm sure he'll send out a search party for you soon."

Uncle Iggy frowned at that. "You know where to reach me. *Melody*."

Ariel left first, walking until her legs decided she needed to run.

LONE STAR MUSIC MAGAZINE
Priscilla Muñoz

Hoo boy, have I got a rec for y'all. I caught this band on a whim with my brother and sister-in-law over the weekend in Dallas. Star Crossed is the splashy new band on the scene. Anything with a pretty front man himbo is usually a pass from me. But from the second they went onstage, I one-clicked their album, and bought their vinyl at the booth. A little pop, a lot of rock, a ton of dope-ass melodies. This is the real deal. I got mega Juanes meets Paramore with a sprinkle of classic arena rock.

Featuring Vanessa G with the mysterious "M" and Le Poisson Bleu, this is a tour where even the opening acts are *fuego*. You'd better get your tix now because they are quickly selling out the southwest leg of their tour. I'm starting to think I'm one of these #StarCrossedLovers after all. Five ole Texas stars from me!

7.7 • Austin, TX • Vanguard Hall – **SOLD OUT**

7.9 • Albuquerque, NM • First Contact Live – **SOLD OUT**

7.10 • Tucson, AZ • The Return of Saturn – **SOLD OUT**

7.11 • San Diego, CA • Rodgers Theater – **SOLD OUT**

7.12 • Los Angeles, CA • The Walter Estate Theater

7.15 • Las Vegas, NV • Vegas Bowl – **SOLD OUT**

7.16 • Portland, OR • Howling Rock

7.17 • Seattle, WA • Seattle Rock Live

7.18 • Missoula, MT • The Norma

7.19 • Salt Lake City, UT • The Canyon

7.20 • Denver, CO • Alpine Cavern

7.21 • Tulsa, OK • River Styx Crossing

7.23 • Manhattan, KS • The Little Apple Music Hall

7.24 • St. Cloud, MN • Cloud Nine

7.25 • Chicago, IL • House of Blues

7.26 • Cleveland, OH • Tenderloin Tavern

7.27 • Rochester, NY • River Run Works

7.28 • Burlington, VT • The Barn

7.30 • Boston, MA • Hunter's

7.31 • New York City, NY • Aurora's Grocery

CHAPTER NINETEEN

ERIC

Dallas → Austin

7.9 Albuquerque, New Mexico

During their VIP meet-and-greet, Eric was bone tired. The previous "day off" had consisted of back-to-back interviews and radio segments, practice, and a promising conversation with the head of their label. He felt held together by espresso shots, Melody's snail under-eye cream, and a prayer. And yet, he'd never been happier. The band signed notebooks, album covers, T-shirts. One girl wanted Eric to sign her chest, and he offered her a selfie instead.

As the fans left, Odelia sashayed her way across the cavernous music hall that was First Contact Live. The outside was a repurposed airport hangar, and the owners had turned it into an alien-themed venue. Oz was positively ecstatic and had probably blown an entire check on merch.

"You're very good at that," Odelia said, perching beside Eric at the edge of the stage. "When I was their age, I was just trying to get the lead singer from Maná to sweat on me from the front row."

Max pursed her lips with surprise. "There is so much I still don't know about you."

Their manager winked. "Never give away all your secrets."

"*You're* in a good mood," Carly said.

"I'm always in a good mood." Odelia turned her multicolored eyes on the guitarist. "Anyway, I have an update from the label."

Star Crossed gathered around her. Eric held his breath and rubbed his saint pendant. Contract. Contract. Contract.

It was not a contract.

"They're giving us a budget for the music video, so we can do your *vision*, Eleanor." Odelia was the only one who called Grimsby by her first name. Their manager held up a long red nail. But she was quiet for so long he thought he might have a heart attack from the anticipation. "They got us Sol Terrero."

It took a second for the words to make sense. Sol Terrero had made every relevant music video for the biggest Latin pop stars. And she was going to work with them. All he could manage at first was "Holy shit."

Max, behind her drums, doled out a loud, joyous clash of sound. She thrust her sticks in the air. The rest of them piled onto Odelia, who allowed maybe ten seconds of hugging before she started telling them to get back to work.

Eric searched the hangar for Melody to share the news. He found her and Vanessa. And Louie, the lead singer from Le Poisson Bleu. He didn't find Louie particularly funny, and every interaction had been him disparaging everything he didn't like about the cities they visited. But whatever he was saying had Melody and Vanessa laughing.

He wanted to be the one making Melody laugh. He wanted to be the one telling her his good news. She was in a see-through neon-pink shirt and a black leather miniskirt that skimmed the sides of her beautiful golden thighs. He watched Vanessa smirk, then Louie reach for a strand of Melody's hair. He wound the dark brown wave around his finger. An irrational sense of protection overwhelmed him. Jealousy gnawing at him like he was fresh meat.

As his bandmates ran around the stage, he decided to go and see what Louie had said that was so hilarious even Vanessa was giggling. Yet a strong force blocked his path: Odelia, arms crossed, her buxom figure accentuated by the black and red roses splashed across her chest.

"She's a big girl," Odelia said.

"I know." He sounded petulant, so very unlike himself. "I was going to say hi."

Odelia clapped her hands together, like a prayer. He could see she was working up the strength to give her unflinching opinion. She was usually so straightforward. It wasn't like her to hesitate.

"We are so close, Eric. We have great traction. Solid numbers. Every day we're doing a little better. Sol Terrero! I need to know you're still in the game. I need you to focus."

"I am." He said it again, with more gusto. "I am."

"Then why are you about to march over there like a jealous prick? Melody doesn't belong to you."

Eric blistered at her words. He couldn't deny it. Melody wasn't *his* in the way he wanted her to be. Odelia had warned him about that complication early on. He sighed hard. "I've never actually felt jealousy before. It's not a natural emotion for me."

She laughed dryly. "Melody smiles at the person who cuts her off in the Starbucks line."

"True enough."

"Has something happened between you two?" Odelia asked, and he couldn't avoid her probing stare. Yes. No. Yes and no. His manager detested indecision.

"No, don't worry."

"That's my secret. It's my job to worry." She sighed, frustrated. "If it's an ego thing, you don't have anything to worry about."

"Yeah," Eric said, all bravado. "He's fine, if you like that European supermodel type."

"I don't believe in stoking male egos, but you're currently a—what did Vanessa call it? A virus. A maymay?"

"Viral meme." He snorted and took her gentle slap of his shoulder in stride. He needed to confide in someone who would give him tough, real advice. Perhaps that's why he told Odelia, "I've never felt this way before. When I'm awake, I think about her. When I'm asleep, I dream about her. I hear her voice everywhere, even when I'm the one singing. I know she likes me, but she's been pulling away. I don't know what I did, or—"

"Eric, I want you to be careful." Odelia had none of her boss-lady attitude, none of the sharpness of the woman he knew he could trust to guide him through an industry that was big and confusing.

"I'm not going to hurt her." He was edging on defensive. It was all jokes with his friends, until it wasn't. Not anymore.

"It's not her I'm worried about. It's you." She glanced away, bit down on her unusual display of emotion. "This is exciting. The whirlwind romance of a tour. It's easy to get swept up in someone. But sooner or later, we all go home."

He wasn't sure what she was saying. "I thought you liked Melody."

"That has nothing to do with it. Just—be careful with your heart. You're a good man. I don't want to see you get hurt."

"I'll be fine," he said, but an uneasiness that hadn't been there before was trying to take root inside him. He wouldn't let it. "Come. I'm starving."

They split up in Central Avenue. New buildings changed the desert cityscape once composed of Pueblo-Deco architecture. He'd only ever spent time in Miami and New York, and he drank in the warmth of each new city's colors and people. Melody found a restaurant called

Aloha Mabuhay, a Hawaiian-Filipino place. Max had been particularly homesick, but the minute they sat down, she brightened.

"How did you find this place?" Max asked Melody, between bites of her adobo chicken over white rice. The first time he'd met Max, he'd been very confused at how Filipino adobo was so different from Latino adobo but equally delicious.

"When we're close to a city, I zoom in on the map for places to eat and visit, and names pop up at me."

"For your never-have-I-ever list?" Vanessa added, with a knowing arch of her brow. She leaned in to see their merch girl's scribbles.

Melody hurriedly closed her notebook. "I feel like you all should have a to-do list, too. Even if it's just a wish list."

"Play a sold-out concert back home," Carly said without hesitation. "Take my parents on a vacation."

"I'd like my parents to see us at the show in Missoula," Grimsby added. "My mom was the one who signed me up for mandolin lessons when I was little. I don't know. Hope she comes."

Max moved on to the syrupy-sweet halo-halo. "To be honest, guys, this is it for me. Tour. My buds. This is the dream! Although I am looking forward to taking down the house in Vegas."

"Can I come with?" Oz asked. "I was going to go on a chupacabra-search excursion, but I've never been to the desert before and I require twenty-four-hour air conditioner."

"*We* can take down the house," Max said.

"Easy, tiger," Vanessa warned as Max and Oz nearly vibrated out of their seats from the sugar and the promise of card-counting schemes. "I would like to find a record label that wants me exactly as I am. So far, everyone we've talked to wants to turn me into a diva or change my sound completely. I appreciate someone with a vision, but I want to stay true to myself."

"You should stay true," Melody said, and they shared a shy smile.

"We'll get there, baby girl," Odelia said, pinching the musubi between her red talons. "Never doubt."

They launched into a guessing game of things Eric Reyes would put on his wish list: a gold statue of himself, to chart on the *Billboard* list, a massive record label, a harem of beautiful models, and so on. They all turned to him, waiting for a response.

Eric crossed his arms over his chest. "I'm not telling."

Looking at his people, his team, his friends, the girl of his dreams, what more could he ask for? There could always be *more*, but if there wasn't, he could say he already had everything.

"Fine," he said. "A six-figure record deal and to write an anthem for the FIFA World Cup."

They kept making their wish lists. Though Melody had been sitting next to him the whole time, it was the first time since they sat down that she grinned solely at him, her chin resting on her palm. "Louie asked me something today."

Eric nodded along coolly. "Did he? Hadn't noticed."

"He asked if you were single."

"And what did you tell him?" He leaned in, like the table and the restaurant had vanished. God, he wanted nothing more than to kiss her.

"I said time will tell."

The same words he'd said in that interview when posed with the same question. Time will tell. Her eyes flicked to his mouth, and she frowned a little, as if she felt guilty for looking. For flirting. He wanted to hold her attention, since she'd found every way to put a buffer between them since New Orleans.

"I like the song you added to our playlist," he whispered.

Melody's lips were glossy, the pink of flowers from his mother's garden. "I was on a nineties R&B kick. It's your turn."

It felt like all his spare time, what little of it he had, was spent cycling through the perfect songs. "What are you in the mood for?"

Melody's cheeks matched her lips then, and she reached for her milky iced tea, leaving a pink imprint on the thick white straw. "*Hmm.* Something . . . that reminds you of your best day."

"Any genre?"

"Any genre."

The slap of Odelia's chair drew their attention. Eric thought she'd fallen, but their manager was standing, her phone in hand. He'd seen Odelia angry, happy, so pissed she'd erupt like a volcano, tipsy, flirty. But he'd never truly seen her shocked. Her eyes teared up, and she clutched at her chest.

"What's wrong?" His mind went straight to Tío Antonio.

"Curséd?" Max asked.

"What?" Vanessa asked. "Mom?"

Slowly, Odelia's composure returned. A smile played at her features. It made her look younger, the girl he'd seen pictures of in Miami. A girl who had dreamed so big, she never let heartbreak and setbacks stop her.

"We hit."

"Hit what?" Carly gasped, whirling on Oz, who in turn jingled the keys in his pocket and said, "Not it!"

Odelia handed over her phone, and everyone at the table gathered around. Eric read and reread the message to make sure that he had read it right. That it was really their name.

"Love Like Lightning," Star Crossed #100.

He wasn't sure who screamed first, but soon they were all joining in, screaming and hugging and bounding up and down the restaurant. Odelia hugged him fiercely, and for a moment, he thought he'd want nothing more than to be held by his parents. His grandfather.

"Gracias, Pedro," he whispered, kissing his thumb and pressing it to his heart, then the ceiling.

Eric was sure he'd hugged everyone, but then there she was. Melody Marín, arms open to him. He gathered her into his arms. He

241

was getting used to the feel of her. The way she clung around his neck and fit, like he'd been carved for her, if she wanted.

When he set her down, he had an idea. In a few days they had to shoot the "Love Like Lightning" video. And Eric knew exactly who he wanted to cast.

THE TUTTLE TELLER

Episode 1375:
Siren Seven: From Humble Beginnings to Music Royalty (Part IV)

Transcript:
In 2016, following the biggest years the sisters had, the family became a subject of controversy when Marilou let it slip in an interview that their father still controlled their finances. When asked about it, Teodoro del Mar issued a no comment stance. Y'all already know what I think!

Young celebrities have pushed boundaries that their parents set. We've all seen stars crash and burn. But Siren Seven has remained true to the "good girl" image they've cultivated since their television show days. What is happening now?

I've heard rumors that Sophia del Mar is going back to college and plans to break her sisters free from their father's grip. Do we think that's why Ariel has gone off the rails?

I hope you know, Ariel, wherever you are and wherever you go next, your fans are rooting for you.

As for Daddy del Mar, shame on you!

Loving Dadager or Overprotective Tyrant? Tell me what you think in the comments.

By the by, what is everyone listening to? I've been into this "Love Like Lightning" song after Marilou del Mar liked the band's post this week.

Tuttle out!

CHAPTER TWENTY

ARIEL
Tucson ✈ San Diego

7.12 Los Angeles, California

Ariel del Mar had experienced the reality-blurring effects of touring when she was with Siren Seven. Sometimes she didn't know what day it was or what city they were in. Once, in Tokyo, she'd thanked Toronto for being such a great audience. Thankfully, she'd been able to play it off, and the crowd had been forgiving.

Now, with Star Crossed, she still barely knew where she was, but she felt more present. Grounded in a way she hadn't when half of her day included a glam squad that had signed an NDA to even enter the same room as any of the del Mar girls.

On the bus, Ariel was the factory-setting version of herself. Like at home, she still woke up first, she still had a penchant for staring at the sky and search for their constellation—the Pleiades, the Seven Sisters from Greek mythology. She still drank unhealthy amounts of ginger ale, and she still spent every moment between songs and backstage jotting down lyrics and thoughts and feelings, or working on her playlist with Eric.

She was the same, and she wasn't. She was different and she wasn't. And why should she have to choose? She decided she was going to tell them all. But as they went from Albuquerque to Tucson to San Diego to Los Angeles, she faltered. The anxiety Troll dolls that plagued her as Ariel del Mar also plagued her as Melody Marín.

When the Beast parked at the soundstage before dawn, Ariel was uncharacteristically the last one out of bed. She'd been avoiding that disappointed look on Eric's face when she declined the offer to be his video girl. She wanted to say yes. How could she not? Grimsby's concept was creative and fun, but she didn't want to chance it. If things went wrong, if all this imploded, she would always be tied to one of the most important moments of his career. She'd seen it happen to other artists. It would be like the musical equivalent of getting a tattoo of a lover and then regretting it, except without the possibility of a cover-up. He hadn't pushed, but she could see his disappointment when he thought she wasn't looking. The thing was, she was always looking.

Ariel quickly yanked on her latest thrift store finds—blue velvet joggers and a white tank top. She felt emotionally hungover from her own anxiety, but pulled it together and followed the rest of the crew out of the bus and onto the lot. When a security guard who'd been working there for decades did a double take at the sight of her, she kept her pink baseball cap low. If it worked for the Avengers, it could work for her.

"How does it feel to be back on your old stomping grounds?" Odelia whispered as the two of them trailed behind the excited band.

"Strange," she said honestly. "It's like walking through someone else's memories, almost. I can't explain it. It was the same way being onstage with Vanessa, but it's freeing at the same time."

"Have you thought about what you're going to do after the tour?"

Ariel nodded. "Eric wants us to write a few songs together. But you knew that."

Odelia made a noncommittal noise. "You want to tell him."

"I mean, those are my two options. I tell him, or I vanish into the ether." She chuckled humorlessly. "I can guess which one you'd choose."

"I'm not the villain, Melody." The manager admonished her with a red claw. "You started this farce. You figure it out. You wanted to be in the real world. Here it is."

They walked in silence for a beat. Ariel remembered what Uncle Iggy had implied. That she didn't know Odelia. What would the older woman say if she knew how closely her family was following the tour? The del Mars were clearly a sore subject, but no one would tell her what happened.

"I'm not saying you're the villain," Ariel told her. "I just know how you feel about my family. That's got to influence how you feel about me."

"Don't presume to know me, Melody." Odelia nodded at the next guard who they walked past. "The last few weeks, I've seen how unlike your father you are. You're kind. You think of others first. You remind me of your mother, actually. I never told you how sorry I was to read about the accident."

Ariel felt a pang of sadness. It was always there, resurfacing at odd moments. When she brushed her teeth and hummed her mom's favorite song, when she laughed particularly loudly.

"But there's so much you don't understand." Odelia let out an exhausted sigh. "You and Eric come from different worlds. He wants fame and tours and the life you're running from."

Ariel had thought of that for days since Sophia had brought it up. She couldn't help but laugh at the irony. "My older sister said the same thing."

Why couldn't everyone see that she wasn't running from music, but running toward a future of her own making? She wanted that future to include Eric, and all her friends from the tour.

"Eric needs to focus," Odelia said, as if Ariel needed a reminder of their first bargain. "There's a label representative coming to Vegas, and a scout coming to see Vanessa. Whatever you decide, do it when the tour is over."

"I will," Ariel assured her. Then she had an idea. She'd already been helping Vanessa as backup with her sets. What if she could help in other ways? She'd never suggest that they work with her father, but Ariel's name still carried influence, even if her sisters were doing a good job turning her image upside down. "Maybe I can help. With scouts for Vee."

It was the wrong thing to say. Odelia glowered at Ariel, but they had no time to continue their conversation as they filed into the soundstage building behind the others. A green screen was set up along with a ginormous pool that reminded her of the set from *The Little Mermaids*. She took a picture and sent it to her sisters.

Thea:
Awww!

Marilou:
You know I still can't swim?

Stella:
You are missing the chance to be a video vixen!

Elektra:
If she doesn't want to be a vixen,
she doesn't have to be!

Alicia:
Will he be in a Speedo? Send pics.

Sophia:
LOL triggered

While the shoot got underway, Melody sat in one of the tall chairs designated for the band members. It was surreal being there, ignored by dozens of crew members. The fear of returning to the movie lot had been scary, but she was surprised at how refreshing, almost *fun*, it was to be on the fringes of the action.

The Mexican American director, Sol Terrero, spoke with her hands, guiding the nervous band across the different sets. According to Grimsby's vision, the video featured Eric and a beautiful model named Adriana walking through glorious landscapes. The Mojave Desert. The rainbow mountains of Peru. The Swiss Alps. A beach in Malta. Every time the couple got closer and closer to each other, they were torn apart with a strike of lightning.

Each member of Star Crossed was a polished version of themself. Grimsby wraithlike in a long black lace dress out of her Stevie Nicks fantasies. Max with freshly cut bangs and her lucky Hawaiian-print shirt. Carly all dewy brown skin and glossy curls blowing from the wind machine, in platform boots that made Vanessa's gaze linger. And Eric—

Eric.

The pit of her stomach fell every time Sol Terrero shouted "Cut!" and the makeup crew fussed over the short waves that kept wanting to flop over his forehead. The brushes dusted matte powder over his tawny complexion. He was in a loose white shirt unbuttoned to the middle of his chest, and the director and assistant director pointed at him like he was a Ken doll.

He made a silly face at her as wardrobe undid another button. Then the stylist brought him another change of pants. Blue this time.

"He looks like a pirate," Vanessa said, plopping down beside Ariel. She munched on a bag of Takis, picking them out with her long stiletto nails.

"I feel like he should be on the cover of one of those old romance paperbacks."

"Yeah, as a pirate." Vanessa laughed, and her black-and-purple hair fell over her shoulders. She cast a long glance at Ariel as the "video vixen" disrobed. Her dress was simple, flowing, pink. Black hair, lush and shiny, sprayed into place. She was breathtaking.

Vanessa snapped a picture of Ariel with the flash on.

"What are you doing?"

"Just documenting the first time you probably ever felt jealous."

Ariel pouted. "I'm not jealous. It's an ugly emotion. And besides, I turned down the job."

"Nope," Vanessa said, throwing a chip at her, which she deflected with her elbow. "Jealousy is hot. Within reason."

Ariel grabbed a handful of the spicy Takis and ate them, watching as the cameras rolled. Eric and Adriana got in the beautifully carved wooden boat. It was something out of a fairy tale, even if, at the moment, it was in front of a green screen.

The song blared and the cameras rolled, the boat spinning and spinning. It happened so quickly, she felt Vanessa react first, gasping as she cupped her hands over her mouth. The director yelled "*Cut!*" and everyone descended on the set.

"Did she fall in?" Ariel had been there. The water was always freezing, and not something she'd wish on anyone during a first take. Thankfully, the model hadn't fallen in. She was throwing up off the side of the boat.

"You are going to hell for laughing," Ariel told Vanessa.

"I can't help it. I laugh when I'm uncomfortable!"

Eric, ever the gentleman, carried Adriana in his arms and carefully handed her off to the medic team. The entire wardrobe and makeup squads then descended on him to get him cleaned up. A few feet away, the director and Odelia conferred, their heads bent conspiratorially. Every now and then, one of them would look up at Ariel, who ignored them and glared at Vanessa.

"How are you still eating?"

Vanessa didn't get to answer. Odelia and Sol Terrero were making a beeline for them. Ariel had a very bad feeling about what was about to go down.

"What happened?" Ariel asked.

Odelia dabbed the sleeve of her blouse on her forehead. "Adriana has an extreme form of motion sickness. She'd never been on a boat before, so she had no idea."

Ariel regretted her jealousy and felt terrible for the model. No one wanted to go through that with cameras rolling and dozens of people watching.

"You're up, Melody," Odelia said, while the director smiled aggressively beside her.

"Me?" Ariel shook her head. "I can't."

Sol pressed her hands together, taking a deep, calming breath. "It'll be B-roll, from the back and clever angles. We have kissing doubles *all* the time when two stars hate each other. All that's left is the boat kiss, and right now you're the closest we've got to Adriana."

"K-kissing double?" Ariel repeated.

"Even if we call one of the alternates, it will take time to get here in this traffic," Sol said, still keeping her prayer hands up.

From her experience, Ariel knew it was such a huge, expensive set piece, no one would want to waste it. Plus, they had a show that night, so they had today and today only. She'd always *wanted* to do it but had been afraid. She needed to have some of Eric's eternal optimism. Needed to believe that things would work out between them, between everyone.

"Do you want to do this?" Odelia asked. Though the band manager was serious, Ariel understood she was truly asking, not only supporting the band, but Ariel, too. Odelia Garcia would not force her to get onstage or sing and dance, not if the answer was no. That support alone made it easier for her to answer.

"I do. I mean, I'll do it."

Because you want to kiss him. Because you've wanted to kiss him for days, for weeks, and this wouldn't break any rules.

Sol Terrero moved like every second was accounted for and had a dollar value, which it certainly did. Ariel was rushed away to change and have some light makeup applied, since they wouldn't need to use her actual face. The beautiful dress was a coral pink that made her feel like her whole body was blushing. The structured bodice and sweetheart neckline accentuated her waist, and the chiffon skirt billowed around her like something out of a dream.

The makeup artists complimented her on how well she took care of her nails, hair, and skin, making their job easier. One of them pushed up her boobs and cinched the ribbon around her waist until she could only just breathe. She took a final moment alone and brushed her teeth to get the spicy Takis taste off her tongue. She laughed, not caring who heard her. After everything she'd done, here she was again.

"There you are," she told her reflection.

This time, though, when she spun on her bare feet, she felt like the entirety of herself. Melody Ariel Marín Lucero. Two parts of the same whole. If the moon could have two sides to her, so could she.

As Ariel walked across the soundstage, she heard distinctly flirty whistles from her friends. She approached the ginormous pool, climbed the steps, and several hands helped her into the boat, where Eric was already waiting. Wardrobe must have stripped him clean, because he was in entirely new clothes. A soft cream-colored Henley (still unbuttoned as far as it would go) that hugged the swell of his muscles, and black pants with a strip of gold piping down the sides. The black waves of his hair were artfully disheveled, and though he'd been touched up, he still looked like Eric Reyes.

He stood when he saw her. Their boat was secured to the pool by a metal contraption, but she felt it wobble. Or was it her own legs giving under his searing gaze?

"You look—"

She tucked her hair behind her ear before remembering to stop touching it. He didn't finish his sentence. He could have said "you look fine" or "you look like you're also going to puke on me, but please don't," and she was fairly certain she'd still react to him the same way—like she was doing her best impression of a jellyfish.

"*You* look," she said, as they took their marks on the benches. Face-to-face.

Strange hands appeared all around and fluffed her dress, spritzed hair spray on her unruly baby hairs, adjusted the gold pendant on his shirt. Somehow, someone found another button on that Henley to undo. At that last one, they broke down laughing.

"You're enjoying this," she said.

"Immensely." He nodded, strong shoulders easing as he got comfortable. Their knees brushed together, and she felt that pull toward him that was impossible to resist. While they adjusted the lights and Sol discussed angles with her AD, Eric whispered, "I'm sorry. I know you didn't want to do this, but thank you."

She took in the slight nervousness in the way he ran a hand along his sharp jaw. And maybe it was because she felt a little bolder, a little more settled in her own skin, but she said, "I wanted to say yes right away. I didn't want you to regret it down the line."

"All right, lovebirds," Sol Terrero said, popping what was either an antacid or candy into her mouth. "Last shot of the day, but the most important one. Eric, you look at her like she's the only person in the world for you. Melody, you look at him like he is an all-you-can-eat buffet and you've been on a three-day fast."

Eric's eyes were wide, lips pressed together to try to stop himself from laughing. Ariel had to quit looking at him because otherwise she would break, and then they'd never start filming.

"Got it," Ariel said, clearing her throat. "When do you, um, want us to, you know . . ."

"Kiss?"

Dammit, she was regressing to her very first on-screen tween romance, when she had to give CPR to a half-drowned heartthrob and could barely get a word out.

"When it feels natural," Sol said, chewing and chewing on the chalky candy. "Talk, talk, talk, act like you're having a deep conversation, and then go for it. So, like, be yourselves, but elevated. Natural, but sexy. Kinetic but approachable. Sweet but spicy."

"Are we getting seasoned, or . . . ?" Eric asked teasingly.

"Cute," Sol said, popping another mystery candy into her mouth. She wound her finger around the air and shouted, "Quiet on set!"

After a final fluff of fabric and hair, the director yelled, "Action!"

As the boat began to gently spin, it felt like the entire lot was holding their breath, waiting to see if Ariel would lose her lunch. (She didn't.) "Love Like Lightning" played in the background, and she tapped her feet to the catchy guitar rhythm.

"So," Eric began, defusing the awkwardness of the cameras with his easy smile. "Be honest."

"Okay."

"Do I look enough like a buffet?"

"Shut up. You know you do." Ariel made the mistake of looking off to the side, where Sol wordlessly signaled for her to look back at her leading man.

"What did you mean before?" Eric asked softly. "When you said you worried I'd regret this."

"Oh, so we're jumping right in?"

"I mean, it's just the two of us and our closest film set friends."

She was thankful they didn't require mics for this. But he was right. Even when surrounded by friends and strangers, being with Eric made the rest of the world easy to forget.

"My life before you met me is complicated," she explained. "I come with a lot of baggage, and there is still so much you don't know about me. About who I am. My family."

"Six sisters and a tyrannical father," he said. "I've heard about this cult."

Ariel laughed, and the director shouted, "Perfect!"

"Tell me," he whispered. "What are you afraid of? You never answered, that day in the elevator."

"I think my answer has changed since then. I would have said I'm scared of horror movies and losing my family the way I lost my mother. I would have said that I'm scared of being myself because I've spent my entire life trying to make everyone else happy and sort of . . . forgot along the way."

He held out his hand. Turned it palm side up. A lifeline. She took it and held on tight. "Tell me."

Ariel's heartbeat quickened. "Now, I'm afraid who I really am isn't enough. That I'm always going to be chasing a version of myself that maybe doesn't exist. Maybe things are always changing, and there's no real point in trying to hold on to a version of yourself that is already gone."

"I might be wildly optimistic, but I'm pretty sure I will want every version of you, Melody."

"You don't know that," she said, her words a little scratchy with how much she wanted to believe him.

"I think I do." He brought her right hand to the center of his chest. She felt the frantic rhythm of his heart, the steady certainty in his eyes. Ariel felt herself pulled to him like a lonely star surrendering to a planet's orbit. That's what being near him felt like. Surrendering.

From behind the blinding light, the director boomed, "Okay, lovebirds, smooch it up!"

Eric's smile twitched, entirely too amused. "Can I kiss you?"

Ariel couldn't speak. The words were stuck. Not because she had any doubts, but because her mind and her body were short-circuiting with wanting too much. With how surreal, how ridiculous, how utterly perfect it was that her first kiss with Eric Reyes was in a boat on a music video set.

Because she'd been silent a beat past comfortable, she nodded at the same time that she leaned in. The only hitch was that he was leaning in, too, and their foreheads collided. There was an audible *thunk*, and she snorted into his chest as he did his best to remain composed.

"Smooth," he said, laughing.

"Cut!" Sol shouted. "Melody, this time let's try it with Eric moving in first."

She wanted to dive into that pool with embarrassment, but was pretty certain that they hadn't fully drained it after the first model's accident.

"I'd honestly thought we'd be better at this," Eric said, wiping a tear from the corner of his eye.

They shook it off, and this time, she did exactly as Sol said. This time they didn't talk, they didn't fall into a fit of laughter. He smiled at her, nervous, sweet. She tried to breathe like a normal human instead of holding her breath as she waited. Waited. And just when she thought he was having second thoughts, Eric's brown stare flicked to her lips, and he came close.

She felt the hitch in his breath, the brush of his nose against hers.

She wanted to laugh because she'd thought about kissing him day and night and in the moments in between. And here he was, shy and careful at first. His cheek brushing hers, the tickle of lashes on flushed skin. He was teasing her, coming close, then pulling a fraction of an inch away.

Ariel tapped her lips against his. A dare. A promise. She felt his smile against hers, then the velvet pressure of his tongue teasing his way inside. He tasted like sour apple Jolly Ranchers, sweet and bright. And then he was gone too soon, pulling away to steady himself.

"Cut!" Sol walked the plank to get closer. "Great. Good stuff. This time, loosen up a bit."

They ran through the song again, their fairy-tale canoe gliding across the surface of the water in steady circles. Eric was an excellent kisser. Gentle, patient. His lips were firm against hers. His hands skimmed her arms, her bare shoulders. She was grateful for the fans because her skin felt ignited everywhere he touched. And yet, during each new take, Eric pulled back first, growing more and more rigid. Second guessing how he touched her, like she was something delicate and fragile.

"Eric," she whispered, as they reset and touched up their clothes and hair. Her lips were sticky with lip gloss, and she finally licked them clean. It's not like her face was in the shot.

"Melody," he whispered back.

"Tell me." She hoped he understood what she meant. They'd spent weeks dancing around each other, trying not to kiss. And now that they were given permission, that they were rehearsing it over and over again, he was showing an incredible amount of restraint. She could see it in the way he ran his palms over his thighs, the way a muscle throbbed along his jaw, the way his eyes were almost hazy from his self-control.

He got close, his breath at her ear so his words were only for her.

"If I kiss you the way I want to kiss you, I'm afraid this video will get banned in several countries."

A delicious liquid sensation pooled low in her belly. She swallowed, her tongue dry, and cleared her throat. She wanted that. She wanted that very much.

"Show me," she said, challenging him.

This time, when the director started rolling, there were no cameras. No people. The set might as well have been an open sea, for Eric and Ariel alone. They met each other halfway. The crush of his mouth was rougher than the first dozen times. He nipped at her lower lip, then chased the sting away with soft, silken kisses. His eyes fluttered shut, and the initial reservation evaporated. There was the roar of her pulse in her ears, the firm pressure of his tongue. Dizzy with want, she held on to him, tugging him closer by the front of his shirt. The rough calluses of his fingers skated up and over her shoulders. One hand rested at the base of her neck, the other pinned her by her waist. She felt the sturdy strength of him, and though they were flush against each other, she wanted him even closer.

"Eric." She gasped his name, just his name, because kissing Eric Reyes was not like falling, as she'd expected. It was like soaring, sailing through a feeling she had tried to capture in song but had never truly felt until that moment. Was this what real love felt like? Heady and molten, like she was unable to do anything but *feel* and want?

"I said cut!" Sol shouted, likely not for the first time, the feedback of her megaphone snapping Ariel's attention. Someone on the soundstage whistled a catcall, and she was fairly certain it was Vanessa.

Ariel and Eric returned to their canoe benches, lips swollen and pink. He grinned at her, and he looked so achingly handsome she knew that no matter what happened, she would remember every detail of that moment.

After a beat of silence when Ariel thought (hoped) they might have to do another take, the director announced, "All right, people, that's a wrap on 'Love Like Lightning!'"

Later that night, after the concert, when she should have been sleeping in her bunk like everyone else, Ariel del Mar was still spinning.

Her phone buzzed. Eric's name lit up her screen. Usually, she was the one who kept odd hours, but her pulse raced again knowing he was up, and he was thinking of her.

> **Eric:**
> Hi . . .

She yanked back the privacy curtain, the crush of fabric so loud in the quiet of the bus. Eric did the same, and they shared a secret smile in the dark. The glow of his phone illuminated the mischief on his face as he typed. Her phone buzzed again.

> **Eric:**
> I know we had a shaky start, but
> I think we finished strong.

> **Melody:**
> The kiss, or your set tonight?

> **Eric:**
> Ouch

Eric:

The kiss

He looked at her then, his eyes so dark they were all consuming. She wanted to ask if he'd meant it. If he would truly want every version of her. If he'd counted every take the way she had. Thirteen. They'd kissed thirteen times.

He was typing again, and she waited for the message to pop up.

Eric:

I want to do it again.

Melody:

Well. You know what they say.

Melody:

Practice makes perfect.

~~ARIEL'S~~ MELODY'S LIST FOR LIVING ON LAND

Ride a bike ✓

Go to a movie alone

Sit at a coffee shop and read a book ✓

Get lost in a city ✓

Have a crush ✓ ✓

Bowling? ✓

Take a long walk

Go on a real date

Eat whatever I want ✓

Fall in love

Make new friends ✓

Get a job I want and love

Buy my own guitar

Get a nonaquatic pet

Laundry? ✓

Epic kiss ✓

Handwrite letters

Take the bus?

~~Tattoo?~~ Tattoo

Learn to say no

Move out

Catharsis

CHAPTER TWENTY-ONE

ARIEL

7.13 Somewhere on the Las Vegas Freeway

On some dusty road across the desert, the Beast barreled toward Nevada. Even though it was the crack of dawn, everyone was up. There was a reservation waiting for them at the Van Luxen Hotel and Casino, and one full weekend off. Because they were never alone on a tour bus, Ariel and Eric worked on the bridge of their song. They didn't talk about their late-night texts, but they sat, with legs touching on the front lounge couch. She'd correct his finger position on the fretboard. He'd untuck her pen from behind her ear to jot down his thoughts.

"Are we slowing down?" Grimsby asked, playing with Monty the guinea pig and the squeaky unicorn cat.

They came to a full stop and followed their frazzled bus driver out onto the road. The cool desert morning and cotton-candy sky were incongruous with the sight before them. The engine was steaming. Big billowing puffs of gray smoke chugged from the front of the Beast. Oz crossed his arms behind his head and made a high-pitched keening sound.

Eric pointed at Max and warned, "Don't say it."

Odelia was verging on her "nightmare" phase. "Oz, where's the list of emergency numbers the coach company gave you?"

Their driver vanished into the bus and returned with a sheet of paper that had been chewed up by something small and furry.

Everyone turned to Grimsby, who was holding Monty protectively. "It's not her fault!"

"It's no one's fault," Eric said. "It's an old bus. Oz, don't you have the numbers on your phone?"

Oz shook his head, phone in one hand. "I'm trying to call my uncle, but he's not picking up."

"Wait, wait, wait, I found a mechanic nearby," Ariel said, pulling up the number. "If the page ever loads."

"I feel like I'm pretty much done with nature," Carly mumbled.

"Where even are we?" Max grumbled.

Eric pointed to a small sign, the green of the metal nearly bleached by the sun. "Paradise Palms."

"Aww, that sounds nice," Oz said.

But as the sun came up, scorching the side of the road, Vanessa pointed out, "The desert isn't my idea of paradise."

Ariel delivered the mixed bag of news to the group. Yes, there was a local mechanic, but the voicemail said he was off getting married. Another mechanic was on her way, but her shop was back in the direction they'd just come from. They waited in the sweltering sun for the longest twenty minutes of her life in a shared disgruntled silence, the heat souring everyone's mood.

The mechanic was named Glenda Sosa, a woman in cargo pants smeared in oil, and a denim shirt over a white tank top. Her black hair was braided into one long ponytail, and her bronze skin had deep wrinkles.

She looked from the Beast to their little motley crew. "Surprise, it's the engine. I can replace the part easily, but even if I have it overnighted from LA, the soonest I can get you out of here is Monday."

Ariel felt their collective intake of breath. The band had a gig at the Vegas Bowl on Monday.

"But," Glenda said, holding her hands up as if the sheer force of her gesture could stop their collective meltdown, "my girlfriend's coming to visit me today. So I can have her drive it to me. I can have you out of here tomorrow morning."

Odelia let out a relieved exhale. "I'll let Le Poisson Bleu know to go on ahead."

Glenda let them borrow a beat-up truck they could hitch the trailer with all their gear to and gave them an address for a nearby hotel called Paradisio. After thanking the mechanic with promises of their first-borns as long as she got them out of the desert on time, Oz, Odelia, and Max squeezed into the cabin of the truck while the rest climbed into the cargo bed.

"I've always wanted to eat dust for breakfast," Eric said, smirking at their predicament. "I think that's a new celebrity diet."

Carly sucked her teeth and squinted under the unforgiving sun. "Next tour, Monty stays home."

"Monty didn't break down the bus," Grimsby said defensively, her face covered in sunscreen and looking like she'd been hit in the face with a cream pie.

Vanessa lowered her sunglasses in Ariel's direction. "Aren't guinea pigs a delicacy in Ecuador?"

Ariel grinned. "That's right. When I was little my dad said that was the reason we couldn't have normal pets, which didn't make sense. Only fish."

"Fish are terrible pets," Grimsby argued, cradling Monty protectively. "They're secretive."

"I always wanted a pet python, but Mom always said no," Vanessa said.

"I wonder why," Ariel mused.

They went on that way, and despite the heat and the arid air, Ariel realized there was no place she'd rather be than sitting in the back of that pickup truck with Eric holding her hand like a silent promise between them.

Paradisio was the kind of hotel that must have been beautiful three decades in the past. It was all pinks and blues and greens, with palm trees that had seen better days, and giant cacti that almost looked like they were reclaiming the mini golf course.

There was a pool, a great big courtyard set up for an event, and then the main building. The place was packed.

"If it's another taxidermy convention—" Carly warned with a grimace.

"Wedding." Vanessa pointed to the welcome sign. "I don't think we'll get a room here."

"We'll see about that," Odelia said. "You all bring in the equipment."

Ariel, who had no desire to do the heavy lifting, tapped her nose and said, "Not it." She left them, a little stunned, and followed Odelia to the counter.

A frazzled man with ruddy cheeks and large glasses waved them forward. "Checking in?"

"Yes, we'd like four rooms, please."

The man, whose name tag read CALE, laughed in their faces, before he realized they were serious. He cleared his throat and typed on his keyboard without looking down. "You're in luck. I have two doubles left."

"Can you check again?" Ariel blinked her eyes and flashed her toothpaste-commercial smile. For a moment Cale seemed transfixed by her. "Please?"

Odelia rolled her eyes.

"There's really nothing I can do beyond that," Cale continued. "We are fully booked up for the wedding. The only reason these rooms are available is because the band canceled. Something about storms down south. I'm mainly worried because we're almost out of the open-bar beer, and it's only day one."

"Oh, goodness," Ariel said, joining in his commiserating.

"We'll take them." Odelia slapped her credit card on the plastic marble counter.

"Wonderful! That'll be five hundred dollars per night, plus a resort fee." He took a sip of his beer and accepted a flower garland one of the groomsmen was drunkenly handing out. "Per person, per day."

Odelia's jaw dropped, and Ariel could see the numbers floating in her head. The band didn't have that kind of money. She thought she could offer to pay, but would Odelia even accept that kind of help from her? And besides, Ariel had already spent half the money Sophia had given her. The solution came to her instantly.

"Actually—" Ariel felt Odelia watching her, felt the protective need to help her crew no matter what the cost. She had told so many half-truths over the last several days, but this was her first outright lie. "I think we have a misunderstanding. *We're* the band."

Odelia grinned deeply beside her, just as Eric and the others were trudging into the open lobby with their instruments. His eyes fell on Ariel, like he could find her in any crowd, and she had that soaring sensation again.

Ariel turned back to Cale, letting her voice climb to that bright soprano she'd used onstage for fifteen years. "Sorry. We should have mentioned that. As you can see, it was a journey to get here."

Cale sighed with relief. "Oh, thank goodness. One less disaster! I'll still need a card for incidentals, but your rooms are covered."

"Not bad, little mermaid," Odelia muttered under her breath as Cale was called away for another wedding-related emergency. "Now you just have to convince the bride and groom we're the band they hired."

"I've got this." Ariel was up for the challenge. She left Odelia to handle check-in and searched the lobby for someone from the wedding party.

The wallpaper was faded exotic flowers, and green glass lamps dotted most surfaces. People zoomed back and forth with wedding preparations. Ariel was drawn to one group's conversation when she heard *band* and *canceled*. A woman with a bedazzled T-shirt that read MAID OF HONOR was holding a pink electric fan pointed directly at the bride's face.

"Hi!" Ariel said, waving at them.

A bridesmaid and the mother of the bride turned to Ariel, who was still dusty and disheveled. "Yes?"

"I'm here with your wedding band." Ariel pointed at the members of Star Crossed. Eric, his thick mane of hair lightly covered in road dust. Carly, who was effortlessly cool. Max, twirling a drumstick in one hand and scrolling through her phone in the other, and Grimsby, who was holding her guinea pig by a leash. They were incongruous, a ragtag group, contradictions of each other, but when they got on that stage, they were one. Perfect.

"Wait, what?" the maid of honor asked.

Ariel waved her friends over. "Guys, I was just telling the lovely bridal party that we're the band, and we're checking into the last two rooms reserved for us."

"No, you're not," the bride said.

"Well, we're *a* band." Ariel softened her voice again, and watched as the women warmed toward her. Innocent, approachable, sweet. It was eerily better than a Jedi mind trick. "Since the other band got stuck because of the storms, the agency sent us."

One of the bridesmaids hiccupped, then asked, *"You're* a country band?"

Before she could panic, Grimsby opened up one of the instrument cases, smaller than her bass and with a sticker that read I ♥ MONTANA, and pulled out a mandolin and a harmonica.

"You bet," the platinum-blond bass player said, glaring at Carly.

"Well, I *am* from the South." Eric smirked, kneeling in front of the bridal party.

Behind Ariel, Carly coughed into her fist, "South *America*."

"I can play whatever you'd like," he said, in *that* voice. Velvet and low and tickling every corner of her heart chambers. There were audible sighs and swoons, and Ariel knew she was so close to having them.

"I present Star Crossed," Ariel said, putting on her best Siren Seven voice.

"Wait." Max's head snapped in Ariel's direction, doing a double take. The drummer squinted, then shook her head. "Never mind."

When she noticed their hesitation, Ariel added, "They've been playing a sold-out tour all month, and they happen to be the ones nearby. They *just* hit the top 100, so you're getting them before they become mega *huge*."

"Oh my god," the bride gasped, her fat tears completely drying up as she fanned herself. "It's fate."

"Fate," Ariel repeated, glancing up at Eric. "That's exactly what I was thinking."

The wedding theme seemed to be "bedazzled," which Vanessa ran with as she styled them. Leave it to the flyest girl on the tour bus to travel with a glue gun and a bag full of rhinestones.

The band took over the adjoining rooms that had been reserved for the original wedding band. Even Odelia had given Ariel a *nice work* pat on the back. Fitting eight people into two double rooms was tight, but they'd been living in a bus for weeks, and the accommodations were free.

Odelia, Vanessa, Ariel, and Max were in one room. Oz, Carly, Grimsby, and Eric were in the second room. They kept the connecting door open, both for ventilation and because it made getting ready easier.

Ariel couldn't find an ironing board in her room and went into the adjoining room to search their closet, without much luck.

Carly set her bag on the bed closest to the puke-pink bathroom. "Eric kicks in his sleep, so I'm sharing with Oz."

"I call first shower," Grimsby announced.

"Second!" Oz shouted at the same time as the others.

Grimsby peered into the bathroom and snorted. "No bears, Melody, in case you were wondering."

Ariel supposed it would've been too much to ask for Eric to let that embarrassing story die just between them.

Oz kicked off his shoes. "Don't worry. I would do the same. Bears are very untrustworthy."

For several hours, the rooms were chaos. It was the camaraderie she missed from getting ready in Sophia's dressing room, clothes and shoes and toiletries all over the place. Music blasting from someone's phone. Oz had nearly cleaned out the vending machine, and Ariel managed to track down housekeeping and promised to return the iron and ironing board. She carefully unpacked the dress Alicia had gifted her. It was a strappy lavender dress covered in iridescent sequins and real crystals. Delicate, but heavy. She hadn't thought she'd have an occasion to wear it, and the twins would be ecstatic to have proven her wrong.

"Where did you get that?" Max asked, stopping at the threshold between rooms. She wore a pretty rainbow print dress with buttons that Vanessa had glued rhinestones onto.

"A gift from my sister," Ariel said. It was the second time that day Max had looked at her strangely. And she was starting to suspect why.

Max frowned, but nodded, and returned to her side of the room, leaving Ariel to steam the wrinkles out of the straps and hem. Vanessa was running gel through Oz's curls one by one when Carly returned with a bottle of hair spray and a box of bobby pins.

"Got these from the maid of honor," she said. "Oh, I left my phone in the bathroom."

"Eric's still in there," Ariel said, grabbing a handful of hairpins.

"So another hour, then." Carly rolled her eyes, putting her ear to the door. "He's just shaving." She opened the door and let herself in.

Ariel wasn't sure who screamed first, Carly or Eric, but the lead guitarist emerged with her hand clapped over her eyes. Odelia and the others piled into the room, searching for the source of the calamity.

"What happened?" Odelia asked.

"I thought Eric was shaving!" Carly said, a big *yikes* smile plastered on her face. Eyes still shut.

Eric appeared at the door, bare chest heaving. His hair was damp and tousled. A tiny pink striped towel was clutched around his midsection. Her belly gave a tight squeeze at the sight of his smooth skin, his muscles.

"I *was* shaving," he shouted.

"I thought you were shaving your *face!*"

They all laughed at Eric's expense. Oz slid to the floor and comically pounded his fists on the ground.

"See, this is why we use locks," Grimsby told Monty.

"I don't get—" Ariel began, then understood with a tiny gasp. "Oh."

269

Eric met her gaze. He was so strong, so beautiful. And ridiculous. That's what she loved about him. That ability to be somehow full of laughter while also incredibly sexy. He winked at her before he slammed the door shut.

They laughed even harder when they heard the click of the lock.

Ariel finished getting ready on her own, since the band needed to set up. She dabbed a pink lip gloss on, brushed her thick, dark brows, and tried to wrestle her straight lashes into something of a curl. She suddenly appreciated her glam squad so much more.

This time, when she caught her reflection, she wasn't surprised. She loved the slight curve of her small nose that contouring had always straightened. The beauty marks on her shoulders and cheeks that makeup used to cover. She gave a final flip of her dark hair, tamed into waves of long layers. The dress fit like a second skin, accentuating her narrow waist, the swell of her hips. She hadn't noticed the long slit until she'd shimmied into the sparkling fabric, but when she gave a little twirl in the mirror, she loved it.

There I am, she thought once again.

Odelia stepped out of the bathroom, wrapped in the same robe she'd loaned Eric at the start of the tour. She seemed exhausted, and plopped down on one of the queen beds. "You really do remind me of her."

Ariel took a deep breath. She'd had more conversations about her mother on the Star Crossed tour than with her father in fifteen years, which made something inside her twist with a mix of sadness and joy.

"Can we talk?"

"It's been a long day, Melody," Odelia said, groaning as she sat on the edge of the bed. "Though you did good today. I don't think I could have pulled this off."

"Thank you."

"All right, out with it."

Ariel wrung her fingers together. She wanted to believe her relationship with Odelia had grown since the first day they met. The woman was no less intimidating in her pajamas. "I want to tell Eric everything. And I don't want to wait until the end of the tour."

Odelia nodded, licking her naked lips. "We had a deal. If I recall, that was your stipulation, not mine."

"I know. You said Eric was off-limits because you want him to focus on everything he's worked so hard for. I want that, too. This thing with us—it's real."

"How do you know that?"

Ariel flinched at the insinuation, but she understood Odelia was being protective. A mama bear for her cubs. But wasn't that what her own father's excuse had been to keep his daughters isolated?

"Because I'm falling in love with him. Because I think he might feel the same way." Ariel smiled tentatively. "Something he said yesterday made me realize that we are going to be okay. It might be a bit of a shock at first, but we *will* get through it."

I will want every version of you. Whenever she thought back on his words, it felt like all the music gods were singing to her.

Odelia chuckled. "His optimism is contagious, I'll give you that. Why are you coming to me?"

"Honestly?" Ariel rubbed the air conditioner chill from her arms. "It's kind of hard to let go of needing parental approval after all these years. I know you're not a surrogate for my father, and you aren't looking for another stray, but I said I could be a help on this tour. I mean it."

"You certainly have been."

"I think if everyone knows about my past, I might be able to do even more."

A fine line creased her brow. "Oh? And how is that?"

"Eric and I are writing together. I wouldn't want to sing on any of the songs—I think that part of my career is over—but I still have industry contacts." She saw Odelia's anger and fear gather, and she rushed to make sense of her words. "Not my father, of course. I would never. But the name Ariel del Mar must carry some weight. I'm sure I can connect you to a bigger label, music scouts for Vanessa, sponsorships—"

"We don't need Ariel del Mar's connections," Odelia said, her voice serious, but tempered. "The head of our current label is coming to see Star Crossed in Vegas. Several scouts are coming to see Vanessa perform. We've done fine without your name."

"But don't you think they could get bigger—"

"I said, we've done fine without it."

Ariel winced at the edge in her tone. "Shouldn't that be for Eric to decide? For Vanessa?"

Odelia laughed bitterly. "Yes, our label is small, but do you know how many predatory label contracts we had to turn down to get to a good place? Hmm? For Vanessa *and* Star Crossed. Do you know how hard it's been for me, clawing my way through this industry, to get people to take me seriously, especially after—"

"No, I don't know," Ariel said, knowing Odelia answered to strength. "Please. Tell me what happened between you and my parents so I can understand."

Odelia, so vulnerable-looking without her makeup, sighed. Ariel thought of the young woman she'd seen on that record cover—so hopeful and full of life. Here she was, decades older, and she'd managed to give that hope to the next generation of musicians, even though her own dream never came true. It only made Ariel admire her more.

"Your mother and I met in Miami," Odelia began, a sad smile tugging at the corner of her mouth. "We waitressed at a nightclub—the Parrot Social, I think it was. We were young, and it was the eighties. That's where she met your father. When I tell you it was love at first sight, I mean it. I'm telling you, it was the kind of love that could burn through the world."

Ariel had fuzzy memories of her parents together, but she could picture it. When she heard Odelia clear her throat, Ariel handed her a glass of water.

"The three of us wanted the same thing." She took a sip, then continued. "To make music. We recorded a demo through one of my friends. Went to New York. 'Luna Mia' was what I'd called the song I wrote."

Ariel sucked in a breath that she didn't let go. She couldn't have heard Odelia correctly. *Her* song?

"It inspired the band name. When we finished the LP, we were ready for launch. But the label wanted the love story. They wanted the dreamy couple whose eyes locked from across the room and started making music together. The inspirational story of a couple coming here from another country, coming from nothing. True love guiding the journey." Odelia's lips twisted with the bitterness of the memory. "Though I had the same story—I came from another country, I came from nothing. But I was the perpetual third wheel. On top of that, too sexy, too loud, too much to fit with the sweetheart dream team."

I know what your family does. You ruin lives. Ariel felt decades of shame at what her father—her parents—had done. There was part of her that didn't want to believe it. She searched her mind for ways to make Odelia's words untrue, but it was like someone trying to find their way out of a maze and hitting dead ends. She'd seen the records herself. Uncle Iggy had warned her away from Odelia, and her gut told her it was because she wouldn't like what she found out.

"I wouldn't sign over my rights, so your father told the label the songs were his. Well, you can piece together the rest."

"I am so sorry," Ariel said. "Maybe I can fix it. I can get your credit back."

"Just let it lie, Ariel." Odelia held up a silencing hand, and that was that. "I put your family behind me, and then you show up and remind me of the worst time of my life. And I tell you to leave Eric alone so he won't go through the same as me, and you won't listen."

"I'm not my father."

"I want to believe that. I think I do believe it." Odelia looked weary with the weight of the past returning. Ariel felt it, too, but didn't know how to help her bear it. "Do me a favor."

Ariel nodded.

"Before you rush into trying to help Eric—hell, help all of us— make sure you know what you truly want. Put on your oxygen mask first. I have learned the hard way, love isn't always enough." Odelia unplugged her phone from the nightstand charger. "Now, go on to the wedding. I forgot to call the mechanic back. Hopefully we can get out of this desert hellhole first thing tomorrow."

Ariel slipped into a pair of sandals she'd borrowed from Vanessa and left Odelia to her privacy. She walked slowly, as if in a daze. She was too stunned to text her sisters all the details about their parents' past.

So tonight, Ariel del Mar would set her sights only on her future.

**CAN'T GET ENOUGH OF STAR CROSSED?
HERE'S EVERYTHING YOU NEED TO KNOW ABOUT THEM.**

Elektra del Mar Steps Out with
New Girlfriend! Click Here to See
Their Central Park Rowboat Outing.

CLICK HERE

*Ariel Del Mar Continues Rebellious Streak,
Racking Up A $50,000 Bar Tab
At A Los Angeles Nightclub.*

**Is the Bermuda Triangle a Hoax?
Meet the Couple Who Lived to Tell the Tale.**

**Here's Why "Love Like Lightning"
Should Be Your Summer Anthem.**

**TREVOR TACHI POSTS EMO PIXAGRAM PHOTO.
ARIEL, HE WANTS YOU BACK!**

CHAPTER TWENTY-TWO

ERIC

7.13 Paradise Palms, Nevada

Eric Reyes watched from the last row as Carrie and Steve Whalen were married with the desert sunset at their backs. Unsurprisingly to any of his bandmates, he loved weddings.

One of the first times he sang in public was at one of his cousins' weddings when he was ten. With his high-pitched little voice, he'd accompanied his grandfather Pedro on a classic vallenato. When Eric really thought about it, all those songs were pretty tragic for the occasion. Either way, it was perhaps the only time his own parents had ever encouraged him musically.

There, in the Paradisio Hotel, a place he'd never even known existed ten hours prior, he smiled as the couple kissed and everyone threw their plastic garlands in the air.

Eric turned around and searched for her. For Melody.

She was taking a picture of the sunset. Probably sending it to one of her half-dozen sisters. He wondered if they were all like her. He wondered what her life looked like before she came into his. He wondered if she'd go back to it without him. If he was just a pit stop on a much longer road he couldn't follow. But when she spotted him in the crowd, and her face transformed with her perfect smile, he knew that there was no way. They were interlinked, somehow.

How often did the universe bring two people together the way it had brought Eric and Ariel?

Always, was the answer.

Everywhere and every second, people crossed paths and didn't even notice. Sometimes, those who listened to the universe were able to make their way to each other.

He crossed the courtyard on unsteady legs. Could barely breathe at the sight of her. That dress. Sexy and delicate. The slit exposing her thigh with every step she took. It shimmered, catching every light, coming alive. A gem in the desert.

"You look—" he started. He could punch himself for not being able to string a sentence together. "You look wonderful."

She smiled, biting her lower lip like she was nervous. "Someone was looking for you, actually. The front desk?"

"Really?"

"Something about a manscaping violation?"

"Carly is a bad influence on you," he said, but deep inside he loved it. He loved that she got along with his best friends. He loved that she simply fit with their nonsensical humor. He was falling in love with her. Perhaps he already had. The thought rammed into him, the same way she had into his life.

He kissed her knuckles, and they strode across the fake grass beneath a blanket of multicolored Christmas lights. She took a seat at the band's designated table, tucked off to the side. He found it almost impossible to tear himself from her.

"Save me a dance?" he asked.

"Always."

Eric gathered the band in a huddle. They all cleaned up extremely well. "Okay, how're we feeling?"

"I don't want to rain on our parade," Carly said, "but we only had one hour to practice."

Eric winked at her pouty frown. "We were a metal band when we needed to pay rent three years ago. And don't forget, before all this, we played covers just to hype up the crowds. Let's stick to the crowd pleasers and lean heavily on Grimsby for the rhythm. We got this."

They hyped each other up, a mosh pit of five, and switched the lineup a bit. Max stayed on the drums, but Carly swapped her guitar for the bass, and Grimsby added the flair with her banjo.

The bride and groom's first dance was a cover of Bon Jovi's "Born to Be My Baby," and lucky for them, they knew almost every song requested by the drunk members of the bedazzled wedding party and guests. When they didn't know the song, they smiled and banged out a soundalike or a Star Crossed original. Eric found that happy, tipsy people only wanted to dance and sing until their bodies gave out. As long as the band kept the music fast and upbeat, the hundred-plus guests, who seemed to have descended upon Nevada from all corners of the country, were happy to party all night to songs from every decade.

When Vanessa took over guitar and vocals for Eric, he loosened his tie and found Melody grabbing two margaritas. That dress on her did unspeakable things to him. All he could think about were the thirteen kisses they'd had, and her text message emblazoned on his mind. *Practice makes perfect.*

"Looks like Oz has been adopted by the bridesmaids," Melody said.

He chuckled, accepted the drink she offered, and clinked his glass to hers, bits of salt falling on his thumb. He licked it away as they sat and did a double take as Star Crossed broke into a country cover of "Despacito."

"So where's this dance I'm saving?" she asked. There was a fleck of salt on her upper lip and he had the impulse to lick it away, but she got to it first.

He couldn't answer because he knew he couldn't control his mouth. He knew the first thing that would spill out would be "I think I love you." So he set their empty drinks down and led her to the center of the dance floor. He twirled her in his arms, gracefully stretching out until only the tips of their fingers touched. She returned to him on her own.

She loves me, Eric thought as Melody rested her head against his chest, even though it wasn't a slow song.

She loves me not, he thought again as she broke their embrace to go and get more drinks.

She loves me, he thought as she laced their fingers together.

She loves me not, he thought again when she accepted the offer to dance from one of the groomsmen.

Eric had never in his life felt this irrationally possessive or jealous over a woman. He knew it wasn't about other men, but about the uncertainty of where he and Melody stood. They'd started off hot, then needed to cool down for the sake of the tour, the stupid bet with his friends. She'd pulled away because of her past, but things had been changing. Hadn't they? Perhaps it was the night to find out. To settle things. If not now, when?

He switched places with Vanessa, and he did what he did best. He sang. Only this time, he sang to Melody, and even though it was a rock ballad most babies born in 1986 were conceived to, he put everything he had into it. And she swayed there, shimmering like his North Star.

When the wedding was over, and only smashed relatives and friends were left dancing to someone's playlist, the band made their way to the glowing blue pool.

"Score," Oz shouted. "We have it all to ourselves!"

"Okay, so I think this is a first thing for all of us," Carly said, sitting on one of the sunbed chairs.

"So when someone says *never have I ever crashed a wedding in the desert*, I can drink," Melody said, kicking off her sandals and massaging her ankles.

"I saw there's a shuttle to Vegas," Max said, waggling her eyebrows. "We can get started on taking the city by storm."

"You know what else I haven't done?" Vanessa asked. Eric caught the sly glance she shot Carly. "Skinny dip."

Max cackled. "I'm game. I didn't bring a swimsuit, anyway."

"I'm more of a hot tub guy," Oz said, but he still began stripping like the others.

Eric remained with his clothes on.

"He walks around the house naked for five years," Grimsby said, "and *now* he's shy. You've changed, bro."

Eric flipped them his middle finger, then began to undo his tie. Everyone hollered. He glanced at Melody, who adorably averted her eyes. He was moving on to his shirt buttons when Vanessa, Carly, and Max cannonballed into the pool, followed by Grimsby and Oz.

Melody pushed off one strap of her dress, and he felt the need to turn around. Back to back, they undressed. Belt buckle rattling, zipper undone, the crush of fabric around their feet.

Eric held his breath and jumped into the deep end. The cold water felt good against his hot skin as he let himself float. He was incredibly aware of the last splash. Of Melody in the water, her curves, when he turned around under the water, backlit by the pale blue light. When the bubbles cleared, they were face to face, smiling and looking up at the surface.

They swam up, the sound of their friends laughing and horsing around seeming to echo across the night. He wasn't sure who called for racing, but Melody went for it, dove into the challenge. That was how it went, for what felt like hours: Eric pushing to keep pace, always just shy of beating her. No one could. She glided through the water like she was born to it.

When they all got tired, Max jumped out of the water and found some inflatable rings and noodles. Oz went to get them some towels, and Carly and Vanessa offered to fetch some drinks. They floated like that for a long time. Max and Grimsby used the noodles to "sword fight" on one end, while Melody clung to her flamingo floatie. Eric had wound up with a blow-up lobster, which resulted in an inevitable joke about how he had crabs, and he had to splash everyone.

"I think this is my favorite day of the tour," Eric said.

"Me too." Melody drifted past.

"You only say that because you've outswum us all. Are you a secret Olympic swimmer?"

She laughed, resting her cheek on her folded arms. "I learned when I was little. There was a Y in Queens right by where we lived. My mom said she had to tie a buoy to me when we went."

He wanted to tell her about swimming in the lake with his cousins, about the pranks he'd pulled during his years at boarding school. Then he realized his friends were incredibly silent.

No, not silent. They were gone. The ancient pink sunbeds were all empty.

Of everything.

Including their clothes.

"Those mother—" He let out a string of curses that had Melody laughing.

She pushed off her flamingo and swam to the center of the pool, where her feet touched the bottom and the water came up to her shoulders. He paddled to her, planting his feet firmly on the slick glass tiles.

"I think they're trying to *Parent Trap* us," she said.

"Subtle." He brushed a water droplet from her chin, saw her shiver. "Let's get you inside."

She grabbed his wrist, held it underwater. "Eric, I have to tell you something."

She loves me. She loves me not.

"I have to tell you something, too." Every muscle in his body tightened with anticipation, dread, delirium. He was going to lose his nerve. His heart stuttered, and then he moved forward.

"You go," she told him.

Fuerza, his grandfather would have said to him. But it was easier to think about being strong than to *be* strong. Physically. Emotionally. Wholly.

"I'm usually better at this," he admitted.

She smirked. "Standing naked in a pool? It's a first for me."

"This. With you. I've never felt this way before, about anyone. It's—"

"New?"

"Terrifying." He hoped she saw in his eyes that he meant every word. "I thought about telling you when the tour was over, and maybe fully dressed and not in a pool, but I've realized a lot of things tonight."

"Like what?" she asked, taking a step closer.

She loves you.

"Like that I wanted to deck the best man for dancing with you. Holding you."

"Holding me like this?" She placed her hands on his shoulders. Heat bloomed at the place where they touched. She laughed at him. "Like dancing?"

"I'm a fool."

"You're not a fool," she said. "Foolish, maybe."

She loves you not.

"Did you mean it?" She let her hands roam from his shoulders down to his biceps, brushing away the chill of the night. "When you said you'd want every version of me?"

"I don't care about what came before, only what comes after."

She still glanced away, her nails running up and down his arms. How could she doubt him? How could he make it clear?

If not now, when? he thought.

"I used to think every song I wrote was for some dream girl I hadn't met yet. That's what 'Love Like Lightning' was. That's what all my lyrics were. But then I met you, and I realized that none of those songs apply. They were about someone nameless. And then here you are, turning everything about me inside out. You're real and you're here, and you're not like anything I said in those songs."

She blinked up at him, her lashes glistening with tiny drops of pool water. "I'm not?"

"No." He cradled her chin, brushing his thumb to soothe the disappointed tremble there. "But every song I write from now on will be about you. The way you look at everything like it's new and wonderful. How you look at me that way, too, and I think—I will do everything and anything to be worthy of that feeling, because I'm in love with you. I am so in love with you, I can't see straight."

"Eric, I—" She didn't finish. She pushed up on her toes and kissed him. The surprise of it made them stagger backward, but there was no way in hell he was breaking them apart. He wrapped his arms around her, tasting the salt still on her tongue as they went under, locked in an embrace. For a moment, he didn't breathe, didn't open his eyes. There was only the beating of his heart underwater and Melody's lips pressed against his.

When they came up for air, laughing and clearing their eyes, he heard shouting nearby.

He climbed out of the pool and noticed a few stragglers from the wedding streaking through the golf course.

"We're about to have company," he said, and fetched the inflated pink flamingo for her, the lobster for him.

They sprinted across the courtyard, the cleanup crew whistling as they ran by. When they got to their room, their clothes had been neatly folded and left in the hall. Their key card was in a hotel envelope with a note that read *Took the after-party shuttle to Vegas! It comes back in the morning. Don't be mad!*

Eric let them in, tossing the lobster to the other side of the room. He grabbed a set of towels from the bathroom, and when he returned,

Melody was there, Venus de Milo emerging out of a pink floatation device. She turned the room's lock, then made her way across the room, her feet leaving wet imprints on carpet.

He opened up the towel for her, but she let it drop to the floor and stepped into his arms instead. Melody's kisses were tentative, almost shy. No one had kissed him this way, soft and careful. Like *he* was the one who needed protecting. It lit a fuse in him as she pressed her lips along his jaw, the pulse at his throat. He felt so lost in wanting her, he didn't feel the bed until the back of his knees hit the mattress. It groaned as he sat back, with his girl on his lap.

"Are you sure?" he whispered, searching her brown eyes.

She tapped her nose to his. Dragged feather-light touches over his lips. "My whole life is unsure, Eric. The only thing that makes sense for me is you."

When he kissed her again, his love for her seared through his skin, deeper still, carved into his marrow, so nothing and no one could remove it.

@TeoDelMar

I remember when you were this small. I remember when you used to look at me like I had given you the world. That's all I've ever tried to do. I know I can be difficult and hard on you girls. But I never, ever want you to go through what I did. I never want you to have NOTHING. Please, my little mermaid. I miss you. Your sisters miss you. Your fans miss you. Please come home.

#ArielComeHome #SirenSeven #SirenSevenLife

CHAPTER TWENTY-THREE

ARIEL

7.14 Las Vegas, Nevada

The road to Las Vegas was paved with the secret smiles she shared with Eric. The Beast was patched up, and every member of the band was the delirious combination of exhausted and energized.

Eric cozied up on the lounge beside Ariel, adding songs to their playlist while they listened to a rowdy reenactment of their friends' time on the strip and their plans for their second day off. Only Odelia kept to the back lounge. Ariel worried she was still upset over their conversation the night before. She wouldn't drop any more suggestions of helping the band until they asked her first. Besides, there was so much Ariel needed to make right between the Garcias and the del Mars. But first, she had to get Eric alone.

When they reached the Van Luxen Hotel, Ariel realized they would go back to their normal room setups, which meant she and Eric had a room to themselves. He must have been thinking the same thing because he took her duffel and slung it over his shoulder to carry it for her. She didn't miss the warning arch of Odelia's brow as she strode past them and into the lobby. Everything was going to be fine, Ariel told herself. She was certain of what she wanted—Eric, the tour, songwriting. It had never been simpler than that.

Oz grinned at Ariel and Eric. "I have a new ship, guys. And it's called *Meloric*. Or maybe *Erody*? I'll work on it."

Ariel's phone buzzed for the hundredth time that day. "It's my sister. I should take this."

"I'm meeting Vee at the gym, but I'll see you upstairs later?"

"Yeah, okay."

Eric brushed a tender kiss against her temple before vanishing into the crowded lobby with Oz.

Ariel answered her phone. Marilou responded with a howl.

"Thank you for shattering my eardrum," Ariel said, walking away from the Van Luxen entrance. All around her were billboards and signs that still shone bright in the light of day.

"I could be dead right now, and you would be feeling like a jerk for sending me to voicemail five times."

"Are you dead?"

"*Duh?* You can't just text a string of eggplant, kiss, peach, fireworks emojis and a happy face and then go radio silent."

Ariel couldn't have stopped smiling if she wanted to. And she very much didn't want to. She felt fizzy all over, like surf crashing against the shore. "I can when I'm on a tour with a million people and don't want to be *overheard*."

"Are you alone *now*?" Marilou asked, more giggly than she'd ever sounded when talking about one of Ariel's romantic prospects. Because Eric was more than that. Eric was it.

"It was nice." Ariel grinned so hard her cheekbones hurt, and she had to press her phone to her chest for a second.

"Babe, salad is nice. That man is a cheeseburger deluxe."

"He's actually a large Hawaiian pizza."

Marilou made a confused noise. "Sorry, you lost the innuendo. I'm happy for you, though. I know we're not supposed to compare, but you haven't had the best track record with guys."

"I really love him," she told her sister. It was the first time she'd said this to her family. They'd had to live through Trevor Tachi, through the terrible publicity stunts before that. Eric was nothing like that.

"You sound really happy, little guppy. I love that for you." Marilou cleared her throat. "But listen—"

"Can I call you later? I'm meeting up with Max since everyone is splitting up until dinner."

"Not to alarm you," Marilou continued, and Ariel was instantly on alert, "but I was actually calling to ask if you saw Dad's Pixagram."

Ariel glanced at her phone. Cars pulled up to the valet parking. Billboards flashed news and advertisements. It was like if Times Square were a Hotel California type of desert oasis.

Her heart sputtered. "No, I haven't. I blocked him."

Marilou cursed, then said, "Texting you the screenshot."

She told her sister she'd call back, then opened the picture. Ariel held her breath the entire time. She read the words under an old photo, and suddenly she was underwater. Her eyes stung. Angry tears spilled down her cheeks as she read and reread his words. The manipulative son of a—

"You." It was Max. She glanced from the phone to Melody. She shook her head like she had to be imagining it.

In the picture, a seven-year-old Ariel crouched at a coffee table with her father. She was a kid, but her face hadn't changed. Her birthday cake read MELODY in surf-green icing. She looked up at the camera with the same smile Eric had told her he loved. Her father hadn't changed much, either, except for the silver in his hair.

"Y-you—you're her." Max grabbed her hair. "HOLY FUCK! I knew it. I thought I was imagining it when Mr. Antonio called you Maia, and then in the lobby when you changed your voice for a second, but I was like, there's no way. There's no flippin' way."

Ariel secured her baseball cap to her head. Glanced around as people began to stare at the screaming girl. She snapped her fingers to redirect her friend's focus. "Max, Max, listen to me."

Her friend was in so much shock, Ariel had no trouble ushering her down the street and into a gaudy coffee shop resembling Venice. Ariel ordered two sugary concoctions and brought them over. Max sat in utter silence, hands crossed like a Catholic schoolgirl. Tiny beads of nervous sweat popped up along her brow like dew. She made a choking sound and lightly slammed her forehead on the table.

"All those things Eric said about Siren Seven! Right in front of you."

Ariel laughed and almost snorted her drink. When she exhaled, she felt a little freer. One less person to tell. "I mean, it hurt a little, yeah."

"He's such a hater." Max recovered, slurping her drink to rehydrate. "He sings 'Te Amo, Je T'aime' in the shower all the time."

A warm sensation unfurled inside Ariel. "Thanks for saying that. I . . . I didn't want you to find out this way."

"I can't believe it. You're Ar—"

"Shhh!" Ariel waved her hands to remind Max they were in public. "Please. No one knows. Well, Odelia and Vanessa knew from the beginning, but that's it."

"THEY'VE KNOWN ALL ALONG?" Max took a break from hyperventilating to sip her drink. "I cannot believe . . . I CANNOT BELIEVE THIS. I was so mean to you that first day, and I love you so much. *Argh!* I mean, not how Eric loves you. Fuck. Eric. He doesn't know?"

"One thing at a time," Ariel said, taking a page from Sophia's notebook. Her oldest sister was usually the most diplomatic of the seven. "The short version goes, Odelia used to be in a band with my parents, and she recognized me on sight. She didn't want me on the bus and only let me come as long as I stayed away from Eric."

Max smiled awkwardly, but seemed to calm down the more she drank her triple-confetti-foam whatever. "Okay. That didn't work out."

"And no, Eric doesn't know. I wanted to tell him last night, but we got carried away. Every time I tried, he said he didn't care about my past, and I was afraid." She stirred her straw in the concoction. "Also, yes, you were mean to me, but it was sort of nice having people treat me like a regular person instead of pretending and fawning over me."

Max's eyes went wide. "I would *never*— Okay, fine, I would have died. I'm actually dead right now." She stared at her hands. "Maybe I never left Vegas."

"Max," Ariel said. "I'm still me. There's just another part of me."

"Shit," her friend said. "All that stuff makes a weird amount of sense. Is it true you all sleep in fish tanks, like the bacta tanks from Star Wars, to keep you young?"

Ariel laughed, truly laughed in a way that felt like exhaling. "No. I have a bed. It's repurposed driftwood, but still."

Max gasped. "*Gross*, you boned Trevor Tachi?"

Ariel rolled her eyes. "Sure, over a year ago. I have him blocked. Assume everything is false unless I confirm it."

"Eric is going to lose it."

Ariel worried the inside of her cheek. "In a bad way?"

Max shook her head. "I've known him for years. The only time I've seen him mad is when Colombia lost to Chile in some World Cup match. That and anytime his father calls the house, but it lasts for two seconds. I think he'll be confused, but you have to be honest with him."

"I know," she said.

"Do you love him? Like for real, for real?"

"I love him." Ariel didn't hesitate. Not for a second. So why hadn't she said the words the night before? He'd bared everything to her, and she'd spoken with actions, but words were just as important. "I'm scared of losing him. Of losing all of you. Even if you'd win the bet."

"Sorry." Max winced. "We did give him a chance to blow it off. But I think he needed it as incentive to make sure he didn't screw up. To make sure you were ready."

"I'm the one screwing up."

"Not on my watch." Max stood up and offered her hand. "Come on. He's probably still at the gym—Wait a minute. Does this mean your sisters know who I am?"

Ariel smirked. "Yep, and they love the band, too. Marilou is actually the reason I went to Aurora's Grocery in the first place."

Max staggered to one knee, making prayer hands, but then recovered quickly. "If you don't introduce us, I will never forgive you."

She wanted to say that she would, but she wasn't ready to make another promise. Not until she finally came clean to Eric, come what may.

Publisher's Deal Place Announcement:

Personal assistant to Ariel del Mar, Chrissy Mahilal, has written a memoir, *The Seaweed Is Always Greener*, a collection of essays, tweets, and sage advice from a decade of living on the edge of Siren Seven's limelight. Mahilal, who has been at the youngest del Mar sister's side for years, says she has followed her truth with the pop princess's blessing. Publication is slated just in time for the holidays, with a foreword from Ariel del Mar herself. The deal was brokered by Sally Herrera, at Townsend & Ramos.

CHAPTER TWENTY-FOUR

ERIC

7.14 Las Vegas, Nevada

Eric spent the afternoon at the gym, pushing his body to the limit, then running two miles to cool down. When he sat down on the bench and poured water over his face, he exhaled slowly.

"Take it easy," Vanessa said, slapping him with the end of her towel. "You're not nineteen anymore."

He crossed his arms behind his head to flex his biceps. "I am eternal."

Vanessa raised her eyebrows. "You had a good night last night, then."

Eric didn't kiss and tell. Still, he couldn't contain his smile. He felt like he could lift a truck with his bare hands. Instead of answering, he shot Vanessa a knowing look. "You nervous for the label scouts tomorrow?"

"Way to change the subject." She picked up a set of dumbbells and began her bicep curls. "And I'm not nervous. I'm either what they're looking for, or I'm not."

"You sound like your mom."

"She'd know better than anyone." Vanessa moved on to a chest press, and Eric spotted her. "I try not to get my hopes up, you know? We've had dozens of scouts come to see me perform. I don't understand why, out of every record label out there, I can't find one that wants me to sound like me."

"It'll happen," Eric said. "You're the whole package."

"The last scout told me I needed to work on my resting bitch face."

"I love your resting bitch face."

Vanessa grunted on her next rep. "Easy for you to say. You get to choose to be brooding or a dreamboat. What about you? Excited for the head of your label to see you play?"

"I'll be more excited if he offers us an advance to cut a new record."

Vanessa's arms trembled, and Eric took the weight from her. She sat and draped the towel around her neck. "Mom seems hopeful."

"Do you think Odelia would ever try to sing again?" All Eric knew of Odelia's mysterious past was that she'd had a deal go wrong. So wrong it had killed her ability to sing and write for years, until Vanessa was born. She'd gone from managing small tours and working publicity for independent labels to representing Vanessa and Eric, and then the band.

"She sings every day. In the shower. When she's cooking. When she thinks we're all listening to something on our headphones. Tío Antonio used to tell me it was in her blood."

"I wonder if I can get Melody to sing." He glanced up at the TVs. The entertainment channel was running a commercial for the latest season of *Before Midnight*—Max was rooting for a cute blond—and something about Siren Seven. Eric rolled his eyes and returned his attention to his friend.

Vanessa picked up the weight again. "She will when she's ready."

"I heard Melody sing in the shower once," he said, remembering the first time they'd shared a room together. "It was the most beautiful sound I've ever heard."

"Excuse me?" Vanessa pointed at herself indignantly.

"Apples and oranges."

His perceptive friend narrowed her eyes at him. "You dropped the L bomb, didn't you?"

"¿Que?" He smirked.

"You understood me, Mr. I Speak Four Languages. Love, dummy."

Eric chuckled. His chest tightened at the memory of Melody in his arms the night before. The way she'd felt against him. The breathy way she'd said his name. "I did."

Vanessa sat up. "I have to hand it to you, Eric. You're different, and you don't even see it."

"In a good way?"

She nodded. "So when you pick out our tattoo, be gentle."

He laughed, and then there was a knock on the glass door. A hotel concierge waved politely. "Mr. Reyes?"

Eric chafed at the name. His father was Mr. Reyes. Not him. "Yes?"

"Your presence is requested," the older woman said.

Vanessa crossed her arms over her chest. "Who's asking?"

The concierge handed Eric a card. He recognized the symbol, a trident at the center of a gold card made of some sort of metal. This couldn't be who he thought it was. An excited, nervous sensation rammed into him.

"Right now?" Eric gestured to his sweaty workout clothes.

The concierge grinned. "Not to worry. If you'll follow me to the restaurant on the deck . . ."

Eric turned to Vanessa, who looked at him like he was getting into some unmarked van at Port Authority, and said, "Text your mom and tell her to meet me."

"You should wait for her."

"Mr. Reyes was requested to come alone. Right this way," the concierge said, cutting her off.

"I'll go see what this is about, and you get Odelia." Eric raked a hand through his hair and sniffed under his arm.

"You smell great," the woman said as they entered the elevator. She hit the button to the roof deck.

When Eric thought back to that moment, he would wonder why he didn't ask more questions. Why he ran like an eager puppy. Why he didn't wait for Odelia or his band. But he knew you didn't keep a man like Teodoro del Mar waiting. He'd dreamed of a moment like this—of being discovered. Sometimes, he'd waited around after a particularly good set and thought, *Today is the day everything changes.* Star Crossed, Odelia—they'd worked so hard for every follower, every download, every click, every door ticket. They'd played concerts for an audience of two, and they'd played sold-out venues. All of it had been to share their sound with the world. Perhaps the world was finally listening.

As the elevator doors opened and they shuffled into a restaurant that was all marble and glass, Eric understood that his life was about to change.

Teodoro del Mar sat in a private dining room overlooking the Las Vegas Strip. A man in a burgundy suit sat to his left, his carefully manicured nails drumming on a black portfolio. Why did he look familiar?

Eric lost his ability to speak. His mouth went dry. His tongue felt like he'd spent the morning licking sandpaper.

"Ah, there he is." One look at the sharp black suit the music tycoon was wearing and Eric knew he should have insisted that he be given a second to change. Shower. Look presentable.

"Mr. del Mar," Eric said, extending his hand. When his nerves fritzed this way, his brain defaulted to his first language. "Es un honor."

Teo stared at Eric's hand for a second past comfortable, then squeezed firmly. Eric squeezed back, never letting his smile drop. All at once he was back in his house in Medellín, getting lectured by his father. He shook off the sliver of doubt that wedged into his spine, leaving a chilling sensation.

He turned to the man in red. "Eric Reyes."

"Ignacio," the man said, quickly returning Eric's pleasantries. "You must be wondering why all the rush."

"I'm sure you're all very busy. Like I said, I'm honored—"

"Then I'm going to be frank with you." Teo sat forward, hands clasped tightly.

Eric clutched the leather arms of his chair, already conjuring the image of Teodoro offering him a record deal. The start of the next phase of Star Crossed. Studio album. World tour. Awards. Music videos. Late night talk shows.

"I need your help," Teo said, his tenor like a roll of thunder.

"Me?" Eric glanced between the two men. Was that a joke? He wouldn't have thought a man like Teodoro del Mar made jokes. "What can I do for you?"

"You can help me convince my daughter to come home."

Eric had seen something that morning on the news, but he never paid attention to that stuff unless Max was watching it at home and he was too lazy to get up from the couch. "What?"

Teodoro chuckled, his features morphing into something angry, impatient. "I don't know how Odelia convinced my Ariel to run away with you—"

"What my brother means to say," Ignacio translated, wincing only slightly, "is that we understand the impulses of youth. Excitement. The thrill. However, we are concerned that Ariel isn't thinking about what is best for her future."

"Ariel?" Eric felt numb.

"Melody," Ignacio said as Teodoro turned redder and redder with silent rage. "Well, Melody Ariel."

This was a misunderstanding. No, it wasn't real. But somehow, he knew it was true. Perhaps he'd known it from the minute he stepped out of that elevator. Perhaps even before then? No, he couldn't have. He reminded himself to breathe.

All at once, Eric remembered. *I'm Ahh—Melody.*

Melody gazing at him. *I have to tell you something.*

Melody who wrote songs and knew her way backstage and told him about her sisters. Six sisters. Siren Seven.

Melody who'd kissed him like she was drowning, and he was her only source of oxygen.

Melody, beneath him.

Melody dancing with him in the desert.

Melody who built a wall between them after that first night, who told him about her manipulative father. Eric had thought that if he ever met the man, he'd tell him what an amazing, talented, strong daughter he had. A daughter he didn't appreciate.

But there he sat, with that very man across the table, and Eric Reyes was stunned silent. How could he have been so foolish?

Ignacio pushed a glass of water in front of Eric. He picked it up. He drank. And drank. He drank every last drop in one long continuous swallow, and when he was done, he was still thirsty.

He had to get out of there.

He had to talk to her.

Teodoro slid the black portfolio from Ignacio and pushed it in front of Eric. "She's spoiled. She won't listen to me. Perhaps with the right incentive, we can reach an agreement."

"What the hell are you talking about?" The words were out before he could stop them.

Teodoro arched a brow, but let the insult slide. "I'm prepared to offer you the deal of a lifetime."

Eric's heart thrummed as he turned the page to read the memo. It was all there: a $750,000 advance to cut an album.

"There are bonuses, of course," Teodoro said, turning the page for Eric. "I will make Star Crossed as big as Siren Seven. We'd start with a name change. Eric Reyes and the Star Crossed?"

Ignacio snapped his fingers. "Eric Reyes and the Star-Crossed Lovers. The fandom is already a hashtag. We can capitalize on it in a big way."

Eric thought about his father's cruel words. He thought about his ex, so disappointed in him when he didn't reach the fame he'd dreamed of. He thought about Melody—Ariel—bathed in desert moonlight.

This was too good to be true. He knew it was. What had Teodoro said? An agreement. He was offering Eric everything he'd ever wanted. Why? Why now? Melody had been with them for weeks.

"We sign this, and what do you get in return?" Eric asked.

"A hot up-and-coming band. I'm surprised I didn't hear of you before my brother brought you to my attention. You're the whole package. You're handsome, and, with the right polish, your band will really shine." The smile Teodoro flashed was arrogant. "Of course, there are two provisions."

Eric let his silence speak for him.

"First, Atlantica Records doesn't do business with Odelia Garcia. You are free to find another manager, or one will be assigned to you."

Eric swallowed. He had the feeling of being severed from his body, watching the scene below from another plane of existence, because this could not be happening. "And the second?"

"You fire Ariel and tell her to come home." Teodoro waved at someone Eric couldn't see. Eric blinked, and three glasses of amber liquid appeared. Celebratory drinks. Because how could he refuse? How could anyone refuse their dream being handed to them on a piece of expensive paper? A genie granting wishes with the stroke of a pen.

"Why are you so sure she'd listen to me?" Eric asked, his body returning to him slowly. He flexed his fingers around the armrests. Who the hell was this man to want to change his band name? *His* band?

A kingmaker, that's who Teodoro del Mar was.

"My daughter doesn't know anything about the real world. Not like you and I do." Teodoro picked up his glass, turned it this way and that to admire the honey color of the drink. "We're the same, you and me. I was once a little boy who left home, made it all the way to New York

City. I fell flat on my face again and again. Trusted the wrong people. Lost everything. Made it all back tenfold. When you want something, and you manage to attain it, you do everything in your power to hold on to it."

Eric stared at his lap. He couldn't walk away from a deal like this. He couldn't. Where was Odelia? He needed her to explain—whatever *this* was.

"Why don't you do business with Odelia?"

Teodoro gave a disconcerted shrug. "Why does it matter? She's the one who called me to come get my rebellious daughter."

Your adult daughter who made her own choice, Eric thought. Then he blinked.

"Odelia called you?" Eric tried to think of a time when she might have mentioned that she had connections to one of the biggest names in the industry, or let slip a sign that she knew who Ariel really was. Why had she kept that from him? And why had she called Teodoro now, not for the band, but to get rid of his girl?

Was she his girl still?

"Ariel's just looking for some fun. Fifteen years of this life, she needed to blow off steam," Teodoro said.

Beside Teodoro, Ignacio stared into his drink uncomfortably, but if he wanted to contradict his brother, he didn't.

"What are you saying?" Eric asked.

"I'm saying my daughter was using you. You were a convenient way for her to taste the real world safely." Teodoro took a nip of his whiskey, checking his phone like he was in a hurry. "Odelia called me, told me where to get my daughter. But she's been hiding you, hasn't she? Hiding your talents from the world, when you can have so much more."

There was too much to think about. What did he mean by the right polish? His band didn't need "polish." And yet, those other things he'd said were right. Eric and Teodoro did leave their countries. They bet on themselves. They followed their dreams. They were the same. Weren't they?

Eric could see the man who'd created an international sensation, a man with a ruthless reputation who the world still adored as a doting dad. He tried to reconcile this man with the emotionally manipulative father Melody had described for weeks.

God. Weeks. He'd been with her for weeks, but he had only ever had half of her. She'd lied to him to protect herself.

I love her, he thought. The words were fierce, a knife severing his ability to speak. He loved Melody. He didn't know Ariel. He shut his eyes against the onslaught of memories. He'd told her he loved her. She hadn't said it. She hadn't told him she loved him back.

"Can I think about it?"

"This is a limited-time offer," Teodoro said, watching Eric carefully. "But I understand you need to talk to your band. My flight leaves at sunset. You have until then. For now, let us toast."

Ignacio raised his glass. "To new beginnings."

Eric repeated the words, but he didn't feel them. Not the way he felt when he sang, when he had proclaimed his love for Melody.

Ariel.

Ariel.

Ariel.

The whiskey burned down his throat and into his empty stomach. He remembered he was supposed to meet the band at the venue. What would they say? There was no way he could do this. He couldn't leave Odelia behind, could he? Even the thought soured his mouth with guilt.

Eric was escorted to the elevator by a restaurant hostess. When the doors closed, he had never felt so alone. He clutched the folder to his chest, absently tracing the record label logo. It should have been the best day of his life. That morning, he'd woken up with the girl of his dreams curled up beside him. He had his friends. His entire world was on a single bus. Now he held their futures in his hands. All he had to do was hurt two women he loved.

Two women who'd been lying to him for weeks.

Foolish, naive idiot.

What was he doing? It was happening again, just like last time. He'd let himself get distracted from the thing that mattered. Star Crossed. He had to prove to his father that he was going to make it. To his grandfather's memory. To himself.

He didn't *need* until sunset to know what was best for his band. They'd worked hard. Every shitty gig that had stiffed them, every time they'd played at an empty venue, every door boarded shut behind them.

He went back upstairs to give Teodoro del Mar his answer.

When Eric walked across the lobby, he was in shock. He couldn't stand the smiling faces around him. Laughing, grinning, cheery strangers, oblivious to the fact that his world had imploded. It wasn't a sensation he was used to, but he'd had so many firsts that day. Why stop now?

He saw her then. As if for the first time.

Melody ran past him, chasing the closing elevator doors. Was she going to her father? Or was she going to find Eric?

A kernel of doubt told him that there was a chance the past hour had been a hallucination. The air in Vegas hotels playing with his mind. Mutating the fibers of his heart into something he didn't recognize.

Please, he thought. *Please don't let it be true.*

He shouted her name. His voice carried, strong and echoing through the cold marble lobby. "Ariel!"

Don't, he thought. *Don't.*

She turned around.

@TeoDelMar

SirenSeven1
What a horrible daughter! ♡

Tink_w1sh
Let's not be quick to judge. ♡

ZoeyCastile
Does anyone feel this has real #FreeJessiLynneMears vibes? ♡

YoSoyTheolinda
Idk, she's an adult. Let her be. ♡

ZoeyCastile
@YoSoyTheolinda If my dad blasted me on main, I'd yeet myself into the sun. ♡

ZaddyDelMarRules
I'll be your little mermaid, Zaddy del Mar. ♡

MuuusicMan33
I've got a business proposition for you. Check your secret folder. ♡

RealSophiaDelMar
Daddy, stop this. ♡

Harharjinx
#ArielComeHome ♡

CHAPTER TWENTY-FIVE

ARIEL

7.14 Las Vegas, Nevada

She heard her name. It was muscle memory. As much as she felt like Melody, she couldn't deny who she'd been for fifteen years.

"Ariel!" he shouted.

She turned around. She didn't need to search to find him. Eric was firmly rooted across the lobby, stragglers staring, parting around their disruption in the pedestrian traffic.

He shook his head once, twice. He looked at her like he didn't know her. Like she'd taken something from him, and she knew she had. It was over. Whatever *it* had been, or could have been. There was no smile masking the hurt on his face. No spark in those brown eyes that always lit up when they found her.

"Eric," she said.

He walked away. Shoved a path through the crowds and stormed out of the hotel. Ariel's legs were heavy, like she was wading against a current. They spun through the revolving doors and slammed into the dry heat outside.

"Eric, let me explain." She grabbed his elbow and he whirled on her, towering and so very solid. She'd never seen that expression on his face. Hurt. Sadness. He clenched his jaw, anger simmering in waves as he waited and waited for her to explain herself.

"I'm sorry," she said.

"For what?" His voice was low, measured. Cold. "For lying to me from the first moment we met? For pretending you were one of us?"

"I didn't lie," she said, and it was the wrong thing.

"Bullshit. Don't give me that half-truth bullshit." He turned to walk away again, but stopped. Faced her. "Was it funny to you?"

"No!" She shook her head. She didn't understand. How could he think that?

"Was it funny pretending that you were like us? That you came from nothing? That you had nothing and no one in the world when you are literally a spoiled rich girl slumming it for a summer?"

Ariel staggered back. Pressed her hand on her solar plexus. She couldn't breathe. He wasn't wrong. He wasn't wrong, and that was the worst of it.

"I wanted to tell you, but I was scared that you'd react the way you are reacting now."

"Because *you* didn't tell me!"

"I'm sorry. I—" That's when she saw it. The thing clutched in his hands. She recognized the trident on the portfolio—her father's label. Her label. He was here, in the hotel somewhere. He'd found her. He'd found *Eric*. "What did he give you?"

Eric blanched, but only for a moment. He licked his lips, had the nerve to laugh. He pinched the bridge of his nose and winced. "I am an epic fool."

"What did he *give* you?" she repeated, harsher, matching his anger note by note.

"The truth, for starters," he said. "So now it's your turn. Tell me."

She couldn't think. She wanted to snatch the portfolio from him to see how much she might be worth. This was what her father did. He used his power to secure bargains. In her heart, she knew Eric could never—would never—make a deal with her father. Then again, what did she know? She was a spoiled rich girl slumming it for the summer.

"Tell you what?" she asked. "You clearly have heard everything you want to hear."

He stepped closer, and it was too much. His scent, his warmth, his hurt. She wanted to take him in her arms and hold him until they disentangled from their anger. They could get through anything. That was the thing about anger. It wasn't reasonable. It wasn't kind. It hooked into your insecurities and magnified them, metastasizing until something broke.

"Was I a convenient way for you to taste the real world?" Eric asked.

Ariel burned with anger. Those were not Eric's words. They were her father's. She knew how her father could be, but this was a new low, even for him. She snatched the portfolio from Eric's hand and saw the offer, her father's signature. She shoved it against his chest. "It's impossible to resist, isn't it? Did you even think of saying no?"

Now Eric stepped back. He pointed with the folder. "Why would I, *Ariel*? He offered me everything I've ever wanted. Everything I've *worked* for."

That stress on the word *worked*—like she hadn't. Like she hadn't broken her body and spirit as her father's puppet. Like she hadn't offered up fifteen years of her life for someone else's dream.

She blinked away tears, knowing this was her fault. She took a deep breath and said, "I hope it's everything you wanted and more."

That's when they noticed they weren't alone anymore. Max was there. Carly and Vanessa. Odelia and Grimsby. She couldn't be sure how long they'd been watching.

"Go home, Ariel," Eric told her. There was no force behind it. The words were sad, tired.

This time he met her eyes. She loved when he looked at her like she was the brightest part of his day. There was none of that anymore. She was just a girl who had broken his heart, who had lied to him, who had kept parts of herself from him when he had ever given his all.

"Go home, Ariel," he said again. "When I get back, I want you out of my room."

This time, when he walked away, he didn't look back.

SevenAteNine Group Chat

Ariel:
It's over

Sophia:
What happened?

Marilou:
Do you want us to come get you?

Ariel:
I think I need to be alone

Thea:
Check in

Alicia:
Just say the word

Stella:
What do you need?

Ariel:
I'm not sure. I'll let you know as soon as I do.

Elektra:
We love you, guppy.

Sophia:
Good news, though.

Sophia:
Spoke to our lawyer

Ariel:
What did she say?

Sophia:
Daddy's been keeping more than his fair share of secrets . . .

CHAPTER TWENTY-SIX

ARIEL

7.15 Grand Canyon West, Arizona

Ariel del Mar had never been alone. Not in the true sense of the word. After she'd gathered her duffel and backpack from Eric's hotel room, she walked up and down the Las Vegas Strip until her feet hurt. Until the sun began to set. Until she felt truly scared for the first time, realizing that she had nowhere to go.

That wasn't true. Ariel could go back to New York City. There was a penthouse with her old bedroom waiting for her. Suddenly she missed her things, the comfort that came with never having to think about where her food and shelter were coming from. She could feel the lure of her soft bed, the baubles and knickknacks she'd collected her whole life. The pool nestled in their balcony that gave her the ability to swim encased in glass over the greatest city in the world. Her own private fish tank, putting her on display.

She hadn't been gone for months or years. It had been days. Weeks. She could go home with her tail tucked between her legs, like her father had predicted. Or she could find somewhere to sleep.

Ariel chose the latter.

The Lucky Clover hotel was past the end of the Strip, where things were more weathered, the lights less bright. Her room was clean enough, but the scent of old cigarettes and spilled wine clung to the worn carpets, and she almost chuckled at what Max and Oz would say.

"The ghosts of the old casino kings who ran away from Cuba are still clinging to these walls."

When she unpacked, she realized she only had some of her clothes, the leather folio full of her personal documents, and a few hundred dollars in cash. That was it. Her records, her notebook, and Tibby the shark had remained behind. Even her lucky boob crystal. She should have never removed it from her person. Look at what happened. The thought elicited a strangled laugh that devolved into crying in the shower.

After, Ariel splurged on a greasy cheeseburger and fries, and she knew she couldn't blame the crystal. She'd told her half-truths and half-lies. She'd chosen to leave parts of herself behind. She'd chosen what to say to Eric and her new friends. She'd let her resentment toward her father poison her relationship with the boy she loved.

Because she did love him.

Loving Eric Reyes was no longer like soaring. It was like watching an asteroid descend from the reaches of outer space. That was the beginning. Now it was everything else. Loving Eric now was the collision, the aftermath, debris strewn everywhere, bits and pieces of herself that she didn't know how to put back together—because the girl who had everything, the girl who could own the world if she wanted to, had never been in love before that moment.

She finished her pity meal and reached into her backpack for her notebook, but remembered again that she'd left it in Eric's room. Was he there now, lying in bed? She'd never seen him angry before, so she didn't know how he would be processing it. Maybe he was back with the gang, laughing with Max or listening to Oz's conspiracy theories. Maybe he was fine without her.

Ariel climbed completely under the covers. Tried not to think too much about wine or the cigarette stench. She lamented all the lyrics she wasn't going to get back, but after a fretful night's sleep, she decided to let them go.

They didn't belong to her anymore.

Perhaps Eric was so angry with her that he'd throw the notebook out. Let Monty make a feast of her scattered thoughts, her silly wishes and attempts at being normal.

There was no normal. There was no ordinary. Her world as Siren Seven's Ariel del Mar was perfectly normal to someone like Trevor Tachi. To the few friends she'd had along the way. To Marilou and the twins, who didn't want to hide from the limelight the way Ariel always had. She'd run away to fix herself and realized, too late, that there had never been anything wrong with her. It had been the only way to break free from her father, and he'd found her anyway. Odelia must have called him. Ariel should have expected it, though she didn't blame the manager.

When she logged back into her Pixagram the next morning, she saw the thousands of notifications she'd missed. More and more came in every second. She zoomed in on the photograph her father had posted of her.

Melody Ariel.

"You little guppy," she told her younger self. "You have no idea what's waiting for you."

Since she didn't want to go home, she gathered her things. She didn't need to check out since she'd paid in cash the night before. The trek to the bus station was only twenty minutes, and after a quick perusal of the board, she chose. Somewhere, anywhere. She boarded a bus heading east, putting as much distance as she could between herself and Eric.

She silenced her notifications when her heart started to race with anxiety and leaned her head on the window. The woman beside her was reading a gossip magazine, and she noticed a photo of the dolled-up version of herself on the cover. A couple of teens watched videos discussing her actions. The damn radio station played "Goodbye Goodbye," and when they got out of the city's range, she was grateful for the crackle of dead air. When the driver changed the station, Star Crossed was playing.

That had been one of Eric's dreams, but he hadn't come across it yet. Of course, the universe was messing with her. It had to be.

Ariel lowered her baseball cap and tucked her necklace under her shirt. She watched the desert pass by and remembered flashes of driving from Los Angeles to Nevada. The moment she'd welcomed the burning sun of Eric's solid body beside her.

She knew it would take time for her feelings to fade, but for the two and a half hours it took to get to Grand Canyon West, she castigated herself, reliving every moment they'd spent together. It was a prism of neon lights and music, of brown eyes and crooked smiles, of kisses and promises neither of them were ready to make.

When Ariel made it to her destination, she wandered around the bus station. She wanted to go to the skywalk, to *see* the Grand Canyon, but she felt strange being there alone. It was still morning, and she just stood there, directionless, until she grew hungry and found a place to scarf down food and coffee. She rented a tiny room, and slept through lunch and dinner, and didn't wake up until sunrise.

She made up her mind and hiked to the top of that walkway. She never thought she was afraid of heights, but her body was numb with fear. As the sky lightened, she got to the farthest point she could, one step at a time. The canyon was all consuming, alien in its beauty. She inhaled the dry air, basked in the morning glow. Just her and a few strangers. She thought of that dark Georgia road where she and Eric had walked in the rain. Lightning had cracked half a mile from where they were standing. She thought of the way he told her he simply took a hike somewhere and screamed. Let it all out in a cry. Catharsis.

She couldn't do it then.

She realized she'd gotten her fears all wrong. Yes, she was afraid of scary movies. Of losing her family. Of not finding her footing in a world that was unforgiving. But maybe she was simply afraid of being alone.

There, surrounded by land that was as old as time, she smiled. Everything changed. Rain eroded the ground beneath her. The moon went through its cycle. Whims passed.

Ariel let go, and she finally screamed.

She screamed even as people watched, as someone checked on her, and she laughed. She smiled for the first time since leaving Vegas and convinced a family of tourists to scream their troubles way with her. To let go, because sometimes that's all you could do to save pieces of yourself.

She wanted to tell Eric that she'd done it, and it had felt good.

Instead, she took a long walk.

She got on another bus, then another, making her way home, city by city, on her own.

She made a new list, and this time it wasn't a pretense at being ordinary. It was everything she wanted. Foods to try. Strangers to talk to. Songs to give a chance to. Eric hadn't added any more songs to their shared playlist, but he hadn't deleted it. Part of her lit up with hope—small, like a lightning bug, but hope nonetheless.

She bought a new notebook and filled it with new songs, even though the entire time she was tapping the rhythm, *two one four*, as if it were Morse code Eric could feel across state lines.

Finally, Ariel del Mar made it back to New York. She got off at Port Authority and took the train. She wasn't going to the penthouse, but she was going home.

Ariel del Mar, MIA?
Where in the World Is the Pop Star?

Is Ariel del Mar Having a Mental Breakdown?
Should Anyone Intervene?

50% Off Waxing
with Promo Code
Tuttle12

ERIC REYES: IS THE ROCK-AND-ROLL
HUNK OFF THE MARKET?

STAR CROSSED PENS STUDIO ALBUM DEAL

CHAPTER TWENTY-SEVEN

ERIC
Denver → Tulsa

7.22 Tulsa, Oklahoma

A week after Vegas, Eric Reyes and his motley crew were in Tulsa. The remainder of their tour was sold out everywhere except Boston and New York City. He had a record deal. But he still couldn't think of anything but her.

A week had gone by.

A week, and it hadn't gotten better.

The seven of them crowded into the tattoo parlor, watching the tattoo artist hunched over their tour manager's calf. The buzzing of the needle was grating, but a welcome distraction for Eric.

"Nervous?" Max asked Grimsby.

Grimsby petted Monty's brown furry head. "No way."

"I am," Carly admitted, knees bouncing. "I know I put on a brave face, but I'm really a big softie."

Vanessa rubbed her girlfriend's thigh soothingly. "It's okay, babe."

A week of two of his best friends making it official.

A week of them proving that they could make a relationship work while he was stuck in heartbreak loop.

"What about you, Eric?" Oz asked tentatively.

He'd heard the question. He heard all of them, but it was like he was and wasn't part of the conversation. He flipped through one of the artists' portfolios to keep his hands and mind busy. (It wasn't working.)

"I'm good," Eric said.

"Come on, man," Max said softly. "We said we'd get these tattoos when we got our deal. Here we are."

Eric put on a weak smile. "Yep. Here we are."

"Are you sure you don't want to see the design?" Grimsby asked, like he was a time bomb waiting to go off.

There were moments when he felt nuclear. His mood radiating and wilting everything on his perimeter. It was why he'd taken to spending more time in his bunk and crashing early. He did the unhealthy thing and scoured the internet for everything on the del Mars, on Ariel, on Siren Seven. The thing was, if he had paid more attention to Max for the entirety of them living together, he'd already have an MFA in Ariel del Mar. The "glam girl next door." He'd snorted the first time he'd seen the article, because all he could see was her in sweatpants and crop tops. Those hideous, but adorable, thrift-store finds that needed to be washed several times before they stopped smelling like mothballs.

A week of sleepless spirals.

A week of pretending that he didn't miss her.

He flipped through another page of the portfolio. Tigers, and dragons, and butterflies seemed to be all the rage. When he got to a page of a beautiful mermaid perched on a rock with waves crashing around her, he shut the book. The band tattoo was a pact they'd had forever, and he couldn't escape it. Even if he'd lost their wager and didn't get to choose the art.

Eric ran a palm over his short hair. He kept forgetting he'd gotten a crewcut. After Melody had left—after he'd told *Ariel* to go—he'd found himself on the Sunset Strip. He'd walked into a retro-looking barbershop, sat down, and said, "Just take it off."

The barber, with a handlebar mustache that rivaled the residents of the O.K. Corral, puffed a laugh. "What, did you lose a bet?"

"Yes, actually."

He'd returned to the venue, hours later, as if nothing had happened. He didn't speak. He strapped on his guitar and ran through rehearsal. He'd needed the feel of his guitar, the deep exhalation that came after singing.

Then, and only then, did he tell his friends everything that had transpired with Teodoro del Mar. Eric had made the right choice. The best choice. He knew it. When he'd turned around in that elevator, he knew that no matter what, he couldn't compromise what his band stood for, or Odelia.

Then why didn't he feel any better?

A week since he'd turned down a six-figure record deal.

Now, Odelia stood up from the tattoo chair. Beneath the clear bandage, her skin was red and angry. Mamoru, the Japanese tattoo artist, grinned at his work transferring Oz's custom art, but Eric looked away so he wouldn't see the design just yet. It wasn't exactly that he wanted to be surprised, and he was certain his girls wouldn't kick him when he was down—but he hadn't wanted to see the drawing. Even with the needle drilling into skin a few feet away, the situation didn't feel real. Losing Melody—Ariel—didn't feel real.

"Sick," Carly said.

"Who's next?" Mamoru asked, sterilizing and resetting his station.

Vanessa gathered the guinea pig from Grimsby as the bass player hopped up on the chair. Odelia took the seat in front of Eric, her one pant leg hiked up.

"I love you, baby boy," she said. "But you need to snap out of it. You told Ariel to go home, and you turned down Atlantica Records. I know you're hurt, but if you have something to say to me, say it."

He glanced up at his friends. He had been taking out his anger on them. Wasn't that what his own father had done? He'd spent every waking moment doing everything possible to not be like the man who raised him. At the first sight of real doubt, he'd turned into the worst version of Eric Reyes. He looked into the foggy silver mirrors that lined the far wall and barely recognized himself. Although, he had to admit, the haircut was growing on him.

"You should have told me," Eric said, straining to keep the resentment from his voice. "You've been there for me when I had absolutely no one. I still trust you. But you should have told me."

"It wasn't my secret to tell, and you know that," his manager and friend said. "But I do regret calling that man."

Eric rubbed his face with his callused palms. "Why, though? I don't understand why. Everything was so—" Good. Perfect. A dream. A lie.

"I got scared," Odelia said. "Ariel came to me. She wanted to tell you the truth, and I asked her to wait. She wanted to go through with it that night of the wedding. She seemed to think she could help the band more as Ariel del Mar."

Eric nodded slowly. Odelia had told him about the bad blood between their families.

"All of a sudden, I was reliving the day Teodoro del Mar stole everything from me. I told her to be careful with you, but I didn't trust that she really listened to me. I panicked. I was scared she would do the same thing to you that her father did to me."

"I would have been able to make the decision," he said. "The same one I made turning him down."

"I honestly thought he'd send his brother to get Ariel." She lightly slugged his shoulder. "But he saw a good thing in you."

The thing was, for all his "kingmaker" glory, Teodoro del Mar hadn't truly seen him. Not the way Odelia had. "It doesn't matter. It's done."

"You don't sound done," Vanessa told him.

"I don't regret turning down Teo del Mar," Eric clarified.

"I mean," Carly interrupted, wincing slightly, "turning down almost a mil is pretty rough. But not after knowing what he did to you, Odelia."

"At least our label came through." It was a modest advance that would let them cut an album and have their own creative input. In the end, it was what he'd truly wanted.

Max grunted her frustration. "Can't you just forgive her?"

Eric glanced away. That was the worst part. He'd forgiven her the moment she walked away. The moment he told her to go. There was nothing to forgive. He loved her then, and his wretched heart still loved her.

"Should I be mad at all of *you* for knowing and not telling me earlier?"

Max brushed her bangs down so they completely covered her eyes. "I found out ten minutes before you. I was the one who told Ariel to find you. Do you even know how scared she was that you would do what you did? I thought—" She cut herself off and left him hanging.

"You thought what?" he asked calmly. "That I'm a fucking fool who was going to laugh and say, 'Wow, the girl I love has been keeping a part of herself from me because she doesn't trust me,' and just move on?"

Chastened, they listened as the needle kicked up again and Grimsby went under. "Oh, that tickles."

Eric instantly regretted what he'd said to Max. He'd hurt his friends because he was miserable. He wanted to stop feeling that way but didn't know how. He could start by apologizing. "I'm sorry."

"You still love her?" Max asked softly.

Of course he still loved her. There was no going back. There was only before Ariel and after. And the after was bleak. The after was ordinary sunsets and sleepless nights.

"She seemed okay at the Grand Canyon," Oz said. "She's been posting on her private account."

Ariel must have removed him from her followers or blocked him. Not that he blamed her. *Go home.* Two words that haunted him every day and night.

Eric inhaled at the revelation that she hadn't gone home. Was she alone? Was she safe? How was she getting around? She didn't have a license. She'd left half her clothes, her notebook. Her bunk in the bus had been left untouched, and, when no one was looking, he placed Tibby the stress shark on his chest. Only then could he truly sleep.

"I thought she'd go back to the city," Eric admitted.

"Would you?" Odelia huffed.

Having met Teo del Mar, Eric knew the answer. No, he wouldn't. He'd avoided going home himself for so long that even the thought of it felt impossible. What *was* home? A father who didn't respect him? A mother who was a ghost of herself? He could imagine the deep disappointment his father would have felt if he knew about the opportunity Eric had passed up. Even if it had been the right thing, the *loyal* thing.

Then again, his father did try. He called several times a year, and Eric simply didn't answer. Ariel's father, on the other hand, worked through other people. He schemed and manipulated.

"That's that, I guess," he said, but he turned to the front doors, as if Ariel would walk in at any moment. God, he wished he didn't know that she was wandering around the country by herself. It had been easier to think of her as returned to her glass castle in the sky, looking down at them. A princess safely returned after a meaningless adventure.

A week since he'd accused her of "slumming it."

It wasn't a fair assessment, but he ached. He didn't know how to stop aching.

"Call her, bro," Carly said, hopping into the chair next.

"Do you want to know your choices, Eric Reyes?" Vanessa asked.

He licked his canine. "No, but I'm sure you're about to tell me."

"Call her and talk like adults." Vanessa held up a second finger. "Or get over it and channel that brooding energy into your Alanis Morissette era."

Eric laughed for the first time in days. Vanessa wasn't wrong about everything. He'd wanted to call her. Every day on the bus, making small talk with the new merch guy, Fergus, a chatty forty-year-old from Los Angeles who had answered their Gregslist ad to replace Ariel.

Then he relived that moment in the hotel lobby again.

Ariel, he'd said.

She'd assumed the worst about him. *What did he give you?*

That's the moment that had broken him. She knew her father would throw the world at him, but she should have thought better of Eric. She should have *known* that he'd choose her, angry as he was. It was proof that she didn't know him at all. Wasn't it?

He inhaled and didn't let go of the breath until it hurt. That's what it felt like, every day without her.

Finally, it was his turn to get on the table. He undid his belt and pushed his jeans and boxers down. Vanessa rolled her eyes, and Oz blinked rapidly.

"Did you have to choose your ass cheek?" Max asked. "You know you could get it anywhere."

He didn't think they would make him get Oz's chupacabra art, or Ariel's name, but just in case, he needed it to be somewhere that he couldn't see unless he went searching.

Eric shrugged and lay on his chest.

The needle's first contact was a constant sharp pain that dulled as adrenaline rushed through his system. It felt good having something to concentrate on, but then his thoughts went back to Ariel, as everything did.

Where was she? Was she safe? Did she need him?

He'd told Ariel that their fathers were the same, but now that Eric had met hers in person, he knew it wasn't true. His father had been driven by his own fears, but he'd never manipulated Eric to make him go home.

What would happen if Eric reached out now? It wouldn't change the past, but perhaps . . . perhaps it might give them a future. That's what he'd told Melody. Ariel. He didn't care about her past. Why couldn't he afford his family the same?

When Eric's skin felt raw, and the pain had gone from pleasant to unbearable, and circled around to numb, it was over. He got up from the chair and studied the tattoo in front of a full-length mirror. The corners of his lips twitched. Oz had drawn them a hamster in an astronaut suit. It was surrounded by a constellation of stars. He loved it, actually. For the first time in days, Eric smiled at his friends. After having his right buttock smeared with a cooling, antibacterial gel and clear bandage, they all headed back to the venue. Eric didn't feel better, but he felt lighter, like some of his anger had drained out of him with every graze of that needle.

Call her, a treacherous little voice in his mind urged.

He didn't. Instead, Eric found a quiet room and took out his phone. He stared at his father's number for a long time before he worked up the courage to finally call him back.

@StarCrossedTheBand Pixagram

We are tired AF but we are coming for you, Little Apple! Thank you all for the love you've shown us along the way. We have some big news and are hyped to get back into the studio. Eric has been hard at work with some new songs. See you on the road! #StarCrossedLovers

CHAPTER TWENTY-EIGHT

ARIEL

7.26 Queens, New York

Ariel hadn't been to the house in Forest Hills, Queens, since the day they moved out. The house didn't look anything like it once had. The previous occupants had updated everything. The faded rose-printed wallpaper her mother had loved so much. The hideous lime-green-and-brown kitchen that had likely been the height of fashion in the seventies. Now it belonged to Sophia.

She dropped her duffel at the entrance, kicked off her sneakers, and went in search of everyone.

"Up here!" the eldest del Mar sister shouted.

Ariel found them covered in paint, with splotchy sections of turquoise everywhere but on the walls.

"You really should have called a professional," Ariel said, running into Sophia's outstretched arms.

Ariel didn't mean to cry. She'd missed them the moment she left home, but they'd never stopped being in contact. And yet, having her sisters back made all the difference.

"The prodigal daughter returns," Elektra said, turning around as she sniffled. She set the paint roller on the floor.

"You got a tattoo!" Alicia pointed at the delicate constellation decorating Ariel's inner left forearm. On her long, *long* journey home, she'd stopped in a quirky Tulsa tattoo parlor Oz had recommended.

"It's us," she said. The constellation was the Pleiades.

They kissed and hugged her, pelting her with more questions than she had answers for. Where had she been? Had she made up with Eric? What were they all going to do next? Where were their souvenirs?

"Wine and pizza first," Marilou said, nearly shaking with excitement. Her brush splattered Ariel's white T-shirt and jeans.

In moments, they'd all changed into pajamas and piled into the only room in the house that was finished. The master bedroom.

Sophia had decorated it in dark wood, deep saturated blues and purples. A flat-screen TV had been set into the wall. The massive king-size bed was a snug fit, but they piled on top of each other like when they were kids.

Part of her wanted to keep her time with Eric to herself, but the more her sisters pulled, the more she let herself get carried away by her memories. She started with that night at Julio's bar. Running to catch the bus. Bargaining with Odelia. The elevator. Playing with Vanessa. Writing a song with Eric that they'd never finish. The first time he'd said out loud that he wanted to kiss her, and when they finally did at the music video shoot. Each memory tumbled into the next, until she got to the ugly, bitter end.

Sophia brushed Ariel's hair back. "I'm sorry it didn't work out."

"I should have been honest from the start." Ariel drank from a seashell cup with a silly straw. It had been Stella's housewarming gift to Sophia. "But that's enough about me. I can't believe you bought our old house."

"I didn't say anything because I didn't want Daddy to find out. There's a lot I've been doing over the last few months," Sophia said. She got out of the bed. Her black fuzzy bathrobe trailed at her feet. She opened a compartment in her wall and brought out a stack of folders. "Now that we're all here, I can get started."

They sat up and turned to their eldest sister. Since they'd disbanded

Siren Seven, she'd stopped straightening her hair, and her beautiful curls tumbled over her shoulders, like black tentacles. Looking around, Ariel realized they had all shed elements of their old personas. Even Marilou had kept only a touch of rose in her hair, although Elektra would likely have electric-blue hair when she was ninety.

"When Ariel asked me about Odelia Garcia, I started to do some digging. The label that put out the record Ariel found doesn't exist anymore, but I found an old producer who told me the whole story."

Marilou drank from her seashell cup. "He just volunteered it?"

"*She* had to be wooed with a nice dinner and my winning smile." Sophia winked, then told them everything.

It went like this: The label had signed Luna Lunita, their parents' band. Only, back then, there were three members. Teo and Maia del Mar, and Odelia Garcia. After they'd cut the record, and right when they were about to release "Luna Mia" as a single, the label decided Luna Lunita would be more appealing as a husband-and-wife duo. They could sell the romance. They could sell the love story.

"Three's a crowd," Sophia said. "That sort of thing. So they fired Odelia, but she wouldn't go quietly. She put up a fight. Without solid proof the song was entirely hers, though, there wasn't much she could do. The contract she'd signed said they could remove her from the project whenever."

"Dad won awards for that song," Thea said, disappointed and horrified as an artist.

"And Odelia never got credit," Ariel added. She filled in the gaps with the details Odelia had given her.

Alicia shook her head. "That's awful."

Sophia held up a finger. "That's not the only thing I found."

"Please tell me it's the jeans you borrowed from me in 2012," Elektra said dryly.

"The jeans are gone, Elektra. Okay?" Sophia returned to the bed with the new folder. She handed it to Ariel, who flipped through the pages. She wasn't sure what she was reading at first. It seemed to be a photocopy of a photocopy, dated a little over fifteen years prior.

"A contract?" she asked.

"Our first contract," Sophia corrected. "The money was put into seven individual accounts that Mom had set up for us. But . . ."

Ariel looked at the account statements with the dates that fit the contract. She followed the highlighted portions that showed the money had been transferred into the accounts. Then transferred out again, leaving a zero balance.

"That was the year—" Stella started to say, and Alicia finished, "Daddy founded Atlantica Records."

"With the money we made on *The Little Mermaids*." Sophia crossed her arms in victory. "I've been talking to our lawyer, and to a law professor from my upcoming classes. They both agree that we have a case."

"Case?" Ariel repeated the word, but she knew what Sophia was thinking.

"That's right," Sophia said, blinking back triumphant tears. "Atlantica Records has always belonged to us."

March 15, 1994

Querida Odelia,

    This is the hardest letter I've ever had to write. Let me start by saying that I'm sorry. I don't know what it's worth, and I know I have no right. I know that I've taken too long to make amends. My heart has always been torn between my dearest friend and my husband.

    I want you to know I did try to talk to Teodoro all those years ago, but you know how he is. When he gets something in his mind, it is impossible to change it, and he wanted this so much.

    We have children now. Number seven is on the way. I heard you're pregnant, too. I suppose I'm writing now to say I'm so sorry about your husband's passing, and, well, selfishly because I started imagining what it would be like if our children could grow up as friends. Like we were.

    Some things aren't meant to be, I suppose.

    I know this is nothing compared to how much I hurt you, but I hope it's enough seed money to get you started.

Love,

Maia Melody Lucero Marín

CHAPTER TWENTY-NINE

ARIEL

7.28 New York, New York

Ariel and her sisters arrived at Atlantica Records with some fanfare. At Thea's behest, they wore sleek black power suits. Their legal counsel trailed behind, as did Chrissy and some of the other assistants.

A couple of Atlantica interns surreptitiously recorded videos and snapped pictures. Good. They wanted the rumors to get started. A coup. A shakeup. A reckoning.

Ariel opened the door to her father's office. She'd never seen him so surprised. Not when they'd won awards. Not when they had their first diamond record. Not even when she'd announced she was moving out. His face was usually calculating, and his default was an eagle eye of observation.

"Ariel," he said. Then he remembered he was on the phone and hung up without apology. "Girls. What are you doing here?"

"Hi, Daddy." Even then, after everything, a small part of her still wanted to run into his arms for the protection he had always offered. *Daddy's girl*, her sisters called her when she was little. But then she remembered what he'd done to her, to Odelia. Who else had her father stepped over in order to get everything that he'd wanted?

Sophia's counsel stepped forward and placed the folder on his desk. She cut to the chase, perhaps sensing a moment of hesitation on Ariel's part. "Mr. del Mar. I'm Annabel Ford. I will be representing your daughters."

"What is this?" Teodoro asked, roaring like a lion that had been prodded. He flipped through page after page.

Everything Sophia had found through her research was there. Every bit of proof they needed to show that he'd used their money to start the label. That he *still* held their rightful earnings hostage.

"What does this prove?" their father asked. "We're a family and this is a family business."

"This shows gross mismanagement of earnings from my clients, who were underage."

Teo was eerily calm. "Why are you doing this?"

He said this directly to Ariel. He knew she had always been the one with the softest spot for him.

"I'm doing exactly what you told us to do," Ariel said. "Think big, Daddy. Atlantica Records was founded with our money, and so we're claiming it." He started to bluster, words angry and slurring so much she didn't understand what he was saying. But she kept speaking, louder and louder, until he had no choice but to sit back and listen. "You'll receive a severance fee and step down as CEO, though you will remain listed as a founder."

"You don't know the first thing about running a label," he said.

"But I do," Uncle Iggy said, entering the room.

Teo del Mar's lip curled, his breathing rapid. "¿Y tu, Ignacio?"

"I will advise," Iggy said, glancing meaningfully at the seven del Mar women, "until they don't need me anymore."

Teo pointed a beefy finger at Ariel. "You wanted no part of this a few weeks ago."

Ariel said the thing she knew would cut him, down to the marrow. "No, Daddy. I want the music. I want it on my own terms. You said it yourself. I *am* the music. What I don't want a part of is you. Not like this."

Teo sat back, quiet, wounded. He suddenly looked so old. When had her big strong father, her shield against the ugliness of the world, gotten so very old?

"All I ever wanted was to give you what we never had," he said. "That's what a parent wants."

"We never doubted that," Sophia said. "We clearly have things to work through as a family. But like you've taught us. This is business."

Teo leaned on his elbow, staring at them like he was seeing them all for the first time. The daughters he'd underestimated. "Is that all?"

"No," Ariel pressed on. "I know about Odelia Garcia. You're going to give her credit for the song. You're going to tell the truth about everything."

"It's not enough you hurt your father?" he asked, snarling with anger and betrayal. "You want to ruin me on top of everything?"

Ariel pressed her hands on the table, strengthened by her sisters, and by knowing that what she was doing was the only way to make amends. "You ruined yourself."

"Don't talk to me—"

"Respect is earned, Daddy. None of this is worth the people you've hurt. None of it."

"Are you punishing me because of that boy?" her father asked, grasping for some kind of purchase.

Ariel shook her head. "We will honor his deal, despite the transfer."

Teo's eyebrows rose. "What deal?"

"The deal you made with him."

Teo was quiet for a moment as they realized, together, what had occurred. "Eric Reyes didn't take the deal I offered. Talented, but not very ambitious. When I was his age, I would have done everything possible for that kind of offer."

Eric had turned down the deal. Eric. Eric. Ariel felt herself unravel. She bit down on her lower lip. Felt one of her sisters squeeze her shoulder. She needed to get through this. "That's the difference between you two. He'd rather be a good person."

Teo chuckled humorlessly. "And a fool."

"I've made a huge mistake," Ariel whispered to herself. She turned to her sisters, who nodded. They'd handle it. They could do anything as long as they had each other. She knew that more than ever.

Before she left, Ariel glanced at her father. She'd never seen him look so defeated. She'd done that. She'd unseated the kingmaker. And yet, she'd somehow hoped that once they talked to him he'd do it himself, instead of making them force his hand. He had made his choices, and, finally, she would make her own.

Ariel's body hummed with adrenaline, with fear and uncertainty. But of one thing she was certain—she had a clean slate. A new beginning.

And she was ready for it to start.

@TheRealArielDelMar

Four million likes

This message is a long time coming. I know you've heard from my father and people who think they know me. But they don't. Not the real me. So I want to set the record straight. I want to tell you everything, and I'm going to need some help. Stay tuned for a big announcement tomorrow 7.31.

Episode 1380:

Ariel del Mar Special! You Don't Want to Miss This!
Live! Live! Live!

[Image description: Scott Tuttle, dressed in a white blazer with a gold Siren Seven lapel pin. Ariel del Mar, wearing a denim jacket, low-cut white tank, and purple jeans.]

"Hello, everyone. I'm literally a ghost. I, Scott Tuttle, am coming to you from beyond the grave because I'm sitting here with none other than Ariel del Mar herself! I see you in the comments. Send us some love!"

Ariel smiles at him and squeezes his hand. "Thank you for having me. I've been following your channel for years."

Scott beams at the camera before turning back to her. "Okay. Wow! Let me compose myself. . . . When you contacted me, I thought it was a hoax."

Ariel holds up her hand and counts. "He hung up on me three times!"

Scott covers his eyes, embarrassed. "Can you blame me? But let's get down to brass tacks. You're here to confess?"

"Something like that," Ariel says. "I know that there's been a lot of speculation since our final concert."

"Tell us, darling," Scott encourages her. "But first, let's address the red elephant in the room. You're not a natural redhead?"

Ariel tosses her deep brown waves over her shoulder. "Surprise!"

"How does it feel?"

Ariel threads her fingers through her hair. "It was an adjustment. I've spent so much of my life in a costume. I loved that girl. She changed my life. But now that Siren Seven is retired, I'm ready for the world to meet me. The whole me."

"So who are you now?"

She smiles wistfully, glancing at the camera, then at Scott. "I thought I'd be entirely different, but I'm not. Deep down, I'm the same person. I'm just not hiding, if that makes sense. Don't get me wrong,

I love the drama and dressing up. So, hello world. I'm Melody Ariel Marín Lucero. But I still go by Ariel del Mar."

"Nothing wrong with a little help," Scott says, patting the side of his silver hair. "But it's nice to meet you again, Ariel. What about the rumors of your mental breakdown?"

They fall into each other laughing. She waves her hands across her body like an X, motioning to get serious again. "Can I tell you a secret?"

"Me and a couple of thousand people watching." He winks at the camera.

"Those were actually my sisters in my old wigs."

Scott covers his mouth. "I knew it. I freaking knew it."

"I'm sorry about the red herrings, no pun intended," Ariel says.

"So where were you?"

Ariel takes a deep breath, steadies herself. "I was finding my voice. And falling in love, actually."

"Trevor?"

Her eyes go wide with alarm. "God, no. Trevor and I weren't right for each other. I thought I made it clear, but his interest was getting to my father, not me."

"If I were any more shocked right now, I'd implode." Scott turns coy and taps Ariel on the knee. "Tell us. Who is this mystery love?"

"Well, he sort of appeared when I least expected it." She levels her gaze at the camera again. "Eric, I want to tell you all the things I didn't say when I had the opportunity. If you still feel the same way as I do, meet me halfway. I'll be at our bridge until sunset. I hope I see you there."

[end of livestream]

CHAPTER THIRTY

ERIC

7.31 DUMBO, New York

Eric had never imagined that he'd be giving his parents a tour of a music venue, but here he was. His father, so old-fashioned he'd worn a suit and tie to a rock club, and his mother, dressed for church, appropriately oohed and aahed at everything. They shook hands with everyone, from Willie the manager to Jake the bathroom attendant.

They sat in the mezzanine VIP lounge of Aurora's Grocery. Vanessa was doing a practice run-through of her set while Odelia made small changes. His mother fussed about how much candy he ate, kept brushing her fingers at the shorn sides of Eric's hair.

Over the past two weeks, he had to keep trimming it to get it to take a shape. He'd let his beard grow out, which the fans seemed to like, though it felt strange.

The night they'd all gotten their tattoos had been the night when he'd called his father. After an awkward, tearful conversation, they'd agreed that his parents would visit New York and come to one of his shows.

They'd high-tailed it after their gig in Boston in order to spend the day together, and he'd learned more about his parents during a single brunch than he ever had in his life. A couple of years after Eric had left, when his abuelo Pedro had passed, his mother had threatened to divorce his father if they didn't start seeing a couple's counselor.

For two people of their generation to even admit their problems felt radical. Eric had his reservations about therapy, but he'd seen the changes in his parents. They held hands. They talked to each other. They listened. He barely knew them anymore, and that old hurt was still there, hooked into his muscles, but he'd figure out a way to move forward. He *wanted* to move forward.

Now he held his mother's hand as if otherwise she'd disappear as soon as he turned around.

"When are you going to visit us?" his father asked.

Eric shook his head. He wasn't there yet. Perhaps he'd never get there, and he knew he didn't have to. But he wasn't ready to shut the door, either. "I think there's a lot I have to do here first."

When the practice set finished, Oz ran up to them, Max and the others following close behind.

"What's wrong?" Eric asked.

"Video!" Oz panted, grabbing his knees for support. "Melody—I mean, Ariel. Message. Look."

Eric glanced around to his friends. "What is he saying?"

Max waved her arms like she was trying to direct plane traffic. "Ariel is waiting for you, and you have to go to her!"

Heat burned at the center of his chest at her names. Melody. Ariel. What were they even talking about?

"No. I—"

That's when Oz tackled him. They rolled onto the ancient carpet of the VIP area. Eric got the wind knocked out of him as Max jumped on next. He cursed and tried to punch them off.

"This is for your own good," Grimsby said.

"It's for true love," Carly added, kneeling and holding the phone in front of him. He cursed and kicked, but he had nowhere to look but at her.

Eric wasn't sure what he was seeing until he read the captions. Ariel

337

had broadcast herself. As Melody. As herself. One and the same. He felt like he couldn't understand what she was saying because he was staring at her beautiful face, and it had been so long. When he put up too much of a fight to be restrained, they let him go. He snatched the phone. His finger trembled when he hit replay, and this time, he understood.

She was waiting for him, halfway.

"Who is Ariel?" Mrs. Reyes asked, scandalized at the scene around her.

Max, Grimsby, Carly, and Oz launched into a comically humiliating reenactment of his heartbreak. And his love.

"Are you going to go?" his father asked. "You know what your grandfather would say."

A viselike sensation tightened around his heart. He knew. But was it the right thing for both of them? Fifteen days, six hours, ten minutes, and a handful of seconds had gone by, and he hadn't stopped missing her. Wanting her. Thinking of her.

"What time is it?"

"You have thirty minutes!" Oz shouted. "I'll drive you."

For the first time, Eric's entire life was under one roof. Except for her. Ariel was missing. Whatever they needed to say, they had to do it face-to-face. He had to go get her. What in the world was he waiting for?

He ran, taking the stairs at a dangerous pace. He barreled out of the side door, stumbling onto the sidewalk. The line of fans waiting to get inside was already looping around the block. His heart soared. Then he realized he was standing in the exact place where they had first collided. Where he'd read her necklace. "Melody." Where he'd returned to meet her for a night that would change his life.

Oz pulled up, driving Eric's beat-up old SUV since the Beast had to remain in Jersey.

"We're coming, too," Max said.

"I'm pretty sure this is some sort of traffic violation," Eric shouted as Grimsby squeezed into the front seat with him. His parents, his band, they were all in there.

He looked down and saw a text from Vanessa: *Your ass better be going to the bridge, or I swear I'll never put up with you again.*

He replied with a rude emoji, and Oz peeled off.

Eric had never had motion sickness before that moment. A combination of nerves and the fear that he was too late made him want to hurl out of the window. That, or Oz's terrible driving was more noticeable in a smaller car.

"Hold on to your butts!" Oz shouted.

The entire car screamed.

And then instantly stopped.

Gridlock traffic spread out in every single direction.

"You have got to be fucking kidding me," Eric said, hitting the headrest.

His mother admonished him, but her voice was drowned out by the blaring of horns. Eric looked to his right, and he smiled. They were right in front of Laucella's Pizzeria.

"I'll text her and tell her you're on your way," Carly said.

"Her number is disconnected," Eric admitted unapologetically. "I might have broken down and called her last week when I hit a very low point. Now let me out."

"This isn't the right time for pizza!" Grimsby shouted as he ran into the parlor.

"I'm going to make it. I will." Eric smiled his old smile. He finally *felt* like himself again. He knew, even if he'd lost himself a little bit along the way, that the universe was on his side.

Eric Reyes was going to get his girl.

CHAPTER THIRTY-ONE

ARIEL

7.31 Brooklyn Bridge, New York

He's not coming, Ariel thought.

The sun was setting on the last day in July. A warm breeze kissed her damp cheeks. Her sisters had insisted on coming along, using the fact that they'd also never walked across the Brooklyn Bridge as an excuse. It would save her having to recount the details later, but now they were witness to her disappointment and humiliation.

What had she expected?

She'd picked up her father's worst habit—hurting people who trusted them.

It stopped with her. It had to.

She watched the sun melt into the horizon, the deep blues of night taking its place in the sky.

She glanced around. There were too many people. Some glanced in her direction, tried to place her familiar face, then kept walking. Others who did recognize her snapped pictures and giggled with their friends. Having had enough of that, she began to march back to her sisters. They had a full set of sympathetic smiles ready.

"Maybe you shouldn't have made a grand gesture on the night of his last show?" Marilou said.

Thea and Alicia pinched her arm, and the sisters burst out into a chorus of excuses.

"See, this is why I don't do romance," Stella said, crossing her arms.

Elektra cackled. "You wish. I see all the books you keep under your bed."

"And," Sophia added, "I feel like this could have been an email."

Ariel knew they were trying to make her laugh. It worked. She cast a final glance at the horizon: a sliver of gold winked at her, the slumbering god of the universe. The thought made her miss Oz.

Then she heard it. A loud, desperate scream that cut through the worst of the bridge traffic.

"WAIT!"

Ariel whirled around. She saw Max, almost doubled over. Grimsby and Carly, and him.

Eric was out of breath, but he kept advancing. He peered down at the pizza box in his hands, then up at her. At the first sight of his wry smile, Ariel wanted to run to him. It took all of her to wait, to be patient.

"My mom said I should have brought flowers," he said, opening the box. "I'm pretty sure I scrambled this on the sprint over."

Ariel looked inside. A small pizza with sausage and pineapple. It *did* look like it had gone through a run in the spin cycle, but she'd never seen a more perfect sight: Eric Reyes holding her heart in his hands. He closed the box and handed it to Grimsby. Ariel waved at her friends, then faced Eric.

"I'm sorry," she said at the same time he said, "I love you."

They tried again.

"*I* love *you*," she said, at the same time he said, "*I'm* sorry."

"Please kiss me," Ariel said, her breath catching, her hands reaching for him. "Please. Please."

As the day gave its final breath, vanishing into night, Eric gathered Ariel into his arms. He tapped his nose to hers, brushed his lips across hers, then pulled back to gaze at her once more. And then kissed her like it was the first time, slow and tender. She tasted the salt of her own happy tears and that familiar sweetness that was all Eric. For a moment, she was aware that their friends, her family, were whistling and cheering them on. That strangers were joining in, and the city was loud and joyous. But then there was only Eric, and her, and the pressure of his lips against hers.

She pulled back first and ran her fingers across his short hair. "They really held you to the bet."

"I did, actually. It's a long story."

"Wait," she said, remembering the second half of that bargain. "I want to see the tattoo."

He smirked. "Later."

She bit her bottom lip. He definitely had her attention.

He rested his forehead against hers. Kissed the tip of her nose. Her lips. He tasted her with so much tenderness, such aching love. Ariel could kiss Eric until the sun came up. When he eased back, he gently cupped her face.

"I didn't take the deal, Ariel."

Her name on his tongue was jarring, and somehow perfect.

"I know," she whispered. "There's so much I have to tell you. I—"

They turned at the same time. Her sisters and the band were watching, silly grins on each of their faces. Grimsby was nibbling on a slice of pizza.

"Don't mind us," Max said, delighted and somehow also annoyed. "We've only got a show to play."

"Right!" Ariel said, smacking her forehead.

"It's a sold-out show," Eric said, winking at the del Mar sisters. "But I know a guy. And I have a surprise."

"What surprise?" she asked.

He dismissed the sentimental moment with a grin. "You know how I lost that bet?"

They raced back across the Brooklyn Bridge, two stars, burning side by side.

Ariel del Mar and her six sisters ran into Aurora's Grocery and filled the VIP mezzanine as Le Poisson Bleu finished their last song. People stared and whispered behind cupped hands. Others took not-so-surreptitious photos of them taking over the entire section, along with Oz, the Garcia women, and Eric's parents. Ariel glanced over her shoulder and waved, which usually encouraged those too embarrassed to take candids without her permission.

Ariel del Mar wasn't hiding who she was anymore. Her red wig was soon to be set aside, one of many cherished mementos of her past, on new shelves. Once she figured out where she wanted to live, that was. But she wouldn't worry about that now. She found that taking things a few days at a time was working.

Marilou linked her arms with Ariel, and they climbed out of their seats and leaned against the balcony railing. "How does it feel to be a normal girl? Well, a normal VIP, I guess."

Ariel was not going to answer that. Seconds later, the lights dimmed. The pit below screamed, and she felt it down to her bones. She did love that sound, that energy of a group of people sharing a moment, a song, a night.

The others joined them at the railing to get a better look at Star Crossed. Blue front light cast the band in a familiar glow.

Eric stepped up close to the mic, one hand on the neck of his guitar. He did this low murmuring chuckle thing she'd felt once before, and she felt it now, like his lips were back at her throat. "It's good to be home."

He let the cheer crest, and Max hit her bass pedal.

"We're going to do things a little differently this time around," he said, eyes cast to the mezzanine. He talked to the crowd like they were all friends, in on the same story, which made him so good, *so* good at that part of performing. "I want to let you all know that at the very start of this tour, I made a bet. It involved a girl."

There was the inevitable *"Awww"* from the audience.

"The most incredible woman, who literally crashed into my life. So, my very mature, very kind friends bet me that if I *'Eric Reyesed'* things between us, I would have to perform a song I hated by a pop group I underestimated."

He let the slightly confused murmur pass through the crowd. Grimsby plucked a bass note, and Eric kept going.

"Spoiler alert, I Eric Reyesed the situation."

While they laughed, Marilou turned to her and nearly shouted, "Did he Eric Reyes you?"

Ariel smiled back. "Twice."

"For the last two weeks," Eric continued, "I've been practicing this song, because I am a man of my word. I listened to it. I played it again and again. The more I did, the more I heard her. I thought I knew what Siren Seven was. I thought it was easy to dismiss something without seeing what was at the heart of it. And I found that at the heart of a song called 'Goodbye Goodbye' is the story of a person letting go of something with grace and love. It's a song about endings and beginnings. And I want to say sorry to our friends of Siren Seven for not seeing that sooner." He pointed up at them, and the crowd absolutely went wild. "This song actually bangs, as they say."

Ariel felt her sisters lean against her. Felt her chest rising and falling with emotion as Carly began to play the intro notes on her guitar and Max kicked in with the drums, Grimsby completing the melody.

"I'm going to need a little help," Eric said, and this time, she knew he was talking to her as he held out his hand. "Ariel, mi vida, mi amor. I need you."

Heads craned in her direction, and her sisters pushed her toward Willie, the venue manager. She already knew the way, taking the service stairs to backstage.

Eric started the song without her, and she welcomed the round of applause as she joined him, standing at his mic, sharing his space. She didn't know it was possible to miss someone so much when they were inches away.

When she sang "Goodbye Goodbye" she changed the key she usually sang it in. Her contralto melding with Eric's voice in a way that transformed the music she'd written, in a way she hadn't realized she needed so badly. Not better, just different.

Eric had been right. It was a song about letting go, about starting over. About being a little different every day. She'd had the words all along; she needed to get a little lost to find her voice.

When the crowd sang so loud they took over, Ariel looked at Eric. The song's crescendo filled every inch of the venue as Ariel pulled him close—her past, present, future tangled up in a kiss that felt like a new beginning.

BREAKING: TEODORO DEL MAR STEPS DOWN AS CEO, ELEKTRA DEL MAR NAMED INTERIM CEO OF ATLANTICA RECORDS.

The Recording Academy Rescinds 1985 Award of Fallen Music Kingmaker.

Marilou del Mar Living Her Best Life At Panda Sanctuary.
See the pictures here.

Atlantica Records Opens Boutique Label "Pleiades." Ariel Del Mar To Head New Project With Vanessa G As First Artist.

STAR CROSSED NOMINATED FOR THREE AWARDS, Including Video of the Year, Album of the Year, Best Rock Album.

ARIEL DEL MAR AND ERIC REYES STEP OUT TOGETHER ON MUSIC'S BIGGEST NIGHT.

Teodoro del Mar Embarks on Sea Voyage to "Soul Search."

Scott Tuttle Joins the Pleiades as Digital Content Manager.

Get Sophia del Mar's Collegiate Look.
25% Off!

Ariel del Mar and Eric Reyes Announce Special Concert. We Hear Wedding Bells!

ACKNOWLEDGMENTS

The Little Mermaid is part of my origin story. It's hard to remember a time when I didn't know all the words or have the melodies in my head. When I was three years old, my grandmother, who had immigrated to New York City before I was born, sent me the VHS as a gift. At the time, I still lived in Ecuador with my parents, and I watched that tape over and over again. As soon as it was over, my dad or mom would rewind it (younger generations will never know the agony of waiting for all the tapes to restart) and we'd watch it again. I used to tell people that it was the way I learned how to speak English, and by the time it was my turn to join my family in New York City when I was in first grade, I had a good grasp of the language.

I consider this story part of my creative DNA, and it has been a privilege to write a love letter to my favorite Disney princess.

Thank you to Jocelyn Davies for taking a chance on me, Elanna Heda for all your work on this project, and the Hyperion Avenue and Disney Books family. This book would not be possible without you all.

To Stephanie Singleton for helping me bring Ariel del Mar and Eric Reyes to life with gorgeous cover art.

To Suzie Townsend, Sophia Ramos, and the best team in the world—New Leaf Literary & Media.

Every writer needs a support bubble. Mine are Dhonielle Clayton, Adriana Medina, Sarah E. Younger, and Natalie Horbachevsky for always being my cheerleaders when I am a brat, and for feeding me while I am in the deadline haze. I love you all.

To my deadline writing buddies, Adriana Herrera and Alexis Daria. You two inspire me to be a better writer and creator. I can't thank you enough for our daily writing sprints. To my romance community for keeping my wheels turning and TBR long—Tracey Livesay, Sarah MacLean, Priscilla Oliveras, Mia Sosa, Sabrina Sol, Diana Muñoz Stewart, and more.

A very special thank-you to Ben Hutcherson from Khemmis, Nick Ghanbarian from Bayside, and Danny Córdova (yup, that's my bro) from The Dreamland Fire for answering all my musician and touring band questions. I hope everyone who picks up this book goes to listen to their music ASAP!

Last, but not least, to my family: You've been in these mentions enough that you know who you are. I'm especially grateful for my uncles Marcos Medina and Robert Laucella for letting me draft and edit this book in their house in Puerto Rico. I cleaned, I promise.

Love,
Zoraida